I0658179

BROTHER BRIGHAM

a novel by

D. Michael Martindale

Worldsmith Stories
Salt Lake City, Utah

What readers have said about D. Michael's novel
Brother Brigham

"Jack London once made my heart pound, but Michael Martindale is the first writer to rock me back in my chair in wide-eyed amazement. LDS readers will not be able to get through *Brother Brigham* without a test of inner character. Whether they like what they learn about their own loyalties depends on who they are before they pick it up."

— Preston McConkie, journalist

"*Brother Brigham* is one of the wildest rides I've ever enjoyed in a novel. Like Stephen King, Martindale captures the earthy rhythms of daily life as the characters get caught up in bizarre, harrowing events."

— Christopher Kimball Bigelow, author and editor

"I just finished reading *Brother Brigham*. Wow! Outrageous, provocative, insightful, courageous and thoughtful. Michael Martindale reminded me of the sensitivities of Orson Scott Card in his novel *Saints*."

— Eugene Kovalenko, blogger

"This novel takes you to heaven and hell and back. You read it in a day and then catch your breath and want a cigarette—and then you remember you don't smoke. *Brother Brigham* is a subversively sensual journey to the edges of Mormon possibility, a weirdly cathartic purging of the darkest fantasy in the Mormon psyche."

—C.L. Hanson, blogger

"At first this book starts out kind of quirky and funny, but it quickly grabs you by the throat and doesn't let go until it's done. It will surprise you in so many ways."

—Kathy Tyner, writer

"Martindale's frank sensuality...is not salacious; it's simply a matter of fact. A lesser book would have found a way to ignore it completely. It is frustrating when people, in life and in fiction, say what they think should be said instead of what they feel. In that light, Martindale's relative profundity is refreshing."

— Sam Vicchrilli , In Utah This Week Magazine

"Martindale...paints a scenario at once believable and shudderingly delusional."

— Kim Madsen, readers group coordinator

"Reading this fast-paced and quickly changing story is like embarking on a river rafting trip that starts out in placid shallows, never suspecting that around the next corner whitewater rapids wait, anxious to engulf you. The ride never slows down until the last few pages."

—*Jonathan Neville, writer*

"One of the things that a novelist, especially one who writes fantasy fiction, is required to do, is get the reader to suspend disbelief, and then sustain that suspension... This is where Martindale succeeds hands down. You will have that little bug in the back of your brain saying, 'Of course that couldn't really happen—could it???'"

— *David Birley, reader*

"His captivating storytelling keeps the plot moving without being predictable or trite. His descriptions ring true, whether he writes about a haggard young mother, a busy bishop, a wistful teenager, or a disaffected rebel."

— *Wife of reader*

"Skillfully written, creating a realistic, complex, difficult world where everything is not as it initially seems. It's a page-turner, a real heavy weight. *Brother Brigham* is a significant, thought provoking, faith affirming, intelligently written novel."

—*Mahonri Stewart, playwright*

"D. Michael has an incredible talent for writing. I was utterly wowed by his characters' inner thoughts."

— *Brian Sheets, digital media specialist*

"I had a hard time putting it down, and as a result I read it surprisingly quickly. I had to know how the whole mess was going to end. It's deep, well thought out, and opens up some interesting and thought-provoking ideas."

—*Lee Penrod, systems programmer*

"The story still lingers in my mind. It was a real page-turner!"

—*Eileen Stringer, reader*

To my sons Matthew and Jason
and to my daughter Natalie
whose mother was scandalized
that I let her read this book.

BOOKS BY D. MICHAEL MARTINDALE

Celeste & the White Dragon
Brother Brigham

Twisted Stories series
Twisted Mind
Twisted Soul

Forward

Theories abound of what *Brother Brigham* is all about and what my motives were for writing it. Some say it's a wonderful book with an important moral message. Some say it's a cautionary tale. Some say it's a Mormon horror story. Some insist everyone should read it. Some warn people away from it, but not because of the quality of the story, but because they feel a need to protect fragile souls from its disturbing influences. Some say it's anti-Mormon.

It's all nonsense!

I wrote *Brother Brigham* as a faithful, practicing Mormon for one reason and one reason only. It's a riproaring great story, and I like to tell stories. I'd read Mormon fiction and found it too preachy or too naive or too encumbered with rose-colored glasses or out-and-out dishonest with how people really behave, all because of a misguided zeal to be faithful and uplifting and—I shiver at the word—"appropriate."

I wanted to write a Mormon story where everybody acts like real people, warts and all. I wanted to write a story that explores the depths and dark recesses of the extraordinary and colorful doctrines and legends and myths of the Mormon mind. Not to preach. Not to condemn. Not to uplift. Not to destroy faith.

To fascinate. To entertain.

I wrote the kind of Mormon novel that I wanted to read, but was nearly impossible to find. Nowadays, Mormon literature is maturing in that direction, but back when I wrote *Brother Brigham*, not so much.

This is a new edition from the original. The story is completely intact in virtually every detail, but I did a rewrite of it, cleaning up clunky sentences, poorly written passages, and outdated technology. While some of my writing skills from the past made me cringe, the story still shines and brings me to tears, even after the zillions of times I've read it.

I love my characters, C.H., Dani, Sheila, Cyndy, even the smaller ones like Moroni and Bishop Schmidt and obnoxious brother Ryan and Special Agent Robertson and therapist Brother Ingols, plus the crew at the bookstore. They are all real people to me, and I ache and weep with them when they're in anguish.

And of course Brother Brigham, a character the likes of which you're unlikely to find anywhere else.

I lament when people avoid getting to know them and living their experiences with them out of fear the story is not "appropriate." Not once the entire time I was writing it did it occur to me I was creating an inappropriate work. I created an honest work that respects the humanity, the strengths, the weaknesses, and the tribulations of each character. *Brother Brigham* wrenches true and honest emotions out of its readers because *Brother Brigham* is true and honest, even as it tells a harrowing, crazy tale that pushes the limits of Mormondom.

As I'm fond of saying, *Brother Brigham* is completely faithful to the Mormon gospel—but not all its characters are!

— D. Michael Martindale, 2018

Chapter 1

Cory Horace Young never could stand Cory or Horace as a name, so when he was old enough to make it stick, he started having everyone call him C.H.

His great-great-grandfather was Brigham Young, something his parents reminded him of often. "You are no ordinary boy," his father would say as they stood before the portrait of Brigham Young that hung in the family room. "You're a descendant of Brigham Young—one of the greatest prophets of all time. God sent you into this family for a purpose. You have a special mission ahead of you."

C.H. would stand before that portrait and stare into the eyes of his great ancestor. The grim expression, the astounding white beard, the pursed lips and piercing eyes frightened and thrilled him. C.H. tried to imagine ever being like him, but couldn't. The man was a towering figure in his family and his religion, almost next to God himself.

C.H.'s father went to graduate school at BYU, and as a young boy fresh out of the waters of baptism, C.H. often visited the campus with him. Behind the administration building stood a life-sized statue of Brigham Young. Whenever they passed it, C.H. scowled at it out of the corner of his eye. He could almost imagine the statue coming to life and Brigham Young growling at him in a commanding voice.

"Cory Horace"—he used C.H.'s two hated names because that made him more frightening—"Cory Horace, are you preparing for your special mission?"

I don't know how to prepare, C.H. answered.

"That's no excuse. You've got my name. Don't you grow up and embarrass me!"

C.H. never liked walking past that statue. but he especially hated it at night. Brigham Young was a dark silhouette then, backlit by the lights from the administration building windows. "Cory Horace!" His name boomed out from that hidden face, echoing throughout the BYU campus. C.H. looked down at the sidewalk and try to ignore him.

But one dark evening as they approached the statue, his father said, "Want to see Brigham Young do the funky chicken?"

"What?"

"Here, get on my back." His father hefted him up into piggyback position. "Now I'll run past, and you watch the statue's legs. It'll look like Brigham Young is dancing."

His father took off, running past the front of the statue about a hundred feet away. C.H. loved how playful his father could be. He couldn't imagine the fathers of some of his friends ever doing anything like this.

He twisted his neck sideways to look at the statue. The light from the windows of the administration building flashed between Brigham's slightly parted legs, and it looked like he was wiggling them back and forth, bending at the knees. Doing the funky chicken.

They fell together onto the grass. C.H. rolled around laughing, and his father laughed with him as he playfully wrestled with him. Students passing by stared at them, and some snickered. C.H. didn't care.

That experience broke the spell of Brigham Young. C.H. could never fear the man again after seeing him do the funky chicken. Several months later when his father died, he made Brigham Young his imaginary friend. At first he stood before the portrait in the family room, talking to him. Before long, he imagined that Brigham Young accompanied him wherever he went. Eventually he began to *see* Brigham. As C.H. grew, he shared his innermost thoughts with him, asked counsel of him, everything he wished he could do with his father. He started calling him "Brother Brigham" after hearing a Joseph Smith quote in Sunday School refer to him that way.

Many times Brother Brigham asked him, "Cory Horace, are you preparing for your special mission?" But it wasn't a frightening question anymore. It was asked with concern and tenderness. He even started liking that Brigham called him by those two names. It was his special name, reserved only for his good friend and proxy father. No one else was allowed to call him that.

"What is my special mission?" C.H. responded.

"When it's time, you'll find out."

"How do I prepare for it if I don't know what it is?"

"You prepare like every other prophet that has come before you. You live the gospel and read the scriptures. You pray and listen. You promise yourself that you will do whatever God asks you to do."

He liked to ask Brother Brigham those questions. It reminded him to keep doing those things so he *would* be prepared for his special mission—whatever it was, whenever it came.

C.H. became a teenager, started seminary, and took up the violin because his father had always liked classical music. He became interested in poetry and started writing some. His English teacher told him that his poems weren't half bad, and the girls seemed impressed by them, so he wrote more. One day after a seminary lesson from the Book of Moses in the Pearl of Great Price, he decided on a pen name and began signing all his poetry *Cain Hell Young*. The girls tittered at it, and his seminary teacher scowled.

After a lesson on patriarchal blessings, he wanted to get his own. His mother set up the appointment, and one Saturday morning they drove to the stake patriarch. He cringed when the patriarch asked him his full name and he had to tell him. C.H. trembled as the heavy hands of the man rested upon his head. What would God have to say to him?

Cory Horace Young was a member of the tribe of Ephraim and would rise in the morning of the first resurrection if he was true to his covenants. Then the patriarch said, "Cory, you are a choice spirit of your Father in Heaven. You have been sent in this time to this family for a purpose. God has a special calling for you. If you are faithful, you will be a great leader in the church and preach the gospel throughout the world."

He could hardly concentrate on the rest. He was glad it was being recorded so he could read it later. He couldn't get those statements out of his mind. *God has a special calling for you. You will be a great leader in the church.*

It was what his father and Brother Brigham had been saying all these years!

The appearances of Brother Brigham died out as C.H. matured. But he kept talking to Brigham like Tevye talked to God in *Fiddler on the Roof*, even though he knew it was a silly thing to do. By the time he attended Brigham Young University as a music major, even those conversations all but faded away. Only occasionally would he indulge in them as a private joke for old time's sake.

Before he could finish school, C.H. was a newlywed husband working as an assistant manager in a mall bookstore in metropolitan Salt Lake City. He got married in the temple, of course, but not to the girl who promised to wait for him. She'd sent the usual Dear John letter one month into the best two years of his life in Hamburg, Germany. Instead he married Danielle, a girl from Minnesota attending BYU as a history major, whom he had known a whopping three months before his bishop, home teachers, and roommates convinced him to pop the question.

That was why he was stuck in a small bookstore in the Valley Fair Mall instead of graduating from BYU with a B.A. in music. One marriage and two children later, with he and Danielle proudly espousing the mother-at-home philosophy, school became out of the question financially—for now. He even had to sell his violin. Some day, he vowed, he'd go back and complete his degree.

Some day...

"What in the world are you reading?" C.H. said one day at work as he sorted through the holds for expired dates.

"*The Satanic Bible*," replied Sheila, a part-time clerk who loved reading more than waiting on customers.

He shook his head and rolled his eyes.

"It's pretty good," she said. "There's a lot in it I agree with. You should read it sometime."

"That'll be the day." He pointedly gazed at a customer coming up to the cash register. Sheila took the hint and waited on the woman, pausing an extra second between ringing up each book to read the title and skim the hype on the back.

It's a good thing she's so attractive, C.H. thought. He didn't think she'd amount to much on her abilities. She was smart but too unfocused.

Milt, the manager of the store, walked up and handed him some papers stapled together. "Here's the week's list of endcaps from headquarters. You want to take care of that?"

C.H. took the papers and started to scan through them.

"Oh," Milt added, "I guess we'd better get some kind of display up for the General Conference visitors. Why don't you set one up with an LDS theme?"

"You bet," he said with a smile. Catholic Milt did this every General Conference—always waited until the last minute to put up an LDS display. "Most General Conference shoppers go to Deseret Book anyway, so why make a big deal out of it?" was his philosophy.

No matter—this was the sort of thing C.H. liked doing, applying a little of his own creativity to an endcap instead of following the carved-in-stone dictates of the corporate suits. What did they know out east about the tastes of readers in Salt Lake City anyway?

One of the required endcaps had a cookbook theme—boring—and another, romance—worse. But one was Orson Scott Card books, thanks to the release of the third volume in his "Obram Wanderer" science fiction series, based on the Book of Abraham in the Pearl of Great Price. Card was a Mormon who had attended BYU and made it big in the real world in a creative field, so he was a hero to C.H. He decided to start on that endcap first.

From Science Fiction he pulled out copies of random Orson Scott Card books and carried them to the end of the aisle where he figured this endcap should go. He filled all but the top two shelves with them. For the second-highest row, he retrieved paperbacks of the first and second installments of the Obram series. He crowned the display with a top row of hardback copies of the third volume, fresh out of the box, keeping one for himself to check out before he left for the day.

Next he tackled the LDS endcap because that was the second most interesting one. On his way to the religion section, he was sidetracked by a customer looking for the latest edition of *The Writer's Market.*

Ah, a creative soul mate! As a writer of music and poetry, C.H. felt a kinship with any artistic person. "What do you write?"

"Oh, it's not for me. It's for my girlfriend," the young man said.

Not a soul mate after all. In fact, he had a look that said he thought the whole idea of writing was silly, but that was what she was into so he'd better go along. C.H. led him to the reference section and handed him the book, then made sure the customer had no other requests before hurrying to Religion to begin scanning titles for interesting LDS books.

The Satanic Bible practically jumped out at him. It was one of those books that a decent employee in a bookstore could only hold his nose and shelve, the same detached attitude he used when customers bought cigarettes or beer at the 7-Eleven where he once worked. But Sheila had made him curious. She was no active member of the church, a de facto apostate who lived in sin with her boyfriend and never did much of anything religious that he could tell. But she was no simpleton either, and he wondered what could possibly be in such a book that would impress her.

Resisting an impulse to look over his shoulder to see if the coast was clear, he picked up the book and gazed at it. The black cover—appropriate—and the picture of its author almost made him put the book back. With shaved head and glaring eyes, the author was doing a creepy satanic hand signal with his two fingers spread along the table. But he thumbed through the book anyway, reading some of the chapter titles:

Wanted: God—Dead or Alive
Hell, the Devil, and How You Sell Your Soul
Satanic Sex
On the Choice of a Human Sacrifice

Gruesome! So far he couldn't see the attraction.

"How're the endcaps coming?" Milt's voice made him jump.

"Oh, fine, fine," C.H. said, feeling like he'd been caught doing something wrong. "I'm working on the LDS one now."

"That's good." Milt glanced at the book in C.H.'s hand, raised an eyebrow, and walked on.

He stuffed the book back onto the shelf and started picking out titles appropriate for LDS customers.

———

C.H. always looked forward to coming home from work. He loved to grab up his two diapered boys and give them hugs and kisses. And he loved to see Danielle, his wife. She was so beautiful with her strawberry blonde hair and one dimpled cheek. Two pregnancies had filled out her figure some, but he thought it made her look better. She had been on the good side of too skinny when he married her.

She usually gave him a deep, lingering kiss when he got home, unless she was in a foul mood. A full eight inches shorter than he was, she always leaned back her head as he held her steady with his hands on her back and leaned down to kiss her. It made him think of Rhett and Scarlett kissing—it made him *feel* like Rhett, and that was fun. He suspected her passionate kisses might have as much to do with welcoming the child-care relief team as with true love, but since he enjoyed them so much, he didn't mind.

When they'd first gotten to know each other, Danielle thought it was a hoot that he signed his creative stuff *Cain Hell Young*. That intrigued him immediately. Most good Mormon BYU coeds clucked or shook their heads in disapproval at his irreverent joke. One even called him to repentance. "How dare you combine the name of a son of perdition and a swear word with the name of one of the greatest prophets of the Lord?"

After explaining to her that Young was *his* last name and telling her to get a grip, he ended the date right there and brought her back to her huffy roommates. All of them turned their noses up at him ever after. Since the roommates were all merely sweet spirits rather than hot like his date, he couldn't have cared less.

But Danielle immediately took to calling him Cain, and he called her Dani, and their romance built from there. On their wedding night, Dani admitted that it intensified her arousal to call him Cain, like she was doing something naughty by making love to the first murderer.

As C.H. walked in the door of their tiny rented duplex, he tossed the Orson Scott Card book that he had checked out—minus the dust jacket, which he was obliged to leave in a file drawer at work—onto the video player on the TV stand. Petey popped a bottle out of his mouth and trotted over. C.H. scooped up the grinning toddler into his arms—dripping upside-down bottle and all—and smothered his face in kisses. The boy giggled.

"How's my little Petey doing?" he said. "You been a good boy for your mama?"

"Gooboy," Petey said.

His two-month-old son was crying from their only bedroom. "Dani, sweetie? What's wrong with Glenn?" He followed the cry into the room.

Dani sat on the bed with little Glenn lying next to her on a blanket, his diaper flopped open and filled with that yellow gooey stuff that reminded C.H. more than anything of scrambled eggs—something he tried hard not to think about at breakfast. It was the kind of waste that exploded up Glenn's back. One look at Dani's eyes, and he knew what he had to do.

"Here, sweetie, let me finish that for you." The new look she gave him as she slid aside made the whole ordeal worth it. He winced as he employed wipe after wipe, which Dani handed to him one at a time. A huge pile of soiled wipes lay in the diaper before Glenn's behind was a sweet baby's bottom again. He wrapped the corrupt diaper around the wad and sealed it tightly shut with its fastening tapes. Dani handed him a clean diaper, and he restored Glenn's modesty, letting out a sigh of relief. Glenn was still crying, but he hadn't squirmed much, and there were no urinary surprises. All in all, not as bad an episode as he'd expected.

He went to the bathroom to dispose of the diaper and wash his hands, then returned and sat on the bed next to Dani and Glenn. He took Glenn from her arms and bounced him gently up and down. The crying soon stopped. Petey wandered in and climbed on his lap. Dani leaned over and kissed C.H. on the cheek. "Thank you," she murmured.

He smiled and stood up. Heading for the hallway, he carried Glenn and dragged Petey beside him. "So what's for dinner?" he called, looking back at her. He stopped as her face filled with a weary and apologetic look.

"I haven't even thought about that yet."

Oops! That joke had been a mistake. "I was just kidding," he said. "Don't worry about it. I'll fix something."

After eating dinner and feeding the kids and putting them to sleep, C.H. and Dani sat on their frayed sofa—one of their "DI wonders" bought from thrift store Deseret Industries—and stared at the TV, a *M*A*S*H* rerun. She snuggled her head on his shoulder and wrapped both her arms around one of his. He took it as an expression of gratitude.

"Sheila was reading *The Satanic Bible* today," he said when the commercials took over.

Dani chuckled. "She's really something else. How many earrings does she have?"

"I think about half a dozen per ear."

"Should I pierce my ears half a dozen times?" she murmured into his biceps. "Do you think she looks pretty that way?"

C.H. thought about it. Sheila was just a few years younger than they were.

Her auburn hair and deep-set eyes appealed to him. Often at work, he caught himself staring at her before turning away in chagrin. But there was no reason to burden Dani with every little trial of temptation he faced. He loved his wife—it wasn't like he had any intention of acting on his casual attraction to Sheila.

"She's cute enough, but not because of all those earrings. I'd just as soon you pass on that idea."

She laughed, a single "hmm."

He pulled his arm from her hands and put it around her shoulders. He kissed her, caressing her arm. His hand slid up her shoulder and down her chest, until it cupped her breast. He started to caress.

She pulled away, gently but firmly. "I'm sorry, Cain. I'm just so tired."

He straightened up and let her put her head back on his shoulder. He'd have to grit his teeth for one more day. He could count on two fingers how many times they'd had sex in the last several months, neither of them since Glenn was born eight weeks ago. But he didn't want to press things. He knew it wasn't just a lame excuse—she usually *was* exhausted with two little boys both in diapers, one exclusively breast fed.

Dani went to bed early and fell asleep immediately. C.H.'s legs and feet felt sore from standing all day, and he knew how much he'd thrash around for a while before he slept, keeping Dani awake. So he stayed up and stared at the TV. He toyed with the idea of starting to read the new Orson Scott Card book, but decided he was too tired. He was always tired after work. Dani was always tired all the time.

What a life they led!

If he'd stayed in school, he'd have graduated by now. This situation was supposed to be temporary until they got on their feet. But he began to wonder if they'd ever escape.

At work, he was officially on track to become a manager. He had to wait for two other assistant managers in other stores in the district to become managers because they had more seniority, then it would be his turn. Then he'd make enough money to go back to school.

But then he'd have absolutely no time to do it. He saw how hard Milt worked. C.H. had to work most Sundays because Milt took them off. But that didn't bother C.H. because Milt worked his butt off the rest of the week. Milt's store was the top one in the district, but he paid a heavy price to keep it there.

And C.H. would be in the same position as a manager. There would be no time for school.

He lay back on the sofa and closed his eyes. A Deseret Book commercial came on. As he started to doze, he thought he heard something about Brigham Young.

"Brother Brigham," he murmured, half asleep. "Where do I go from here? How do I get out of this trap?"

He thought of his patriarchal blessing. "And when is my special calling coming?" He chuckled a little. A special calling seemed like the last thing that would ever happen to him. Nothing special happened in their lives. Just the same old grind like everybody else.

When Glenn's crying woke him, C.H. crawled into bed since Dani would be awake now anyway. Both boys woke up several times during the night, Glenn for his feedings and Petey just on general principle.

When C.H. awoke the next morning, Dani and the boys were still asleep. He checked the clock. Ten-thirty—General Conference had started half an hour ago! With a groan, he clambered out of bed, padded into the living room, turned on the TV, and rummaged for a VHS tape to recycle that didn't have anything important on it. He always taped General Conference so he could listen to a little bit of it every morning before going to work, to get him into a good frame of mind for the day.

At least, that's what he always intended to do. Somehow every day for six months he never got around to it. At the end of every six months, when the next General Conference rolled around, he would repent and say, "This time for sure!"

Sliding the cartridge into the slot brought him back into a funk. He couldn't even afford to get his family a Blu-ray player or even cable, and those things were already on their way to becoming outdated. He sighed and pushed the feeling away.

When he finally got the machine recording, he sat back into his recliner with a sigh, popped out the footrest, and leaned back. He missed the first half hour. He'd have to make sure he read the *Ensign* Conference report, this time for sure.

His recliner was a hand-me-down from his mother instead of a DI wonder like most of their furniture, and it was in a little better condition. He always sat there unless he wanted to sit next to Dani. Almost immediately his eyes drooped, and he dozed. When Dani came out and lay on the sofa, he woke up. Some unfamiliar General Authority was speaking, probably one of the Seventies. He was warning his listeners about the danger of apostasy.

"Keep your eye on the prophet," the man said. "He will never lead the church astray. We have that promise from God."

After a few more words, the nameless General Authority said amen and sat down. A regional youth choir from Davis County broke into a rendition of "We Thank Thee, O God, for a Prophet." How appropriate for that song to follow that talk, he thought. He wondered if it was deliberately planned, inspiration, or just dumb luck.

Grateful that the boys were both napping, he dozed again, letting the waves of music wash over him and break up into incoherent ramblings of his half-asleep mind. Dani began to snore, partially rousing him to consciousness, but not enough to open his eyes. He dreamed Brother Brigham standing at the podium, looking as he must have looked in real life all those years ago. He was speaking, but C.H. couldn't make out the words. It was the same deep, resonating voice he'd always imagined for Brother Brigham.

"Cory Horace," said a whisper.

"Hmm?" One eyelid lifted halfway open and stared at the TV. The choir was still singing.

"Cory Horace."

His eye slid closed again. He could see Brigham standing at the podium, gazing straight into the television camera, lips pursed, eyes piercing C.H.'s soul. "I have a task for you to do."

"Mm-mmm," said C.H.

"The salt flats," said Brother Brigham.

"Mm-hmmm-hmm? What?" C.H. muttered.

"In the Great Salt Lake Desert."

Dani snorted loudly, startling herself and C.H. awake. She giggled with embarrassment and fell back asleep.

The hymn was over, and another nameless General Authority was speaking. "Many are called, but few are chosen," he said. "Who does the calling? The Lord, usually through his inspired servants. And who does the choosing? We do. We choose ourselves by accepting the call and fulfilling it."

C.H.'s stomach growled, and he got up to make himself a ham sandwich. He had a vague feeling of something communicated to him in a dream, but it slipped away as he spread the mayonnaise and sliced the tomato. When he accidentally tipped over the saltshaker as he reached for the head of lettuce, he suddenly remembered. "Salt flats," he murmured. Brother Brigham had said something about the salt flats. What in the world was that all about?

C.H. shrugged and pressed the slices of bread together, poured a glass of milk, and returned to the recliner. The next few speakers were actual apostles with names and faces he recognized. It amused him how many of them were former BYU presidents. That must be some sort of boot camp for apostles.

After the sandwich, sleep took over once more, Dani's soft snoring notwithstanding. Glenn's cry woke them both, and Dani hurried into the bedroom. Commercials played, meaning that the morning session was over. C.H. got up and stopped the VCR, rewound the tape until he found the end of the morning session, then left it loaded and ready for the afternoon. He couldn't do all that with the remote control these days because it was long lost. Probably Petey dropped it in the garbage and no one noticed until the garbage man drove away. He'd put it there before.

C.H. smacked his mouth several times at the dry and disgusting flavor inside. Probably a jillion bacteria had grown off the remains of his sandwich and milk while he slept. He walked to the bathroom, brushed his teeth, and rinsed with a mouthwash loaded with alcohol to kill the unwelcome creepy-crawlies in his mouth.

"How about mowing the lawn?" Dani said as she came up behind him and embraced him.

"But it's Sunday."

"It is not!" she said with a swat on his butt.

"Oh, yeah." General Conference always did that to him, made him feel like Saturday was Sunday. Still, it seemed disrespectful to do something as mundane as mowing the lawn between spiritually uplifting sessions of Conference.

Not that he'd gotten much inspiration staring at the back of his eyelids.

"Glenn's back asleep. I'll make breakfast while you're out there." Dani gave him a squeeze, kissed the nape of his neck, and headed out of the bathroom.

"Thank you," he said, keeping quiet about the ham sandwich. It hadn't filled him, and he knew the smell of more food would get him hungry again.

He retrieved the mower from the shed. It required three tugs to start it sputtering and smoking. He mowed the front yard first. Other mowers droned in the neighborhood, guided by other husbands who'd been banished to the lawn to get in one more mowing before winter took over. It was a nice, sunshiny day, after all, even if the temperature was a bit nippy.

The new guy across the street was deep into working on his car. He had headphones on—did that mean he'd been listening to Conference, or just some raucous music? C.H. had gone over and met him last Saturday when he moved in. He was single, named Moroni. C.H. assumed that meant he was a member of the church, which was a good thing. No one in the ward would pressure him to spread the gospel to the new neighbor. He hoped the man *had* been listening to Conference—otherwise he might be inactive, and everyone would expect C.H. to fellowship him. He had no idea if Moroni had been to church last Sunday, since C.H. had been at work. But the fellow's long blond hair and stained tank top made him doubt it.

Moroni waved, and C.H. waved back.

The chill air lost its bite as his body warmed up from the exertion. When he finished the front yard, Moroni was still working waist-deep in engine. Trying not to breathe in the burnt oil fumes, C.H. dragged the sputtering mower into the back and started on that lawn. It really belonged to the other half of their duplex, but since the back apartment was currently vacant, he'd offered to keep the yard up for a cut in rent.

"Cory Horace."

The sound made him jump. In spite of the mower roaring in his ears, the words were clear and soft. C.H. looked from side to side and saw nothing.

"Cory Horace."

He whipped around and looked behind him. Brother Brigham stood there in full view, a vivid image in the sunlight. It was as if he reflected more light than what shone on him. He seemed to be outlined with a thin layer of glistening sun rays. He had a robe on, open at the chest, and C.H. immediately thought of the angel Moroni visiting Joseph Smith. Brigham's feet were bare and stood inches off the ground. The colors of Brigham's robe, face, and beard shimmered with unreal ferocity.

"Brother Brigham," C.H. said, the hairs all over his skin creeping.

"I have a task for you, Cory Horace." Brigham's voice reverberated against the grumbling of the mower.

"The salt flats," C.H. said with a sudden rush of memory.

Brigham nodded. "Yes, go toward the salt flats and the Great Salt Lake Desert. Take Interstate 80 to the Clive exit. Follow the frontage road west until you get to mile marker forty-five on the freeway. Walk perpendicular to the road one hundred yards. You will find a backpack there. Bring it home and wait for further instructions."

"When?"

"*Now!*" Brother Brigham barked, then smiled cryptically and vanished.

C.H. blinked and rubbed his eyes. His head swam with shock. Brother Brigham hadn't appeared for years, even though C.H. still talked to him occasionally. And he'd never appeared like that, so vivid in appearance, so vibrant in color, speaking so forcefully and succinctly. Always he spoke more like a patient, understanding father. Always he was a bit vague and drab in appearance, a bit dubious in location, shifting here and there, with his voice coming from no particular direction. This visitation was strong, intense, authoritative, and *real*. Or so it seemed, compared to all the others.

And that robe! Brother Brigham had never worn a robe before.

C.H. absently shut off the mower and, leaving it where it stood, walked around to the front door and entered the house. Dani stood at the stove, still trying to get some eggs scrambled with Petey, now awake, clinging to her leg. "Done?" she said.

He stared at her, trying to understand her word. "No, I—I've got to go somewhere." He grabbed his wallet and car keys sitting on the counter.

"Where are you going?"

He tried to think what he could say, but only shook his head. "I'll tell you when I get back." He slammed the door behind him as he rushed out to the carport, climbed into their rusting Corolla, and drove off with a slight squeal of tires.

He felt disconnected from the world. They lived just south of I-80 on 400 East. In a moment he was on the freeway heading west. As he drove, his thoughts started to collect, and he chanted, "This is nuts! This is nuts!"

What on earth was he doing? His imaginary friend shows up and tells him to go get a backpack in the middle of nowhere, and he actually goes? Was he out of his mind?

"What's going on, Brother Brigham?"

But it was so easy to keep traveling in the direction he was already headed. The freeway jogged north for the short stretch where it combined with I-15, then west again. He drove past the Salt Lake City International Airport, the Airport Hilton fountain glistening in the sun, past the Saltair resort building with its onion-shaped domes. The faint stench of Great Salt Lake brine shrimp filled his nostrils.

"Did you really appear to me, Brother Brigham?"

Of course not—it was absurd. Certainly as a Mormon he believed that supernatural visitations were possible, theoretically. But a visitation to him?

Nonsense!

As he approached the Oquirrh Mountains on the left, the smokestack of the Kennecott copper plant belched out smoke. His feelings of foolishness deepened, and he told himself he would get off at the Tooele exit and turn around. The Great Salt Lake shone to his right, a vast sweep of grayish-blue extending to the horizon, with Antelope Island and Stansbury Island further ahead breaking the view.

But as the Tooele exit neared, he asked himself, *Why was it nonsense?* Joseph Smith was fourteen when he received his first heavenly vision. Samuel in the Old Testament was called by the voice of God as a young boy. Why should it be nonsense for C.H. to receive a vision? God had worked through common people before.

Because C.H. wasn't valiant in his service to God, that's why. He hardly ever went to church, thanks to working so many Sundays. Slept through Conference. Couldn't remember the last time he'd prayed, not personally, not with his family. Hadn't cracked the scriptures for personal study since his religion classes at BYU. Didn't even have a church calling anymore.

Not valiant—that's what described him. Just like the passage in the Doctrine and Covenants said. Bound for the terrestrial kingdom. He never did anything really *bad*—he just wasn't valiant in doing good.

The Tooele exit beckoned to him. No, he couldn't have had a heavenly visitation. Not him. He wasn't worthy of such a thing.

But Brother Brigham had appeared so different, so real.

It was absurd to think there could be anything valid about all this. So he visualized his imaginary friend more vividly than ever before. So what?

But what if it *was* real, and he didn't go? Once more he would be unvaliant in obeying a commandment.

The exit passed without him making a decision. The bottom line was that he knew it would drive him nuts if he never found out. So he'd drive out to mile marker forty-five, count out a hundred paces, find nothing, and go home feeling silly but satisfied that it was just his imagination acting up, punishment for falling asleep during General Conference.

Mile marker ninety-eight was the first one after the exit. What would he tell Dani after driving halfway to Wendover for no reason? He already felt chagrin at not telling her anything before he left. It wasn't like he was in the habit of keeping secrets from her. He was just in a daze—who could think straight after seeing Brigham Young in a vision? While mowing the lawn.

And when he drove out there and found nothing, what would he say then? He didn't know if he could admit to the love of his life what an utter fool he'd made of himself, especially when it was costing a large portion of the gas in the tank. They weren't exactly swimming in money.

The freeway made its wide arc across the Tooele Valley, avoiding the Great Salt Lake. Eventually the Morton Salt plant appeared on the right with its piles of white salt. Dull gray mud covered with patches of grass and sagebrush took over the landscape. C.H. began to hope a backpack really was there so he wouldn't have to excuse his trip to Dani.

But if a backpack *was* there, then the real Brigham Young *had* appeared to him, *had* told him to perform a task, *had* promised him further instructions.

Could this be his special mission?

He shuddered. No, it had to be a ridiculous daydream. Why would God call someone who was unvaliant? Even Saul, persecutor of the early Christians, had been valiant in what he believed was right. Why hadn't God just spewed lukewarm C.H. out of his mouth, being neither cold nor hot?

Mile marker sixty passed, then fifty-five, then fifty. A sign announced the Clive exit. He turned off. The frontage road was gravel, but he didn't slow down much. He watched anxiously for the little spot of green on a post that said forty-five. The freeway mile markers were easy to see, the frontage road being so close.

His heart began to pound as forty-five appeared. There had been no traffic on the gravel road, so C.H. stopped in the middle of it and shut off the engine. Grass stalks waved and sagebrush quivered in the wind. A small herd of what he thought might be elk meandered off in the distance, munching on the vegetation. A semi zoomed by on the freeway, rattling the car windows.

C.H. spent a moment repressing feelings of embarrassment, then climbed out of the car and slammed the door. The elk startled and wandered farther away. C.H. walked over to the edge of the road and stared at the field before him.

"Technically, Brigham, this isn't the salt flats," he said out loud. Those were farther west, next to the Nevada border. They were white and devoid of growth, and maybe even flooded a couple feet deep for the winter by now. Then he remembered—it was the "dream" Brigham who had told him to go *to* the salt flats. The "real" Brigham had said go *toward* the salt flats. He pursed his lips in shame at his careless criticism of a prophet. The expression became a frown as he realized he was thinking of the Brother Brigham apparition as real.

C.H. strained to see anything unusual. Just grass and sagebrush. He tried to visualize a hundred yards. A football field. He imagined himself sitting in the end zone of the BYU stadium—something he'd done often enough with various dates—and tried to determine where the far end zone would be, then looked hard for anything unusual around there. Nothing.

He almost turned to leave, but that *had-to-know* feeling was still there. He checked right and left for any highway patrol approaching on the freeway, not quite understanding why he felt guilty, then headed north away from the road, peering ahead intently, counting paces as he went.

By the time he was a first down's worth of distance away from the far end zone, he saw the backpack, partially hidden behind a swatch of grass. C.H. shivered, suddenly wishing it hadn't been there. This should not be happening! Brother Brigham had to be a figment of his imagination—the real Brigham Young wouldn't appear to him. The backpack had to be an elaborate, vivid mirage, as vivid as the hallucination of Brother Brigham. That must have been some ham sandwich he'd eaten earlier.

He stopped before the backpack and studied it. An olive-green, Army-surplus backpack, made of canvas. Filthy with the residue of evaporated raindrops. Well worn, but still in decent condition. How long had it been there?

C.H. dreaded to pick it up. Slowly he reached for the strap. The tips of his fingers touched it—it was real. He grabbed the strap and had to yank the pack free from dried mud, leaving a moist imprint. A handful of bugs skittered away.

A blast of chilly wind made him shiver, grateful for the faint warmth of the sun. He hefted the backpack, testing its weight. Something was inside, moderately heavy.

"What's in here, Brigham?"

He opened the flap and peered in. A musty smell of mildew assaulted him. Inside was paper, countless bundles of green paper. Money green. He pulled out one bundle. The band around it was imprinted with "$100." From his bookstore work, he knew that was the standard band for one-dollar bills that came from the bank in bundles of one hundred. But these bills were not ones—they were hundreds. At least the top one was. He riffled through them—they were all hundreds. That would be ten thousand dollars! He rummaged through the rest of the bundles. They all seemed to be hundreds. C.H.'s breath came in short gusts. How many thousands of dollars must be in there!

Instinctively he swung his head around, peering guiltily at the freeway. A couple of cars passed by, but no cop had appeared. The elk were way off in the distance. He scanned the area around where the backpack had lain. For an instant he thought of skyjacker D.B. Cooper, but that was too outlandish. So where had the money come from? Who would leave it? Did someone come out here with it and die? Then where was the body, or the picked-over bones? Where were the footprints? No, there wouldn't be any footprints if this thing had sat out here for as long as it appeared.

C.H. headed with a forced stride back to his car, trying not to look guilty. Now more than ever, he didn't want a cop finding him out here with a bag full of hundred-dollar bills. At the car, he opened the front passenger door and flung the backpack onto the floor. It poofed out a cloud of dust. He slammed the door shut and leaned his back against it, breathing heavily and trying to calm his pounding heart.

"What am I supposed to do with all that money, Brother Brigham?"

Part of him wished he'd have another visitation right now so he could get those "further instructions" Brigham had promised. Part of him hoped the second visitation would never come.

He finally felt recovered enough to drive, but he couldn't bring himself to get back into the car with that backpack lying inside. He stared straight ahead to where it once lay on the ground. Why did it have to be there? What would he tell Dani? Coming up with some other excuse for why he went on a gas-wasting wild goose chase seemed the better option now.

A brief siren pulse blasted behind him, and he nearly jumped into the air as he let out an involuntary cry. He turned and found a highway patrol car stopped along the freeway shoulder, nothing more than a barbed-wire fence between it and C.H. An officer exited the vehicle, leaned on his open door, and stared inscrutably through dark glasses. "Is there a problem, sir?"

"Oh, no," C.H. said, trying hard to keep his voice calm. "Everything's fine, officer."

"Why are you stopped in the middle of the road?"

"Oh, I dozed off at the wheel and thought I should step out for a minute and wake myself up." C.H. stared at the officer, trying to read his face, trying to figure out if he was buying his lie. A lie from someone called of God!

"Good idea," said the officer with no emotion in his voice. "Are you okay now?"

"Yes, I'm feeling pretty alert." That was certainly true, with about a thousand gallons of adrenalin pumping through his body.

"Alright, then, move on." The patrolman gazed around one more time, as if hoping to find probable cause for something. C.H. held his breath to keep from visibly panting.

The officer climbed back into his car and drove away.

He had to wait another several minutes to calm down again, then he rushed into the car and started it. Torn between getting out of there as fast as possible and not wanting to attract attention, he forced himself to make a careful U-turn and drive at thirty miles an hour back to the freeway ramp. Once on the freeway, he continually pulled his foot off the gas pedal to bring his speed back down to the speed limit. All the way to Salt Lake City his head swam, and he breathed shallowly with apprehension.

"Dammit, Brigham, what the hell is going on?" he shouted. He was too agitated to feel bad about swearing.

Chapter 2

Over two hours! Where was Cain?

Dani tried to ignore the cold, drying breakfast sitting on the kitchen counter as Glenn sucked. So far Petey had amused himself on the floor with the set of blocks her sister Crista had given him for his birthday. They were the old kind, wooden and cubed with letters and numbers, well worn. Crista probably got them at DI before she flunked out of her second freshman semester at BYU and went back home to Minnesota.

Dani prayed Petey would keep playing until Glenn finished. Or until C.H. got home. Or maybe she'd feel better if Petey *did* distract her from the images in her head. Car lying upside-down in a ditch. C.H. in a coma bleeding to death.

She shook her head angrily. She hated it when she did that to herself.

But where was he?

General Conference was over. She tried concentrating on the TV show that came next, but it was too insipid. With Glenn nursing, she didn't want to get up to change the channel. The commercials were more entertaining than the show. Until that lawyer came on...

"Have you or a loved one been injured in an accident?"

Where was Cain?

Glenn's sucking weakened. He was falling asleep. Dani closed her eyes in anticipation of the sweet moments of freedom she would soon get. When the sucking stopped, she opened her eyes and looked down. Yes, he was asleep.

Petey stood in front of them, block in hand. "Baby play block," he said and rammed the block down on Glenn's cheek.

Glenn screamed with his infant voice.

She cried, "Petey!"

Petey said, "Baby play block," with his big-eyed innocent look.

A drop of blood formed on Glenn's cheek where the corner of the block had cut through. Dani struggled to her feet with Glenn in her arms, rushed into the bathroom, tore off a wad of toilet paper, and moistened it under warm water. Glenn's wail filled the small room, and the drop on his cheek became a trickle. She wiped the blood away. Another drop formed immediately.

Dani opened the medicine cabinet and pulled out the box of bandaids. She set it down and pried it open with one hand. As she rummaged in it with two fingers, she knocked it onto the floor. Band-Aids scattered.

Behind her Petey cried, "Ban-aid!" He reached between her legs and shuffled them around.

"Out of here, Petey!" she cried, trying to step over his arm and crouch in the cramped room without knocking him over. Glenn's cry felt like a pounding on both sides of her head.

Petey stood and held out a bandaid. "Ban-aid?"

It was the small size that she wanted. Petey had redeemed himself. Dani took a deep, calming breath and said, "Thank you, honey. Now go play with your blocks."

"Baby play block," Petey said.

"No, Petey play with blocks. Baby got hurt."

"Baby hurt?"

She wanted to scream *Get out!* but she clenched her teeth and said, "Yes, baby hurt. Now go play with your blocks."

Petey finally left. Dani shushed Glenn as she rocked him a moment and dabbed at his cheek once more. When he calmed a little, she ripped open the Band-Aid wrapper with her teeth, barely caught the Band-Aid as it flew out, used her teeth again to remove the plastic linings, and covered Glenn's wound. In the mirror she noticed that her breast was still exposed.

On the way back out, she stopped at the TV and flipped through the channels until she found something tolerable. She noticed that the VCR was still taping and shut it off, then dropped onto the sofa with a grunt and, leaning Glenn on her shoulder, covered up her breast. Glenn still whimpered, and she caressed his back.

Where was Cain? He'd never done anything like this before.

I'm going to kill him when he gets home.

Anger felt much better than fear.

But fear was more insistent. She wished desperately to see his face again, to hold him, even though she knew that when he came home she'd yell at him.

The door burst open, startling her. C.H. stood there gazing at her. An angry *Where have you been!* nearly escaped her lips, but she saw the wild look in his eyes. Something was wrong.

He strode to the coffee table and lowered a backpack onto it, holding it by one strap. She noticed how dirty it was and cringed. "What's that?" she said, holding back all her seething emotions until he had a chance to explain. The television show droned on.

Petey dropped the block he was holding and waddled over to investigate, leaning his hands on the table. He pointed and said, "Whassat?"

C.H. peered at Dani, breathing heavily. "You remember my imaginary friend, Brother Brigham?"

Brother Brigham? He hadn't mentioned him for a year or more. "What's going on, Cain?" she said as calmly as she could.

He began to pace back and forth, a short trip in that living room. "I—saw him today."

"You saw Brother Brigham today?"

"I saw—" He stopped and looked at her, eyes shining fiercely. "I saw Brigham Young."

Dani could smell a musty odor coming from the backpack. She closed her eyes and tried to calm herself. Why was he talking in circles? "You saw Brigham Young." She opened them again. "In the flesh?"

His gaze unfocused as his forehead wrinkled, and then he chuckled humorlessly. "I don't know."

"Cain, tell me what's going on."

His finger shot out and pointed at the backpack. "*That's* what's going on!" He picked it up, opened the flap, and turned it upside down. Bundles of cash tumbled onto the table, some spilling onto the floor.

She gasped. "*What is going on, Cain?*"

Petey began knocking bundles off the table, crying, "Money!"

C.H. dropped the backpack to the floor and fell back into the recliner. The musty smell filled the room. The TV offered a great return on money market certificates.

Staring at the ceiling, C.H. said, "Brother Brigham appeared to me while I was mowing the lawn. I mean Brigham Young. He said to drive out toward the salt flats, pick up this backpack, and bring it back."

She focused on one of the bundles lying on the floor. The bill on top was a hundred! Carefully she laid Glenn on the sofa, barely noticing that he was asleep, got down on her knees, grabbed the bundle, and fanned it slowly. "They're all hundreds?"

He nodded.

"How many?"

"I don't know yet."

A sickening feeling gripped her heart. She knew their financial situation bothered him. She knew it needled him to be making so little at the bookstore, even as an assistant manager. He should have graduated by now and started a career in music. Instead he was in *retail*, of all things.

She glanced at the TV. A commercial for laundry detergent was running. *Retail.*

She knew he expected to be stuck as a manager in retail for the rest of his life. And he hated the idea, even though he tried not to let on.

Dani felt tears brimming in her eyes. She didn't want to think the thought that was forming, but it wouldn't let go of her. C.H. was a good man. Yes, his job kept him away from church too much, and his despondency over his career made him complacent in a lot of ways, but he was still a good man. He loved her and the boys. He helped around the house more than any man she knew. He was that way with his mother too. He was handsome and funny and talented. A good man. True, he'd been arrested for shoplifting once, but that was a long time ago. He would never do anything like that now.

Would he?

"Dani?" He gazed at her from the recliner, his jowl muscles tense. She stared into his face, trying to read his emotions. The noisy commercials ceased, and the regular programming resumed.

What would a man who felt like a failure resort to? She suddenly began to wonder just how much of a failure he felt like. Frantically she searched through her memory, trying to think of anything she might have said or done to help him feel that way. She didn't think she had, but could he have read accusation into innocent things? Had she ever talked about wanting to get something she knew they couldn't afford? Had she ever scolded him for not doing something he should? Of course she had.

"What are you thinking?" he said.

The tears wouldn't hold back any longer. *Don't ask me that*, she thought. She blinked her eyes and let the tears spill onto her cheeks. Petey handed her a bundle of cash and said, "Want money, mommy?"

She accepted the bundle and stared at it, then looked at C.H. "Cain, I love you. Everything will be alright. You don't have to do this."

He peered at her with a confused expression.

"I love you as you are. I'm proud of you *right now*." She felt a desperate urgency to say what was bottled up inside her. "We'll get by, and things will get better. We'll do it together. That's all that matters."

"What?"

She held the bundle up. "We don't need this." She tossed it on the table. "We'll manage. I don't care that we're struggling right now."

Horror seeped into his eyes. He stood up, walked over to the TV, jammed it off, and leaned his head and arm against the wall.

Petey handed her another bundle, but she ignored him. She stood and came up behind C.H.

"Cain." She put a hand on his shoulder and waited until he turned around. Holding up the bundle, she said, "Cain, how did you get this?"

His eyes narrowed. "You really think I could do that? Is that what you believe?"

A moment of anger flared inside her. *What am I supposed to believe? That Brigham Young visited you and sent you off to pick up a backpack full of money? Is* that *what I'm supposed to believe?* "Please," she almost whispered, "just tell me what happened."

He gazed at her an instant, then took her hand and led her to the sofa. They sat together, barely fitting into the space not occupied by Glenn. He held her hand in both of his and said, "I know this sounds crazy, but I promise you it's the truth."

She nodded, barely able to breathe, wondering what he would say.

"I was mowing the lawn. Brother Brigham appeared to me. He told me to drive out on the freeway toward the salt flats until I got to mile marker forty-five. Then I was supposed to walk out a hundred yards and find *that*." He nodded at the pile of money. "I was supposed to bring it home and wait for further instructions."

Dani waited for him to say more, but he didn't. He just gazed into her eyes expectantly. She tried to process the information. She tried to think of something to say. All that came to her was *Are you serious?* but she knew that wouldn't go over well. She studied his unflinching eyes, watched him wet his lips, felt the slight trembling in his hands, and realized that she didn't need to ask. He *was* serious. And he was afraid she wouldn't believe him.

Did she believe him? Could she?

"Is that everything?" she finally thought to say. He nodded.

If she didn't believe him, then not only had he brought thousands of dollars home under suspicious circumstances, but he was lying through his teeth about it. To *her*. To the police, she could understand. But to *her*—that was unthinkable. He'd never been deceptive with her before. He confessed the shoplifting to her when she never would have known about it. He told her about the girl he'd done some heavy petting with back in high school. He even told her about the time he snuck into a movie with his friends back in sixth grade. He wanted no secrets from her, he said, big or small. He wanted her to know who she was marrying. He wanted to know that she accepted him as he was. And she always had.

No, she couldn't imagine him lying to her.

But if he wasn't lying, then Brother Brigham *had* appeared to him. Hallucination? Nervous breakdown? Had the pressure gotten to him? Was he subconsciously trying to manufacture his "special calling" that he used to talk about?

She looked at the bundles of hundred-dollar bills, all on the floor now thanks to Petey. Hallucinations don't hand over thousands of dollars in cash.

Brother Brigham had appeared to him. No, Brother Brigham was an imaginary friend. *Brigham Young* had appeared to her husband. So he claimed.

"Cain—" she started to say, then shook her head. Either he was a thief or out of his mind. Or, she thought, looking at the cash, he really saw Brigham Young.

Which was the most likely possibility? Thief—she couldn't bring herself to believe that. Out of his mind—possibly, although he didn't seem to be. And how does a crazed hallucination hand over money?

There it was, the pile of hundreds, staring at her, daring her to dismiss it. She couldn't, of course. C.H. had run out of the house agitated and returned with a backpack of money.

She put her arms around him and whispered next to his ear, "I believe you."

He squeezed her tightly.

"But I don't understand it," she added.

He broke the embrace and gazed into her eyes. "Neither do I."

"Money, mommy?" Petey said, offering a bundle again.

Dani accepted it. "How much is there?"

He blinked. "I guess we should count it."

On hands and knees, they stacked the bundles back on the table. Fifteen of them. "These bands are what the bank uses to bundle dollar bills together," C.H. explained. "A hundred in one band."

"So if these hold a hundred bills each..."

He slipped the band off one bundle and counted. She had to stop Petey from picking at the band on another bundle. "One hundred," C.H. announced.

"A hundred times a hundred times fifteen," she said. "A hundred and fifty thousand dollars." They gazed at each other with eyes wide. She could hardly breathe. "What are we supposed to do with it?"

He studied the bundles. "We wait for further instructions." He leaned over the table to grab the backpack off the floor, then stuffed the bundles back in. Petey whined when he took the last bundle from him.

C.H. marched to the closet and shoved the pack onto the shelf above the coats. She cringed at the streak of dirt she knew was on the shelf now. As a consolation, she went to the kitchen, wet a paper towel, and wiped the dirt that had settled on the coffee table. She'd get the closet later.

He stood there, gazing at her as she wiped the table. He seemed more at peace now—calm, no pacing, no clenched jaw. She didn't want to disturb that calm, but there was a question gnawing at her. Whether the actual Brigham Young had sent her husband to get it or not, someone had left that backpack out there in the first place. In a mild voice she said, "Where do you suppose the money came from?"

His calm expression disappeared. His eyes squinted a little and looked down. Slowly he shook his head, then suddenly he peered at the wall clock. "I'm going to try and find out."

Dani glanced at the clock. It was shortly after five. "How?"

"The library. A missing hundred and fifty thousand dollars ought to show up in the news somewhere."

"Sir, the library is closing."

C.H. looked at his watch. Five fifty-nine. He nodded to the woman, closed the browser on the computer, and stood and stretched. The library lights began to dim as he walked out and down the mall of specialty shops to the elevator. He rode it down to the underground parking and got into the car. He slid the key into the ignition, then stopped, gazing straight ahead.

He'd spent forty minutes looking for bank robberies, embezzlements, kidnappings, drug deals—anything that might generate a hundred and fifty thousand dollars in cash in a backpack. He planned on making a list of any episodes involving that amount of money and work from there. Based on the condition of the backpack, he planned on covering a year or so of online *Salt Lake Tribune* articles, but he could cover only four months before the Salt Lake library closed.

It wouldn't have mattered anyway. Any possible news story reported "an undisclosed amount of money," and C.H. despaired of ever finding out anything that way.

He really didn't know what he was doing. Musicians don't learn how to do research. He spent his education studying music theory, history, and appreciation, not to mention practicing piano and violin. His experience with research amounted to a few papers in English 115. He'd turn this whole mess over to the authorities to figure out, if it weren't for how he found the money.

I'll wait for further instructions, he told himself. *I'll ask Brother Brigham where the money came from. There must be a satisfying explanation.*

He needed to pray about it—that was the Sunday school answer. But since he couldn't remember the last time he prayed, he felt embarrassed coming before God now. What was it about prayer that made it so easy to overlook, to neglect, until finally you got so out of the habit you didn't even feel bad about missing it anymore?

Why would God select someone who hadn't prayed in months?

But he remembered that God *had* selected someone else who neglected prayer—the brother of Jared in the Book of Mormon. And look what happened to him. He saw the Lord by the irresistible force of his own faith. If God was determined to choose C.H., he wouldn't let him off the hook just because he hadn't been praying. He'd expect him to repent.

The admonition in that morning's Conference came back with full force. "Who does the calling? The Lord, usually through his inspired servants. And who does the choosing? We do. We choose ourselves by accepting the call and fulfilling it."

He vowed to accept whatever call came to him and fulfill it valiantly. He'd been complacent far too long in his service to God. He'd do all the things he'd been taught over the years. Pray to verify the truthfulness of the calling, then accept it with all his heart. Read scriptures and pray every day—alone and with his wife. Have family home evening each week. Work harder to attend as many of his meetings as he could. Maybe he should even get a different job, one that didn't make him work so many Sundays.

He thought of praying on the spot, but with all the people heading for their cars from the library, he decided that the privacy of his home would be better. He started the car and drove out into the street.

When he walked through the door at home, Dani sat at the kitchen table eating soup and a grilled cheese sandwich, and Petey sat in his high chair, spoon in hand, soup everywhere. Glenn must have been asleep in the crib.

"Did you find anything out?" she asked.

"Not a thing."

She gave him a tight smile as he pulled a paper towel off the roll, wet it, and swabbed up spills on the floor. "Is Glenn asleep?" he asked.

"Yes. Are you hungry?"

He realized that he was—he hadn't eaten since that ham sandwich seven hours ago. But he had more important things to do right now, and besides, several hours of fasting could only help his praying. "I'll wait. I'm going into the bedroom for a minute. I need to be alone."

"Don't wake Glenn," she said emphatically.

Don't worry, he thought, *that's the last thing I want to do.* He walked down the short hall and carefully opened the door, crept in, and sat on the bed. Glenn slept peacefully in the crib that was crammed against the wall. C.H. peered around the room, dark with the curtains drawn. Their double bed, a dresser, a closet door, and the crib. In the corner, a basket of laundry waiting to go to the laundromat. What a cramped life they lived! Their small bedroom could barely hold even those furnishings. Glenn would sleep in the crib by day. At night, Petey would sleep in the crib and Glenn in bed with them so Dani could feed him easily. Since the first boy's arrival, most of their lovemaking had occurred in the living room. His pittance of a paycheck could do no better for them.

What they could do with that money in the backpack! Get an apartment actually big enough for the family. A car that wasn't rusting and didn't require work each year to pass inspection. More interesting meals than grilled cheese sandwiches. Furniture and clothes purchased somewhere besides DI.

He could buy another violin.

Guilt seized him. What a way for someone called of God to think. Certainly this money wasn't entrusted to him for his own gain. He thought of Joseph Smith on his way to find the golden plates for the first time. Joseph had imagined what he could do for his poor family with such riches. It made C.H. feel a little better, knowing that he shared this weakness with the Prophet. In spite of Joseph's lust for the gold, he'd still been accepted—after some chastising. C.H. would probably need double the chastising Joseph Smith received.

He realized he was doing it again—putting off praying. He felt embarrassed, unworthy. Months without thinking about prayer, then when he needed something—*bam!*—on his knees. He wondered if God ever got tired of that.

But he had to do it. One thing was sure, God must be used to it by now. With difficulty he knelt on the floor, leaned on the bed, and closed his eyes.

"Father..." His heart burned with a miserable feeling of unworthiness. What should he say? "Father, I'm sorry for going so long without praying. Please forgive me." The dismal feeling intensified. His conscience was convicting him with a vengeance. Well, good! Maybe it would help motivate him to change. "I promise I'll do much better from now on. But I need to ask a question. Father—" He felt a dark feeling. It made him want desperately to turn his life around and live the gospel valiantly, just to end the sensation. "Father, I need to know if the visitation I had from Brigham Young was real."

A light shone through his eyelids. He opened them and found the room glowing with a warm, golden color. Brother Brigham stood before him on the opposite side of the bed, just next to the crib. The glow emanated from him. Glenn stirred momentarily with a sweet infant moan, then fell silent.

"Yes, Cory Horace, it was real," Brother Brigham said. "I appeared to you and sent you on that task. I now have further instructions for you."

C.H.'s heart pounded. The ugly feeling of unworthiness clung to his soul. Did Joseph Smith feel like this when he saw the Father and the Son?

"You have noticed by now that the backpack contains money, a great deal of money."

"Yes."

"You are to hold onto that money and protect it. You will have need of it at a later time. For now, you are to use some of it to take care of the modest needs of your family."

He felt relieved that his desire to help his family with the money had not been an evil desire. Still, he couldn't seem to shake the dark feeling.

The instructions Joseph Smith had given in the Doctrine and Covenants for testing an otherworldly visitor popped into his head. *The three grand keys* they were called. Ask to shake hands with the personage. If he did and you felt something, he was a resurrected being. If you felt nothing, he was a spirit. But a good spirit would refuse. Only a devil would shake hands with you.

A devil!

Fighting a sudden surge of dread, C.H. stood on wobbling legs. He gazed at the manifestation before him. Brother Brigham—was he Brother Brigham?— peered back with a neutral expression. He felt like he might faint, but he fought the sensation and held out his trembling hand. "Brother Brigham, would you shake hands with me?"

Brother Brigham looked at the offered hand. "If I did, you wouldn't feel anything. I haven't been resurrected yet."

A thrill shot through his body.

"Do you still want me to shake hands with you?" asked Brother Brigham.

C.H. watched him. Was he refusing?

"Because I would rather not."

He was refusing! Whenever C.H. thought about the three grand keys, he'd always pictured the heavenly messenger obstinately refusing to shake hands, eyes closed, head turned to the side, nose slightly in the air. But Brother Brigham had refused politely.

And why not? Why wouldn't heavenly messengers be polite?

He lowered his hand, smiling. Brother Brigham returned the smile, satisfaction showing on his face. "I'm glad you accept me now."

"What do you want me to do?" he asked reverently, determined to obey.

"Shortly you will be called to do a great work. But first, I want you to take care of your family's immediate needs."

His head spun with the magnitude of what was happening. A great work!

"Find better transportation for your family." Brother Brigham lifted his hand in the direction of the carport. It made C.H. think of the statue of Brigham Young in downtown Salt Lake at the Main Street plaza. "Your current vehicle is inadequate for the work you'll be doing. Find something good for your whole family. Whatever you decide is best. I trust you."

His panting was loud and obvious and embarrassing, but he couldn't help himself. His consciousness was already fragile, and if he didn't keep the oxygen coming, he would surely pass out.

"Provide adequate nourishment for yourselves." Brother Brigham smiled. "Especially for those two growing boys."

"Yes, Brother Brigham," he gasped out.

Brigham's smile broadened. "Get a better television. It's not respectable for the General Authorities to have green faces." And then he winked.

C.H. was nearly bowled over by that one. It seemed almost flippant. Yet somehow it fit with the image of Brigham Young he'd had over the years.

"Get cable television to go with it," Brother Brigham said. "Danielle needs some intellectual stimulation, and she'd love to watch the History Channel while she's taking care of your children."

The History Channel? C.H. was astounded. It was so obvious, yet he'd never thought of it. And she'd never mentioned it. Because they could never afford it—that's why.

"And—" Brigham waved his hand casually. "Get that violin back. Don't bury your talent in the earth. Let your light shine. Quit hiding it under a bushel."

He nearly fainted and caught himself on the bed. He tried to cover it by falling to his knees and saying, "Thank you, Brother Brigham. Thank you!"

Brother Brigham gave him that enigmatic smile again, then vanished. The natural shadows of the room swept back in.

The ugly feeling of unworthiness was gone now, replaced with the thrill he felt about the calling and the blessings he had just received. "And thank you, Father," he said with eyes raised to the ceiling.

Dani heard Glenn give out a wail. *Oh no, Cain woke him up!* And just as Petey had dozed off on the sofa next to her.

She waited for C.H. to appear in the hall with Glenn in his arms and an apologetic look on his face. After a few minutes he did, with a balled-up diaper in his hands—but minus the apologetic look. He positively beamed.

"I'm sorry," he said. "Glenn woke up." His tone sounded more like he'd said, *Isn't it great that Glenn woke up!* He disappeared into the bathroom for a moment and reappeared without the diaper.

"Is he hungry?" she asked, stifling her irritation. After all, he *had* changed the diaper.

"Probably."

After she unbuttoned her shirt, he handed the baby to her. Then he sat in his recliner and stared as she nursed, a wide grin on his face. He looked too silly to get mad at, so her curiosity flared up. "What happened in there?"

"I saw Brother Brigham again." He jumped up and began to pace. This time the pacing was lively and filled with nervous energy.

Brigham appeared again? Twice in one day? "What did he say?"

"I'll be called to an important work soon." He stopped and faced her. The strangest déjà vu sensation struck her. He seemed to be doing the same things he did when he first came home with the backpack. Except before, he was agitated, morose. Now he seemed excited, exuberant. "But first," he went on, "I'm sup-posed to use that money to provide for our family."

A thrill and dread shot through her at the same time. They were to use the money to improve their circumstances—the thrill—and they were to use *that* money to improve their circumstances—the dread. "That's what it's for?"

His grin faded, and he shrugged one shoulder. "Well, not all of it. Most of it's for the work I'm supposed to do." The smile returned. "But Brigham gave me a list of things we're supposed to get."

A shopping list from an angel? But she decided to give him a chance to ex-plain first. "What are we supposed to get?"

He started ticking off things on his fingers. "Better transportation. Better food for the family."

Yes, these were obvious things they needed.

"A better TV."

What?

He stopped as he reached for the fourth finger. His smile disappeared. "Have you been wishing you could watch the History Channel?"

"Brigham Young told you to get the *History Channel*?" Her voice held more sarcasm than she meant to put into it.

"He said you need your intellectual stimulation as much as I do."

That caught her attention. To have something meaningful to do as she for-ever breastfed Glenn or cleaned house. To stare at something more energizing than mind-numbing soap operas or game shows or deteriorating Disney vid-eos. The History Channel, Discovery Channel, Biography Channel...a better TV and cable. Suddenly Brigham's instructions didn't seem so ridiculous. Suddenly Brigham Young seemed like a very wise man.

Nodding, Dani said, "Yes, I've been wishing I could watch the History Channel."

His eyes gleamed strangely. Her answer seemed to mean more to him than she would have expected.

"Did he tell you to get anything else?"

Quietly he said, "A new violin."

"For you." She nodded again. Brigham *was* wise. They'd both been starved of their main interests for years now.

Glenn popped off her nipple, asleep once more. C.H. sank back into the re-cliner. "I'm supposed to let my light shine. Stop hiding my talent."

It made sense. He sacrificed his dream in life so he could support his family, symbolized by the selling of his violin to get into this tiny duplex. Now God was repaying him for the sacrifice, giving him back his dream.

"Can this really be true?" she murmured. C.H. gazed at her with a smile.

But the more she thought about it, the more it just seemed weird. God giving them a car, a violin, cable TV? She still wasn't sure she could accept it. In fact, the more she thought about it, the crazier it got.

This was nuts! She couldn't keep going back and forth like this. Would she trust her husband or not? Would she have faith in God or not? Was she going to waver every time she didn't understand some little thing? If God wanted them to have cable TV, then fine—they'd get cable TV.

But the dread remained. She searched inside and pinpointed the reason. It was because of the money. "Did he say where the money came from?"

He scowled. "I forgot to ask him." He looked into her eyes. "You're not sure you believe me yet."

"No, I believe you." She laid the softly snoring Glenn onto the opposite side of the sofa from Petey, closed her shirt, and went over to C.H. Sitting in his lap, she put her arms around his neck. "I just can't believe this is happening to our family."

He nodded.

"It's such a blessing." She said it with more conviction than she felt.

He nodded again. "I'll have to be more diligent living the gospel. I haven't been very valiant." His eyes widened with alarm. "I forgot about Conference! We missed the whole afternoon session."

Dani smiled. "I taped it for you. You can still watch it."

He let out a sigh of relief, but then his expression became alarmed again. "Priesthood session!" He looked at the clock. "I've missed half of it already!" He shook his head. "Geez, off to a great start."

She embraced him with her cheek pressed against his. His stubble prickled her skin. "Oh, honey. You don't have to become perfect all at once." She kissed him hard on the lips. "Just make sure you go next time."

"But I'm always saying that. Next time—but I never do."

"This time you will. I'll make sure you do."

He kissed her again. "There's one thing I *can* do right now."

She tilted her head questioningly.

"We can go shopping for a new car."

The dread stirred again. But no, she wasn't going to do that. She wouldn't let her concerns interfere with his obedience. Brigham Young commanded her husband to get a new car. She'd just have to trust that the money was okay.

Chapter 3

They drove toward the sprawling car mall along State Street with the two boys strapped into car seats in the rear and four bundles of cash stuffed in Dani's purse. She tried hard not to tremble as she huddled protectively over forty thousand dollars.

C.H. insisted they stop to get something to eat. "I'm famished! I haven't eaten all day."

The last thing Dani wanted to do was make stops along the way, but she realized he was right. "Petey's probably hungry too." She craned her neck back and called, "Petey, you want a hamburger?"

"Hangabur!" he cried with delight.

They grabbed something at the drive-through window and ate while they traveled. "What kind of car should we get?" she asked.

"I thought we'd just get another Corolla, a new one."

The money still bothered her—she couldn't shake it. She could almost feel evil vapors oozing out of her purse. As they turned into Larry H. Miller Toyota, she said, "How are we going to pay for it?"

He gave her an *Are you nuts?* look. "With the money from the backpack."

"No, I mean—" She took in a deep breath. "What if it was a bank robbery?"

He pulled into the Toyota dealer lot and parked.

"What if it's marked?" she said.

He turned to her. "I don't think Brother Brigham would give us marked money. That wouldn't make any sense."

That was what she kept trying to tell herself. "I suppose."

"Hand me the money."

She gave him the bundles, and he pulled out several bills and studied them. "They're not new, that's for sure." He turned them over and around. "No dye on them from a canister exploding in the sack. Serial numbers aren't sequential." He looked at her and shrugged. "I don't know how else they'd mark money, but they look fine to me."

"Won't it look strange paying for the car with cash?"

He raised one eyebrow. "Well, no. I've heard of that being done before."

"Wouldn't it be better if we deposited it in our checking account?"

He chuckled. "I think that would look more suspicious. Depositing a hundred and fifty thousand dollars in hundreds all at once?"

"Out, Mommy," Petey called, extending his arms as far as he could reach.

"We could deposit a little at a time," she said.

"How little? If we buy a car tonight, we'd have to deposit enough Monday to cover the check."

"Mommy, out!"

She felt foolish at how desperate she sounded, but she had to work this out to her satisfaction. "We could get a car loan and just deposit enough to cover the payments each month."

"Dani, sweetie, I doubt we could qualify for a car loan. Besides, I'm not going to feel guilty about using the money. God gave it to us and commanded us to buy a car. I'm going to have faith that he knows what he's doing. I'm not going to skulk around with a guilty conscience."

"Okay," she said without conviction.

"*Mommy!*"

C.H. handed the cash back to her, climbed out of the car, and opened the back door. He unstrapped Petey and picked him up. After stuffing the money deep into her purse, Dani did the same with Glenn.

"Come on, Petey," he said as he set the boy down and took his hand. "Let's go look at cars."

"Look cars," said Petey.

They barely walked through the showroom door when a salesman came up and smiled a toothy smile. He held out his hand and said, "How're you folks doing tonight?"

"Fine," C.H. said, shaking hands.

"My name's Willy," the salesman said. "What's yours?"

"I'm C.H. Young, and this is my wife, Dani."

"C.H. What does that stand for?"

Dani hid the smile that broke out on her face. He loved doing this to people. "Cain Hell Young."

Willy's smile froze as he gazed at C.H. for an instant, then he crouched before Petey and said, "And what's your name, Mister?"

Petey pointed to the nearest shiny vehicle and said, "Look cars."

"That's right," Willy said. "We're here to look at cars." He stood back up. "Do you have a particular model in mind?"

"A Corolla," C.H. said.

"I see you're already driving one. Satisfied customer, huh?"

"They never seem to quit."

Willy nodded knowingly. "Will you be trading in your old car?"

They hadn't talked about that. When C.H. didn't answer right away, Dani said, "How much would we get for it?"

Willy shrugged one shoulder and gave a cynical smile. "Probably a few hundred."

"Wait," C.H. said. "Maybe we'll just keep it."

Keep it? Two cars? Dani looked at him with a concerned squint. "Cain, can we afford two cars?"

"Cain?" Willy said with surprise. "C.H. really does stand for Cain Hell?"

C.H. ignored him. "We can now."

"But Cain—" She glanced at Willy and became guarded. "Are you sure that's wise, considering?"

"Could you excuse us for a minute?" C.H. said to Willy.

"Certainly," he said with a knowing smile and headed in the direction of some office.

Dani studied C.H.'s face, trying to think of a tactful way to say what she was thinking. "Two cars? We shouldn't get extravagant, should we?"

"Brigham told me to get better transportation for my family. He didn't specify any details—he didn't even say how many vehicles. He just said it was my choice, and he trusted me."

She thought about it. Better transportation didn't have to mean one vehicle, she supposed.

He took her hand and held it. "It's always bothered me to leave you home alone with two little kids and no transportation while I'm at work. I'd feel so much better if you had a car when you need it."

She had to admit that she'd feel much better too.

He kissed her hand. "It's not like we're *buying* two cars. We don't owe anything on the old one, and the insurance on that piece of junk isn't much."

A thought came to her. She squeezed his hand. "He said it was up to you?"

"That's right, sweetie."

Better transportation echoed through her mind. *I trust you.* Quietly she said, "What do you think about getting an SUV?"

His eyebrows shot up, then he gave her a half-smile. "Now who's being extravagant with the money?"

Petey tugged on his hand. "See cars, Daddy."

"Small cars are dangerous in an accident," she said with greater determination. "Little boys are hard to reach over the back of my seat in a small car. With an SUV, they'd be safer, and I could reach them easier when I needed to."

She grabbed his wrist as another thought occurred to her. "Let's get a hybrid. It'll be—"

"Better on gas," he said, and he grinned broadly. "We'll get a RAV4."

But it bothered her that he answered so quickly. "Don't say that just because I asked. Brother Brigham said he trusted *you*, not me."

"No, you're right." He put an arm around her. "About all of it. A larger vehicle would be better for our family. Safer, easier to take care of the boys. And perhaps better for whatever Brigham has in store for me. He said I'd need a better vehicle for the work I'll be doing. If it's for the work as much as for our family, then I say let's do it right—let's *really* get better transportation."

"Are you *sure* you're not doing this just for me?" He would, after all.

He squeezed her tightly. "I'm sure. It felt right the minute you mentioned it. It's *my* choice."

That's what she needed to hear.

Willy sauntered back. "Did you come to a decision?"

"We'll be keeping our old car," C.H. said.

"Fine. Now how about looking at some new Corollas. Are you partial to a certain color?"

C.H. looked at Dani with a smile.

She smiled back. "I think—maybe we'll want to look at hybrids instead."

Willy gazed at them with his first genuine smile. "Hybrids it is then."

He showed them the models they had in stock, demonstrated all the power controls, and explained the keyless remote locking system, complete with a panic button that Dani could use if she ever got into trouble on her own. He let them drive up and down the local streets and a stretch of the I-15 freeway as the cabin filled with a Vivaldi violin concerto from KBYU radio. Eyeing the two little boys, Willy emphasized the safety features.

C.H. insisted on metallic blue for the color. Willy sat them down in his office and played good salesman/bad salesman with the manager, fighting for a low, low price. When he asked how they wanted to finance it, C.H. said, "We'll just pay cash."

He smiled broadly. "Well, make your check out to—"

"No, *cash*." He nodded to Dani.

She glanced through the open office door. This late on a Saturday night, there were no customers visible. She pulled all four bundles of hundred-dollar bills from her purse. Willy's eyes nearly popped out. Dani stared at the cash in her hand.

She began to feel less excitement and more discomfort. Buyer's remorse already? Or her conscience pricking her? C.H. had intended to buy only a little

Corolla, and she had talked him into a vehicle costing thousands of dollars more. "Whatever you decide," Brother Brigham's words rang in her ears. "I trust you." She imagined his voice as a deeper, more reverent version of C.H.'s voice.

Better transportation. It was such a vague instruction. That could mean anything from a used car slightly better than their old one all the way up to a brand-new Rolls Royce. Was the vagueness of the instruction a test of their character, to see how they would interpret the open-ended command? If so, were they failing the test—all because of her?

It wasn't like a RAV4 was the ultimate in luxury. It was a solid family vehicle, and after all, that's what they were supposed to get. They could have chosen a Lexus or Mercedes, but they chose a Toyota. Perhaps it wasn't the lowliest vehicle their family could get by on. But they were already getting by on a lowly vehicle. That's not what Brother Brigham wanted. He wanted them to have better transportation than what they had now.

She decided to take Brigham at his word. It was better transportation, good for their family without being ostentatious.

She handed the salesman three of the bundles. "That's thirty thousand." She pulled the band off the third bundle and counted out the rest as Willy fanned the first two bundles. He had to leave to get forty-seven dollars and fifty-three cents in change. She imagined he was also meticulously counting the bills. After a good ten minutes, he came back with a fifty in his hand. "Keep the change."

They turned down the protective undercoating and the extended warranty and finally stood in front of their new vehicle, dark and metallic sparkly in the parking lot lights.

C.H. let Dani drive the van home. As she zoomed down I-15, the ride was so smooth compared to the Corolla that she accelerated to eighty-five several times before finally setting the cruise control just to keep to the speed limit. KBYU played Dvořák's *New World Symphony* on the radio, filling the cabin with a fullness she hadn't experienced since she'd listened to her parents' stereo the Christmas before getting married. It was like discovering music all over again.

Cain will love this, she thought with a warm glow.

The boys fell asleep immediately. The traffic light at the bottom of the State Street exit was red when she pulled up to it. She unfastened her seatbelt and reached back to caress Petey's cheek and then Glenn's, just to try out the easier access to her babies. When she arrived home, the Corolla was parked in the street. She pulled into the carport, shut off the engine, and sat there breathing in the new car smell until C.H. came out to help carry in the boys. She felt convinced they had made the right choice.

———

C.H. extracted an ironclad vow from Dani to record both Sunday sessions of Conference while he was at work. He'd have taken the Corolla to work, leaving the SUV for her and the kids, but she insisted he take it. "You haven't had a chance try it out yet."

As he headed for work, the second movement of Rimsky-Korsakov's *Scheherazade* filled the van's cabin through four speakers. The sound of it was exquisite, like the taste of fine chocolate after abstaining for months. Not since he'd met Dani's parents their first Christmas had he heard such fine reproduction. All they had at home was the tinny clock radio in the bedroom.

He was the acting manager for the day because Milt had his usual Sunday off. His shift started at 9 a.m., one hour before opening and the same time church started when it wasn't General Conference weekend.

I should find a new job. Someone called of God really should attend church.

Someone with a hundred thousand dollars in his closet shouldn't need to work at all. His family could last five years on that with as meager a lifestyle as they were used to. He wondered if that was how the money would be used so he could concentrate on his calling. Guilt from coveting tried to rise up again, but he clung to the reassurance that Joseph Smith had coveted too. Maybe C.H. wasn't hopeless after all.

He pulled into the empty parking lot of Valley Fair Mall behind the service entrance to the store. Sheila was already waiting by the door. "Nice wheels!" she cooed. "Did you just buy it?"

He felt the blood drain from his face. He hadn't thought of that. Of course everyone would ask him about the vehicle. He wished he'd beaten her there so she wouldn't have seen him climb out of it. "Yes," he muttered as he fumbled for the key to the service entrance and opened the door.

"How'd you afford it?"

He knew that would be her next question. That would be everyone's next question, whether they actually spoke it or not. He blurted out his first thought, "Someone gave it to us," and immediately realized it wasn't a lie. "A friend."

"Wish I had friends like that," she said as they entered the store.

He switched on the lights. Her dozen earrings caught the illumination and sparkled. She turned to him with a smile, which made her look very beautiful. "Guess what I did yesterday."

He shrugged his shoulders. "What?"

"I bought *The Satanic Bible*." She grinned, waiting for his response.

He decided to oblige her with the reaction she hoped for. "Disgusting."

She laughed with satisfaction. "I've been reading it. It's fascinating." She grabbed a corner cart of paperbacks that needed shelving as he twirled the dial on the safe and pulled out two cash register drawers. "It talks about the hypocrisy of Christianity over the years. Boy, do I agree with that!"

He shook his head as they walked out of the back room, him carrying the drawers and her wheeling the cart.

"It also explains how to do some rituals."

"Satanic rituals?" This went beyond morbidly amusing. "Are we talking virgin sacrifices?"

"No." She laughed. "Satanists don't do that. There's one where you can do a symbolic execution of your enemy, but they don't do real sacrifices."

He wasn't too sure he believed that, even if she did.

She veered off into the Horror section with her books, and he continued to the registers. He punched in the initialization codes, counted the money in the register drawers, and slid them into place. He combed through the holds in the cabinet, removed the ones that were expired, and carried them over to Sheila.

"I have a present for you." He plopped the books onto her cart.

"Thanks a lot."

He checked the endcaps and filled in empty spots, straightened up the bargain book tables, and made sure the floor dumps were full. Being Sunday, there was no shipment to unpack and shelve, so he decided to pull overstock for Science Fiction. Milt was a big science fiction fan too and had been developing that section into an impressive collection for such a small bookstore. Science fiction sales had increased twenty percent as a result.

The first wall section was almost entirely taken up by Isaac Asimov and Piers Anthony. He pulled over the ladder, its wheels squealing on the rails attached near the ceiling, and climbed up to compare overstock copies with missing titles on the shelves. When he had a good handful selected, he climbed down and shelved them. Most of them were from Anthony's Xanth series.

By then Sheila had finished shelving from her cart and was pulling overstock for Romance, which suited him since Romance was an inscrutable genre to him. Annie, who usually worked evenings during the week, was the shop's Romance expert. She claimed romances were becoming sophisticated, with modern, take-charge heroines. Somehow that didn't titillate his curiosity.

At 10 a.m. it was time to open. Already one customer waited at the gate, foot tapping. C.H. isolated the correct key from his collection and slid it into the lock near the floor. He turned the key and held it as the gate lifted with a drone of its electric motor. The customer looked familiar—a young man with long hair and a nose ring, stooping to get through before the gate had completely opened. He ignored C.H.'s greeting as he passed.

All along the mall corridor, gates rose or glass doors slid aside as shops opened. The aroma of hamburgers and pizza and Mexican food and chicken nuggets wafted in from the food court across the hall. Some of the shops remained dark and brooding, closed on Sunday. He eyed them enviously, now that being more valiant in living his religion was on his mind. Until he started noticing what kind of shops they were: jewelry boutiques, office supplies, a pet store, women's overpriced designer clothes. Working in any of those places with their cluttered, tedious inventory would drive him nuts. As it was, he could barely stand dealing with the forever-disorganized Children's book section.

The customer was in the back talking with Sheila, and that triggered his memory. He was her live-in boyfriend. Their conversation looked heated. He cringed and wondered what was going on.

A woman and her daughter strolled in, asking where the books on braiding hair would be. He brought her over to Hobbies and Crafts and showed her two books he'd noticed the other day while facing that section. Sheila's boyfriend sailed past with a grim expression. C.H. had a hard time concentrating on what the woman was saying. He wanted to ask Sheila what that was all about.

The mother and daughter decided on one of the books. He carried their selection to the cash register for them, fulfilling a corporate obligation.

Sheila approached as he finished counting out change and thanking the mother. "C.H.," she said, and then hesitated. "Could I take the rest of the day off?"

Any other time he'd have blurted out, "Are you out of your mind?" But he saw the troubled look on her face. "I don't know. I'd be alone for a couple of hours until Maria gets here."

"Please. Something serious has come up." Her face was flushed with emotion, and her eyes glistened with excess moisture.

"Well..." He assessed the state of his bladder. Nothing was worse than having an urgent call of nature while alone in the store. "Let me go to the bathroom first."

She grabbed his forearm and squeezed. "I owe you one."

He wanted to ask her what happened, but instead he asked, "Is there anything I can do for you?"

"No, thanks." She tossed him a melancholy smile as he headed for the restroom in the back.

Dani tried to watch General Conference, but she felt too much excess energy to sit still. "Oh, well, it's being taped," she told herself and searched for things to do. There were plenty of possibilities: dishes, laundry, dusting, vacuuming, decluttering kitchen surfaces, and diapers, diapers, diapers. Petey must have eaten something that didn't agree with him because his output of solid waste was unworthy of the label *solid*.

She turned up the TV loud so she could at least hear Conference as she worked. There was a time when she'd have felt bad about doing housework on Sunday. With two young boys, she'd given up that luxury long ago. She squeezed in the work whenever she could.

That afternoon she finally sat down for a minute of rest, ignoring Glenn's crying and Petey's demand for food because C.H. would be home in moments to take over—how she loved him! As she relaxed, she finally let herself notice what she'd been doing all day. She'd been avoiding what was on her mind.

The money still bothered her.

And if the money bothered her, there could be only one reason. She hadn't resolved once and for all in her own mind that an angel had appeared to C.H. *He* was convinced—he had a pack full of money to prove it—but she still hadn't accepted it, not completely.

Or was it the angel's identity she couldn't trust? She thought for a moment. Exactly how did he know it was Brigham Young who appeared to him? Because the vision looked like his imaginary friend? That was no proof. Because he looked like pictures of Brigham Young? Because the visitor said so? Were any of these enough?

Dani realized that she *did* accept his claim that he'd seen a vision. He was convinced, and she trusted him. But if it hadn't been Brigham Young, who did he see?

She felt a cold fist wrapping itself around her heart and squeezing. No, it couldn't be that!

But she couldn't deny it to herself any longer. Yes, it could be *that*.

She remembered, there was a way you were supposed to be able to tell. Something about shaking hands. Had C.H. thought of that?

He must have. He was intelligent. He knew the scriptures pretty well, even if they hadn't been reading them a whole lot lately. She felt confident that he must have. Reasonably confident. Pretty confident.

Therefore it couldn't be Brigham's identity that bothered her, she insisted to herself. So what *was* bothering her?

It was the money itself. That damned money!

Where does a hundred and fifty thousand dollars bundled in a backpack sitting in the middle of nowhere come from? Did God create it himself, like the Liahona compass sitting in front of Lehi's tent one morning? Dani didn't think so. Would God create used, musty-smelling money in a dirty backpack? Someone, some mortal person, must have left it there.

So who?

She couldn't think of one legitimate reason for such a thing to happen. And she couldn't think of one *illegitimate* reason for such a thing to happen unless something had gone very, very wrong. People dealing with large sums of illegal money didn't just misplace a hundred and fifty thousand dollars and forget about it. Whose was it, why did they leave it there, and when were they coming around to look for it?

And why couldn't she trust that Brigham Young knew what he was doing?

Questions started flooding her mind now, questions she knew she'd been holding back all day with her nervous energy and bustling activity. Why Brigham Young? Why her husband? Why a pile of suspicious money for a spiritual calling? Why such a dramatic method of giving the calling? Why didn't the bishop call C.H. into his office and give him the calling? Or the stake president, or a General Authority, if the call was *that* important? And why cable TV?

Why hadn't she prayed about it?

There it was, the question at the core of her anxiety. If she was unsure, why didn't she pray about it and find out?

Because she didn't want an answer. She didn't want to find out that her husband was wrong.

She'd prayed a couple of times since his first visitation yesterday. Thank you for blessing my husband in such a marvelous way. Thank you for the new car. Thank you for this and that wonderful thing. But never, "Dear Father, is it true?" And now she realized why. What if he said no? What if all she received was that dreadful stupor of thought?

And if she received it, how would she know—absolutely *know*—that it was because C.H. was wrong? What if it was because she didn't have enough faith to get an answer or wasn't spiritual enough to discern the answer? It was easier to ignore the problem and do housework on the Sabbath and go on supporting her husband like a good Mormon girl.

But the money. Who was out there in the world, wondering what happened to it? There must be somebody.

C.H. burst through the door with his usual grand entrance, distracting Petey from his whining. Dani quickly gathered up Glenn and started nursing him to hide her consternation.

"How's my Petey?" he cried, and Petey giggled at his kisses. He came to her on the sofa, riding Petey on his arm, and leaned over to kiss her warmly. "And how's my incredibly beautiful sweetie?"

She gazed up at him with a tight, closed-mouth smile, hoping he wouldn't notice that she was biting her tongue to hold back tears.

He went to the TV and examined the VCR. "Did Conference tape okay?"

"Yes," she rasped.

"Good." He heaved Petey into the air, and the boy laughed with delight. "Is everybody hungry?"

"Hungey, eat," Petey said.

"What should we eat?" He dropped Petey to the floor and headed into the kitchen where he started banging cupboard doors and opening and closing the refrigerator.

Dani quickly wiped at her eyes while he was out of the room. Maybe she should talk to him about what she was feeling.

"Guess what happened today at work," he said as he pulled out a can of something and started cranking on it with the hand-held can opener.

Dani cleared her throat and spoke loudly to keep her voice from catching. "What?"

"Sheila and her boyfriend got into a big fight or something, and she asked for the rest of the day off." He poked his head out of the kitchen. "I wonder if they're going to break up again."

Not now, Cain! Of all the topics to bring up, not Sheila, not now. Dani always felt a twinge of jealousy whenever he talked about her. But she tried not to let it bother her. Sheila was attractive, and Dani could tell that he noticed. But she knew there was nothing behind it—just the usual male attraction to a beautiful girl. Dani wasn't about to demand that her husband stop being a man, not when he never let the attraction amount to anything. She trusted him completely, knew that he loved her only. She wasn't about to become a shrew over a harmless attraction.

But *not now!* Even though she knew it wasn't his fault, she resented him for mentioning Sheila now. Not while Dani was struggling with fears and concerns about him and this thing that had come into their lives. The last thing she wanted to hear was *that woman's* name on her husband's lips.

He gazed at Dani, and she knew that she'd failed to hide her agitation. He set the half-open can onto the counter and came out to kneel down before her. "What's the matter, sweetie?"

That did it. Her tears spilled over. He embraced her until her weeping slowed down enough for her to say something.

"I'm sorry, Cain. I'm just feeling nervous about the money."

He released his breath noisily through his nostrils, pursing his lips and shaking his head. "I'm sorry. I was supposed to ask Brother Brigham where it came from. If I had, you wouldn't have to be worried now." He stroked her cheek with the back of his hand, then wiped her tears with his finger. "This whole situation is pretty nerve-racking, isn't it? Well, I'll tell you what."

He leaped to his feet and headed for the phone on the corner end table. He leaned behind the table and lifted up the unplugged end of the cord. "There! We are now officially on vacation from the rest of the world. I have tomorrow off, and we're not doing anything for the next twenty-four hours except have fun together. No obligations, no responsibilities."

Yes, that would work fine for a man and his compartmentalized mind. But would it work for her? Could she be distracted enough to stop worrying and have fun?

No, not until she took care of one last thing. "Cain?"

"Yes, sweetie?"

"Can I ask you a question?" She was trying to be matter-of-fact, but she could tell it wasn't working.

"Dani, if something's bothering you, you'd better ask." He sat next to her and caressed her arm. "I don't want you to be upset."

She nodded and took a deep breath. This was generating as much anxiety as the thought of praying about it did. Did she really want to know?

"When Brigham Young appeared to you, did you...did you test him?"

A smile broke out all over his face. Her rush of relief was immense.

"Yes, I did. He refused to shake hands with me."

That was it—she remembered now. A spirit from God would refuse to shake hands. C.H.'s apparition had refused. It had to be Brigham Young. A righteous spirit wouldn't deceive. If he said he was Brigham Young, then he must be.

Wait—did he? "How do you *know* it was Brigham Young? Did he say so?"

"Uh, yes, he did."

She started playing with his tie as relief calmed her. "Are you mad at me for asking these things?"

He laughed and smacked a big kiss on her cheek. "No, I'm not mad! I'm glad you're watching out for me—keeping me honest. Do you feel better now?"

"Yes." No. Not completely. But she would try. She'd try to have fun with him for twenty-four hours. But the next time he saw Brother Brigham, he'd better ask him about that money. That damned money!

Chapter 4

C.H. woke up early Monday morning and rushed to the grocery store, where he stocked up on the food he needed: ham, canned mushrooms and olives, orange juice, eggs, bacon, cheese, multigrain bread—a nice change of pace from that cheap, spongy white stuff—real butter, strawberry jam, tomatoes. He also grabbed an actual omelette pan because he wanted to do the surprise right.

Dani woke up to a tray steaming with an egg, ham, cheese, mushroom, olive, and tomato omelette. A tall glass of orange juice and toast with jam sat to the side. Her eyes went wide.

"Better nourishment, sweetie," he said with a grin.

The boys stayed mercifully asleep, and he crossed his fingers, hoping it would continue that way. If Glenn woke up, the nursing would have to come first.

She almost finished the whole meal before Glenn finally woke up, and C.H. occupied the last bit of time she needed by changing his diaper. By then she was ready to nurse, and he breathed a sigh of relief that his surprise had gone well.

Glenn's cry woke up Petey. C.H. grabbed him out of the crib and said, "Let's make ourselves something to eat, Petey, while Mommy feeds the baby."

As his own omelette cooked, he whipped up some scrambled eggs and bacon for Petey because he didn't like "yuckies" in his eggs. He stubbornly concentrated on his cooking because today he didn't want his mind occupied with troubling thoughts.

After breakfast, the four of them headed on foot for the nearby Lions Park, a narrow strip one block long butted up against the hill to the freeway. Petey laughed wildly as C.H. pushed him on the swing, spotted him carefully on the monkey bars, and coaxed him down the slide. The rubbery soles of Petey's shoes kept catching on the slide's surface, so C.H. removed them. Instead of enjoying a slicker surface on the slide, however, Petey took to trotting around barefoot in the grass. Better let him enjoy it while he can, C.H. figured. There couldn't be many warm days left to this Indian summer.

Dani sat at the picnic table in the shade of the pavilion, holding Glenn and shaking her head as she watched Petey cavort. She was probably anticipating the bath Petey would need when they got home, so C.H. silently resolved to take care of that for her before she had a chance to act. He made a vow to himself years ago at a BYU fireside. The speaker discussed how the little things make or break a marriage. "I'll make sure I do all the nice things I can think of for my wife," he told himself.

It was one vow C.H. did keep—most of the time—and in the intervening years he'd come to realize how fortunate he was to have done so. Three months of intensive courtship at BYU had seemed like plenty of time to get to know Dani, but since then he saw several whirlwind BYU romances turn into ugly divorces in a frighteningly short time. He trembled at how risky his three-month courting of Dani had been, and he felt sure his willingness to do the little niceties for her kept them in love while other marriages foundered.

The funny thing was, it didn't seem like work to him. Doing nice things for her was fun—it felt like a completely natural thing to do, as did spending time with his sons. Glenn was too little to do much with yet, but C.H. delighted in his time with Petey. He couldn't imagine why other husbands and fathers found such things a challenge to do. Why did they start families in the first place?

When everyone got hungry again, they walked home, and C.H. decided to splurge and go for a bucket of KFC. The new vehicle was still a novelty for Petey, so he had to come with. C.H. bought the chicken with their own money— he doubted deep-fried breaded chicken would count as "better nourishment." The enticing aroma wafting out of the bucket overwhelmed the new car smell.

Dani gave him a big kiss when she found him getting a bath ready for Petey. It wasn't until he finished and sat in the recliner that he remembered his vow to watch a little Conference every day. He couldn't believe it—already he was slacking. Sure, that's how it played out every time, but this time really was supposed to be different. He made a mental note to do it tonight, after their twenty-four hour vacation from the world was over.

Dani had been upset last night, and her *yes* answer to feeling better hadn't been convincing. But she seemed in a much brighter mood today. He was pleased that his idea seemed to be working out.

For her *and* for him. He needed to take his mind off books and customers and heavenly visitations and worthiness. He felt those concerns lingering in the background all day but successfully ignored them. He understood Brother Brigham's instructions about TV better now. Recreation was as important as everything else, if a man was to keep his morale charged up.

"Do you know what I'd like to do next?" Dani said as she sat next to him.

"What?"

"Go to a movie."

He grinned at that idea. They hadn't been to a movie since—well, he couldn't remember when. Months and months. He immediately ran out for a newspaper—another luxury they'd done without along with Internet and smart phones—and let her choose the movie. He knew it would be a chick flick, but he was feeling generous today.

They could still make it to the 4:15 show and pay matinee prices. "Who should I get to babysit?" she said.

"Very funny." They both knew who they'd get. Young Cyndy McGarry would drop anything to babysit for them. They hadn't figured out which reason was the stronger one—how much Cyndy liked their two boys, or the crush she obviously had on C.H. They'd given up feeling bad about taking advantage of her. Whenever they tried asking other girls, she was always hurt that they hadn't asked her.

"I'll call her," Dani said.

Cynthia McGarry had been Cindy throughout her childhood, and that was well and good for a little girl. But it was much too precious for a mature woman of fourteen, so she changed the spelling to Cyndy. Whenever anyone asked her name, she'd say, "Cyndy with two Y's." She thought it looked exotic and sophisticated that way.

Of course, her insufferable brother Ryan would spell it Cindyy just out of meanness. She was glad he was three years younger—she'd be leaving middle school just as he arrived.

As she lay on her bed reading, the landline phone rang, and Cyndy decided to ignore it, even though the phone was outside her door in the hallway. That way Ryan would have to answer it.

It rang again. And again. Dang it! He was trying to make her answer. When the fourth ring started, she angrily jumped up to go for the phone, but the ring cut short. Good! He *had* answered it.

She could hear his muttering in the hallway. Then Ryan called in his taunting voice, "Cindyyyyyyyy," emphasizing the Y's at the end so she knew he meant *his* spelling. "Telephone!"

"Who is it?" she called back.

"It's your lover boy, Brother Young."

Bad mistake! She should have answered. She hated when Ryan said that. Brother Young wasn't her lover. He was just a nice guy. Sure, he was about the most gorgeous man she'd ever seen and as friendly to Cyndy as anyone she could remember, but that didn't mean she *loved* him. Not *that* way. Just in a normal, love-your-neighbor kind of way. Her heart palpitated and her breath was shallow right now only because she was so angry at Ryan.

She hopped off the bed. "Big fat jerk," she muttered under her breath as she came out of her room, but not *too* under her breath. He slugged her shoulder as he handed her the phone. She cried "Ow!" and "Jerk!" but secretly smiled. He wasn't really all *that* fat—just hadn't grown out of his baby fat yet. But at eleven and just starting to notice girls for the first time, he was terribly self-conscious about it. That was her ace in the hole when she really needed to get under his skin.

He stuck out his tongue as he turned the corner to his own room.

She lifted the phone to her ear, cursing her mother with euphemistic Mormon cuss words because she refused to let her have her own phone. If she did, this kind of fiasco would never happen. But her mother was all this-and-that about how they're a waste of time and become an addiction and how kids sext with them. As if she'd do anything so disgusting. As if 99.9% of the girls in the ward didn't have their own phone, and the 0.1% consisted entirely of Cyndy.

"Hello?" she said, trying to speak calmly, fussing with her hair in the hallway mirror.

"Hi, Cyndy, this is Danielle Young."

She felt a touch of disappointment at the female voice. It wasn't Brother Young—it was his wife. She told herself the disappointment was because she'd been snookered by Ryan. "Hi, Sister Young," she said.

"We were wondering if you could babysit for us this afternoon while we go to a movie."

"Sure, what time?"

"In half an hour. Will that be okay?"

"I'll be there."

"Thanks so much."

Cyndy hung up with a warm feeling. She liked babysitting for the Youngs. She wouldn't do it for anyone else, being a mature woman of fourteen. That sort of work was for twelve- and thirteen-year-olds. But the Youngs were an exception. Sister Young needed all the help she could get with two baby boys to take care of. And those boys were so cute! Took after their father for good looks. She would never let the Youngs pay her, although they tried hard for a while because she knew how little money they had. And they didn't ask her to babysit often, not wanting to take advantage of her generosity. Frankly, Cyndy wished they would. All she had here was Ryan.

She didn't want to tell him where she was going and endure more taunting, so she went downstairs and left a note on the refrigerator door for her mother who'd be home from work before she got back. After half an hour, Cyndy walked one block to the Youngs' tiny duplex. The first time she'd ever seen it, she hadn't realized it was a duplex because the entrance to the other half was in the rear. It was the only duplex in the neighborhood—unless there were some others disguised like that.

There was a shiny new vehicle in the carport, and the Young's rusty car was parked in the street. Had someone moved into the empty rear apartment? But she thought that carport belonged to the Youngs. She was sure of it—their car was usually parked there. She shrugged her shoulders and rang the doorbell. Maybe the Youngs had company, and they were all going to the movie together.

Did that mean Cyndy would be babysitting other kids too? She shuddered at the thought of dealing with strange kids who would probably be bratty. But no, Sister Young would have said something if that were true. She wouldn't spring it on Cyndy without warning.

Brother Young answered the door with a big smile. "Come on in, Cyndy."

She smiled back as warmly as she knew how and entered. She could never get over how small their living room was. One sofa, one easy chair, one recliner, one coffee table, one end table, a small bookcase, a TV stand with a mere 32 inch TV and a cheap VCR sitting next to it. The picture on their TV was tinted slightly green at all times, and the sound came from two tinny little speakers on the bottom. They had only a small handful of Disney videos stacked on the lower TV stand shelf. If Cyndy's reason for babysitting had been electronic entertainment, she'd have stopped doing it for them a long time ago.

Sister Young came out from their one bedroom and said, "Thanks so much for doing this on such short notice, Cyndy."

"No problem," she said as she picked up a book on top of the bookcase and looked at it. "You can ask me anytime." The book was hard cover without a dust jacket. She read the author's name: *Orson Scott Card*. Dumb name. She'd never heard of him. She set the book down.

Wait—didn't some movie come out a while ago from one of his books, some dumb sci-fi thing about a kid fighting aliens? Whatever.

"I just fed Glenn, and he's asleep. He shouldn't need feeding again until we get home. Petey's napping too right now. If you're lucky, they'll both stay asleep until we get back."

Cyndy shook her head. "That wouldn't be lucky. It's fun playing with them."

Sister Young looked genuinely pleased when she smiled. Brother Young took his wife's hand and said to Cyndy, "Thanks again," and they both walked out the door.

Cyndy moved to the easy chair, knelt on it backwards, and pulled the drapes back from the window just a little. She watched as the Youngs strolled to the carport, hand in hand, talking together and smiling. They were so much in love.

She sighed as she tried to imagine what that must be like. She thought back to how her parents had been before Papá left. No comparison.

She always called him Papá, with the second syllable accented. It sounded so European. Besides, it irritated her mother and made Ryan shout, "Cut that out! It's stupid!" She imagined that Papá, who wasn't a Mormon, might be in Paris right now, wearing a beret and sipping champagne with a beautiful French woman at a sidewalk café. How romantic!

The Youngs disappeared from sight into the carport. She heard one door close, then several seconds later the other. She smiled. Brother Young must have opened the door for Sister Young. What a gentleman! The engine started, and the new blue vehicle backed out.

She forgot about that! It *was* theirs! But how could they afford it? A warm feeling swept through her body. Things were getting better for them. If anyone deserved it, they did.

After watching them drive off, she turned on the TV, but all the shows were dreadful. How could they stand living without cable or satellite or something—anything—to stream with? She toyed with the idea of turning the TV loud and waking the boys so she'd have something to do, but that would be mean. She'd seen their Disney videos a million times already, and the few books in their bookcase that interested her she'd already read.

She stared at the TV for as long as she could stand it, then went into the kitchen and checked the refrigerator. Whoa! It was stocked fuller than it had ever been. That got her wondering. New car, lots more food. What was up? Did Brother Young get a promotion or a new job?

The Youngs were practically family, so she didn't feel too many qualms about poking around. Maybe she could find out something. The cupboards in the kitchen all looked about the same, except for extra food. There was nothing different about the bathroom. She wished she could check the bedroom—the most interesting room—but not while the boys were asleep in there.

She tried the closet in the living room, just inside the front door. The instant she opened it, she caught a whiff of something unpleasant—old and moist. Dirty shoes or something? She looked around and saw the usual coats, the ancient vacuum cleaner, some winter boots. Nothing that hadn't been there before. Only the smell was new.

She looked up on the shelf above the coats. Now *there* was something she'd never seen before. It was a backpack. She stood up on tiptoes to get a better look. Sure enough, that was where the smell was coming from. It certainly looked old and dirty enough to be smelly.

It wasn't lying flat—there was something inside it. She was supposed to be figuring out how the Youngs could afford a new vehicle, and surely a beat-up old backpack would have nothing to do with that. But curiosity got the best of her. She reached up to grab the strap that hung slightly over the edge of the shelf, but just then she heard Glenn cry.

At last! When Glenn cried, Petey would cry. She could play with the boys now! She shut the closet door and rushed toward the bedroom. Sure enough, Petey began to whine. She opened the bedroom door and said, "Hi, Petey, it's Cyndy."

"Cynny!" he said, standing up on the bed and holding his arms out.

She gave him a hug, then grabbed Glenn. Petey followed her into the living room. Glenn had a wet diaper, which she changed immediately. Petey wanted to "See Nocchio," so Cyndy grabbed the *Pinocchio* video. When she went to slide it into the VCR slot, she noticed that a tape was already there. Out of curiosity, she pushed play. General Conference came on. She watched it for a moment, filled with admiration. The Youngs were so spiritual! Not only did they tape Conference, but they left the tape in the machine so they could turn it on any time and watch it over and over. She made a mental note to put the tape back into the machine after *Pinocchio* was finished. She didn't want to disrupt their spiritual habits.

The wooden puppet who wanted to be a real boy kept Petey engrossed, and Cyndy played mother with her live doll Glenn, holding him, rocking him, baby-talking to him. She couldn't wait until she could have little babies like him. She never understood why so many women wanted to get out of the house for some stupid job. Being a mother seemed like the greatest thing in the world to her, just taking care of these sweet little angels from heaven all day long. Any woman who would choose a job over that must be some kind of cold, heartless witch—like her mother. It was one of the things she admired Sister Young for. She chose to stay home.

Petey insisted on watching the video a second time. The Youngs returned as Pinocchio and Geppetto were smoking their way out of Monstro. They walked to the door arm in arm and kissed before they entered. Cyndy was careful to open the drapes just the tiniest slit so they wouldn't notice her watching. As Brother Young reached for the doorknob, she flopped back into the easy chair in a normal position, Glenn in her arms, and stared at the TV. Pinocchio and the gang rode a big wave from Monstro's enormous sneeze. The door opened, and Petey jumped up and shouted, "Mommy!" He ran to her, and she scooped him up into her arms.

"You little devil," she said. "You didn't sleep for Cyndy."

"Cynny," Petey said, pointing at her.

"I hope they were little angels for you," Brother Young said.

"Always," Cyndy replied, looking down into Glenn's face as his gaze darted about the room and his tongue flicked in and out. "How was the movie?"

"Great!" Sister Young said. "Cain even liked it." She smiled at him and squeezed his hand.

It was so cute how she called him Cain.

"Are you sure you don't want us to pay you anything?" Sister Young said. They only asked halfheartedly anymore, since Cyndy always refused.

"No, thanks. It's my pleasure."

Cyndy walked home in waning daylight. In a couple more weeks when daylight savings ended, they wouldn't let her walk home this time of day. It'd be too dark. One of them would accompany her. She always liked it when Brother Young did.

How in love they were, she thought as she walked up to her big, stuccoed home. What a contrast it was to the Youngs' small, well-worn house. But she was willing to bet they were happier. He treated his wife like a queen. What would it have been like to have parents like them? What would it be like to have a husband like him?

As she walked through the door, Ryan smirked. "Did you kiss him?"

She didn't even get mad at him. She was too busy enjoying the image that put in her mind.

Dinner at Denny's—hardly fancy, Dani thought, but for them it was a treat. Then off shopping for a TV set. C.H. had been right after all. A one-day vacation from the world had done her a lot of good. She was in too good a mood now to let yesterday's dark clouds bother her. She was actually excited about buying the television.

They went to Walmart because they didn't want to get too extravagant with the money. Only loose hundred-dollar bills sat in her purse this time, tucked away in her wallet.

C.H. eyed the big screens with lust in his eyes, but he didn't even try to suggest them. She was almost disappointed, but she knew there was a big difference between splurging on a useful hybrid car and splurging on a monstrous television that would take up half their living room. So she remained quiet as he moved on to smaller screens.

"These are probably as big as our TV stand can handle," he said.

"Especially with our VCR next to it," she said.

A smile curled up one corner of his mouth. He walked over to some Blu-ray players, put his hand on one, and said, "What VCR?"

"I don't remember *that* on Brigham's shopping list."

"Don't you think part of having a better television is to be able to watch better things on it? Aren't you sick of Disney videos? And we can get DVDs out of the bin for just a few bucks."

She rolled her eyes and shook her head. "I'm not even going to argue with you anymore. You're the one Brigham trusts. Just make sure he understands you're the one going to hell for it, not me, *Cain Hell Young*."

They picked out a moderately sized TV and a modestly priced Blu-ray player. Now that the deed was done, Dani imagined watching the History Channel on its screen, and couldn't wait to order the cable service.

They told the salesman they wanted to do more shopping before picking up the TV. They wandered the store for over an hour, browsing departments they usually never entered. Dani thought how easy it would be to slip the remaining hundreds out of her purse and load up on new outfits and new pairs of shoes, or buy one of the books or CDs that C.H. had been enamored with. She wondered if he was tempted. Whether he was or not, he never said anything, and she wasn't about to put ideas in his head.

On their way back to pick up the TV, with C.H. holding Glenn and Dani dragging Petey along, they passed the music section. C.H. stopped dead in his tracks in front of a display table loaded with multiple-CD sets on sale and zeroed in on a collection of all nine Beethoven symphonies for $19.95.

"What a deal!" he murmured, examining one.

She gazed at him. Even in profile she could see the desire in his eyes. And why not? He'd been a music major. Music, especially classical music, had been his life and his dream, and for more than two years he'd been virtually starved of it.

And Brother Brigham had told him to buy a violin, an obvious sign that he was to involve himself in his dream again, remove his talent from under the bushel and let it shine. Dani wondered if that might be what his mysterious calling was about, making music for the building up of the kingdom of God, preaching the gospel through music. The great classical composers for centuries had written plenty of music in praise of God: cantatas, masses, requiems. There certainly was historical precedent for spreading the gospel through music. Could it be possible that he'd be the next Bach, the next Mozart, the next Beethoven?

He gave a resigned smile and put the package back down. "Ah, well."

"Get it," Dani said.

"What?"

She picked up the package and handed it to him. "Buy it."

He stared at her with a faintly irritated expression and put the package back in place. "I can't."

She set her purse on the display table, opened it with one hand, fumbled for a twenty in her wallet, and handed it to him. "Buy it! This isn't from the backpack.

This is our money."

Petey's hand squirmed in hers. "Go home, Mommy," he whined.

C.H. stood still without attempting to take the bill. "That doesn't help. It just means we'll have to take twenty out of the other money later."

"You're supposed to buy a violin with the backpack money."

He shrugged his free shoulder. "Right."

"You're obviously supposed to get involved with music again."

"But Brother Brigham didn't say a thing—"

"He told you to buy a violin and a TV set. Don't you see a pattern there? We're supposed to enrich our lives, not just survive. If we can buy a new Blu-ray player, we can buy some CDs. You've been dying to have music in your life again, and I'm tired of feeling guilty that you don't. *Buy it!*"

He scowled darkly and stared at her extended hand.

"I'll skip breakfast for a while to pay for it," Dani said.

"No, you won't. You're a nursing mother."

A realization hit her. "We're supposed to use the backpack money to buy our food. So we *can* afford it!"

She was getting through. The scowl lightened to an expression of mere hesitation. His eyes slowly returned to the CDs, and he stared for a long moment.

"Please, Cain," Dani said. "I want you to have it."

He looked up. "Only if you get something for yourself too."

"I am."

He looked at her empty hand. "What?"

The sweet lug—he didn't get it. "I'm getting a set of all nine Beethoven symphonies so my husband can enjoy them and I won't feel guilty that marrying me took him away from the music he loves."

He studied her face intensely, then whipped the twenty out of her hand. "I'll buy it for *you* then."

They glared at each other for an instant, then burst out laughing at the same time. "As long as you're doing it for me," she said.

With the boxed-up television in back—another reason the larger vehicle came in handy—and Beethoven's Pastorale Symphony playing on the stereo, C.H. hummed away at the pleasant themes. Images of centaurs and naked cherubs from Disney's *Fantasia* pranced in Dani's mind. She felt better than she had in weeks. What a fool she'd been to doubt God and Brigham Young. Look at how much happier they were already. The sweet music and the smooth ride quickly lulled both boys to sleep. Fortunately, they arrived home before the noisy storm in the third movement started.

With Petey sprawled on the recliner and Glenn asleep in his car seat on the living room floor, C.H. and Dani carried in the TV. Working together, they unpacked it and set it up. When they turned it on, a show's theme song flowed from the stereo speakers with a grandeur that almost seemed to mock the mundane show it represented.

"What do we do with the old TV?" he asked.

"Give it to DI?"

He smiled, and she knew he was thinking what she was. How nice it would be to *donate* something to Deseret Industries for a change!

He carried out the TV to store in the back of the SUV until they could transport it out of their lives. She flopped down on the sofa and soaked in the contentment that hung in the air like a haze. When he returned, he stood in the middle of the room looking around for an instant, then headed for the end table. Reluctantly he held up the phone cord and shrugged, then plugged it back in.

"It was a nice vacation," she said. "Thank you, Cain."

"You're welcome." He gathered up Petey and carried him into the bedroom.

The phone rang, startling her as she was drifting off to sleep. She leapt to answer it before it could ring again and wake up Glenn. "Hello?"

"Hi, Dani?"

It was Mother—C.H.'s mother. Dani couldn't bring herself to call her Mom because that was *her* mom. Mother seemed to like it better that way anyway.

"Hi, Mother. Are you in town?" She rarely called from St. George. Usually her phone calls meant she was in town and wanted to stop by.

The hybrid! What would they tell her about the hybrid? And the TV!

"No, I'm home."

Dani felt relief, until she realized that her voice sounded odd.

"Is everything alright?" said Mother.

Her apprehensive tone rubbed off onto Dani. "Yes, we're fine. Why do you ask?"

"I just felt like I should call and see if everything's okay."

Dani took in a deep breath. "Yes, Mother, everything's fine up here."

"I've been trying to call all day, but no one ever answered." There wasn't any discernible accusation in her voice, but Dani swore she could hear it.

"We've been gone all day. C.H. had the day off, so we've been playing." Mother never liked the name Cain, and Dani had learned long ago not to use it with her.

"Cory still has his job, doesn't he?"

"Yes, Mother."

"You two are doing okay together, are you?"

"We're doing great."

He appeared and looked at her questioningly. "Your mother," she mouthed to him. "Here's C.H. now," she said and handed him the phone.

Mother felt like she should call and see if they were okay? What was that all about?

"Yes, we're fine," he said. "We're doing good, in fact."

It was completely true—every word of it—yet Dani felt a gnawing sensation that they were lying through their teeth.

"No, no problem. How are *you* doing?"

She felt irritation that he could appease Mother so easily, as if she expected Dani to obfuscate whenever possible. And yet wasn't that exactly what both of them were doing? Hiding what had happened to them?

But what would they tell her? *Yes, we're doing fine. Things are great. Brigham Young gave us a hundred and fifty thousand dollars.*

"When are you coming around again?" he asked.

Dani didn't dislike his mother, and she didn't think Mother disliked her. They just hadn't warmed up to each other very well. Dani's mom was a pleasant, affectionate, outgoing sort who always made people feel good to be around her. Mother was a more reserved, no-nonsense kind of person who never verbally expressed disapproval, yet somehow seemed to emanate it. At least that's how Dani perceived her. Maybe there was no disapproval—maybe she only assumed it because she wasn't used to Mother's personality type.

"Yes, yes, okay. I love you too. Bye." He hung up the phone and gazed at her. "She felt like something was wrong and wanted to see how we're doing."

The way he put it only strengthened the apprehension she felt. She hated that the feeling intruded on her pleasant emotions of a few moments ago. And she'd had enough of trying to deal with it tactfully anymore. "Cain, that money's still bothering me. Where did it come from?"

To her surprise, he nodded. Mother's call must have disturbed him too. When a person's mother calls with a "feeling" soon after an extraordinary thing happens, it's hard to brush it off as nothing.

"I'm going to ask Brother Brigham the next time he appears to me."

"Do you promise?" Her question sounded childish to herself, but she had to hear his answer before she could relax.

"Yes, I promise."

The phone call from his mother spooked C.H. Now he felt uncomfortable leaving the backpack full of money in the closet next to the front door of the house. He tried to think of somewhere safe to put it. Under the bed? In a dresser drawer? In the tiny, musty basement full of spider webs, where they hardly ever went? At least the smell would match.

Everywhere he could think seemed like a typical place a burglar would look.

What about a barrel of beans, like where Joseph Smith hid the golden plates? C.H. smiled. That wouldn't be a bad idea, if a barrel of beans were handy.

Instead he hid it at the bottom of the clothes basket. Kind of similar. What thief would search dirty clothes for valuables? He carried the backpack into the bedroom, dumped the clothes out of the basket, dropped the backpack in, and shoveled the clothes on top of it.

"Good idea," Dani said as she watched, sitting on the bed nursing Glenn.

Chapter 5

Special Agent Robinson filled his cup with steaming black coffee and trudged to his desk, wishing he were still in bed. A stack of memos and reports lay in the middle of the desktop—a very messy stack, dropped so the individual pages had scattered. It looked like an ecological blight in the middle of his hyper-neat desk.

Robinson sighed as he set his cup on the coaster that sat permanently to the left, in the perfect spot for his hand to reach. He gathered up the stack and, sitting down, tapped the papers against the desk until they were aligned. He took a sip of stinging coffee, strong and black because he needed that jolt to get going in the morning.

Only a couple other agents in the Salt Lake FBI field office were non-Mormon. Robinson was finally getting accustomed to being surrounded by Mormons at work and at home. He was approaching his first anniversary in this office since his transfer from North Carolina.

"Don't accept it!" his neighbors had warned him. "Those Mormons'll drive you nuts!"

Then they regaled him with all the horror stories they could think of about stealing wives and secret devil worship going on in the temple in Salt Lake City. At first Robinson began to worry about living in Utah. Then one fellow told him how all Mormons were born with horns, but they were dehorned as babies so you couldn't tell. That finally made him come to his senses and ignore all the idiocy. After all, living among a bunch of Mormons couldn't be any worse than living among a bunch of Southern Baptists.

The reality turned out even better than he'd hoped. For the most part, the Mormons were intelligent and friendly and hardly the religious fanatics he'd expected, especially his colleagues. Oh, there were a few zealots in his neighborhood who had already tried to convert him or call him to repentance for his smoking, but it was par for the course when you lived among a high concentration of a religious denomination. Sure, his family had a hard time fitting in, but he'd experienced the same thing among the Baptists. It was just human nature to associate with people who thought like you.

Even the strict liquor laws in Utah didn't bother Robinson all that much. He wasn't much of a drinker. As a new agent, he'd seen the damage alcohol had done to the careers of some older agents who had let the pressure get to them. He swore that would never happen to him, so he was always careful to keep his drinking light and very social.

But the anti-smoking laws really bothered him. Coming from tobacco country where parents would blow smoke in the faces of infants to get them used to it, Robinson found Utah's rabidly anti-smoking laws to be the part he hated most about living here. He couldn't even smoke at work all day unless he stepped out and away from the building. In the winter, that got pretty uncomfortable. Couldn't they set aside even one smoking room?

But the skiing here was fantastic. A man could put up with a lot for some fantastic skiing. And the family-oriented attitude made the perfect environment for raising his own kids. All in all, Robinson was happy living in Utah.

Including work. Ironically, Utah was a popular conduit for drugs coming into the country, and working with the DEA in chasing them down offered many enjoyable challenges. At times Robinson even felt like one of those FBI agents in the movies when things got jumping.

Now, however, the most interesting thing going on was surveillance of a small-time pusher by the name of Steven Coulter. Hopefully this guy would lead them to someone higher up the chain. He maintained three residences, each with a different woman. Apparently he'd abandoned one of those residences and probably the woman living there too because he hadn't visited for a while.

Robinson scanned through his stack of papers, finding run-of-the-mill memos and reports, until one caught his eye. The Larry H. Miller Toyota dealership had submitted a routine report about a new van that had been paid for in cash—all one hundred dollar bills. When the deposit was checked at the bank, the bills turned out to have certain significant serial numbers—every single bill!

When Robinson had first come to the Salt Lake office a year ago, he was dropped into the middle of a sting operation. The DEA was about to pass a hundred and fifty thousand dollars of cash in unmarked, nonsequential bills with carefully registered serial numbers so they could be traced. They were hoping to fill in some blanks on the organizational chart of a local band of dealers. But the cash completely disappeared. None of the registered bills ever showed up.

Until now. The purchaser was named Cory Young, a young father and husband living in a small rented duplex in South Salt Lake. He worked at a mall bookstore as an assistant manager. How in the world had he gotten hold of that money?

It couldn't have been through normal circulation, otherwise only some of the bills would have turned up registered. Maybe he found the money somewhere. Or maybe he was involved in its laundering. Regardless of how it happened, this Cory Young knew something that Robinson wanted to know!

Sipping his coffee, he decided he wouldn't bring in Young for questioning right away. He'd order up surveillance first, see what they could find out before they tipped Young off.

With a satisfied grin, Robinson dropped the report on his desk, kicked back in his chair with his feet on the desk, and sipped. Interesting things should start happening now!

The twenty-four hour vacation from the world was over. Time to buckle down and get to work. And for the next couple of days, C.H. did work—diligently—to remember his promises. He prayed when he got up in the morning, watched one General Conference speaker on tape as he ate breakfast, and made sure his family prayed together at night. He called Monday's picnic family home evening and the movie with Dani date night. Before going to bed, he made sure he cracked open his scriptures and read at least a few verses out of the Book of Mormon.

And still he felt a gnawing feeling that something wasn't quite right.

"Please help me be worthy of this calling that's coming to me," he prayed. "Help me do everything I'm supposed to do. Help me feel good about it."

He must have been spiritually weaker than he realized. The good feelings were slow in coming.

He wondered when he would hear from Brother Brigham. Each day Dani asked, "Has he appeared again yet?"

He heard her unspoken question: *Do you know where the money came from yet?*

By Wednesday evening, the tension grew worse. Where *had* the money come from? What would his calling be? Was he still worthy of it, or had he done something wrong? He thought of the times when Joseph Smith had lost his prophetic powers due to mistakes.

He tried to imagine what else he should be doing. The Word of Wisdom was no problem. He wasn't interested in tobacco, alcohol, coffee, or tea, and certainly not drugs. Maybe home teaching was the problem. He wasn't even sure if he was assigned any families, it had been so long. He vowed to talk to the elders quorum president about that next Sunday, which was one of those rare ones he actually had off from work.

Genealogy crossed his mind, but he decided that there was such a thing as biting off more than he could chew, even in living the gospel. Too many changes at once, and he might get discouraged and fail in all of them.

Temple attendance at least once a month. His temple recommend had expired a a while ago—Dani's too. It had been easy to put off renewing it, since he rarely went to church.

"We should renew our recommends soon," he said to her that night as they lay in bed, Glenn asleep between them.

She remained quiet, and he thought she must be asleep already. But then she said, "I've been thinking about Sunday. What do we drive to church?"

"What do you mean?" But in that instant, he knew exactly what she meant.

"What do we say when people see our new car? They'll ask us how we can afford it."

Would people really ask such a nosy question? Sheila had, but that was Sheila. He shook his head. "They don't know that. And it would be rude of them to ask."

"The bishop will know."

The bishop. Yes, he'd know, thanks to the tithing that Dani made sure they paid regularly, along with all their other bills. Frankly, C.H. wasn't sure how she managed to stretch his paycheck to cover their expenses. Once he suggested jokingly—half-jokingly anyway—that they skip tithing that month. Her reaction banished that thought from his mind for all eternity. The bishop had told her he'd rather have them pay a full tithing and receive assistance from fast offerings than skimp on tithing. They had taken him up on that suggestion several times, including the month of C.H.'s tithing joke.

Yes, it would look awfully suspicious to the bishop for a family struggling as they were and receiving occasional financial assistance to suddenly show up at church with a gleaming new RAV4.

I got a raise at work.

Dani's parents gave it to us.

Shame engulfed him. Here he was, called of God and thinking up lies to tell the bishop. Why should he lie at all? Why should he feel ashamed for doing what Brother Brigham had instructed him to do? Why couldn't he just go to the bishop and tell him what happened?

"We'll just drive up smiling," he finally answered, "and if the bishop asks, I'll tell him what happened. Why should we hide that God called us?"

She remained silent until they fell asleep.

Thursday was supposed to have been his second day off for the week. He planned to go violin shopping that day. But Milt called and asked him if he could work anyway. "Sheila called in sick again. I'll make it up to you."

Sheila had called in sick all week. There was no doubt in C.H.'s mind that her absence had more to do with whatever happened between her and her boyfriend, but kept that to himself. All week he worried about her, wondering what had happened, what she was doing, how she was doing. She was usually pretty responsible about showing up for work. Whatever the answers to those questions were, they couldn't be good.

Every time he came near the Religion section, he could sense *that* book as if it burned with an internal black fire, even though Sheila had purchased it off the shelf days ago. Satanism and depression couldn't possibly be a good combination. He shuddered as he thought what she might be getting mixed up in.

No, he tried to reassure himself. She was eccentric, but she wasn't batty. She wasn't interested in the *Satanic Bible* because of some dark mysticism. She just liked how it criticized Christianity. She wouldn't take it seriously.

But he didn't feel reassured.

Friday was Sheila's scheduled day off. The next morning, Saturday, she didn't show up again, and this time she didn't call either. Whatever Milt had in mind for making it up to him, it didn't include having his Sunday off, not with Sheila mysteriously disappearing. "I don't know what's up," Milt said on Saturday afternoon. "I can't get hold of her. I hope she's alright."

On Sunday Dani insisted on driving the old Corolla to church. "You won't be there to explain it to the bishop," she said.

He almost protested, but he didn't feel good about making her explain it either. It was his calling, his vision, his responsibility. "Can you set up an appointment with the bishop then, for our recommends? He does his appointments on Tuesdays, right? I'll explain it to him then."

That was why he ended up driving the SUV to work while Dani and the kids took the rusty Corolla, even though it made him feel like a jerk. No matter—it was just for this once. In two days he should have everything straightened out.

Maria, the lead cashier, was already at work when he arrived. She'd have been the acting manager for the day if C.H. hadn't come in at Milt's request. Surprisingly, Milt was also there. He was at his desk slumped over a scheduling form. "I still can't get hold of Sheila, and she usually gets here by now. I think we'll just have to let her go." He held up the sheet of paper. "I'm reworking the schedule for the rest of this week. Need any specific times off?"

"Just Tuesday evening."

C.H. was surprised how much he felt concern for Sheila. He couldn't blame Milt for letting her go—he *tried* to find out what was wrong, and he had a store to run. But she was losing her job now on top of whatever else was upsetting her. And what was upsetting her must be pretty bad for her to lose her job. It didn't pay much, but she loved reading, and working in a bookstore was her dream job.

After work, Dani let him know that the Tuesday appointment with the bishop was all set.

"How was church?" he asked her.

"Nice," she said. "How was work?"

"Sheila wasn't there again, and Milt's going to let her go."

"Oh, that's too bad."

He stifled a feeling of irritation at her casual tone. He couldn't expect her to feel as concerned as he was. She wasn't fully aware of the situation, and she barely knew Sheila. Not like him who worked with her almost every day.

"You hungry?" she asked. "I've got dinner ready."

Only then did he notice the delicious aroma coming from the kitchen. He must be more preoccupied than he realized if he hadn't noticed steak cooking.

Part of his mind concentrated on the good meal, but another part kept thinking about Sheila and Brother Brigham and the money. With Joseph Smith, three years passed between his First Vision and when Moroni actually got him started on his calling. Would Brother Brigham wait such a long time before returning?

The thought appalled him. With all that money buried in his laundry, would he have to wait three years to find out what he was supposed to do with it? Three years before he could ask Dani's question for her and ease her mind? Patience and faith were virtues, but for *that* long?

Then he remembered that Joseph Smith's Moroni vision had occurred when he finally got around to asking for one. For three years he'd played around like teenagers do, then one night he started feeling bad for his frivolous behavior. He prayed for forgiveness, fully expecting another visitation. Sure enough, another visitation came: the angel Moroni. If he'd prayed sooner, would Moroni have shown up sooner?

Brother Brigham had already appeared to C.H. a second time, and it had been in response to a prayer. He started feeling a combination of guilt and foolishness. Brigham was probably just waiting for an invitation. C.H. might have already found out what his calling was and where the money came from if he'd only asked. *Ask, and it shall be given you.*

"I'm going into the bedroom and pray," he announced to Dani.

The way he said it made an impact on her. "You're going to talk with Brigham Young?"

"I'm going to ask for it, yes. I just realized I haven't asked."

In the bedroom, he sat on the bed for a moment, meditating. If he received what he asked for, he was about to find out what his calling was. He trembled with excitement and nerves. What could it be? How hard would it be? Would he balk at fulfilling it?

No, no way would he. He was determined to fulfill it, no matter how hard it proved to be. How had Nephi put it? "I will go and do the thing that the Lord commanded me, because I know he wouldn't command me if he hadn't prepared a way for me to fulfill it," or something like that. Nephi had to go up against an evil man who sought after his life and finally had to kill that man with his own hands. Joseph Smith went through all sorts of persecution establishing the Church of Jesus Christ in modern times, eventually giving his life as a martyr. Brigham Young had to lead thousands of people across thousands of miles of desolate country and spend decades carving a civilization out of desert. In C.H.'s times, the church was established and respected, and life was easy with modern conveniences. Nothing Brigham Young required of him could possibly measure up to the great challenges Brigham and other prophets of the past had faced. He made a firm commitment that he would accept whatever calling Brother Brigham gave him.

Trembling, he knelt down and leaned against the bed. It felt a little strange, but he didn't close his eyes, since he expected as much as Joseph Smith had that he'd receive a visitation. At first, he almost began his prayer to Brother Brigham, but years of conditioning made that feel all wrong, so he addressed it to his Father in Heaven.

He spent several minutes giving thanks for everything he could think of: the SUV, the good food, his family, the gospel, this wonderful world we live in. Giving thanks was the next step in the prayer formula, and he wanted to be sure he got it right.

When he ran out of ideas on what to be thankful for, he paused, trying to think of a good way to word his requests. *Just say it*, he thought. *God already knows anyway. Why phrase it in some kind of fancy language?* "I'd like to know what my calling is, Father," he said with forced boldness. "And Dani is very concerned about the money. Please don't think of her as faithless. She's just concerned about where it came from. It would help her feel better to know. In the name—"

The golden light shone through his eyelids. Without realizing it, he'd closed them while praying, the habit of a lifetime. He opened them, and Brother Brigham stood in the same place as before, next to the empty crib. C.H. felt some of the same feelings of unworthiness as before, but with less intensity this time. That made him feel better, to know that his daily efforts were making a difference.

"Cory Horace," Brother Brigham said. "You would like to know where the money came from."

"Yes, Brother Brigham."

"Are you sure?"

The question suddenly made him not so sure. But he couldn't face Dani without finding out. "Yes, I'm sure," he said with forced conviction.

"That money was part of a drug deal."

A cold thrill shot through his body.

"One person dropped it off where you found it and picked up a package of drugs at another location along the freeway. The person who was supposed to retrieve the backpack was murdered before he could do so."

Drug money! C.H. tried hard to keep from panting. The musty smell of the money billowed into his memory, adding to the filthiness he felt about the bills.

"The money was forgotten and has been there for quite some time."

C.H. breathed deeply in an effort to calm himself. "Yes, Brother Brigham," he half-gasped.

"And now..." Brother Brigham raised his eyebrows and let a small smile lift one corner of his mouth. "How do you feel about this?"

"I... I..." How did he feel? "I think that God has turned an evil thing into a good purpose." Yes, that's how he felt about it. It was God's prerogative to do such a thing. His negative feeling was about Dani—how would she feel about this? "No one knows the money was there?"

"The only one who knew is dead. It was an anonymous exchange. The one who dropped it there doesn't even realize the other was murdered."

"And the bills weren't marked?" He felt a little foolish for asking these things, but he knew Dani would ask them, and he wanted to be able to answer her with certainty.

"Would drug dealers use marked money?"

Now he really felt foolish. Dani's concern about marked money was because she was thinking of a bank robbery. Of course drug money wouldn't be marked. When Brigham had first mentioned drug money, C.H. worried that Dani would balk at that, thinking of it as somehow dirtier than a bank robbery or something. But it might actually make her feel better. No marked bills, and nobody was looking for it.

It was a lesson in faith. There'd been nothing to worry about all along. God was taking money intended for evil and turning it to a good cause. The foolishness of mortals! All this time he only needed to have faith.

"And now, grandson"—Brother Brigham's face filled with a warm smile and crinkling eyes—"you want to know what your calling is to be."

C.H. burned with anticipation. "Yes." He felt like the time he was in a violin competition, seconds before the winner was announced.

"Then hear me well, Cory Horace." Brigham suddenly spoke in a commanding, officious voice, as many angelic visitors before him must have spoken. "You are called to become the prophet and president of the Church of Jesus Christ of Latter-day Saints."

"What!"

"Thus saith the Lord, 'If my prophet shall ever lead this church astray, he will be removed from his office, and another placed in his stead.' I say to you, the current holder of that office is leading the church astray. You, Cory Horace Young, my great-great-grandson, will be put in his place."

C.H. was on the verge of toppling from his knees with dizziness. This couldn't be! It was all wrong! This isn't how it should happen. "How—why—why isn't this calling coming to me through the priesthood line of authority?"

"What makes you think it will not?" Brother Brigham barked with a scowl. "David was anointed king by the prophet Samuel in private with no one's knowledge years before he received the public anointing. You are being called in private so you can prepare for the time when the calling comes through official channels."

He had to lean forward, touching his head against the side of the bed, to keep from fainting.

"Hear me well, my young descendant. The president of the church was given a revelation restoring an important principle of the gospel, and he has rejected that revelation. The Lord has given him ample time to repent and comply, but he has not, and the time is long overdue for that principle to be put into practice. You are being called to live that principle now, and when the time is right, you will be called to lead the church and proclaim that principle to all the Saints."

The words kept coming, bombarding him without respite. C.H. wished Brigham would pause so he could take a moment and soak it all in.

"Cory Horace Young, you must now listen and accept that revelation. Thus saith the Lord, 'It is time again for my people to live that most sacred principle of celestial marriage in its fullness. I have spared them from this requirement for a season, that my people could grow and strengthen themselves against the fiery darts of the enemy. But the time is at hand that they obey me in fulfilling the new and everlasting covenant. They are strong, and when their enemies come against them, I will fight their battles for them.'"

Celestial marriage? What did Brigham mean? Wasn't that getting married in the temple? But the church was already doing that.

The torrent of Brigham's words wouldn't stop. "'Hear me, Cory Horace, for I the Lord am one God. I change not, and I require this of your generation as I have required it of generations past from faithful Abraham to my servant Brigham Young. Listen and obey. You shall take to yourself wives, given to you by me, for the raising of a righteous posterity and for the glory of God in the eternities. You shall marry them according to the new and everlasting covenant, for time and for all eternity. When the time comes, you shall accept my call to lead this church as its president of the high priesthood. Remember, Cory Horace, that many are called but few are chosen. Accept this call, or you shall be destroyed in the lake of fire of which my servant John has spoken.'"

The silence seemed to thunder through the tiny bedroom with a magnificent echo. C.H. had to put a hand on the floor to steady himself from the force of the shock. Polygamy? He was supposed to live polygamy? It was impossible! How could he do such a thing? How could he do that to Dani?

Through his mind ran all the examples of splinter groups he'd heard about that broke from the church over this very issue. The prophet has led the church astray, they always said. The Principle, as they called it, should be lived now. He remembered the legendary tales he heard on his mission—stories that were probably gossiped through every mission in Europe—about the missionary in France who thought he received a vision commanding him to live polygamy and teach it to others. He converted a small group of members, and when they were excommunicated they formed their own church.

C.H. had always considered those people fools. And now he was supposed to become the same sort of fool? Except that he didn't just *think* he received a revelation. He really had—the backpack of money proved it, if nothing else. And he'd tried Brother Brigham with Joseph Smith's three grand keys test.

But that meant God really had called him to live polygamy.

No, he couldn't live it. How could he face Dani and tell her that?

Dani—his first wife! According to the scripture governing celestial marriage, the first wife had to give permission for the husband to marry other wives. In a million years, he couldn't imagine her doing such a thing. She'd refuse permission, and he wouldn't be allowed to marry without it.

He breathed a sigh of relief. He was off the hook.

C.H. straightened up on his knees, wiping his eyes. Brother Brigham stood silently, perusing him with a neutral expression. "Brother Brigham, I—my wife, Dani, my *first* wife. I don't think she'll give me permission to marry."

Brother Brigham's face grew grim. "Did that stop Joseph Smith from obeying God?"

A chill ran down his spine. Marry behind her back? No! No! That was worse than telling her to her face. "I—I can't deceive her."

"Your wife *will* give her consent," Brother Brigham roared. "Will you obey this commandment, Cory Horace?"

Impossible! There was no way Dani would agree to such a thing.

Would she?

Yes, she would. He knew she would. It would kill her, but she would if she was convinced it came from God.

Quietly—*profoundly* quietly after the resounding commands he had just uttered, quiet with intensity so the words pierced deep into C.H.'s soul—Brother Brigham said, "Will you say no to *me*?"

He peered into Brigham's eyes, his sharp lances of eyes. Say no to Brigham

Young, his hero, his great-great-grandfather? Say no about living polygamy, to one of the most married men since the days of Solomon? Say no to the man who, when first hearing about polygamy himself, preferred to trade places with a dead man in a coffin than to marry a second wife, but who obeyed anyway, and with only the word of the prophet Joseph Smith to go on, not an angel back from the dead?

Now he understood why God had sent Brigham Young to him. Unless Jesus or the Father himself came—and he trembled at the thought of such a thing—Brigham was probably the only man in heaven and earth that C.H. could not say no to. Not about this.

"I have been entrusted with the keys of the principle of celestial marriage, Cory Horace." With a fleeting smile, Brigham added, "That should come as no surprise to you. And as a faithful, albeit recently slothful, descendant of mine, you have been selected to inherit these keys from me."

It hurt—it physically hurt somewhere between his heart and his gut—to contemplate what he was being asked to do. He understood exactly how Brigham Young must have felt. Right now, lying in a coffin sounded like a pretty good alternative to telling Dani he was marrying another woman. But he could not say no to Brigham Young. He could not go back on his commitment to accept the calling, whatever it was. He could not so soon turn his back on the lesson he'd just learned about having faith. If this was the thing the Lord commanded, then he would do it, putting his trust in God that he'd prepare a way for him to do this impossible thing.

But, dear God, how it ached to think of telling Dani.

"Will you accept this calling, Cory Horace?" Brigham said firmly.

C.H. bowed his head and closed his eyes. Tears immediately spilled out. The ache in him was devouring. It was the special calling he'd been anticipating all his life, the calling his father had talked about, his patriarchal blessing, even his imaginary friend. The special calling that he'd waited for, wished for, prayed for. And now that it came, he wished he'd died before ever hearing it.

"Yes," he whispered.

"You shall be blessed for your obedience, Cory Horace," he responded with gentleness. "Now go and tell your wife, and command her to be obedient."

A moment of silence passed, and C.H. looked up. Brother Brigham gazed upon him with his lips pursed tightly together and his forehead knotted, a look that communicated empathy for what C.H. was going through.

"Yes, Brother Brigham," C.H. said, steeling himself for the struggle ahead.

Chapter 6

Dani sat on the couch nursing Glenn as C.H. plodded out from the bedroom. He looked like he'd received a death sentence. His face was white and sullen. His shoulders and back were hunched, and his eyes held a look of resigned determination. His jaw muscles trembled with a tight clench. He glanced at Petey curled up asleep on the recliner, but he wouldn't meet Dani's gaze.

She broke the seal of Glenn's mouth from her breast and laid him on the sofa, ignoring his soft cry. Then she walked over to C.H. and hugged him. "What happened, Cain?" she asked him, even though the apprehension inside her made her certain she knew.

He returned her hug with a fierce embrace that squeezed the breath out of her. Relaxing, he held her for some time without moving or speaking.

It had to be the money. Someone was looking for it. They would find the Youngs and do something awful to them.

She led him to the sofa and guided him down, then sat next to him and gathered up Glenn. "It's the money, isn't it?" she said as she aimed her nipple back into the baby's mouth.

"Dani, the money's fine," he said in a dull voice. "It came from a drug deal—an anonymous drug deal, Brigham called it. One person dropped the money where I found it, and another person was supposed to pick it up. They didn't know each other. The guy that was supposed to pick it up was murdered before he could pick it up. That money's been sitting there ever since, and no one even knows it was there."

The money's fine. It was what had been bothering her for days, and that was the answer she wanted to hear. But she didn't feel any relief from it. "Drug money doesn't sound so fine to me."

"No one knows it was there. No one's looking for it. It's not marked. God took an evil thing and turned it to a good purpose." He droned on as if there were no life in him. "*The money's fine.*"

If there was no problem with the money—and he obviously thought so, even if she didn't—then why was he acting like this? Something else was wrong. Something she should have been worrying about all along instead of the money.

He wouldn't look at her—just gazed straight ahead as if in a trance. "The money's fine," he repeated in a whisper.

For the first time since he dumped the bundles of cash onto the coffee table, she wished there *was* something wrong with the money. At least that would be a familiar fear.

"So Brigham Young did appear to you again?" she said, trying to coax some words out of him.

"Yes." He still wouldn't look at her. What was so bad that he couldn't even look at her? She couldn't take it anymore. "Cain, please tell me. What's bothering you?"

Finally he looked at her. Some kind of struggle was going on behind his eyes. "I learned what my calling is." He seemed to force out the words.

"What is your calling?"

"I'm going to become the president of the church."

At least three full seconds passed before the words sank in. "What? You're going to be the *prophet?*" This was too preposterous. No one became the president of the church. Not regular people.

He nodded slowly, eyes looking away from her again.

"You're joking, right?"

He shook his head.

She studied his face, as much as she could see of it. He sure didn't look like he was joking, and she'd kill him if he was under these circumstances. "You can't be the president. You're not even an apostle."

"So?" he said. "You think God can't choose his own prophet from wherever he wants?"

"But it's never been done that way before, not since Joseph Smith."

"So?"

"So you're serious?" She finally began to realize he might be. "You're really going to be the president?"

He nodded.

This was incredible news—unbelievable news—incomprehensible news. But she started thinking about it. All his life he'd expected a special calling to be a great leader in the church, to preach the gospel throughout the world. His patriarchal blessing said so. This certainly would satisfy those prophecies!

But it still seemed so ridiculous. Her husband who calls himself Cain Hell Young, the prophet?

A scripture ran through her head, chastening her: *A prophet is not without honor, except in his own home.* That was certainly true! She was too used to him as a real human being, with all his strengths and all his weaknesses. It seemed absurd to her that God would choose him to run the church.

Just like it seemed absurd to the people of Nazareth that the carpenter boy Jesus who grew up in their midst could be the Messiah.

Okay, she'd accept his statement...for now. But if it were true, it wasn't a bad thing. So what was bothering him?

"And you don't feel worthy? Is that it?" She almost felt angry with him for scaring her so badly.

"No, that's not it."

That's not it? She grabbed his chin and yanked his face toward her. "Cain, what *is* the problem?"

Forced to look at her, he studied her with mournful eyes. "Our prophet has received a revelation, but he won't accept it. One day he'll be removed from office, and I'll be called to replace him."

"Shouldn't the president of the Quorum of Twelve replace him?"

"I'm Brigham Young's great-great-grandson. He holds the keys to...the new and everlasting covenant. I guess I'm going to receive them by patriarchal inheritance or something."

Dropping her hand from his chin, she stared at him, trying to make sense of his words. "I don't understand what you're talking about."

He peered deep into her eyes, making her want to flinch. "God's restoring the practice of polygamy. The prophet won't accept it. I'm supposed to prepare myself to take his place." Keeping his eyes on her, he paused as if to gather strength. "And I'm supposed to begin practicing polygamy now. Brigham says the time has been delayed too long already."

Dani could only gape at him. What was this nonsense he was speaking? Suddenly everything he told her since he first ran out to pick up the backpack seemed outrageous. "Brigham Young told you that?" She let out an incredulous laugh. "That's crazy—that's impossible. Restore polygamy? Become the prophet? That's nuts! You just imagined it."

Why wouldn't the words stop? They kept flowing out of her mouth with a will of their own, words that she was aghast to speak, words that must be hurting him to the core. But they wouldn't stop. They sprang from some fountain she could not quell.

"This whole thing is crazy. You haven't received a calling. You never saw Brigham Young. You stole that money. Tell me where you got it! I demand to know—"

He grabbed her by the shoulder with one hand. "Stop it!" he cried.

His demand broke the flood of words. She thought about what she just said, and she couldn't decide if she was more appalled at that or at all the claims he'd made. *The prophet is leading the church astray. You must practice polygamy again.* This was standard apostasy talk. This was the road to excommunication. What was happening with her husband? She couldn't just accept this.

"Cain—"

"I know what you're thinking."

"Cain, this isn't right."

"I have to obey God, Dani. I have to have faith."

"It's adultery. You'll be excommunicated."

"No, Dani, listen!"

His image swam in her tears. This couldn't possibly be happening. Why did he keep saying all this nonsense? "I can't listen to this."

"Dani, please! Brigham Young gave me the commandment. Don't you remember how he felt when he learned about polygamy?"

"Horny?"

He stifled a laugh.

"How dare you laugh at me!"

His face got very somber. "I'm sorry. You caught me by surprise."

"So what *did* Brigham Young feel?" She squinted angrily at him.

"There was a funeral going by, and he wanted to trade places with the man in the coffin."

So was she supposed to feel sorry for poor Brigham? Tears spilled from her eyes. He wiped at them desperately with his fingers.

"Brigham was as horrified as we are, but he obeyed anyway. He was commanded by Joseph Smith, and he obeyed."

Dani shook her head over and over. She wanted to shout, *Stop talking!* She didn't want to hear this.

"Dani, I'm sorry. I don't want to do this. But Brigham Young commanded me. *Brigham Young.* How can I say no to him?"

"Like this!" She jumped to her feet and gazed up at the ceiling. "Brigham Young, listen to me. *No!*"

The shriek woke up Glenn and Petey. They both began crying, and C.H. scrambled to pick up Petey and comfort him. Dani gazed at him as he sat on the recliner rocking his son. Slowly she backed to the sofa, picked up Glenn, and began gently rocking him. She felt completely numb inside. Her shriek had drained all emotion from her. She gazed at her husband, who was studiously ignoring her by giving all his attention to Petey, stroking his hair and encouraging him back to sleep. What was he feeling? She couldn't tell, and she wasn't sure she cared. How could he demand this thing from her?

In the middle of the living room, four feet above the floor, a faint patch of golden light formed. A chill ran through her as she froze in place, staring. The glow intensified, and the small patch enlarged. Dani wanted to turn away, but she couldn't take her eyes from it. The glow became vertically oblong and differentiated into a human form. She wished she could close her eyes, wished she could even blink, but she couldn't.

"Danielle," said a rumbling voice. It was thin and distant, yet clear and commanding.

A figure stood in the middle of the room radiating the warm glow. C.H. and Petey looked jaundiced in its glare. The figure looked like Brigham Young from pictures she'd seen. Not the older man, stocky from age with a frazzled white beard stretching down to his chest. But a younger Brigham, hair curled up above his forehead, beard darker and trimmed. She had seen only one picture of him at that age and didn't remember it well, but it seemed to be Brigham Young.

"Danielle," the figure said again, "will you keep your husband from obeying the commandment of God?"

She felt horrified as she thought of the things she said moments ago. A sickening feeling permeated her, as if hell itself were grasping her and pulling her down. What had she been doing? Trying to get her husband to disobey God.

She glanced at C.H., who was looking back at her. Brigham was looking at her. They were waiting for an answer. What was the question again?

"Will you, Sister Danielle?"

She hated this feeling that gripped her, this feeling of despair and filthiness, but she couldn't bring herself to form words of acceptance. Share her husband with another woman? Her mouth opened and her lips quivered as she tried to say something—anything—but her brain had no idea what to produce.

"Will you be like Emma?"

The figure remained in the center of the room, and the voice had actually grown softer, yet she felt as if Brigham were inches away from her, staring her down, whispering the accusation in her ear. *Will you be like Emma?*

She'd always felt condescending toward Emma Smith. Married to one of the greatest prophets of all time, and the minute he dies, she turns her back on the church he established and drags his children away with her. All because she couldn't accept the commandment Joseph had received from God to practice polygamy. Emma's refusal to accept the doctrine caused her and Joseph no end of grief. Joseph, torn between loving his wife and obeying God, practiced polygamy in secret, slinking around like an adulterer. It may have cost him his life.

And now Dani, placed in the exact same position, was reacting in exactly the same way Emma had. Refusing to accept the commandment. Demanding that her husband not obey. Forcing him into an impossible situation. Would he also obey anyway behind her back? Would she hate him for it if he did, or love him for being obedient to God?

"The promises God made to Emma are the promises he makes to you, Danielle, and the warnings she received are also yours. Thus saith the Lord, 'You are an elect lady, and the office of your calling is to comfort your husband Cory Horace in his afflictions, with consoling words, in the spirit of meekness. You will be ordained under his hand to expound the principle of celestial marriage to your fellow sisters in the church, preparing them to receive it. You do not need to fear for the temporal needs of your family. The gift of money that Cory Horace received at the hand of God is for your support. For I have called him to do a great work, and he is to diligently fulfill this calling without the distraction of temporal matters.'"

In a small part of Dani's soul, a glimmer of hope ignited. The Lord had called her an elect lady in spite of her hostile reaction to the news. She was being called to an important work, as much as her husband was being called. Maybe she could endure this trial by immersing herself in the work she was called to do. She could fill her life with the Spirit, and that should strengthen her to carry this burden.

And maybe she could accept that the money really was fine.

"'But let my handmaid Danielle receive all those that shall be given to my servant Cory Horace. I will bless him and multiply him and give to him a hundredfold of fathers and mothers, brothers and sisters, wives and children, and crowns of eternal lives in the eternal worlds. But if she will not abide this commandment, she shall be destroyed. For I am the Lord thy God, and I will destroy her if she abide not my law.'"

The chastening made her feel better. It seemed to cleanse her of her defiant words, and now she could begin fresh again.

"'Keep my commandments, my handmaid Danielle, and you shall receive a crown of righteousness, and shall delight in the glory which shall come upon your husband.'"

Suddenly Brother Brigham turned to C.H. "And you, Cory Horace, shall continue to love your wife through all that comes to pass. You will begin to practice the new and everlasting covenant of celestial marriage at once, as the time is long overdue. You will give notice at your place of employment so you can free up your time to prepare for your new calling. The money you have received is for the support of your family, to be used at your discretion. And now, Cory Horace, do you accept this calling?"

"Yes, Brother Brigham," he said with determination.

Brother Brigham turned back to Dani. She knew what his next words would be, and she dreaded them.

"Do you, Danielle, accept these things from the Lord?"

Picturing Emma's face vividly in her mind, she forced out a whispered, "Yes." The word seemed to burn as it came out. She understood Emma better now and felt grateful for the lessons she could learn from her experiences. Perhaps Dani could avoid making the same mistakes, if she tried hard enough.

"Good. Here is your first mission, Cory Horace. Go immediately to the home of Sheila Matthews. She is involved in satanic rituals at this very moment. She needs you to pull her away from the precipice. You will go to her and stop her, then teach her the things you have learned. She will be contrite and repentant. She will be the first wife given to you under the restored principle of celestial marriage."

"Sheila?" C.H. said, and he looked at Dani.

Our Sheila, Dani thought, *who works at the bookstore?* She'd never heard her last name before, but from C.H.'s reaction, she was certain it was her. Crazy, rebellious, fornicating Sheila with the twelve rings in her ears.

"Go at once!" Brother Brigham barked. "She needs you at this moment."

C.H. jumped up and laid Petey back on the recliner, then came to her and crouched down, gazing at her at eye level. "Dani?" he said in a tone that asked permission, asked if she was okay with this, and apologized all at the same time.

"Go," she said forcefully. "She needs you." She tried and failed to keep the sarcasm out of her voice.

He hurried out, and soon she heard the sound of the Corolla driving away.

"You have done well, Danielle," Brother Brigham said with a smile. "I know how difficult this is for you. God will bless you for your courage, your devotion, and your faithfulness." His image faded quickly, and the glow shrank into a pinpoint and disappeared.

She held tight to Glenn, clinging desperately as if she might lose him in the next moment. She rocked back and forth slightly like she always did when trying to calm him, even though he was sound asleep. His face was sweetly angelic, like all sleeping babies, and as she gazed at it, she realized her breast was still exposed. The whole time Brigham Young had been there! Mortification would have been her normal reaction, but after all that had happened, that small humiliation hardly seemed worth getting worked up over.

"Go," she said to the front door. "Sheila needs you."

Like I don't?

C.H. had to make a stop at work because he didn't know where Sheila lived. The parking lot was dark and deserted. His watch said almost 10:00 p.m.

He fumbled through his keys as he headed for the service entrance to the bookstore. *Open the door, turn on one light, and head for the filing cabinet.* He felt a little like James Bond rifling through the villain's papers. His hair crawled on the back of his neck, waiting for the hand of Milt or some security guard to come down on his shoulder. This wasn't exactly kosher, pulling the private file of an employee so he could drop by her home unannounced, definitely *not* for company business.

He breathed freely again as he pulled out of the parking lot, the address scribbled on a torn piece of paper lying on the passenger seat. Thank heavens Brigham Young had designed the streets of Salt Lake City with a coordinate grid so he wouldn't have to waste time figuring out where some street was.

The apartment complex was not far, still within the limits of West Valley City. He searched for the correct building, then parked in a vacant handicapped spot because there was nowhere else nearby to park. "Keep the cops away, Brother Brigham," he prayed. "This errand is your idea."

He bounded up to the third floor, taking three steps at once. *Satanic rituals? What in the world's gotten into you, Sheila? Are you out of your mind?* He stopped in front of the door, raised his hand in a fist ready to knock, and paused. What Satanic ritual could she be doing? Was she actually evoking the powers of Satan? Would the apartment be full of evil forces? Would Satan himself be in there?

He shivered with anxiety. It wasn't like she was dabbling in magic, something he didn't believe in. The beings of hell were real, and so was their power— he might be jumping into some pretty serious stuff. But he had the priesthood and could command the devils with it. On paper, anyway. How strong was his priesthood after he'd neglected to magnify it for so long?

No, he wasn't going to start that again. God had called him, and it was time he put his lackluster past behind and concentrate on the future. Apparently he had enough priesthood authority left to satisfy God, and he was supposed to minister to people with it. Brigham said Sheila needed ministering right now, so he'd do it even if he had to face demons from hell.

He knocked. Nothing happened. He knocked harder. Still nothing. He pressed his ear to the door and listened. Faintly he could hear Sheila's voice calling out, but he couldn't make out any words. He knocked a third time and then tried the knob. It was unlocked. Thank heavens for small blessings.

Slowly he opened the door. It stopped after a couple of inches. One of those stupid chains held it in place. Sheila's voice was louder now.

"Shemhamforash! Hail Satan!" A gong sounded, sending a shiver through his body.

The room was dark except for flickering lights. "Sheila?"

"I request the forces of darkness to destroy my enemy Steven Coulter in the most horrible manner possible. He has betrayed me and mocked my pain. He has left me stranded in the world after promising to be with me forever. Let him die a terrible death!"

He expected to witness a satanic ritual, but the reality chilled him. He shoved himself against the door and popped the chain loose, then caught the door before it could swing too far.

He gasped.

Furniture had been shoved aside indiscriminately to clear a space along the west wall. A coffee table sat against the wall, serving as an altar. About a dozen tall, thin candles stood on the table in two groups on either end. The candles were all black except for a single white one in the group on the right. In the middle of the table was a glass chalice, empty but for a small puddle of red liquid at the bottom. Near the chalice was a small gong hanging by a frame and a large schoolmarm-style bell standing upright. On the wall hung a chain with a medallion at the end. He couldn't make out the engraving on the medallion. On the far right end of the coffee table stood an eight-by-ten glossy of Sheila's lover—former lover—in a cheap gold frame.

Her back was to him. She wore nothing but a black teddy that barely covered half her back and buttocks. In one hand she held the hammer for the gong and in the other an impressive sword straight out of Camelot, with a sheet of paper impaled on the end of it.

Where in the world did she get all that?

"Shemhamforash! Hail Satan!" she cried and banged on the gong. She dipped the paper into the flame of the white candle and set it on fire. Holding up the sword, she let glowing ashes drop to the table. Smoke danced up to the ceiling like an apparition.

"Now you die!" she growled as the last of the flame spent itself. She swung the sword broadside onto the top of the picture frame. He jumped as the sheet of glass covering the photograph burst into flying shards and the frame toppled onto its back. A black candle tipped and rolled. For an instant he thought it would roll off the table, but the roll followed an arc that just barely missed the edge. Wax dripped onto the tabletop as the flame sputtered and flared.

Sheila stabbed the photograph with the tip of her sword, gouging the table, and choked out some word that sounded more like a feral snarl. She lifted up the picture—the frame hung precariously by its cardboard backing—and slashed down, smashing the frame onto the floor. Her face swung into profile, and C.H. shuddered at the grimace on it.

She flung the picture with a sweep of the sword. It sailed away and crashed into a lamp on an end table, denting its shade. The lamp tipped, almost recovered, but then fell to the table. The light bulb shattered.

"Sheila, stop!" he bellowed.

She spun around and held out the sword at him, a wild look in her eyes. "You are dead!" she shrieked and charged him.

He jumped to the side, but the point of the sword snagged his sleeve as she rushed past. "Damn it, Sheila! What are you doing?"

She pulled the sword out of the puncture it had made in the drywall and whirled around, aiming it at his heart once more. She glared at him, but then her eyes softened as sanity seemed to take over. "C.H., what are you doing here?"

"Why did you do that?" He fingered the tear in his sleeve.

The tip of the sword sank to the floor, and she scowled. "Why did you come? You ruined the ritual."

With the sword out of the way, he walked to the table and blew out the tipped candle. A puddle of wax had formed, and a few drops had dripped to the floor. He noticed the engraving on the medallion hanging on the wall: an upside-down five-pointed star with a goat's head inside. He shuddered. "What ritual are you doing?"

"I'm killing Steven!"

"Who's Steven?"

"My *boyfriend*." She uttered the word like a curse. "He dumped me and sold the lease to our apartment, and I've got to be out of here in two days. I don't have any money to get another apartment." Her eyes squinted with rage.

He carefully approached and reached out to take both her hands. The sword clattered to the floor. The light from the candles danced on the walls like fiery imps from Disney's *Fantasia*. The smell of candle wax and smoke was thick in the room. Sheila's earrings sparkled in the fluttering illumination. She peered into his eyes, the rage melting away.

"You almost killed *me*," he said softly.

She burst into tears and buried her head in his chest, flinging her arms around him. "Oh, C.H. Why are you already married?"

The words shocked him. He'd never been aware of such feelings. She always acted so smug, even a little cocky around him. She was condescending about the religion that she'd rejected and he continued to espouse. All this time, it was a facade? Covering up her true feelings toward him?

But now things made sense. When Brother Brigham told him Sheila would be his second wife, he'd nearly fallen out of his chair, Petey and all. Sheila marry him? Even if he wasn't already married, he couldn't imagine her being interested in him. What could they possibly have in common? She mocked what he considered sacred. She lived as a radical free spirit, while he was a card-carrying conservative in his lifestyle. She read the *Satanic Bible* and acted on it, while he read the Book of Mormon and strove to apply its principles.

Now she was saying she wished he wasn't married, and that could mean only one thing. And he was learning this not one hour after an angel tells him she should be his wife. It was like the money all over again: an improbable situation turning out to make sense.

He lifted her chin with his fingers and gazed at her face, streaked with tears. Her deep-set eyes, her dark-red hair, even those absurd twinkling earrings—they all came together to make her beautiful, and he felt a sudden rush of arousal. He'd always been aware that she was attractive, but had always put it out of his mind since he loved Dani so much. Now God was telling him he could enjoy his attraction to her without guilt.

The gaze in her eyes was longing but despairing. At least, that's how he interpreted it. Actually, he realized, he was reading a lot into a single sentence, and maybe he'd better verify his assumption. "Why do you say that?"

She lowered her face, but not before her cheeks flushed. "Don't you know? I thought it was obvious, even though I tried to hide it."

If she meant what he thought, her attempt to hide it had been fabulously successful. "I—I'm not sure."

"I've seen how you treat your wife." She looked up again. "There were lots of times I wished Steven was you so I could be treated that way. Hell, you *did* treat me better than Steven. And you're—" She let out an embarrassed chuckle and lowered her eyes again. "You're so handsome. I had the hots for you the minute I saw you."

He needed her to say it clearly. "Are you saying you wish I was married to you instead of Dani?" He nearly held his breath waiting for the answer.

Her playful smile and mischievous eyes returned again, like a curtain descending over the vulnerability that had been there a moment ago. "Married? Hell, no. I don't believe in marriage. I just wanted to live with you. Or even just sleep with you."

He felt another shock. He should have known she'd think that way, but he hadn't imagined she'd apply that lifestyle to him. She laughed at his reaction, that delicious, bell-like giggle of hers that communicated ridicule and affection all at once. Immediately her face became serious. "I could never let you know. You love her—I can see that. And those damn religious beliefs you have. I just let it go."

Not so perfect a situation after all. He still had work to do to fulfill his duty. And his duty didn't start with proposing marriage. First preach to her, bring her to repentance. *Then* start worrying about the rest.

"Sheila." He broke their embrace and swept his arm around the room. "What about all this? What's this talk about killing Steven?"

A little of the darkness from before clouded her face. "I wasn't really going to kill him. I was just doing a ceremonial assassination out of the *Satanic Bible*.

I perform the ritual and let fate bring about his death naturally. Fate or magic or Satan—whatever."

"And you believe all that?"

She looked at the sword lying on the floor, the makeshift altar full of candles, and shrugged. "I don't know. But it sure felt good doing it." She picked up the sword and held it before her, examining its blade. "It would still feel good—the bastard!"

She marched over to the coffee table and placed the sword on it. The movement of her body beneath the teddy electrified him. He shut his eyes. He was supposed to be helping her spiritually, not fantasizing about their wedding night.

"What am I going to do, C.H.?"

He opened his eyes. Her provocative back was still to him.

"I don't have anywhere to live. I don't have enough money to put down a deposit on a new place. I don't have any good enough friends to move in with. I sure don't want to go back to my mom's." She turned to face him. With that sheer fabric, this view was just as provocative. "My paycheck at the bookstore wouldn't be enough to live on by myself anyway, even if I could get a place."

"I'm afraid you don't work there anymore."

She nodded her head. "I kind of figured that. But what would be the point of going back? I couldn't survive on that job anyway."

A hundred thousand dollars in the bottom of a clothes hamper. A command to make her his wife. Puzzle pieces falling into place.

Suddenly she peered at him with a quizzical look. "Why did you come here?" She looked at the door and rushed toward it. "Look what you did!" She held up the dangling chain and fingered the gouge in the wall.

"I'm sorry," he said. "I'll pay for it. But you didn't hear me. I had to get in."

"Why?"

"Well—" He began pacing back and forth. "Something incredible happened to me. I don't know if you're going to believe it."

"Try me."

"I was—well, I was mowing the lawn—" It already sounded stupid to him. Oh, well—he wouldn't be the first prophet to sound stupid to others. "An angel appeared to me."

Watching her, he debated how much detail to give her. She stared at him with a somber expression. He couldn't tell what she was thinking. At least it wasn't her usual scornful half-smile.

"I was told that I'll become the next president of the church."

"The *Mormon* church?" It was strange to hear her say it without any condescension. She sounded like she was only after clarification.

"The prophet was given a revelation, and he rejected it. He's going to be removed from office, and I'll be called to replace him."

Her somber look hardened, but still she didn't smirk. "Okay," she said in a noncommittal tone.

He continued to pace. "The revelation he rejected says that polygamy is supposed to be restored—"

"*What* is supposed to be restored?"

"Polygamy," he said weakly.

Now she thinks I'm making all this up so I can have sex with her. Would she be disgusted? Or pleased that he was deluding himself into having the affair she wanted with him?

"That's...bizarre." She pondered a moment. "But why are you *here*?"

"The angel that appeared to me was Brigham Young. He told me you were performing satanic rituals and that I should come here and stop you before you got too deep into it."

Her eyes widened, and she turned and absentmindedly fingered the hilt of the sword on the table. "Are you serious about all this?"

He peered at her with as much confidence as he could muster. "Yes."

She turned back to him. "Please leave." Her tone and her eyes were cold now. Her hand wrapped around the hilt.

"Sheila, there's something I have—"

"*Now.*"

She backed defensively toward the wall, raising the tip of the sword toward him. He wasn't sure if it was a reflexive or deliberate gesture.

A familiar golden glow appeared to his left, washing Sheila's face in yellow. Her eyes popped wide open, and she cried out as she fell back to the wall with her sword straight out.

"It's okay, Sheila," he said. "It's Brigham Young."

He wanted Brigham to say, "Fear not!" like all the other angels did, but then he wondered if it ever did any good. She stared with her mouth gaping and her outstretched sword trembling.

"Sheila Matthews," said Brigham's deep voice. "I am Brigham Young, as Cory Horace has told you. I have appeared to him as I appear to you now. He has been called to perform a great work for the Lord. I sent him to you to lead you back onto the path of righteousness. Listen to him, and heed him! He has been called to restore polygamy, and he has been commanded to begin practicing it at once. You have been chosen to be his wife."

The sword dropped out of her hand, clanging on the hardwood floor.

The glow dissipated. The flickering illumination of a dozen candles returned, playing harshly on her face. C.H. crossed to her and caught her just as she began to slip to the floor. Her eyes stared ahead at nothing. He led her to the sofa and sat her down on it, then sat next to her. She looked at him finally. "It's true?"

"Yes, it's all true. I'm sorry. It must have been quite a shock."

The wild look in her eyes agreed. "That was Brigham Young?"

"Yes."

"Oh, God!" She buried her face in her hands. "The things I've done!"

"It's okay." He stroked her hair. "God understands. He sent me to call you to repentance. You don't have to be afraid. Would God do all this if he didn't love you and want to forgive you?"

She looked up at him with a dismayed expression. "I don't know if I can go back to all that."

"All what?"

"All those—oh C.H., I *left* that religion. I don't know if I can go back."

"Is it really that bad?"

"It's not the smoking and drinking and all that. It's all those hypocrites. All that mind control. All that sanitized church history and—"

"Sheila, Brigham Young just appeared to you. Doesn't that tell you anything? We can deal with all that other stuff. We can work it out together."

She dropped her head onto his shoulder and sat still and silent, letting him continue to stroke her hair. He tried hard to keep his eyes off her partially dressed body. With the positions they were in, it was natural for his eyes to gaze down, and there were lots of interesting curves and folds to study, most of them in full view. He had to consciously move his eyes elsewhere.

"You're going to be president of the church?" she said.

"Yes."

"When?"

"I don't know."

Her face lit up. "When you are, you could have revelations that clean up all the negative parts of Mormonism."

"I'm not going to make up revelations from God."

"No, I didn't mean that, but—I mean, you could use your influence to change the way things are in the church. Weed out the hypocrites, change attitudes and interpretations of scripture and all that."

He wasn't keen on this liberal approach to the gospel, but he knew Sheila's faith was fragile right now—that visitation had only planted the tiniest seed in her, and it needed time to grow. So he remained silent.

"This feels nice," she said softly.

He realized he was still stroking her hair. He almost stopped because the immediate need of comforting her had passed, and now he felt like he was taking too much liberty with her. But she hadn't complained, and this *was* his wife-to-be. Besides, it felt good to him too.

"I'm supposed to be your wife?"

"Yes. I'm sorry about that. It was a jarring way to find out."

Her hand lifted to his cheek and caressed it. An electric thrill shot through him, a dazzling arousal that took his breath away. She sat up and kissed him, a deep kiss with her tongue exploring all the recesses of his mouth. His body flamed with desire. He pulled her hard against him and kissed back with equal passion. Her hands wandered over his torso. His own hands moved with a life of their own, fondling her arms, her shoulders, stroking her back. They wandered precariously close to her buttocks before he realized what they were doing, and he pushed himself away from her.

"I thought"—he gasped—"you didn't want to marry me."

Her breathing came as heavily as his. "You damn fool! I love you! But I couldn't say that before, could I, because you're married. But now..."

So her reaction to marriage had also been a show? She continued to hide her real feelings because at the time he was inaccessible to her. But now she was given to him by God. How much more accessible could he get than that? "So you *will* marry me?"

"I haven't cared much about marriage." She stroked his hair. "But I know you do. So I guess I should too. All I really care about is being with you. If marriage is what it takes...I'll marry you."

He desperately wanted to kiss her a second time. She looked like she desperately wanted him to. But he said, "I don't think we should kiss again. I almost couldn't stop myself. We're not married yet."

"Then you better go, because I don't give a damn about your precious Law of Chastity."

"Yes, I'll go." It was both easy to say and one of the hardest things to say.

But he didn't move. It was even harder to do. He knew he'd better leave fast before he lost his resolve. "Sheila, I don't know what to say. I just need to go."

"I understand. Go."

He headed for the door. As he opened it, she said, "C.H.?"

"Yes?"

"What do I do? Two days from now I got nowhere to live."

Somewhere down in his subconscious was the solution, rattling around waiting for that question to be asked. It sprang instantly to mind as she asked it, and it felt like he'd known all along what she should do.

"The other half of our duplex is vacant. You'll move in there."

"But I don't have enough—"

"I do. And I'm going to be your husband, so..."

"You don't make a whole lot more than I do—did. How can you—"

"I'll tell you about it later." He smiled. "Just trust me. I'll get everything arranged, then help you move."

Her face filled with relief. "Thank you."

He smiled at her once more and then took a step out of the apartment. "C.H.?"

He stopped. "Yes?"

"Does Dani know?"

Dani. He hadn't thought about her this entire time. Was he a total jerk for being so uncaring about his wife? Or was he doing well obeying this new commandment, concentrating his attention on his new wife while he was with her?

"Yes, she knows. She understands." He spent an instant wondering how accurate that was.

She nodded. As he looked back once more while pulling shut the door, the candles flickered sweet highlights in her hair and glittering ghosts in her eyes.

Back in the car—the car he'd shared with Dani for their entire marriage—and away from his future second wife, he had time to feel the terrible guilt that had lain dormant in his heart. For the first time since he married Dani, he kissed another woman, passionately, and had burned with the desire to take all of her. It had been a long time since he felt such raw passion with Dani. Was it forbidden fruit syndrome?

But giving it a name and a rationalization didn't help. For all the attraction and passion he felt for Sheila, Dani was still the one he loved. The mother of his two delightful boys. The wife who sat home alone at this instant, feeling God knows what, while he visited another woman and proposed to her. Maybe he'd been the good little polygamous boy with Sheila, giving her all his attention while there. But now he was returning to his other wife. Now it was time to give *her* all his attention. And that meant empathizing with the horrendous pain she must be feeling. Sheila was getting a piece of something she thought was forever out of her reach—she'd be happy. But Dani was having to share something that she thought would always be hers alone. And she had to like it or be damned.

Then there was C.H.—Cory Horace Young—Cain Hell Young—great-great-grandson of Brigham Young. He got the best of both worlds. He got to go home to the woman he loved, the home that was warm and comfortable and nourishing in spite of its humble trappings. And soon he could be with a woman who was exciting and exotic and delicious and not even have to dilute his elation with feelings of guilt because God had approved. What happy circumstances for a red-blooded American boy!

Except his happiness was being purchased with the anguish of the woman he loved. And he couldn't do anything about it because God not only approved of it, he commanded it. Nor could C.H. remain faithful in spirit if not in fact to Dani because that would be completely unfair to his new wife, who deserved his love as much as Dani did. He was obliged to be the best husband he could to both wives, to love them both, to enjoy the company of both—in all ways. He was obligated to enjoy the circumstances that would torture his beloved Dani.

"We're not the first ones to go through this," he repeated to himself. "If they can survive it, so can we."

But as he passed a cemetery on his way home, he almost wished he could trade places with one of its inhabitants.

Chapter 7

Sheila stared at the door after C.H. left, then at the dangling chain next to it. What in the hell had just happened?

She slumped onto the sofa. The candles on the table blazed silently. Arousal burned in her veins. She could still feel his lips pressed against hers, his body pressed against her body. She still couldn't believe it happened.

Her hand wandered down to her crotch and unsnapped the teddy there.

It didn't take long. In the warm aftermath of spent arousal, she could now think. It was time to make sense out of what just happened.

Did Brigham Young appear to her? C.H. said so. But what an insane notion! She *had* seen something. And in a state of shock, she'd taken his word at face value. Brigham Young had appeared to her! That made her feel horribly guilty for turning her back on Mormonism and doing all the things she'd done since then.

But she'd also been in a frenzy of hatred for Steven, slashing at his picture with a sword. She wasn't thinking straight. She was so agitated that she attacked C.H., thinking he was Steven.

She attacked him! What if she'd hurt him?

Finally she realized it was him. And there she was, alone in her apartment with the man she wished she could be living with, standing in front of him with nothing on but a scanty piece of lingerie. And he was noticing. Oh boy, was he noticing! Noticing while trying not to notice. She knew that look from too many Mormon boys in her youth.

How titillating that had been, no less so because she knew he wouldn't do anything about it. That made sex wicked again, something she hadn't experienced for a couple of years, and *that* made fantasizing about it more exciting than it had been in a long time.

Then he started talking about seeing Brigham Young and becoming president of the church and polygamy. And he didn't even do drugs!

That was too much, even for her. She got afraid. Maybe she didn't know this sweet, all-American Mormon boy like she thought she did. Maybe he was just as whacked out as the rest of them. All she could think at that point was to get him out of her home.

Then *she* saw Brigham Young. Well, she saw something. How could she be sure it was Brigham Young? But it sure as hell was *something*.

Maybe the satanic ritual worked. Maybe she called up a demon. But C.H. acted like it was old hat to him. He'd seen the apparition before, several times. She couldn't retroactively summon a demon to appear to him in the past...could she? Hell, she didn't believe in the ritual anyway. It just sounded like a good thing to do—curse Steven to death.

So what appeared to her?

Then C.H. started talking about being forgiven, and marrying him, and it was all legit, and all she had to do was agree and repent. Then she could live with the man she loved.

He said he'd be president of the church. Her own husband, the president. What an opportunity that would be! Together they could turn Mormonism into what it should be. It wasn't that she hated the *whole* religion. She grew up with it, and her mother and most of her relatives were still active in it. She just couldn't accept huge parts of it. The silly claims in its history. All that holier-than-thou shit about forbidding things that were harmless. What did it hurt if someone masturbated? Or drank a little alcohol, or did a little cocaine? Anything to excess was bad, but done in moderation, what was the big deal? What did it hurt if two people in love lived together? Sheila was careful about safe sex. She wasn't going to bring any bastard children into the world or contract any disease. So who did it hurt?

But those goody-goody Mormon boys, blessing the sacrament on Sunday and then practically raping girls during the week—*that* hurt other people. Sheila hadn't been ready for that kind of relationship, but she got suckered into it by some nice boy three years older than her that she thought she could trust. Her life was changed forever, and he just thought it was funny.

Never again. From then on, Sheila would decide when and where her body was penetrated. No one else would decide, not even God.

But with C.H. as president, he could change that repressed attitude toward sex that pervaded the church, so those boys wouldn't be so wound up like corkscrews about it. Maybe, over time, the whole state of Utah could develop a healthier attitude toward sex.

Sure, C.H. didn't take to the idea right away of reforming the church, but there was plenty of time to change that. It all sounded like a bargain to her.

Except for Dani, his wife. Mormons might consider Sheila's lifestyle wicked, but she did have her own moral code, and sleeping with another woman's husband wasn't part of it. She detested anyone who would do such a thing. That's why she never let on to C.H. that she wanted him. She couldn't do that to another woman.

But according to C.H., God commanded her to have him. All she had to do was believe that the apparition really was Brigham Young, and she could have him, everything legal, signed, sealed, delivered in the eyes of God. Hell, even Dani already knew about it and said it was okay. What more could a girl ask for?

It was all easy to believe when she was aroused and semi-naked in the presence of the man she wanted. Now that she dealt with her arousal, now that she was alone in her apartment with reminders of Steven all around, it sounded asinine. Brigham Young appeared to her? Ha!

But *something* appeared to her. If not Brigham Young, then what? She hadn't taken any hallucinogens lately. She was crazy with anger, but by the time the apparition appeared, she'd cooled off. What would have caused her to hallucinate? Her subconscious desire for his batshit insane claim to be true? But if it was a subconscious hallucination, why did C.H. see it? Why did he say, "Sheila, meet Brigham Young"?

She felt the icy grip of depression closing in on her chest. What she wanted for more than a year was now in her grasp, but she had to believe in outrageous hocus-pocus to accept it. She had to return to that religion she turned her back on. In that light, it didn't seem like such a bargain after all.

She decided she could use a little help feeling better right now. In the bedroom she pulled a jewelry box out of a drawer and set it on top of the dresser. She opened the lid and pulled out a little plastic bag. Carefully she poured out a strip of white powder on the dresser's surface, then formed it into lines with a razor. She placed one end of a tube in one nostril and sniffed hard, then did the same with the other nostril.

Lying on her bed as the familiar euphoric feeling crept over her, Sheila decided that believing in Brigham Young wasn't such a bad deal after all. Just for that small price, she could have a place to live and could hold C.H. and make love to him. She imagined what it would feel like holding him right now. She wondered what kind of a lover he'd be. Gentle, she guessed, and considerate— he seemed the type. At least, Dani seemed the type who wouldn't marry any other kind of lover.

Sheila could use a little gentle, considerate lovemaking these days.

When C.H. arrived home, Dani and the boys were already in bed asleep. He lingered at the bedroom door with the light from the bathroom casting a faint illumination into the room. Petey and Glenn sprawled out in all directions.

Dani snored faintly, her bare arm resting on the covers. She liked to wear a long nightshirt to bed. The sleeve had ridden up her shoulder, exposing the sleeve of her garments.

Her nightshirts covered her body quite modestly, whether she wore anything under them or not. In fact, he usually couldn't tell if she had on anything underneath when she climbed into bed. She liked to surprise him that way—when he cuddled up to her, he never knew if she wore garments or was stark naked underneath the nightshirt. At least, that's how it was when there wasn't a sleeping baby between them.

Which there had been for more than eight weeks now. Eight weeks without sex as Dani recovered from childbirth, plus about three weeks before that as well. Her small frame dragging around that bloated belly had made the logistics of sex difficult, and her exhaustion didn't help either.

Three months without sex. No wonder he'd been so aroused by the sight and touch of Sheila in a flimsy teddy. It was more than just forbidden fruit—any fruit would be appetizing right now.

These thoughts made him feel even worse than he already did. He loved the one and desired the other, and he couldn't really blame himself for the feelings he had. They came from biological wiring, reinforced by God's command to marry Sheila. In all this, Dani came out the victim every way he looked at it, through no one's fault.

Except God's.

That thought intensified his wretched feelings, so he rejected it. God had been requiring difficult things of people since the beginning of time. C.H. and Dani were in no different shoes than many other prophets and disciples of God. Instead of feeling put upon, maybe he should feel honored that God considered him up to the challenge.

Thinking that way helped lessen his guilt. Not much, but a little. He gazed at Dani, admiring her beauty. He never truly wanted any other woman—honestly, he hadn't. He never in a million years would have wished for all this to happen. Not like some people he knew at BYU. Some of his friends spoke dreamily of the days when polygamy might be restored. Well, those friends were going to be very happy when the new revelation became public.

Why didn't God call one of them to do this? They would have loved it.

That was probably why God didn't call one of them.

He ached to hold Dani. But he didn't dare crawl into bed with her. Her face looked so peaceful, and he didn't want to wake her. Let her have a few hours of peace.

He went to the living room, lay back on the recliner, and kicked off his shoes. Armed with a new remote for a new TV, he flashed through the handful of stations available through broadcast television. Most of them were playing infomercials. He wished they already had the cable TV. Dozens of distracting options would be very useful right now. He needed to remember to order it soon.

The new television had been exciting when they first set it up. Now it left a dry sensation in his soul. "Brigham," he murmured, "you can have the TV back, the SUV, the good food, the money—all of it—if you don't make me do this to Dani." He would even be willing to forego the violin.

When some loud commercial woke him, he realized it was after sunrise. He dozed again until Glenn cried. His heart jumped, knowing Dani would be awake now. What would she be thinking? What would she be feeling? He didn't want to know. What could he do about it?

For the first time in his life, he didn't want to see his wife.

Dani emerged from the bedroom with Glenn in her arms. She paused and stared at him, then forced a smile and said, "Good morning." She sat on the sofa and started nursing.

"Good morning." He tried to read her. Certainly she was feeling something, but he couldn't tell what. Without knowing how she felt, he had no idea what to do or say.

"How long have you been out here?" she asked, not looking up.

"Most the night." He could tell it was a charged question. What did she think, that he'd spent the night with Sheila?

"Why didn't you come to bed?" She did look up this time, and her pupils were pinpoints.

"I didn't want to disturb you," he answered weakly. Obviously he made the wrong choice. "You were sleeping so peacefully."

She nodded as she gazed down at Glenn. "Peacefully," she murmured.

Peacefully with a tiny baby and a husband off visiting his new fiancée? Another bad move. "I'm sorry." He didn't know what else to say.

He rushed through his morning preparations and left a little early for work. It was probably a cruel thing to do to her, but he was too uncomfortable and too uncertain to remain any longer than necessary.

I've already failed as a polygamous husband, he thought as he drove, *and I haven't even married my second wife yet*. He hadn't given his first wife the love and attention she needed. But he did leave her the new car. At least he wasn't enjoying himself with good music and a comfortable ride while Dani sat home neglected. Small penance, but penance.

At work he gave his notice first thing. Flabbergasted, Milt asked what happened to his plans to become a manager. He responded with vague statements about personal reasons and things coming up.

Now he got to feel guilty about letting Milt down too.

During lunch he contacted their landlord and arranged to have Sheila move into the back of their duplex. Friend of the family, he could vouch for her, and all that. The landlord was an easy sell. He said the Youngs had been his favorite tenants—respectable, quiet, trustworthy—so he was thrilled to have someone they recommended take his other apartment. Sheila could move in immediately.

After work he sat in the car in the mall parking lot. The day at work had been a godsend, keeping his mind off his circumstances, but now it was time to face them head on—and do it much more effectively than he did that morning. He had to get this right.

Suddenly he realized that he had not prayed or listened to Conference or read any scriptures in the last twenty-four hours. Get it right, indeed! But could he really blame himself? The last twenty-four hours were a nightmare.

"I'm sick of feeling like this!" he blurted. The past was the past. He was determined to do better, and he *had* been doing better, right up until his life had been blown apart yesterday. A super-saint might have maintained the daily rituals, but he was only human. He slipped momentarily for very good reasons, and now he should worry only about getting back on track. In fact, right now was an excellent time to pray.

He rested his forehead on the steering wheel and closed his eyes, not caring who saw him. He pointedly thanked God for the gifts he asked Brigham to take back the night before. He thanked God for his trust in C.H. and for giving him such an important assignment. He prayed for the wisdom and strength to carry it out. He begged for the Spirit to comfort Dani and strengthen her in this ordeal, since her trials would be the hardest. And he prayed for Sheila, that her repentance would be sincere, that she could develop faith in the parts of the gospel she didn't understand, that the Spirit would fall upon her and convert her.

He prayed for the ability to love both wives equally, to give them both what they needed, to make them both feel important to him. He prayed for the safety of his family and of Sheila. He prayed for the soul of the president of the church who would soon be removed from office.

A knock came on the window. He tried to ignore it, but it came again. An older woman peered at him and said in a muffled voice, "Are you okay?"

He nodded and forced a smile. She smiled back and left. With his train of thought broken, he hurriedly closed his prayer, then started up the engine. Time to go home and put his praying into action.

Sheila slept all morning. That afternoon, as she cleaned up the mess from her ritual, C.H. phoned her from work. Everything was arranged. She'd move into the rear apartment tomorrow as soon as he got off work.

She didn't say a word about her doubts. So what if she hadn't decided yet whether she believed the real Brigham Young appeared to her? She still needed a place to stay.

But if she didn't marry C.H., she'd be accepting his help under false pretenses. That didn't sit well with her moral code either. If she did move in, that was tantamount to confessing her belief in his claims and her agreement to marry him, if she wanted to maintain any sense of integrity.

She had some serious thinking to do for the next twenty-four hours.

Could she return to the Mormon Church? Even if he were willing to change things, it wouldn't happen overnight. She'd be expected to stop drinking, stop swearing, go to church. She sure as hell couldn't do cocaine anymore.

The worst part had to be going back to church. She'd be married to the man she wanted to sleep with, so her sex would be legit. She wouldn't have to give that up. Following the Word of Wisdom didn't seem like that big a deal. She was only a social drinker, and she made sure her cocaine use was infrequent. She had no intention of getting hooked on the shit. Using cocaine was so tied to Steven that without him around she could probably shake that habit completely. More than anything, the way he treated her was what drove her to use it. And besides, she wouldn't know where to get any now. Steven had always gotten it for her—she didn't want direct contact with drug dealers. And Steven was the one who could afford it.

Speaking of affording, C.H. still hadn't told her how he was paying for all this. It couldn't be from his paycheck at the bookstore. He complained about how little he made as much as the rest of them.

Maybe he pushed drugs, and he could keep her in coke.

She laughed at her joke, even though it wasn't very funny, because the image of him pushing drugs was too ridiculous. Then she sobered immediately. This *was* no joke. She might not take Mormonism all that seriously, but he sure as hell did. And it wasn't any go-along cultural thing—he was sincere. She wasn't just after sex with him. She wanted the whole relationship to work. She was smart enough to know that if she only pretended to change, it wouldn't last. He'd notice soon enough.

Was he worth converting back to Mormonism for? Was he worth attending church for?

She looked around the kitchen where she sat. The refrigerator was getting empty—she'd eaten almost all the food Steven had left. After the coke wore off last night, she trembled alone in her bed like she'd done for over a week. Every unidentifiable noise, day and night, made her jump. She hated being alone.

But she was sick of taking up with assholes like Steven. He'd been the nicest, and she'd have stayed with him if he hadn't left, but he was no picnic. He disappeared a lot, and when he *was* with her, his treatment veered wildly from wonderfully sweet to indifferent to on-the-edge frightening. The sweet moments were what sustained her. But now that she was on the verge of living with a decent guy like C.H., she wondered how they'd ever been enough.

What would she have done if C.H. had come to her with this proposal before Steven left? Was she taking his proposal seriously because she really loved him, or because she was desperate for a place to stay?

As she thought, she went to the refrigerator and grabbed the last beer. She sat back at the kitchen table and drank, amused at the irony of drinking beer as she contemplated becoming a Mormon again.

To hell with it! This was her last beer. It didn't taste all that good anyway. Beer had never excited her, with that yeasty smell and biting flavor. She just started drinking it, like any teenager, because it was the thing to do, and she never bothered to stop. Eventually she acclimatized herself to the flavor, but she never actually *liked* it.

Wine was better, but she could probably live without it too. Maybe she could switch to power drinks or something. The thought made her smirk.

The idea of quitting cocaine was a little scarier. She took it because Steven sent her into a depression now and then. That was the story she told herself, but was it really true? Would she really lose interest in it without Steven around? After all, she headed for the jewelry box last night at the first sign of non-Steven depression. That wasn't a good omen. Maybe attending church wouldn't be the hardest part.

She set the beer bottle on the table and marched into the bedroom. Stopping before the dresser, she opened the drawer and gazed at the box. A gift from her dead grandmother—what would she think now if she knew what Sheila used it for?

Slowly she opened the lid. There was her paraphernalia and the plastic bag of powder. Still many doses of euphoria in that little bag. Since Steven always bought it, Sheila wasn't sure how much it cost, but she knew it had to be a lot. Could she live without it?

She looked at the bed, imagining herself lying there in C.H.'s arms. The fantasy was appealing. But did she love him or just want to sleep with him?

She thought she felt a kind of love for Steven, even with the way he treated her. Surely she'd love C.H. more. Would he really treat her like she expected? Or would he be a big disappointment, as so many before him had turned out to be?

She thought of Dani. There was no question Dani loved him, and Dani didn't seem like a fool. Even if Sheila wasn't sure she could trust C.H., she felt sure she could trust Dani's judgment. If she loved him as much as she seemed to, Sheila probably would too.

She looked at the powder and tried to imagine turning him down. Face it, girl—he's not worth it! Too much baggage comes with him. You'll make all these changes for him, then he'll turn out to be an asshole like every other man. And you won't have your cocaine or even a can of beer to help you through the rough times. Screw him!

She saw his face gaping at her forlornly, brokenhearted at her words. As he turned to leave her for the final time, she panicked. She wanted to cry out to him to stay, but he closed the door too quickly.

The images gave her a depression and caused the cocaine to beckon to her. She felt the familiar urge for its white happiness whispering to her.

She smiled. That clinched it. Thinking of life without C.H. depressed her and made her crave cocaine. It might be depraved, but that was the persuasion she needed—that was her burning in the bosom. Mormons might be appalled at her version of spiritual confirmation, but it worked for her. She *would* believe in Brigham Young.

Sheila lifted the bag by two fingers and dangled it before her eyes. The crystals sparkled as the bag twirled. She stepped into the bathroom, emptied the powder into the toilet, and flushed. Goodbye coke, goodbye Steven, hello C.H.

The paraphernalia went into the trash, and as a token gesture she removed ten of her twelve earrings and placed them in the jewelry box. Her grandmother could rest easier now.

Chapter 8

Dani lay in bed staring at the ceiling as dawn crept through the window. She knew C.H. was finished rescuing his new wife-to-be from satanic rituals because she could hear the TV running. So why hadn't he come to bed with her?

As she lay with Glenn breathing peacefully beside her, the sound of the car driving away last night still echoing in her ears, her mind went numb because it had to. Otherwise she would have to think about everything that happened.

Brigham Young had appeared to Dani. If any doubt remained that C.H. had been lying or crazy, it was gone now. Brigham had appeared to her and told her to share her husband with another, *or else*. And C.H. had gone off to visit that other woman, to save her from the clutches of Satanism. At the command of Brigham Young. At the command of God.

Dear God, she prayed. Why did you pick *that* woman as his first polygamous wife? An apostate Mormon. Six pierced earrings in each ear. Living with her boyfriend. Probably smokes and drinks too.

And into Satanism. At least Joseph Smith got to marry wives like Eliza Snow. Why Sheila?

Thank heaven her mind was numb, so she didn't have to think about all this.

But Brigham said that C.H. would convert Sheila and get her to repent. He took off to *save* her. The angels have greater joy over one soul that repenteth than ninety-nine righteous souls. This was a good thing that was happening, right? A lost soul would be found.

She felt so tired. She wondered if she slept at all last night. Why hadn't C.H. come to bed? Did he feel guilty about something? Had they already been married? Had they already consummated their marriage?

What would everyone say? How long could they hide this relationship? Where would Sheila stay? Please, God, not with them!

She imagined turning the TV up loud so she couldn't hear the bed creaking down the hall.

What horrible diseases would Sheila give him that he'd pass on to Dani?

She couldn't think about all this now. Her mind was too numb. She drifted off to sleep, but in minutes Glenn woke her.

How long had it been since Dani and C.H. made love? Weeks before Glenn's birth. Dani had felt some stirrings of arousal, but sex with her huge belly had been so difficult and tiring, and sex for six weeks after the birth was forbidden by the doctor. That six weeks was already up by now, and then some. She'd been planning on making their first time again a special occasion. Lately he made some tentative advances, but she gently shrugged him off because she hadn't had time yet to plan the special occasion.

No, that wasn't completely true. She was really just tired all the time. She *wanted* to plan a special occasion, but kept putting it off. A newborn's feeding schedule was exhausting.

Had this interloper beaten her to it? After—what, three months?—had his first sex been with another woman?

Dani couldn't stand lying in bed thinking all these thoughts any more, even though she was still tired. She got up, grabbed Glenn, and went into the living room.

C.H. lay in his recliner, looking up at her. She stopped and gazed at him a moment. His eyes were puffy and his clothes rumpled. Had he slept in that chair all night?

She felt relief, but then she thought that he might look just as rumpled if he spent the night with Sheila. She forced a smile and said good morning. He replied. His gaze was intense, and his fingers fidgeted absently. He had to be wondering what she was thinking.

Dani sat on the sofa and started to nurse. She didn't know what to say to him. He probably didn't know what to say to her. What does one say when one spouse goes to see another person who will become a lover, and everyone knows it, and everyone is obliged to accept it? She had no behavior in her repertory to deal with this situation. He wouldn't either.

But why had he slept out in the living room and not with her?

She asked him. His answer both relieved and bothered her. "Peacefully," she murmured. Wouldn't he realize that waking her up for a moment would be a small price for the comfort of having him beside her all night? Especially under the circumstances.

He said he was sorry. Maybe he did understand now.

He worked today, right? Monday—yes, she was pretty sure he did. *Then, please, Cain, please just get ready and go. I need some time alone to think about this.*

Whether by chance or by sensing some vibes, he got up and started getting ready. Not a word passed between them until he said goodbye to her and self-consciously kissed her. She breathed a sigh of relief when the door closed.

It was daylight, her mind was no longer numb, and her husband was gone—but not to the other woman. Even Petey was still asleep. She could let everything crash in on her now. Her body shook from the sobs that burst out. Glenn became fussy and wouldn't nurse.

He didn't sleep with Sheila last night, but sooner or later he would. Dani would no longer be the only woman in his life. As he slept with her, he would no doubt grow to love her. Perhaps he'd grow to love her more. Sheila wasn't hampered with two children. She was bold and exciting. He often came home from work and talked about some crazy thing she said or did. He already had a sort of affection for her. Dani knew he wouldn't do it intentionally, but what if he ended up loving Sheila more?

She couldn't bear the thought. That was the worst thing she could imagine happening in her life, other than the death of one of her children. To have C.H. slowly grow away from her because he loved another woman. And Dani would just have to sit and watch because God commanded it. She couldn't even have the satisfaction of hating him for cheating on her.

When the tears exhausted themselves and the empty feeling they left behind drifted away, she felt disgusted with herself. So Sheila was more exciting than her? Then Dani would do something about it! Sheila was going to draw him away from her? Not without a fight! Dani was his wife, his first and only love—so far—and she was going to make it hard for him to forget that. It wasn't like she was some middle-aged matron who didn't hold a candle to young Sheila. Dani wasn't much older and was rather attractive, if she said so herself, even after two babies. There was no reason in hell she should take a backseat to anyone! *Forgive me, God, for my French.*

In moments she formulated a plan. A phone call to Sister Vandermeer, the Relief Society president, and Petey was taken care of for the day. She'd have to lug Glenn around with her, but that wasn't so bad, and she could take him over to Sister Vandermeer's right before the evening started. He'd be good there for a couple of hours.

Feeling a bit of defiance toward Brigham—*if you're going to ask this of me, then you'd better not say a word about this little bit of cash*—she grabbed a bundle of hundreds and spent the day getting everything prepared.

Cyndy always passed Sister Vandermeer's house on the way home from school. On this Monday, she noticed Petey playing in the back yard. Cyndy felt betrayed. *She* was the Youngs' babysitter! Had she done something to make them mad at her?

No, you idiot, she scolded herself. They just needed someone to babysit while she was still in school.

At home she found Ryan glued to the TV set watching some kid anime show that she didn't recognize. Cyndy had sworn off that Japanese-style crap years ago, but Ryan was still fascinated by it. Big weepy eyes and silly mouths, horrible English translations, idiotic plots. Mature women found better things to amuse themselves with.

She dropped her backpack on the hall table and headed for the kitchen. As she stole a few cookies out of the cookie jar and poured herself a glass of milk, she wondered if Sister Vandermeer would let her take over the babysitting. Probably not, she thought glumly. As an adult, she wouldn't trust Cyndy well enough to hand over someone else's kids she'd taken responsibility for.

Cyndy crept into the family room and laid her glass and cookies on the end table as quietly as she could. Ryan was oblivious so far, with his butt parked on the floor three feet in front of the television screen. The remote lay on the carpet next to him, and if Cyndy was *real* careful, she could slide it back and grab it without him knowing.

Holding her breath, she inched forward on hands and knees, reached her hand out, and touched the remote. No reaction so far. Her fingers closed over it and pulled slowly back. After sliding it back about a foot, she scampered back to the easy chair next to her snack. Ryan whirled around and glared at her, but she tucked the remote behind her before he could notice.

"Hey, I want cookies!" he cried.

"So go get some." She popped one into her mouth and licked the crumbs off her fingers.

"You'll change the channel."

She pulled out the remote and pointed it. The TV image flashed, and a nature show about birds came on. "I will anyway."

"*Turn it back!*" Ryan yelled as he lunged for the remote.

Cyndy secured it behind her back.

He hovered over her, hands outstretched, fingers curled into threatening claws. "I'll tickle you."

"Alright," Cyndy pouted, throwing the remote at him. "I was just kidding anyway. Can't you take a joke?"

She hated that she was so ticklish. It was Ryan's trump card against her. She glared at him as he settled into place and switched the channel back to the dumb animation. Staring at his round backside, she decided to play *her* trump card against him.

"Go ahead and get some cookies. I won't change the channel."

He turned and eyed her suspiciously, remote tight in his hand, then stood up and headed out.

"Eat some extra for all those girls swooning over your hunk body."

Ryan glared all the brotherly hate he could muster but still continued toward the kitchen.

Maybe she could at least *help* babysit, Cyndy thought. Great idea! She immediately consumed the rest of her cookies and gulped the milk as fast as she could. Ryan barely made it back with his snack before she was out the door and marching down the sidewalk, ignoring his question about where she was going.

But before she went far, the Youngs' new car zoomed by on its way home. Darn it! Sister Young had probably picked up the boys already. Maybe she'd like a little help herself so she could make dinner or something.

Cyndy whirled around on her heels and walked toward the Youngs' home. She passed an unfamiliar car parked on the other side of the street with a man sitting in it reading the newspaper and munching on some kind of sandwich. The man looked up, smiled, and went back to his reading.

Sister Young had parked the car in the driveway, and the door was open. But she only unloaded one boy—Glenn. Where was Petey? Still back at Sister Vandermeer's?

Sister Young carried Glenn into the house. Cyndy was about to head over and offer her help, when Sister Young came back and pulled a beautiful white evening gown out of the van. The gown was covered in sequins flashing brilliantly in the sun. She pulled out a couple of other sacks of stuff and carried it all in, leaving the van door and the door to the house open.

This was intriguing! Cyndy held back, keeping a tree between Sister Young and herself. What sort of plans did they have that she would need such a beautiful gown? And that gown didn't have sleeves or even straps. Would Sister Young actually go out somewhere dressed like that? Cyndy couldn't decide if that was scandalous or exotic.

Sister Young appeared again and unloaded a few boxes. This time she closed the car and house doors.

Cyndy stood on the sidewalk contemplating for a moment, gazing at the empty yard. They had some big deal planned, that was for sure. She was dying to know, but she didn't have the nerve to go find out. Instead she decided to head back to Sister Vandermeer's where Petey must still be. She could help there. She wondered how long he was supposed to be there.

There was that man again, staring at her. He looked back down at his newspaper and took another bite. What was he, some kind of perv?

Sister Vandermeer *was* glad for the help, and Cyndy took over most of the babysitting duties. She could stay only a couple of hours until her mother got back from work and fixed dinner, but she learned that both Young boys would be there that evening. Now her curiosity gnawed at her.

Later, helping her mother fix dinner, Cyndy was much quieter than usual.

"Where are you today, honey?" her mother asked.

"Huh?"

"You've been distracted ever since I got home."

"She's dreaming about her lover boy, Brother Young," said Ryan.

"Shut up!" Cyndy cried as her mother smiled. She was getting real tired of his one-joke humor. Couldn't he at least come up with a fresh taunt?

After dinner, she announced she was going for a bike ride. She wished she could get her license already—riding a bike was such a childish thing for a mature woman to have to do.

But she couldn't yet, so she pedaled around the neighborhood feeling like a ten-year-old, grumbling to herself. There were lots of neighborhood streets to wander around on, but somehow she kept going past the Youngs' house. She never saw anything because the drapes were drawn and no one came out. At least that pervert with the newspaper was gone, thank heavens.

Cyndy passed several of her girlfriends' homes and wished she had someone to talk to about what she'd seen. But since her best friend Sue Ann had moved away last summer, she had no friend close enough to trust with her most intimate gossip. The other girls would just tease her about being in love with Brother Young like Ryan did.

So she rode aimlessly, feeling a slight chill from the cooling air, wishing something interesting would happen. And finally, something did. After one of her trips around the block, the Youngs' new car was parked in front of Sister Vandermeer's house. Glenn was being dropped off! On the next trip around, the car was back home.

Things should start happening soon.

As C.H. parked along the curb in front of his home, he got the same queasy feeling he'd once felt when called to the principal's office. He would just have to learn to ignore it because guilt over his new lifestyle obviously wasn't going to go away easily. Right now he needed to concentrate on Dani and her needs.

When he opened the door to the house, a blast of roast beef aroma hit him. No Petey ran to greet him. The drapes were drawn, and the room was dark. He crept in almost as if he were entering a wolf's lair, wondering what was about to happen.

The kitchen table was in the living room, covered with a white tablecloth. A vase of flowers sat in the middle of the table, framed by two place settings, two champagne glasses, and a pair of candles flickering, casting dancing apparitions on the walls that looked like—

Like the fiery imps in Disney's *Fantasia*.

In the kitchen, the single light bulb in the hood of the stove glowed, and on the burners two pots of something simmered. The light in the oven gleamed through its window. The corner of the coffee table was visible through the kitchen doo, where the kitchen table normally sat.

"Dani?"

She entered from the hallway like Cinderella appearing in the palace ballroom from those millions of times Petey had watched the video. A shimmering white gown hugged her body, slinky and strapless, glittering with sequins in the candlelight. Her strawberry-blonde hair waved around her head in perfect curves, and ringlets hung from her temples in tight curls. Every nuance of her body showed through that intimate gown, even the tummy bulge from her pregnancy, which somehow added to her attractiveness.

Her eyes sparkled as she peered at him. She was trying to keep her face neutral with a faint smile, but he saw the anticipation in it. No matter how he might feel, there was only one possible response for a husband to make. But that was no problem because he wanted completely, heart and soul, to give her that response.

He approached her and gazed down into her eyes. A perfume scent drove the roast beef aroma from his consciousness. "Dani, you look beautiful."

She smiled brightly.

He embraced her and kissed her deeply, leaning his head down to reach. Rhett Butler never had it so good! His hands touched bare skin—an open back to the gown. This risqué choice in clothing for an LDS woman married in the temple excited him. He didn't want to think about how she had afforded it.

When the kiss finally subsided, Dani said, "I love you, Cain."

"I love you," he said forcefully. "I always will. You're the only one I will ever need, no matter what other—"

She placed her finger on his lips and shook her head. "Are you hungry?"

"Yes."

"Have a seat." She gestured toward the table.

"Would you like me to help—"

"Sit! I can manage."

He obeyed as she disappeared into the kitchen. Even though he wore dark slacks, a white shirt, and a tie—his work uniform—he felt grossly underdressed compared to her. He should have a tuxedo on.

The flickering candlelight played on the wall. The image of a satanic altar intruded, Sheila in a black teddy swinging a sword. How unreal it seemed now, like a dark horror movie. Now he was in the midst of a fairy tale right here, with a beautiful princess preparing to serve him. He felt ashamed for receiving such treatment from someone he was obliged to hurt—

Don't start that again! It wouldn't help anything. It would certainly ruin the wonderful evening Dani had spent hours preparing. For her, he would enjoy himself tonight.

Yeah, some sacrifice!

She brought out two plates filled with slices of roast beef, scalloped potatoes, and broccoli in a cheese sauce. She had even added a sprig of parsley for a garnish. As she set a plate in front of him, its aroma bathed his face. She disappeared again and returned with a bottle of sparkling cider—the Mormon version of champagne—and filled their glasses. He wondered where the glasses had come from. They'd received some similar glasses as a wedding present but had exchanged them long ago for things they really needed.

Brother Brigham, he said silently, *if Dani was wrong to use that money for all this, please forgive her. With everything she'll be facing, she deserves this small indulgence.*

He remembered the words Brother Brigham had uttered last night: *to be used at your discretion.* Well, C.H.'s discretion was that this money had been well spent, so if there were any blame to lay, lay it at his feet.

"This looks fantastic," he said as she took her seat.

"Thank you."

"How did you do it all? Where are the boys?"

"They're with Sister Vandermeer. She said to take our time."

He swallowed a lump in his throat, feeling foolish for choking up so easily. But he couldn't help it. That dear Relief Society president! He thought about how much the church meant to them, even though they took so much for granted. Sister Vandermeer probably thought she was just helping them have a pleasant evening away from the kids. She could never realize how important this night was to C.H. and Dani.

He lifted his champagne glass. "Shall we make a toast?"

She took her glass in hand. "I'll make it." She held the glass up high and gazed into his eyes. "To my sweet husband, the wonderful father of my children, my tender lover. I know you'll be going through a lot from now on, and I know it'll be as hard for you as it will be for me." Her voice wavered a little, and she swallowed. "I promise I will always love you, and I will stand at your side through everything. All I ask—" Her voice broke again, and this time her lower lip quivered. She cleared her throat and dabbed at her eye. "All I ask is that you continue to love me as you always have." She held the glass forward and waited, eyes moist.

"I will!" he said. "I'll always love you. You are my wife, my one true love, and nothing can change that."

They clinked glasses and sipped, gazing at each other. He couldn't imagine a woman looking more beautiful than she did at that moment. He couldn't imagine burning with love for a woman like he burned for Dani right now. He couldn't remember why he felt the way he did while kissing Sheila last night. Sheila was the last thing he wanted to think about right now.

I guess that means I'm being a good polygamous husband, he thought. *I'm concentrating fully on the wife I'm with at the moment.* He began to think that maybe a polygamous lifestyle was doable after all.

Dani was thrilled. The evening was sheer magic. They talked like they hadn't talked in a long time, focusing on each other and nothing else in the universe. Pleasant small talk, little jokes that would mean nothing to anyone but themselves, trivial memories that held sweet nostalgia for them. It had been too long since they spent a moment like this together. Too long since they felt this way with this much intensity.

He told her the meal was exquisite, and she had to silently agree. There was no dessert—she had other plans for that, and thinking about them positively aroused her. At last she'd prepared her special occasion for their first time after months, and now she wondered why she ever put it off.

She disappeared into the bedroom and peeled off her gown as fast as she could. Before putting on the negligee, she gazed at her nude figure in the full-length mirror attached to the closet door. That tummy bulge streaked with fading stretch marks leered at her. Well, he'd just have to deal with it! He'd gotten two wonderful sons out of it. The rest of her body was fine, and her milk-filled breasts were something to behold. *Eat your heart out, Sheila with the small breasts! Your hair isn't even blonde.*

She slipped on a long, flowing negligee, white and heartbreakingly sheer. She unwrapped the new CD and went out, her heart thumping so hard she felt like she'd have a heart attack. She was greedy tonight. Most women would be happy with one grand entrance. She was going for two.

C.H. had cleared the table and was wrapping the leftovers. That silly, wonderful man! Just couldn't resist helping out. He glanced up as she came out, and the look of desire on his face made her tingle all over. She kept her hands coyly behind her, holding the CD out of sight.

Without a word, he approached her and placed his hands on her sides. His touch through the sheer fabric shot a thrill through her body. He bent to kiss her, but she said, "I have a present for you."

His eyes widened. "You've got *more* to give me?"

She went to the Blu-ray player and inserted the CD. With the press of a button, the gentle notes of Pachelbel's *Canon in D* drifted from the new TV's speakers. It was one of his favorites. "Schmaltzy, but emotionally touching," he said once. The sound wasn't quite as rich as the new car's speakers, but this tiny apartment had never been filled with such a transcendent sound since they moved in.

"A girl could ask me to do anything while this is playing," he said with a suggestive look on his face, "and I'd do it."

"I know," she said and kissed him.

They stumbled to the sofa. The negligee slid from Dani's body and tumbled to the floor. She almost giggled with his lips pressed against hers, thinking how little use that negligee had been put to.

Sheila was a brief image in C.H.'s mind as they made love, and only as a comparison to what he felt now. There *was* no comparison. The desire he felt for Dani was colored deeply by their years together, the struggles they shared, the love they felt for each other, the children they created together, even their petty arguments. His desire was colored most of all by the recent challenges they faced, challenges they could never have imagined. Mere lustful passion could not begin to compare.

He wondered how he could ever feel this way with Sheila. But it didn't matter now. He was with Dani.

Cyndy couldn't believe how rotten this night was ending up, after starting out so intriguing. She returned from another swing around the neighborhood and found the Youngs' old red car parked in the street. Brother Young had come home and gone inside without Cyndy seeing him. She kept missing everything!

She wondered if he brought home anything exotic for this night. Maybe he picked up a tuxedo or something. Maybe they were going to a ball. That would mean that if she waited long enough, she could see them leave.

She rode and rode, getting more and more tired and more and more irritated. Why didn't anything happen? Surely Sister Young wouldn't get an evening gown like that if they weren't going somewhere. Maybe it was for some other night.

But why were the boys not home then?

Would Sister Young even go out with a gown like that? It was pretty racy, and although no one in Cyndy's family wore garments, she'd learned about them in Young Women lessons on temples and modesty. That gown couldn't be worn with garments, so for Sister Young to go into public wearing it would be a little bit wicked. She couldn't imagine Sister Young being even a little bit wicked.

A thought suddenly occurred to her. They must be having their big deal at home right now! Maybe a candlelight dinner, maybe their own private ball.

That had to be it! They were having their own dance right at home, the wife all dressed up in that sexy gown, and the husband probably decked out like James Bond. Dancing to ballroom music in their little apartment.

Gosh, how romantic!

Twilight surrounded her, and Cyndy knew she'd be in trouble if she didn't get home soon. But she was overwhelmed by the image of Brother and Sister Young dancing a waltz, gazing dreamily into each other's eyes. She wished she could just catch a glimpse. She could never fall asleep that night if she couldn't get just one little peek. It would be like attending the king's ball and never once glimpsing Cinderella and Prince Charming dancing together.

But how? She understood why the drapes were closed, but how she wished they weren't!

As she passed their window for the millionth time, now that the daylight had waned, she could see a flickering of light in the middle of the window. Her heart leaped in her chest. The drapes were parted slightly, enough to show some light through. The candlelight dinner! Cyndy was right.

Peeking into someone's window—what a perverted thing to do! But Cyndy couldn't bear the thought of just going home. It wasn't like she was some dirty old man trying to catch a glimpse of an undressed woman. She just wanted to see a romantic moment between two people who loved each other, and who Cyndy loved. Just a glimpse of one sweet moment. That wasn't wicked, was it?

But no one would understand it that way, so she didn't dare do it while the slightest daylight remained. She'd have to wait until it was dark enough. And to do that, she'd get into real trouble with her mother. Dang daylight savings! Why hadn't it switched back yet?

Her mother would ground her for a week but then forget after a while, sometimes even the next day. It was worth it. She didn't have anyone but silly, immature girlfriends to visit anyway. *This* had to do with grown-up stuff. This was much more interesting.

She waited until night closed in, then hopped off her bike and walked it up the Youngs' driveway into the carport, wincing at the clicking sound of its wheel. She leaned her bike on a post and crept along the side of the house until she got to the window. Gazing around to make sure no one was watching, she raised up on her toes and pressed against the window.

Through the slight part in the drapes she saw a candle—no two—burning away on a table with a white table cloth. And some flowers in a vase. The dinner! Except there was nothing else on the table.

Faintly she could hear music playing. Nothing she recognized, but it sounded pretty. Of course! The dinner was finished, and now they were doing the ballroom dance.

Why wasn't this slit wider? She couldn't see them. Why didn't they dance past the slit?

She slowly moved her head from side to side, trying to see more. To the right she noticed movement. It was a foot, a leg.

Oh my gosh! A naked leg! Brother Young's naked leg! And his naked—he was—and there was Sister Young's naked—

Cyndy gasped and covered her mouth with her hand. They hadn't heard her, had they? *Don't be silly.* She was outside, and they had music playing. Pretty, romantic music playing as they—

Oh my gosh!

She couldn't move. She couldn't breathe. She knew she was being as evil as those dirty old men, but she couldn't pull her eyes away. She knew she should be *feeling* evil right now, but what she felt was anything but evil. She felt so... so...

Alive!

She kept swinging her head side to side so she could piece together the whole image in successive slitwide glimpses. It was so beautiful! She'd tried before to picture it, and all she ever imagined was lying quietly nude with a boy, holding him and giving him little kisses on the lips. But the Youngs weren't lying still, and their kisses were amazing! It looked almost rough and yet...thrilling.

Cyndy heard a car coming. She turned and dropped as fast as she could, hoping the bushes and shadows would hide her well enough. The car passed by and disappeared.

She panted hard as she sat with her back against the house. The bushes pricked her in a couple of places, and a chilly breeze caused her to shiver, but she barely noticed. She was too busy enjoying the tingles that blazed through her body and the dazzling thrill of adrenalin from almost being caught by the car. Her mind pieced together a composite view of the slices of images she'd seen through the drapes. Brother Young loving Sister Young passionately, and she loving him back. Gosh, how beautiful, how incredible it had been!

Another car approached, waking Cyndy out of her trance. She'd better get home now! She was in trouble already, and if someone found her *here*, she'd be in even more trouble. She waited for the car to pass, crept back to her bike, and walked it down to the street, peering all around to make sure no one saw her. Then she hopped on the bike and rode like mad.

Her mother chewed her out good when she got home and grounded her, but

Cyndy didn't even notice for how long. During the chewing out, Ryan piped in every chance he got. Finally her mom sent her to her room. She was delighted with *that* punishment because that's exactly where she wanted to be.

She flopped onto her bed and wrapped her arms around herself, basking in the delicious feeling that still lingered. Why didn't she feel wicked? Hadn't she done a horrible thing?

Had she? She didn't *mean* to see them doing—that. She just thought they'd be dancing. It was all a mistake. And the Youngs hadn't been doing anything wicked. They were married. They were supposed to do that.

But should Cyndy feel so good after watching? Was it wicked to feel like this after seeing what she saw? Shouldn't she feel bad, or embarrassed, or something? What *was* this feeling?

It was—*oh my gosh!* she realized in shock. It was because, deep down, she was imagining herself doing—that—with him. This feeling must be a little of what it felt like for them, a hundred times stronger. Gosh, was she evil! Imagining doing it with him and feeling *good* about it.

But she wasn't really imagining doing it with *him*. She was imagining making love with her own husband. And he looked like Brother Young only because that was the husband she happened to see tonight.

Heavenly Father, she prayed silently as she lay on her bed. *Please forgive me if I did something wrong. I didn't mean to. And please forgive me if I'm doing something wrong now thinking about it. I'm really just thinking about when I'll be married. Please, send me a man as wonderful as Brother Young. That's why I'm imagining him, because I want someone as wonderful as him.*

That's what her mind said. But as she prayed, her heart couldn't seem to separate Brother Young from her imagined husband. She hoped God would understand the difference.

Dani hadn't realized how much tension she'd been feeling until it was gone. Lying together on the sofa, sleek with perspiration, listening to whatever classical selection had followed Pachelbel's Canon, was almost as good as making love. All the cares of the world had disappeared, and she couldn't imagine them coming back.

But of course they would. And although the two of them had spent an evening together as the only people in existence, there was a whole world out there waiting to intrude. It wouldn't be denied much longer. But now Dani had a promise from C.H., and she made sure he wouldn't forget her too easily. Now she could deal with that world.

As she stroked his back and he played with one of her ringlets, Dani said,

"Okay, tell me what happened with Sheila."

His pleasant smile faded. "Are you sure you want to talk about that just now?"

"Yes. I'm ready."

He nodded. "Well, she was doing a satanic ritual alright. A ceremonial assassination, she called it, of her boyfriend. He left her and sold the lease to their apartment, so starting tomorrow she has nowhere to live."

"Sounds like this is good timing for her."

"Yeah, I guess so." He attempted a smile.

"Did you stop her from performing the ritual?"

"I suppose. She had some paper skewered on the end of a sword and was burning it. She had on black"—he gave her a guilty glance—"clothes, and—"

She chuckled. He was so transparent. "Please, Cain. Don't hold anything back. I'll be able to deal with this better if I know you're being completely honest with me."

He studied her face for a moment. "Okay. She had on a black teddy and looked very sexy in it."

She maintained her interested smile and was surprised how little that comment bothered her. He paused an instant, assessing her, then went on.

"There were black candles and one white candle, and a medallion hanging on the wall by a chain with—I guess it's a satanic symbol. An upside-down star with a goat's head in the middle. It was all pretty creepy."

"Sounds like it."

"There was a picture of Steven—that's her boyfriend—and she started destroying it with the sword. She got pretty violent, and that's when I stopped her."

He gave her a sheepish grin.

"What?"

"She tried to kill me."

"*What?*"

"I think she thought I was Steven. She seemed pretty out of it."

Tried to kill him! "What did she do to you?"

"She lunged at me with the sword. But she missed, and after that she came to her senses."

Dani had been ready to accept things. Now all she could do was wonder what kind of a lunatic Sheila was. She sucked in a breath and tried to put that train of thought out of her mind. "Did you tell her about—everything?"

"Yes, I told her about Brother Brigham and my calling to become president—and about the polygamy. I told her she was chosen to be my next wife."

"And what did she say?"

He shrugged his one free shoulder. "I think she thought I was nuts. She told me to get out."

Hope surged inside her. Would Sheila reject this? Would they be freed of this impossible demand? But disappointment followed immediately. If Sheila refused, God would probably just choose another.

At least the next one might be better than Sheila. How could she be worse?

"Right then," he continued, "Brother Brigham appeared to her, told her everything himself, and commanded her to accept it."

Damn that Brigham! Couldn't he leave us women alone? First he appears to me so I have to accept it. Then he appears to Sheila to make sure she does. If he didn't keep showing up, we could reject the whole thing a lot easier.

She calmed her anger with regular breathing, and of course, as the anger dissipated, remorse flowed in. Where had her resolve to accept everything gone?

She knew when it disappeared: when she felt hope that Sheila wouldn't cooperate. If only he hadn't been so chronological with his narrative, getting her hopes up. Time to cut to the chase.

"So did she finally accept everything?"

"Yes, she did. I guess..." He gazed into her eyes. "You don't want me to hold anything back?"

What now? "Nothing."

"She was in love with me all along." He looked embarrassed. "But she knew I was married and loved you, so she never let on."

Dani felt stunned. She never guessed that. Was that why God chose Sheila, because she already loved him? It made sense, but she felt betrayed—and at the same time flattered that the man who chose her was desired by other attractive women. She appreciated the respect Sheila had shown for their relationship. A woman like her might easily have decided to steal her husband away.

It was strange to feel appreciation toward the woman she was trying hard not to hate.

"So when are you going to marry her?"

He turned a little red. "Uh, I don't know. We didn't discuss that. I—had to get out of there right away." He flashed his guilty look again.

"Why?" she said, trying to leave out the irritation she felt.

"Well, we kissed. It was a pretty passionate kiss. And I—I got excited." He wouldn't make eye contact with her. "I'm sorry, but I couldn't help it. She had on that teddy, and..." He shrugged and shook his head. "It's been eleven weeks..."

"So what happened?" She said it darkly, even though she tried not to.

He looked at her with alarm. "Nothing! That's why I had to leave so fast. I wanted to make sure nothing happened."

She breathed a sigh of relief. She tried to tell herself that she was simply afraid their lovemaking tonight had not been his first in—eleven weeks, he said?

So he'd been counting. But she knew it would be like this every day he was out of her sight, wondering when the inevitable would happen. She couldn't take that.

"C.H., promise me something."

"I promise."

His eagerness to do whatever she asked began to bother her. It wasn't out of love or consideration—it was because he felt guilty. She didn't want kindness motivated by guilt.

"Promise me you'll tell me when you make love to her—before you do it."

A look of consternation crossed his face.

"Please. I can't just sit here and wonder every time you're gone."

"I won't have sex with her before we're married."

"Please. I might not like it that night, but I'll rest easier every other night."

He pursed his lips and sighed.

"Besides," she said, "you already promised."

He looked at her with surprise. She deadpanned for as long as she could, then grinned. He smiled back. "Yes, I did, didn't I?"

She caressed his cheek. "Promise me again. Now that you can mean it, now that you know what I'm asking." She hoped he got the hint.

"I promise." He returned the caress on her cheek. "I just don't want to hurt you. I don't know what's right to do under these circumstances."

"I know. Neither of us do." She kissed him. "We both understand what's happening, and we've both accepted it. Let's just act like it's normal—as much as we can."

His eyes were misting.

"You're going to marry Sheila," she went on, "and you're going to make love to her. That's what you're supposed to do. I know all that, and I accept it. Okay?"

A tear slipped from his eye. He wouldn't look at her. She pulled on his chin until he faced her. "*Okay?*"

"Okay."

"Just keep the promise you made to me at dinner. Love me like you always have. Love me as much as you do anyone else."

"I'll do better than that," he said, wiping away the tear. "I promise I'll love you more than anyone else."

Her eyes began to tear up. She was trying hard to be magnanimous to the other woman, keeping the two of them on equal footing. But that's what she'd *really* wanted to hear from him. She was his first wife—he had chosen *her* to love and live with. She should be the one he loved the most.

"Just don't let Sheila ever hear you say that," she said.

He chuckled. "I kind of already said it to her."

That almost made her feel happy again. He promised to love Dani more, and Sheila already understood that.

She snuggled her head into his chest. "I love you, Cain," she murmured.

"I love you, sweetie."

"And she never gets to call you Cain."

They lay together for a few more minutes, then Dani sat up suddenly, pressing her palms on both breasts. "I think we'd better get the boys back. I need to nurse Glenn."

He rose to his feet. "I'll get them." He started dressing. "And don't you touch those dishes! That's my job tonight."

He rushed out the door as Dani sat on the sofa pressing her breasts and peering about the silent room. She hadn't even noticed when the CD stopped playing. The candles had burned down an inch or two. The scents of the meal and her perfume had nearly faded, but the flowers were still noticeable. The love she felt for C.H. burned fiercely in her heart.

Sheila, she thought, *do you have any idea how lucky you are?*

By tomorrow she has nowhere to live. C.H.'s voice popped into her head, giving her a sinking feeling. Where *would* Sheila live tomorrow? Where could she go on such short notice?

Please, Cain, don't bring her here. We don't have room, and I couldn't bear to have her under my own roof, not even for a few days.

Then she thought of the vacant apartment behind them. It would be perfect. Perfect for Sheila, perfect for C.H.

And for Dani?

Still under the same roof. Turn up the TV so she wouldn't hear the bed creaking.

Her dread at having Sheila live with them had never been too strong because it was too absurd to think it would ever happen, if for no other reason than there wasn't enough room.

But the apartment behind them—that made sense. It *was* too perfect not to consider, yet was it all that much different from having Sheila actually live with them? Just an extra wall—that was it. A quick trip around the house. Dani knew how sound carried through that wall from when the last tenants lived there. They'd heard lots of unpleasant noises from the bedroom as they lay in their own bed. When they moved out, Dani was relieved.

She stared at the wall through the kitchen door. How noisy was C.H. when he made love? She hadn't paid that much attention—there were more interesting things to focus on. He couldn't be too noisy because she never noticed anything unusual.

But what about Sheila? She was a wild sort, living in sexual sin, dabbling in Satanism. Who knew what kind of things she liked to do and what kind of noises she might make while doing them?

What if she was a screamer?

When the time came, how could Dani casually listen to even a creaking bed, knowing what was going on back there? She would definitely be turning up the TV, or playing some music. But not Pachelbel's *Canon*. She couldn't bear to play that while *they* were...

But from a practical standpoint, she couldn't think of a better arrangement. So close—C.H. could see both families easily. He would never be far when Dani lay in bed alone at night or if something went wrong. It was too perfect and too obvious. If he hadn't already thought of it, she would suggest it.

Oh God, can I really do this?

By the time C.H. returned with the boys, Petey whiny and sleepy and Glenn crying, Dani still sat naked on the sofa, pressing on her breasts. No doubt to him it looked as if she'd done nothing. But in that time she accomplished some important things. She wrestled with her feelings and came to a decision—a *final* decision this time. She would stop oscillating once and for all and truly accept what was coming.

"Cain," she said immediately, to prove to herself she was serious, "where will Sheila live after tomorrow?"

He frowned and steered Petey onto the recliner. "I'm sorry, sweetie. I wasn't trying to keep this from you. I just forgot—"

"It's alright." She knew he already thought of the rear apartment, or why would he be so apologetic about it? "She's going to live behind us, right?"

He nodded weakly and handed Glenn to her. She immediately urged the baby's mouth onto a nipple and continued to press the other to keep the milk from leaking out.

"It's the best arrangement."

His head jerked up with a stunned expression. More confidently, he added, "And we'll be using money from the backpack to pay for it."

That caught her by surprise. She assumed Sheila would pay her own rent. But of course, why should she? She'd be married to C.H., and Brigham had told him that the money was for the support of his family. God had planned everything well. Brigham had simply used the wrong word. He should have said *families*. And with more than a hundred thousand dollars to work with, how many families were on the drawing board?

"Okay," Dani said, determined to live up to her decision.

Chapter 9

C.H.'s stomach churned as he left work. To this point, the call to practice polygamy had been theoretical. He was about to take the first step to make it reality. He was about to help Sheila move into the other half of their duplex.

He climbed into the SUV, which Dani had insisted he drive to work so he could transport Sheila's stuff afterward. As he drove, he tuned into KBYU for some nice, distracting classical music, but they were in the middle of airing BBC news. He tried the smooth jazz station instead—anything but pop or country—and found something passable playing.

He swung around first to the West Valley Deseret Industries store to drop off their old TV set that had been rattling around in the back all this time. As he pulled into the parking lot of Sheila's apartment complex, he slowed to a crawl. His churning stomach had become positively nauseated. Could he possibly go through with this? A determination to obey God and some fantasizing about being intimate with Sheila had sustained him while everything was an abstract future event. But this first definite step toward marrying a second wife was too much.

He found the closest available visitor's slot, pulled in, and stopped the engine. Feeling lightheaded, he leaned his forehead against the steering wheel and closed his eyes.

"Father in Heaven, give me the strength to go through with this." How many times had he declared his commitment? Yet he was still vacillating.

He wondered how Sheila felt about it. She wouldn't feel like she was betraying any spouse. But she had her own concerns—returning to the religion she rejected, giving up certain behaviors, sharing her new husband with another wife, being the second wife. She probably had a few butterflies in her stomach as well.

It was time to be a man *and* an obedient disciple and go do what he must do. He yanked off his tie, got out, and climbed the stairs to her apartment, this time only one step at a time. He knocked on the door, and this time she answered.

"Hi, C.H.," she said brightly—maybe a little too brightly.

"Hi, Sheila. Are you ready?"

She shrugged and smiled guiltily. "Mostly." She opened the door wide.

He found packed boxes scattered randomly, some suitcases, and a lot of loose things strewn about. He tried hard to stifle a sigh. He didn't mind helping people *move*—carrying out boxes and furniture and loading them onto the truck. But he hated helping them *pack*—he never had any idea how they wanted things organized or what should be thrown out.

But Sheila wasn't some member of the ward he was obliged to help as an elders quorum service project. She was his fiancée. He'd have to swallow his feelings and help in any way she needed.

She must have seen him looking at the clutter with discouragement. "Don't worry about this stuff. I'll finish packing as you carry things out." Her eyes gleamed mischievously. "I'm leaving most of it anyway. It's Steven's lease—let him worry about it."

That did make C.H. feel better. No packing, just moving. And it was a much better way to get back at Steven than magical assassinations.

He noticed the coffee table that had been the altar, still against the same wall, still set up for the ritual. Candles standing but unlit. Goat-head medallion hanging from the wall. Bell and gong in place. And the sword lying lengthwise across the table with Steven's smashed picture leaning against the hilt.

"I set it back up again," she said with a grin.

"You still going to do the ritual?" His queasy stomach returned.

"No, I just want him to know I did it. He read the *Satanic Bible* too—he'll know what it all means. Besides, it's his sword."

He shook his head with half a smile and hoped Sheila would never get too angry with him. He rolled up the sleeves of his white shirt and started carrying things down the stairs as she went back to packing. They didn't say much beyond logistical necessity as they worked. He was glad to have a routine to settle into so he could ignore how weird this all felt.

He needed every cubic inch of the SUV's space to cram everything in. A couple of times he had to pull out some things and rearrange them to squeeze it all in. When boxes and suitcases and tote bags and whatever else she'd found to stick things in were all loaded, they stood next to each other surveying the living room. Self-consciously he put his arm around her waist. She stiffened for an instant, then relaxed and leaned into him.

"Nothing else?" he said.

"That's all."

"No furniture?"

She smiled. "I thought about it. But—" She turned to him. "What the hell, you don't have any more room anyway."

"We can make another trip or two. Whatever it takes."

"It's all his anyways. I figured he owed me some of it, but—" She dismissed it with a wave of her hand. "I've been without furniture before. I can manage again."

He noticed the dangling chain by the door that he promised to pay for. She noticed him noticing. "Let it come out of his deposit," she said and pulled him out the door.

They climbed into the car—a tight squeeze, since he'd moved up the front seats to accommodate all of her stuff. He turned the ignition, and the interior filled with a smooth jazz number. As he pulled out of the parking lot and started driving down the street, he glanced over and was surprised for a second to see Sheila and not Dani sitting next to him. His squeamish stomach returned. He almost felt like he was in the Twilight Zone.

It was completely unfair of him to think that way. Sheila hadn't intruded. She respected their marriage in spite of her feelings. Brother Brigham had intruded. God had intruded.

Not that that line of thinking made him feel any better.

"What's with the elevator music?" she said.

He switched to playing a CD. The middle of the second movement of Beethoven's *Eroica Symphony* burst out.

"Much better," she said with her half-smile. "*High class* elevator music."

He realized he had no idea what kind of music she liked. He knew all sorts of things about what books she liked, but not music. It hit him that there was a whole world of things he didn't know about her.

"Okay," she said after several moments of wordless driving. "How are you paying for this?"

He pondered, trying to decide how to start. "Well...Brigham Young again. The very first time he appeared to me, he told me to drive out west on I-80 and pick up a backpack."

"Brigham Young told you to get a backpack," she repeated with one eyebrow raised.

"Yeah. I was supposed to drive to mile marker forty-five, walk out one hundred yards, and pick up a backpack lying there."

"Oh, I thought you meant go *buy* a backpack."

He smiled apologetically and shrugged. "Sorry."

"That would've been weird to specify exactly which direction and which interstate to go to buy a backpack."

"Trust me, it was weird anyway."

"So why *that* backpack?"

"Because of the hundred and fifty thousand dollars in it."

That perked her up. She stared at him with wide eyes for several heartbeats. "How much?"

"A hundred and fifty thousand dollars."

"Holy sh—shucks!" She gave him an apologetic smile.

He chuckled. *Shucks* was not how she usually put things. But he was touched that she made the effort. That was a good sign.

"What are you supposed to do with it?" she asked.

He gestured toward her. "Support you. And my family. Polygamy isn't cheap, I'm sure."

"Polygamy." She shook her head. "If you'd have told me I'd be living in polygamy one day..."

He noticed she didn't ask where the money was now, and that made him feel better. Then he remembered she chose to do this without knowing about the money and mentally kicked himself for thinking that of her.

"So what happens next?" she said after a pause.

"We move you into the back of our duplex—"

"No, I mean what happens next with *us*—with *me*—and the church?"

He waited to answer until he passed a particularly slow car. "I'm not sure. Brother Brigham hasn't given me any further instructions yet."

"Brother Brigham?"

He smiled sheepishly. "That's what I call him. I had Brigham Young as an imaginary friend when I was younger, and I called him that."

"That's interesting." *That's weird,* her tone said.

"Hey, he's my great-great-grandfather. It's not that weird." He was beginning to feel more comfortable. This was the sort of banter they had at work all the time.

She patted him on the shoulder. "It's okay. You can have any imaginary friend you want."

He was almost enjoying himself, and that felt strange. The situation was too bizarre to be enjoying himself. He felt unreal.

"So we sit around and wait for him to tell you what to do next?"

He shrugged. "I guess so."

"Well, we know we're supposed to get married, right?"

"That's right."

"How? Where? By whom? This isn't exactly legal, you know."

That was a thought he'd been trying hard not to think. "I know," he said glumly. "And how, I'm not entirely clear on. Brother Brigham—"

When he glanced at her, she smiled at him. He suddenly realized that most of her twelve earrings were gone.

"What?" Sheila said, her smile fading.

"I'm sorry. I just noticed your earrings."

"Oh." The fading smile became a smirk. "Is that okay?"

"Sure. Although it'd be fine with me if you left them all in."

"Liar. I was thinking of getting tattoos all over my body instead."

"Liar." But her enigmatic smile made him not so sure she wouldn't.

"Are we supposed to get married in the temple?" she asked.

"I don't know."

"Am I going to have to wait a year?"

He took a deep breath, gripping the steering wheel tightly. "*I don't know.*" He was feeling a little stupid for having no answers to her questions. You'd think he'd have been as curious as she was. "Brigham says the Lord's already been waiting too long for polygamy to be practiced again. So maybe you won't be waiting a year." It was the best he could offer her.

"How's the big guy going to pull that off? I'm disfellowshipped right now."

He gunned the engine through a yellow light. "I have no idea."

"You're the boss."

"Actually, Brigham is. I don't have a clue what's going on."

"You mean God."

"Huh?" He looked at her. She was staring at him with a hint of disapproval.

"You keep saying Brigham Young is doing this and doing that. Isn't he just the messenger? Don't you mean God is running the show?"

He knew his face was beet red. He *had* been doing that. "You're right." His voice broke, and he cleared his throat. "He's just—since he's been my imaginary friend and all—"

Sheila laughed. "Relax. You don't have to justify it to me."

That didn't help his face become less red. Any other time he'd have recognized she was teasing him. She was right—he should relax.

She settled back in her seat and looked forward. "So...who are we inviting to the wedding?"

"Uh..."

"My dad will have to give me away, you know, and my mother will want to plan everything." She stroked her chin thoughtfully. "Who should I get for bridesmaids?"

He pointedly concentrated on his driving.

"Where are you taking me on our honeymoon?" She leaned over and pecked him on the cheek. "Or is that supposed to be a secret?"

"I have no idea, Sheila! I haven't thought about any of it."

Again she laughed. "You're no fun these days."

"Maybe it's because your questions are serious ones. What *will* we do about your family and friends?"

"And yours?"

He let out a single humorless chuckle. "My family's easy. They're not going to hear about it."

"Well, I'm not exactly on speaking terms with my family," she said with a wave of her hand. "Not since I went heathen on them. So we don't need to tell them either. You'll just be another guy I'm shacking up with."

Putting it like that didn't make him feel any better. He stopped at a red light. She gazed at him an instant. "May I kiss you?"

His heart jumped. "You just did."

"I mean *really* kiss you."

He wanted to, but... "What if someone sees us?"

"So what if they do?"

"I mean someone who knows me."

She sighed with exasperation. "C.H., if I'm going to marry you, you have to be more fun than this. The car is packed full behind us, there's no one in front of us, and do you recognize the man in the car next to you?"

He looked. "No..."

She leaned over, and he followed her example. She kissed him deeply on the mouth, stroking his tongue with hers. The excitement it kindled made him breathless. The car next to him moved, and the person behind honked.

Without breaking the connection of their lips, she said, "Light's green." But she didn't stop kissing him. The horn honked again. He finally pulled away.

She laughed wickedly as he accelerated. "I'm a bad girl, aren't I?"

"Maybe, but your kisses aren't bad."

"Aren't you afraid I'll corrupt you?"

"No, you'll repent too much."

She settled back into her chair. "Okay, I'll start repenting now. Let's see, what were the steps again?"

"First you—"

"Don't tell me. Let's see if I can remember." She muttered voicelessly as she counted on her fingers. "Okay, first I admit that I've sinned."

"Admit to who?"

"To myself, of course. I can't repent if I don't think I've sinned."

"So do you?"

"Think I've sinned?" She stared ahead quietly. "Good question."

That caused his heart to sink. She wasn't sure if the things she'd done were sinful? This could take a while.

"I know by the standards of the church I've sinned. If I believe that was really Brigham Young, then the Mormon church must be right, so the things I've done are sins."

"*Do* you believe?"

"Hey!" She pushed his shoulder, which caused the car to veer. "What if Brigham Young was cast into hell for being a false prophet? Maybe we *weren't* visited by an angel." She gave him a gleaming conspiratorial look. "Maybe it was a demon."

He chuckled. "You *were* doing Satanic rituals."

She sat back decisively. "If it was a demon, then God didn't command us and we can't get married. Therefore...it was Brigham Young."

He knew she was playing around, and it wasn't exactly a conversion by the spirit. But if it was enough to get her started, it was enough for now. "So do you acknowledge your sins?"

"I think I already have." She gave him a vulnerable look.

"Then what's the second step?"

"To feel remorse about them."

"Do you feel remorse?"

"Hell, no." She grinned at his shock. "It's not like I hurt anyone."

He began to feel like this was one step forward, two steps back.

"But I guess I feel better that I've decided to stop them. Is that remorse enough?"

Okay, maybe two steps forward and one step back. "Enough for now."

"Now I have to confess my sins to whoever I hurt and ask their forgiveness."

"But you don't believe you hurt anyone."

"Check that one off!"

He didn't think he was pouting, but she said, "Oh, stop pouting. I'm just teasing you."

"Then who *do* you think you hurt?"

"You," she said softly. "And me, because you'll have a harder time accepting me because of them."

He glanced at her. The expression on her face was one he'd never seen on her before. A deep, earnest sincerity.

"Sheila, you don't have to worry. I know you've done those things. They won't drive me away from you."

"I'm not so sure. You don't know what some of them are."

Her eyes began to moisten. This really was a new Sheila to him. "I know you've had sex with people you weren't married to. You must not have committed adultery since you said you'd never do that to another— " He cast her a sudden glance. "Have you?"

She glared at him. "No!" Then she looked forward again. "I've been saving that one to commit with you."

She wasn't going to get him with her teasing this time. "Well, fornication isn't as bad as adultery. So unless you've committed murder or eaten babies, I don't think you have much to worry about."

"That's true," she said. "I'm several notches down on the Mormon list of top ten sins."

"You don't have to confess to me if you don't want to."

"But I *did* try to get Steven killed," she said reflectively. "Does that count as murder?" She turned to him. "Yes, I do need to confess to you. If we're getting married, I'm not going to hide things from you."

That resonated with him. It's what he said to Dani. "Did you really believe all that Satanism stuff?"

"No, I don't think so. It just seemed like a good thing to try. Therapy or something."

"If you didn't believe it would really work, then I don't see how it could be considered murder."

"Thank you," she said with mock formality.

"So do you want to confess now?"

She swallowed hard. "Sure, why not." She took a deep breath. "I've had sex with seven men, only three of whom I had a relationship with. But we always used a rubber—I was very careful about that."

He kept his eyes glued to the road ahead and maintained his best poker face—not that he had a clue how good his poker face was. He hadn't thought of that. What if she had a disease? He wasn't about to bring that home to Dani. Should he trust her word that she'd been careful? Or had she become infected even though she was careful? He heard that condoms weren't *totally* reliable. There was always a possibility.

"Uh, Sheila." He swallowed nervously. "I don't know how to say this—"

"I'll get tested," she said. "I understand. You've got Dani to think about."

"Thank you."

"The least I can do for my husband, right?"

Get tested so he didn't pass a disease onto his other wife? Sure, that should be on every couple's to-do list.

"And I've drunk alcohol. Oh, and coffee. I didn't think about coffee. Do I have to give up coffee?" She said it like it was a deal-breaker.

He shrugged. "I'm afraid so."

Sheila stared ahead long and hard, then spat out a vile word. "Alright! I'll become a Dr. Pepper addict. Oh, and I swear now and then."

"Yeah, that I knew."

"But that's such a fun one. Do I have to give that up?"

"Well, don't use the Lord's name in vain—that's one of the Ten Commandments. Just try and keep it to the milder words, especially around other members. Out of respect for their sensitivities."

"What the hell, I suppose I can handle that, damn it!" She smiled innocently at him. "Was that mild enough?"

He rolled his eyes. "Is that it?"

"I've seen plenty pornography, but it's not an obsession or anything. I can avoid that okay."

He nodded. Actually, the progress she'd already made was impressive.

"And..." She paused. The silence grew long.

"And what?" he prodded gently.

"I've used drugs."

He raised his eyebrows. It wasn't that big of a shocker, he supposed. But he hadn't known. "What, you dabbled in marijuana or something?"

"I snorted coke Sunday night after you left."

His face jerked toward her. That *was* a shocker. "You're kidding."

She wouldn't look at him. "No, I'm not."

For a moment he was sure she was pulling his leg again, but gradually he realized she was serious. This was what she was afraid to tell him. This was what she thought might drive him away. He hated to admit it, but she might be right. That was an *addiction*—extremely difficult to break.

She gazed straight ahead, waiting for his reaction. He turned into the street that led to their house. How did he want to react? It didn't help to know she did it so recently, and *after* she agreed to marry him.

"Will you keep using cocaine?" he asked.

She shook her head.

"Can you be sure about that?"

"I was careful not to get addicted."

He wanted to believe her, but weren't these the exact things an addict would say? "Are you *really* sure about that?"

Finally she looked at him. Her jaw muscles were tight, her eyes squinting, and her lips pursed hard. "The next day, I took my supply of coke and flushed it down the toilet. And I threw all my paraphernalia away. It was quite a bit of coke too—expensive. Does that answer your question?"

It was a heroic demonstration of her intent and all she could be expected to do in such a short time. He decided he needed to give her the benefit of a doubt. But he also decided he better keep a watchful eye on her.

"Yes, that answers my question."

He noticed as he passed his home that the Corolla was missing. He wondered where Dani might be. Probably wanted to be anywhere but here as he brought Sheila into their lives.

"Anything else?" he said.

"No, that's it. Oh, except—" Her grim expression turned into defiance. "I don't want to go to church."

He laughed as he pulled into the driveway of her new home. Frankly, that sounded like a good idea anyway. How would he explain her to the ward? "Alright, you can stay home from church, at least for a while. You've turned over enough new leaves for one day. Maybe I can administer the sacrament to you myself." He wondered if that were really true. Sure, he *could*. But would it be appropriate on his own initiative? He needed to ask Brother Brigham.

Her defiant look softened. "Then...do you forgive me?"

"I forgive you." He reached over and hugged her tightly before it occurred to him to wonder if someone was watching. He decided not to worry about it. What harm was an innocent hug?

She held the embrace a moment, then gave him a kiss on the cheek. "And I forgive you," she whispered in his ear.

"For what?"

"For being such a prudish twit since the day I met you."

He pulled back and looked at her. There was that half-smile. "But I never confessed that," he said snobbily.

Maybe this could turn out fun after all.

"Need any help?"

With his grip on the box not quite solidified, C.H. craned his neck to look. It was the new neighbor across the street, Moroni. "Uh, sure."

"So who's this lovely lady we're moving in?"

Sheila appeared around the van, gazing intently at Moroni.

"My name's Sheila." She extended her hand.

"I'm Moroni." Their eyes locked as they shook hands.

She grinned. "You're kidding."

"That's what it is."

"My condolences."

He smiled back at her. "I don't mind. I like the reactions I get from people."

C.H. swore the tank top Moroni was wearing was the same one he'd worn working on the car the day of General Conference—the day all this had started. He wondered how long it had been since Moroni had washed his long, stringy hair.

"Well, if C.H. will get out of the way with that box, I'll help too." Moroni stepped up beside him. C.H. hefted the box and walked slowly toward the door.

"How do you know C.H.?" he heard Moroni say.

"Oh, he's a—relation," Sheila answered.

C.H. walked even slower, straining his ears.

"A very close relation?"

"Not too close—so far. But we hope to change that now that we're living near each other."

"Blood relations, or are you related to his wife?"

"Oh, definitely not his wife. No, we're the ones who're related."

C.H. couldn't help it. He had to turn and look. He saw Moroni glance at him and then back at Sheila, who was hidden behind the car. Moroni nodded absently, but his eyes seemed to gleam.

Probably thinks she's my mistress, C.H. thought—which wasn't all that far off, he supposed. Move his mistress into the same duplex as his family? Even if he were the mistress type, he wouldn't be that brazen about it.

He had to move on since Moroni was closing in on him fast. He dropped the box in the middle of the living room next to the ones they already moved. Moroni immediately added his box. Sheila wasn't far behind with one of her own. They all paused an instant to look at each other as they stood, and C.H. noticed something extra in the glances Sheila and Moroni exchanged with each other.

He was shocked to realize he felt jealous of Moroni. Over a little flirting. What Dani had to be going through!

"Well, I guess I'll make another trip," Moroni said and walked out.

She leaned over and kissed C.H. briefly on the lips. "Relax, big boy. Just because I think he's cute doesn't mean I'm going to do anything about it."

He stared at her with pursed lips, feeling embarrassed she could read him so easily. She looked him up and down. "You've got a lot of nerve pouting like that, when I have to share you."

He nodded his head toward the door. "Let's go get another load."

She smiled and kissed him again. That relaxed his lips quickly. He focused on the kiss, trying very hard to ignore his dislike for Moroni and his long, blond hair, his well-etched muscles under the tank top.

After working all day at the bookstore, then carrying Sheila's stuff down three flights of stairs and unloading it into her new apartment, C.H. was beat. And starving. He strolled through his front door into an empty house—Dani was still away—and checked the clock on the wall. Just enough time for a quick bite to eat, then a shower and a change into clean clothes before the interview with Bishop Schmidt.

He plopped into the recliner and laid it back, planning to relax a moment before he got ready.

"Cory Horace."

It startled him awake. Brother Brigham shone before him in the middle of the room in the exact same place where he'd appeared to Dani. He pulled up the recliner and stood.

"Brother Brigham. I—I'm sorry. I fell asleep."

Brother Brigham smiled and nodded. "I know. You have done well by moving Sheila here. And God is pleased with the way you have handled the money you were given so far."

That made him feel better. In the back of his mind, it gnawed at him whether he'd made the right choices.

Brigham motioned with his hand. "Please sit down, Cory. We've got a lot to discuss."

He sank back into the recliner.

"You still have not ordered cable TV for Dani."

Oops. He planned on doing that today.

"And you still haven't purchased a violin for yourself."

His nice feeling was fading fast. "I'm sorry. I'll be sure to do all that tomorrow." It was his one day off this week.

Brigham nodded. "That will be fine. And now, we must talk about what will happen with your calling."

Then, to his surprise, the spirit of Brigham Young sat down on the sofa and leaned forward with his hands folded, elbows resting on his knees. A spirit sitting and relaxing on some furniture? He never imagined such a thing. What did a spirit have to rest from? He had no body.

Maybe Brigham was doing it as a gesture to put him at ease, to make this moment more intimate. He wanted to stare down and see if his rear end made a depression in the cushion, but he couldn't bring himself to gawk at an angel's butt.

"Cory Horace," Brigham said, "tonight you will meet with your bishop to renew your temple recommend."

He nodded.

"It's important that you receive a recommend for yourself—and for Sheila. Shortly you two will be sealed together in the temple."

In the temple! This was becoming very real very quickly.

"The time is long past for the restoration of celestial marriage. God desires that you act with haste."

"But Brother Brigham, Sheila hasn't been active. And she's done things that she'll need to confess and repent of. She's been disfellowshipped. They'll make her wait a year."

"Has she not confessed to you?" Brigham said somberly.

He nodded. Already he could see where this was going.

"And are you not called to be the president of the church?"

Again he nodded.

"That confession is sufficient. She has changed her life already. She is ready to enter the temple."

"But Brigham, what about waiting a year?"

Brigham's face grew angry. "Do you think God is constrained by the policies of the church? Man sees only the outward appearance. God sees the inner heart. He has seen Sheila's heart and declared her worthy."

Chagrined, he said, "Yes, Brigham. But—"

"Oh, ye of little faith!" Brigham said as he sat straighter. "Go to the interview tonight. Everything will be laid out before you. When the time comes, you will know what to do. You will obtain a recommend for yourself and for Sheila. You must do it at any cost."

C.H. frowned.

"This is vital to your salvation and the salvation of the church. Do not tell your bishop anything about your calling."

What?

"I know that disturbs you, but if the prophet was not able to accept this new revelation, do you think your bishop will?"

He took a deep breath, remembering the promise he made to Dani about telling the bishop. "Yes, Brother Brigham, I understand."

"You will marry Sheila soon in the temple. Sometime within the next year, the president of the church will die. The Quorum of the Twelve will meet together to select the next president. But contrary to previous successions of the presidency, they will not come to an agreement on who it will be. They will feel unanimously that they must wait, and the chosen man will present himself."

Brigham shifted in the chair, and he marveled that a spirit would feel the need to do that. Or was it more sympathetic body language for his sake?

"That is when you, Cory Horace, will go to church headquarters and present yourself to the president of the Quorum of the Twelve. He will realize that you are the chosen man. The quorum will unanimously accept you as the next president of the church and ordain you."

A tear came to his eye. Learning how it would happen made it seem much more real. He really would become the prophet—within a year, Brigham said. The magnitude of the calling began to weigh on him. Was he worthy of it?

Of course not! Not even remotely worthy. Every new president must feel this way, although he bet none of them felt *quite* as unworthy as he did. After all, they were apostles for a long time before it happened to them.

"After you are ordained," said Brother Brigham, "you will announce the revelation on celestial marriage in General Conference."

His head was spinning—something that seemed to happen often in Brother Brigham's presence. He pictured himself standing at the Conference Center podium where dozens of prophets and apostles had stood before. He would *be* the prophet, the one running the show, with the eyes of the world trained on him. Deeper and deeper the realization sank in.

It was his special mission—finally coming within the year. All those years he never dreamed it would be this grand.

"You will announce that you have already been practicing it. You will be arrested, tried, and convicted of bigamy."

What?

"You must appeal the decision. However, the judgment of the lower court will stand—"

What? He was going to jail?

"—until it reaches the Supreme Court. They will overturn your verdict, and on grounds of religious freedom overturn all laws that made polygamy illegal. The church will finally be free to practice the celestial system of plural wives legally and openly."

Brother Brigham seemed to beam, even through his usual golden glow, and C.H. thought he understood how the man felt. He himself was excited over the events to come—the sheer elegance with which God had planned it all. So simple and succinct. Maybe that's what all the rush was for—God knew this Supreme Court would be the one willing to overturn the original decision.

He needed to practice polygamy for a while and then publicly confess to it so it could enter the legal system and be appealed all the way to the Supreme Court. It was the most efficient way to get the decision overturned in America. Again he marveled at the wisdom of God and how everything turned out exactly right, even when he couldn't figure out the point of any of it.

A car drove up, and its ignition shut off. Brother Brigham looked toward the street, even though the drapes were drawn. "Remember what I have told you, Cory Horace. Get those recommends at any cost. You will know what to do when the time comes." He stood and, without another word, vanished.

A fleeting moment later, Dani came in alone carrying two bags of groceries.

"Where are the boys?" he asked, jumping up to help her with the bags.

"Asleep in the car. Cyndy will be by in a moment to watch them." She looked him square in the face. "You did remember about the appointment tonight, didn't you?"

He smiled. "Yes, I did." But he realized that, after Brother Brigham's appearance, he didn't have time to shower or change. He'd have to go with dried sweat and the same clothes he wore all day. Oh well—a minor inconvenience with all that was happening, and maybe the suit coat he'd put on would hold the smell in.

She nodded and began putting things away in the cupboards. "Did you get Sheila moved in?"

"Yes." He couldn't see her face, so he couldn't tell what she was feeling. But he could probably guess.

As C.H. and Dani entered the church building and sat in the foyer, waiting for their temple-recommend interviews, it was all he could do to keep from shaking. How he would get his own recommend was no mystery. But how would Sheila get hers? He supposed this was part of the fun of being led by the Spirit, not knowing beforehand what to do.

The bishop took Dani into his office first. As C.H. sat in the foyer waiting, he heard some boys playing basketball in the cultural hall. What a typical sound in a Mormon church on a Tuesday night! It brought back unpleasant memories because that sport had never interested him growing up, yet everyone acted like he was an apostate if he didn't participate. A Mormon boy who didn't play basketball, who liked classical music instead? He might as well have lit a cigarette in church.

That reminded him of the violin he had yet to buy. It was a commandment he hadn't fulfilled yet. Not that he wasn't willing—he was downright excited about it. He just hadn't had time yet. He couldn't believe it had been only a week and a half since he mowed the lawn. He never even finished the lawn in back.

"Interesting haircut the grass has," Sheila had mentioned before he left her to her new home. He walked her to the spot where the cut part stopped and pointed. "This is right where I was when Brigham appeared." She overacted like it was a shrine.

Well, tomorrow was his day off, the only one he'd get this week with Milt's labor shortage. The poor guy had to fill two spots as fast as he could. C.H. planned to go to Peter Prier and Sons in downtown Salt Lake to buy the violin. After that, maybe he'd take care of Sheila's lawn. Oh, and order cable for Dani—mustn't forget that.

She emerged from the bishop's office clutching a new recommend. They exchanged smiles as he went to the bishop and extended his hand. When they shook, his bones nearly cracked in the bishop's viselike grip. Not surprising from a machinist foreman.

"How are you doing, Brother Young?"

"Fine, thanks, Bishop Schmidt."

The bishop directed him to the chair on the other side of his desk. As the bishop sat, C.H. gazed at his desktop. The booklet of recommend forms sat open, several to a page. Dani's name was on the last one at the bottom of the page, and the first thing the Bishop did after sitting was flip over the page, exposing a new page of blank recommends.

"How's your job going?" asked Bishop Schmidt.

"Oh, it's fine." He was glad he hadn't left it yet so he didn't need to fib to the bishop.

"We don't see you much in church."

"It's my job. I have to work a lot of Sundays."

Bishop Schmidt nodded. "That's too bad."

C.H. wondered if he should have said anything about his job and Sundays. When he started coming to church regularly all of a sudden, how was he going to account for it?

"How's your family?"

Ugh! How should he answer that one? "They're great," he said with forced enthusiasm, ignoring his pricking conscience.

"Those boys giving you trouble?"

"No, they're little angels." That was an easy one.

Bishop Schmidt laughed his loud guffaw. "It's not nice to lie to the bishop!"

That made his heart jump before he realized it was a joke. "No, they really are. I love 'em to death."

"That's wonderful." He adjusted his glasses and grabbed his pen. "Well, shall we get started?"

"Okay."

As the bishop began reading the questions, C.H. focused on the man's gray temples, then on his shock of black hair on top, as thick as a twenty-year-old's. C.H. hoped his hair would weather aging that well.

Yes, he believed in God the Father, his Son Jesus Christ, and the Holy Ghost.

Yes, he had a testimony of the restored gospel.

Uh, yes, he sustained the president of the church as the prophet, seer, and revelator, the only person on earth authorized to exercise all priesthood keys. He had to think about that one for an instant. The president of the church had refused to accept a revelation from God and would be removed from office sometime in the future. But for now, he was still the president. It was God's job, not C.H.'s, to reject the man. As long as God kept him in place, he believed he could truthfully say he sustained him.

It suddenly occurred to him that one upcoming question was going to be *very* hard to answer.

Yes, he sustained the other church leaders. Yes, he lived the law of chastity. So far at least, the devil inside him quipped, which he immediately squelched. No, there wasn't anything in his conduct toward members of his family that was out of harmony with the teachings of the church. He actually sighed after answering that one.

"Do you affiliate with any group or individual whose teachings or practices are contrary to those accepted by the Church of Jesus Christ of Latter- day Saints, or do you sympathize with the precepts of any such group or individual?"

There it was. The first half was fine—he didn't affiliate with any apostate groups. But he was now required by God to sympathize with one of their precepts: polygamy. There was no getting around this question. If he said no, he would definitely be lying. If he said yes, he would definitely not get a temple recommend.

He could only sit and stare at the bishop. He didn't know what to do. He was under divine instruction to get a recommend, but he couldn't bring himself to lie to the bishop.

And the Spirit wasn't leading him anywhere on this one.

Bishop Schmidt's brow wrinkled a little as the pause stretched out. He stared at C.H. with piercing eyes. C.H. stared back, frozen.

At any cost, Brigham had said.

But he couldn't lie.

"Bishop," he said, not even sure what would come out of his mouth next. "I don't believe—"

A loud knock jolted both of them in their seats. The bishop scowled as he looked toward the door. "I've got the interview light on," he growled. "Why are they disturbing us?"

The knock came again, multiple poundings. "Bishop!" a voice called, muffled by the door.

Shaking his head, Bishop Schmidt strode to the door and opened it. One of the boys who'd been playing basketball stood there.

"Donny," the bishop said. "I'm interviewing. What's th—"

"I'm sorry, Bishop," the boy said, clearly agitated. "But Sean's been hurt bad. He's unconscious."

The bishop glanced at C.H. "You'd better excuse me a minute," he said, then rushed away with Donny.

C.H. stood and walked to the door. The doors to the cultural hall were open, and he could just see the feet of a boy lying on the floor of the basketball court, with all the other boys gathered around him. The bishop was out of sight. One of the boys was kneeling down and crying shamelessly. "I didn't mean it! I'm sorry, Sean!"

What in the world had happened? He couldn't remember the name of the crying boy. In fact, he couldn't remember most of the boys' names, even though their faces were familiar. He really needed to attend church more often. Well, soon he could.

He returned to his chair. As he was about to sit down, he looked at the blank recommend forms lying on the bishop's desk. Instantly a thought occurred to him, and instantly he balked at it.

C.H. needed a recommend, but he couldn't bring himself to lie to get one.

Sheila needed a recommend, but as far as the church was concerned, she wouldn't be eligible for at least a year.

Brigham said to get recommends for both of them at any cost and that he'd know what to do when the time came.

The time had come.

But if he wasn't willing to lie, was he willing to *steal*?

The forms lay brilliant-white in the fluorescent light of the bishop's office. A completely blank page of forms. C.H. knew that the forms were two-part and the second part remained with the booklet. Under normal circumstances when only some of the forms on the page would have been filled out, if C.H. tore out a whole page of forms, the bishop would notice at once that all the forms on the open page were blank.

Unless, of course, the bishop had just turned over a new page.

Fate couldn't have offered a more blatant invitation. The bishop was called out of the room, and the blank page sat before him practically begging to be re-moved. Sure, there were serial numbers on each form, but what chance was there that the bishop would check serial numbers from one page to the next? C.H. could leave with more than enough blank recommends for both him and Sheila. And he wouldn't have to lie to do it.

Just steal and forge signatures for the bishop and stake president.

Which crime was worse? Which was the lesser of "any cost"? He didn't have much time to decide.

It wasn't like he'd be taking anything of economic value: the cost of one page of forms would be negligible. What mattered was what they stood for. And right now for him, they stood for obeying the commandment of God. It would be like Nephi taking the brass plates from Laban because he was commanded to, and C.H. wouldn't have to kill anyone to do it.

Besides, lying to the bishop would not get a recommend for Sheila.

At any cost.

He ripped the page from the booklet, folded it along the perforated seams, and stuffed it into his suit coat pocket. Then he rushed out.

Dani stood at the door to the cultural hall, watching the emergency. She turned her head when he appeared and walked toward him.

"Sean's hurt pretty badly," she said. "I think he tripped and ran into the wall—"

"Dani, we've got to go."

"Why?"

"Donny," the bishop said from the cultural hall. "Call 9-1-1. I'm going to call Sean's parents and tell them what happened."

The bishop would use the phone in his office, no doubt. C.H. gripped Dani by the arm and pulled. "Please don't ask. I'll tell you later." They scurried down the hall, exited the building, and climbed into the SUV. He jabbed the key into the ignition, yanked the lever into reverse, and shot back, squealing the tires. He barely paused to look as he pulled into the street.

"What's going on, Cain?" Dani said, gripping the armrest.

"I did something," he said, feeling his heart rattle like a castanet. "Oh Dani, I really did something!"

"What?" She sounded frightened. And why not? He was terrified.

"I did something, and I don't know if it was right or wrong. I don't know what you're going to think of me. I hope you don't hate me."

"I'm going to hate you if you don't *tell me what you did!*"

"You remember the brass plates?" What an idiotic way to start! But he couldn't bring himself to blurt it out—not just yet.

"Huh?"

"Just think of the brass plates and Laban. And what Nephi did."

Dani took a deep breath. "Alright, I'm thinking. So tell me."

"I took some temple recommends."

"What do you mean?"

He fished the folded page out of his pocket and tossed it onto her lap. "I took some temple recommends."

Dani unfolded the page and stared in horror. "You *stole* temple recommends?"

He turned left at the street to their neighborhood with another squeal.

"How could you do this?" she said, waggling the page near his face. "What were you thinking?"

"I didn't know what else to do." His decision seemed pretty stupid now. "I was supposed to get recommends for me and Sheila. At any cost, Brigham said. He said I'd know what to do when the time came."

Dani stared at the page, her face wrinkled with perplexity. "Brigham told you to steal blank recommends?"

"He told me to do whatever I had to do to get them!" He immediately felt bad for shouting. And his own excuses weren't working, even on him.

"You've got to take these back. *Now!*" She tossed the page onto his lap.

The car barreled into their driveway, and he had to hit the brakes hard to stop. "Don't you remember about Laban and the brass plates?"

"What the crap is this Laban thing you keep talking about? What does that have to do with *this?*" She grabbed the page and held it in front of him.

He peered at her as he tried to catch his breath. She stared back with a dark expression. A lock of her strawberry-blonde hair hung down over her forehead.

"God commanded Nephi to get the brass plates," he said, trying to keep his voice calm. "He killed Laban and stole them to obey that commandment. I was commanded to get recommends for me and Sheila. Brigham said at any cost. I obeyed."

He glared at her. As his heart calmed down and his excitement ebbed, he started feeling anger—anger that she wouldn't accept what he said, that he'd been forced into this impossible decision in the first place. Anger that he felt stupid afterward.

"Isn't the bishop going to wonder why you suddenly left in the middle of an interview?"

That thought had already lurked in the back of his mind. "The last thing he asked me was if I sympathized with any teachings of apostate groups. I didn't know what to answer, and he noticed my hesitation. That's when Sean got hurt. The bishop will probably assume I didn't want to stick around to answer that question."

"Then he'll assume you *do* sympathize with teachings of apostate groups."

"Well, don't I?" he said, more belligerently than he intended. "Anyway, that's better than knowing I—" He held up the recommends.

Tears trickled from her eyes. "Are you sure this is right?"

"No," he said, and it almost came out as a childish whine. "I'm not sure." His anger evaporated as he recognized how unfair he'd been, directing it toward her. It was her tears that did it, the power of a woman's tears. "But I did fulfill the commandment that Brother Br—*God* gave me."

And I'm sick of worrying about whether I did it right, he didn't add.

Taking her hand and squeezing it, he decided he wanted to voice that thought after all. "I'm tired of feeling guilty about things I have to do. None of this is normal, and I can't tell what's right or wrong anymore. I'm just going to do what I'm told to do. I'll let God sort it all out."

She sat with tear streaks and a deep frown on her face, shoulders slumping. "Okay," she whispered. She wiped at her eyes and opened the door. "We'd better go in so Cyndy can get home." She left without waiting for a response.

He sat in the van, holding the page of recommends in his hands where Dani had dropped them. He was too drained to feel anything. Soon he'd have to fill out two of those forms. Name, ward, stake—and two signatures that would have to look different from each other, even though he would sign them both. There was no way he was going to ask a second person to forge a signature for him.

He wondered what happened with Sean. Did God really arrange to hurt a boy so C.H. could steal some recommends? Or would the injury have happened anyway, and God just took advantage of the unfortunate accident?

The door to the house opened, and Cyndy came out. He decided to let her walk home by herself. Normally he thought the crush she had on him was cute, but not tonight. Tonight he wasn't up to dealing with anybody.

Cyndy tapped on the window and waved. He forced a smile and opened it.

"I just wanted to say goodnight," she said.

It would be cruel to brush her off, no matter how he felt. "How were the boys?"

"Little angels." She always said that.

"And how are you doing?"

"Fine." She glanced deeper into the car. "So how come you're still sitting here?"

"Oh, I was just thinking." He wanted to say something to make her leave, but how could he do it without hurting her feelings?

"Thinking about what?"

He swore she was actually gazing dreamily at him. He'd never been sure if her crush was a harmless thing that would ride its course or if he should do something about it. Every sitcom on earth had done an episode about childish crushes on adults. They always ended with the child being disillusioned about the crush but understanding the wisdom of moving on. Yeah, right.

What harm did a crush do? So the girl would dream about a man she thought she was in love with. It wasn't like she actually expected anything to come of it, not in real life. She'd probably be terrified if it did. So why not let her enjoy the fantasy until she grew out of it, and nobody had to get hurt.

"I was thinking about how nice it is that you babysit for us," he answered.

She grinned. "No, you weren't."

He smiled back. "Maybe not, but it's still true."

"I like to do it. Petey and Glenn are so adorable."

He couldn't argue with that. "Well, I guess I'd better go in now."

"And I guess I'd better go home." She stepped back so he could open the door.

He climbed out, and they both stood looking at each other. Cyndy was cute in a puppyish way, like so many teenaged girls were. Mousy brown hair and large brown eyes. Full lips. He wondered what kissing full lips would feel like, compared to Dani's thin lips.

Cyndy had on shorts and a sleeveless top that exposed her bellybutton. She often dressed like that—in a way that couldn't help but catch a male's eye for an instant, even one older and married and hopelessly in love with his wife. He didn't think she did it on purpose. She was probably unaware of the effect she could have on males. A girl who would babysit at the drop of a hat probably didn't have much of a social life, so her experience with boys was probably limited. He hoped the way she dressed and her obvious passion for babies wouldn't get her into trouble one day.

Suddenly her eyes flicked down his body and then back up. It was an act he'd seen many boys do to attractive girls, but surely Cyndy couldn't mean the same thing by it. Still, it gave him an exhilarated feeling.

And that gave him a sudden blast of angst. Where did that exhilarated feeling come from?

She said goodbye, and they parted. As he walked in, he thought, *Dear Lord, what is your command to practice polygamy doing to me?*

Inside, Petey ran to him with arms outstretched. C.H. grabbed him and swung him up, smothering his face with kisses. Petey giggled. Adorable! He completely understood Cyndy's love for babysitting them.

I wonder what my kids with Sheila will be like, he thought.

He pictured Sheila in her apartment behind them at this very moment. She'd be unpacking her things right now. He made sure she was stocked up with enough food and other supplies to get her through the night, until they could do some serious shopping tomorrow during his day off. In a moment of pure stupidity, he offered to let her sleep on their sofa until she could buy a bed tomorrow, but she politely declined, and only then did he realize how awkward that would have been.

She would sleep on her floor tonight with all the blankets the Youngs could spare for cushioning. "Don't worry," she said. "I've done it before."

When the moving was finished, they parted with a kiss, but not too passionate—it was still too strange having both women living under the same roof. He wondered if he'd ever get used to doing his husbandly duty with one wife while the other was one wall away.

But with Petey in his arms, and thinking about having children with Sheila, he worked up a touch of desire to do his husbandly duty with her right now. With that feeling pulsing warmly through his veins, he was convinced that, when the time came, he'd manage somehow.

Dani was on the sofa nursing and watching TV. When he wandered over with Petey, she smiled up at him, and even managed to put a little warmth and affection into it. It made him feel good—even better than usual, considering the recent tension about the recommends.

He wondered how long it would take before Bishop Schmidt stopped by to ask him what apostate teaching he sympathized with.

Chapter 10

Special Agent Robinson stood and reached for his suitcoat. It was time to bring in the Youngs for questioning. It seemed clear there was nothing directly drug-related in anything they did. They just spent the money a little at a time.

A very little—except for the car purchase, their restraint was remarkable, and even the RAV4 was not exactly ostentatious. Many people would have blown the whole wad by now. Robinson finally had to admit to himself that the couple probably had nothing to do with any drug organization. They just found a huge sum of cash somewhere and decided to spend it instead of turning it in, a crime well below the interests of his current focus. Probably a courier had been killed and the money was lost.

Still, they were a lead. Maybe the DEA could piece something together by how the couple found the money.

But as Robinson slid on his coat, an agent popped through the door of his office. "Something new came up in the Young case." She handed him a report.

He scanned through it—a surveillance report about the couple, Cory and Danielle Young. Out of the blue, Cory Young had picked up a woman and moved her into the apartment behind his own. This was the same woman, Sheila Matthews, who he rushed over to visit the other night. The same woman who'd shacked up with Steven Coulter, their current person of interest. Now all of a sudden, a man who was spending drug money moved the girlfriend of a drug pusher into his own duplex. The agent tailing Young even saw them kissing.

What an interesting development! Obviously he guessed wrong—there was more going on here than an innocent couple finding some money. The Youngs wouldn't be brought in for questioning today. Instead, surveillance would continue. He wanted to see what would happen next.

C.H. stood before the mural that filled the side of the building, showing luthiers crafting away at violins in an Old World setting. He remembered being fascinated by it as a child, his first memory of being interested in violins. Since then, he always felt fond of Peter Prier and Sons in downtown Salt Lake City. They ran a violin shop and a violin-making school in the building. He'd purchased his first violin there, and now that he was ready to purchase his second, he hadn't even considered going anywhere else.

For a while in his youth, he toyed with the idea of attending the Violin Making School of America, as the Peter Prier school was called, until he learned the difference between an artist and a craftsman and came to realize he was *not* a craftsman. Most craftsmen didn't have ten thumbs when it came to woodworking. But C.H. found out that his ten thumbs holding a bow and fingering violin strings produced beautiful music.

He never felt the motivation to aspire to Carnegie Hall virtuosity. The relentlessly focused life necessary to accomplish that seemed too much of an excess to be worth it. But he could become good enough to play in a prominent orchestra and perhaps aspire to a solo now and then. And he could compose.

But all that had fallen by the wayside when he got married—even the composing, which he could have squeezed in at odd times here and there. He loved Dani and didn't regret marrying her for one minute. However, like so many other young people—especially BYU students—they had no clue what they were getting themselves into. He sold his violin to afford a place to stay, thinking he would buy another one before long. But that time never came.

Only by the grace of God was he walking through the door of Peter Prier and Sons now as a customer ready to purchase. Without God's command and gift of money, he had no idea when, or even if, he would ever hold a violin again.

Standing just inside the door, he drew in a slow, deep breath, his eyes closed. The earthy smell of fine woods and the crisp aroma of varnish filled his nostrils. He could make this visit with a clear conscience because he already ordered the cable TV for Dani and gone shopping with Sheila to get all her necessities.

He crept toward the first violin he could see and ran his fingers along its side. The hourglass curve felt as exquisite as Dani's naked waist. He plucked a string, and the staccato note sent a chill down his back.

The salesperson offered his assistance. C.H. asked to see orchestral violins, new, with a bright tone. He hefted several of them, searching for the right size and weight. Those that felt right he placed under his chin and tested the width of the neck in his hand. He gripped the bow and tried a couple of experimental draws across the strings, trying out their lengths. He narrowed down his choices to two violins. Then the real test began.

With a slightly trembling hand, he positioned the first violin under his chin and lifted the bow above the strings. He hadn't played in more than two years. He knew the first note would sound awful in his ears, and he felt terribly self-conscious with another person standing next to him for this first time—a man who must surely know what superb violin playing sounded like. But he needed to play it now. There was no other way he could be sure it was the right instrument for him.

"It's been a while," C.H. said. The salesclerk nodded with an understanding smile.

He took only an instant to decide what to play. Such a momentous occasion in his life deserved nothing less than Beethoven's violin concerto—the same piece he slaved over and perfected while at BYU. The same piece he still imagined himself playing every now and then, sometimes fingering an imaginary violin and drawing an imaginary bow like lesser artistic souls pantomimed playing an air guitar. Profound and magnificent, but simple in its first notes, that concerto seemed like the perfect piece to break his long fast from playing.

He dove in forcefully with the bow. The first note came out slightly sharp, and each note was far from confident.

The salesman smiled faintly. As C.H. finished the first phrase of the opening theme, the man said "Boom boom boom boom boo-oo-oom" in a low, rumbling voice—the timpani that were supposed to come in at that point. C.H. grinned and started on the second phrase. As that one finished, the salesperson lifted his hands like a conductor and blurted out the strings part: "Pa pa pa pa *paaaaaaaaaa!*"

C.H. joined the second phrase of *pa*'s with the violin, using his one instrument to stand in for the entire string section. Together they continued performing the first movement of the concerto, the salesman conducting with wild, caricatured movements and both of them filling in the brass, wind, and percussion sections with their voices as C.H. played solos and entire string sections on his violin. For it was *his* violin now. He wouldn't even consider the other. This one felt wonderful and sounded delightful, and the other could not match this instrument for the instant nostalgia it had acquired with this experience.

Eventually they both lost track of where they were in the score, and they laughed together as their performance fizzled out. "I'll take this one," C.H. said.

The salesman raised his eyebrows as C.H. peeled off hundred after hundred in cash, but he took the payment without comment. C.H. left the shop reluctantly, pausing before the windows of the violin-making school to watch the fledgling luthiers hard at work. He felt good about how confident his playing had become the further into the music he'd gone. It began to sound almost as good as he remembered playing before.

But he still had long hours of practice ahead to put a professional edge on his performance. The average person might call his playing good right now, but any professional musician would detect the deterioration of his skills. However, that was fine with him. Long hours of practice would be no chore at all. It would be heaven.

While C.H. was off buying a violin, Dani piled the boys into the SUV and headed for the Salt Lake City library. They had plenty of money to buy books, yet Dani still thought of the library first.

With a flourish, C.H. had ordered cable TV for her that morning, but right now Dani needed a different kind of history than she could get on the History Channel. She knew it was going to be tough finding books with two babies, especially with one of them toddling around getting into things, but Cyndy was still at school and Sister Vandermeer wasn't home.

As she parked in the underground lot beneath the library, she decided to forego the stroller. It was too much bother muscling it out of the back of the car, unfolding it, and strapping Glenn in. How hard could this be? Go in, grab a couple of books, check them out, and leave. She should manage okay—she was a pro at handling her two boys by now.

Inside, Dani pecked quickly at the computer terminal, trying to do this as fast as possible. She typed P-O-L-Y-G-A-M-Y into the search field and pressed enter. A long list of titles popped up, with several additional pages of titles available. Dani memorized the most common Dewey decimal code among the listed books and went to the information desk to ask what level that number was located on.

When she found the correct shelves, she scanned the books and pulled out the ones that sounded remotely applicable. Sitting on the floor and struggling to keep a whiny Petey from wandering too far afield or pulling more books off the shelves, she thumbed through each book and created two piles, one for books that looked like what she wanted and one for rejects.

Petey was becoming impossible, and Glenn was starting to fuss loudly. She wished she could just pull open her blouse and nurse Glenn on the spot, but in a library full of kids that would be scandalous. She considered the bathroom but dreaded Petey's echoing cry as he was forced to wait in a cramped space with nothing to do. Why couldn't America let mothers be mothers, even in public? There was nothing sexual about breastfeeding.

When she picked out four books, she lifted Glenn onto her shoulder and rocked him with her arm around his bottom, trying to quiet him, and then she slid the four books into that same hand, barely able to grip them all at once. With her other hand she grabbed Petey, who had managed to slide two books from a shelf to the floor. Dani sighed in exasperation and reluctantly left them. The library staff would just have to earn their pay today.

Down the elevator and halfway to the checkout desk, as Petey tugged at her hand trying to get away to explore some unknown attraction, the books slipped out of her hand and tumbled to the floor, one hitting flat and making a loud *whack*. A couple of readers at a nearby table jumped and looked at her. She bit her lower lip to keep it from trembling. How was she going to pick up the books while holding Glenn and hanging onto Petey? If she let go of her toddler, he'd be off in a flash.

When a teenaged girl came up to her, Dani stepped back in shock. The girl's ears were peppered with rings, her hair was colored a bright and unnatural orange, and her sleeveless shirt was too short to cover her tummy, showing off her pierced bellybutton and allowing the chain from that ring to reach to the belt loop on her pants. The rings through her eyebrows and one of her nostrils disgusted Dani, and her bare shoulder displayed a tattoo of a dragon. Her jeans looked like she'd walked through a minefield with them. She gnawed away at a piece of gum, making smacking noises as she chewed with her mouth open.

"Here, let me get those." The girl crouched down and grabbed the books.

"No, that's okay," Dani said, but the girl had already stood back up.

"I'll carry them for you."

The girl headed for the checkout desk without waiting for a reply. Dani followed with Petey whining as he struggled to get away. The girl placed the books on the counter and then said, "What a cute little boy you have!" as she crouched down to Petey's level. "What's your name, little fella?"

"He's Petey," Dani said, feeling anxiety creep up and down her skin.

"Hey, Petey! Look at this." The girl lifted him up and carried him a few steps to a Muppet poster on the wall. "Cookie monster!"

Dani realized the girl was occupying Petey so she could dig in her purse for her library card and check out the books. She blinked back a tear. The girl was only trying to help.

"Cookie mahster," Petey said as he pointed at the poster.

"You want your mommy back?" the girl said when Dani finished.

"Mommy."

She put Petey back down, and he ran to Dani and took her hand.

Grabbing the books, the girl asked, "Did you drive or walk?"

"Drove. I parked below."

The girl carried the books as Dani led her out the door into the indoor mall of tiny shops and to the elevator that took them to parking level 2. She helped Dani strap the boys into the car and leaned over and waved. "Bye, Petey!"

"Bye-bye," Petey said, waving back with an open-and-closed hand movement.

"Thank you so much," Dani said.

The girl smiled and disappeared into the elevator.

At home, Dani started nursing Glenn while Petey watched a video. Lifting one of the books, she began reading. If she was going to live this polygamy thing, she was going to learn all she could about it. She was going to find out how women dealt with it in nineteenth-century Nauvoo and Utah.

But she couldn't concentrate on her reading. She kept thinking about the teenaged girl with rebellion written all over her. Pierced body parts everywhere, tattoo, raunchy clothing, grotesque hair. Dani had actually been frightened of her, especially when she showed an interest in Petey.

Instead of reading about polygamy, all Dani could think about was the parable of the Good Samaritan.

Before C.H. returned home to Dani, Sheila shared a pleasant meal with him from her new supply of groceries. All he could talk about was his new violin, but he said he wouldn't play it for her until he'd played for Dani first. It was only fair, he said, and Sheila agreed, though she wasn't too happy about it. At least Dani had heard him play before. Sheila never had.

After he left, she stripped off all her clothes and climbed into bed nude, the way she always slept. She decided to spend the evening in bed reading the new book she bought that day just because she felt like indulging herself.

Three chapters into the book, the music started. A sweet, penetrating melody she didn't recognize, caressed from the strings of a violin. The melody was quiet and longing, filled with promises and tender passion. It was a melody a man would play for a woman, and Sheila knew he was playing it for *her*, that other woman in his life, the one who'd been there first.

She lifted away the bedclothes and slid over to lean her back against the wall while she hugged her bent legs. The wall was cold against her bare skin. She could feel the faint vibrations of the lower notes.

As she became familiar with the repeating theme of the melody, she began to hum along. She pictured him playing it for her, sitting next to her on the bed. Because Sheila was nude, she pictured him nude as well. His eyes gazed at her as he played, full of affection for her. After a few moments he set the violin down and crept to her and embraced her. Somehow the music kept playing anyway. He kissed her gently, pressing his body against hers.

"Do you love me?" she murmured against his lips.

"Yes, I love you," he replied.

"More than her?"

He pulled away with a pained look on his face, a guilty look. With difficulty he forced out his answer in an intense whisper.

"God help me, I do."

She flung herself forward and squeezed him tightly. They kissed deeply and caressed each other passionately.

Suddenly the music stopped, tearing Sheila away from her fantasy. Arousal swam in her, so she jumped up and went into the bathroom, splashed some cold water on her face, and cursed. Any other time she'd take care of her own passion, but she was trying to be *good* now, though she couldn't understand what harm it caused.

After toweling off, she stared at herself in the mirror. Her face was ugly with a scowl. She compared her dark-red hair to Dani's blondeness. The scowl deepened.

She wondered if he'd ever play like that for her.

She fingered the holes in one ear where earrings used to be. The holes would start closing up before long. She didn't really want that to happen. Maybe she should wear the earrings again.

Would C.H. be disappointed? She knew he would.

She returned to the bedroom and walked over to the jewelry box lying on the new dresser, pausing for a moment before she opened it. The earrings glittered faintly in the subdued light of the reading lamp near her bed. It still felt strange not to see a bag of white powder there.

She ran her hand across the surface of the dresser. She realized that her new furniture must look nicer than the stuff in the Youngs' apartment, which C.H. said was all thrift-shop garbage from DI. It made her feel guilty for harboring jealous feelings toward Dani. It wasn't Dani's fault she got to him before Sheila. And he was doing an amazing job trying to be fair and considerate to both his women. He might have played his new violin for Dani first, but he bought Sheila new furniture before he bought any for Dani

She slammed the lid closed, leaving the earrings inside, and crawled back in bed and opened her book. She read several paragraphs over and over without understanding them, then she gave up and let the book drop to the floor as she settled into prone position.

The music started again, this time a livelier tune. Sheila closed her eyes. A tear streaked down the side of her face and tickled her neck. As she fell asleep, she wished the bag of powder was still in the jewelry box instead of those damned earrings.

Sheila woke up in a sweat over some disturbing dream. But the dream's images fled quickly from her mind, and she couldn't remember what it was about.

She dragged herself out of bed and shivered as the crisp air hit her moist skin. The floor was cold against her bare feet. When she heard the heater start blowing, she moved to the floor vent and crouched over it, letting the soothing, heated blast hit her buttocks and glide up the front and back of her torso. Shivering away her chill, she thought, *Being naked feels great.*

Would Brother Brigham make them get married in the temple? Would she have to start wearing garments? She shivered again, and not because of a chill.

The call of nature began to press, so she went into the bathroom and relieved herself. Then she stretched out on her new sofa and flipped on the television he'd bought her that day. Infomercial after infomercial.

She wished she had cable so she could watch some of the racy shit on Cinemax, then remembered she'd repented of pornography. She sighed.

The heater had no concept of nuance, and the room reached the overheated stage. She stood and walked to the front door. What time was it? A little past two o'clock, a glance at her new clock-on-the-wall told her. Everything in the apartment was new—and tacky. At least Steven had some taste in furnishings. C.H. went for inexpensive and functional, trying to be responsible with God's money.

Two a.m. was plenty late for everyone in the neighborhood to be asleep. She opened the door and took one step out. The air hit her nude body with a cool blast, but not too cool, and it felt good after the excess heat in the room. Off to the east she could see a pile of clouds above the mountains, slowly creeping into the valley. A haze below them warned of some precipitation. The cold front she heard about on the news that would end the Indian summer.

Sheila took one more step, gazing around for signs of life in any of the surrounding homes. Everything was dark and peaceful.

She took one more step. Her tender sole hit a small rock. "Ouch!" she cried in a whisper. She went back inside and slipped on some sandals, then stepped out again. The brief immersion in the heat made the cool night feel good again. This felt much too good to resist. And her time was limited. Rain—maybe snow— was heading in from the mountains.

With her senses in a hyper-alert state, she crept down her short sidewalk and onto her driveway. Some of the grass still stood tall—C.H. promised to finish mowing it, but hadn't gotten around to it yet. Too busy buying tacky furniture for her.

She heard no sounds but crickets and the breeze. The wind fluttered all over her body—the sensation was exquisite. Taking a deep breath, she strode down the driveway, keeping out a sharp eye in all directions. There shouldn't be any traffic in this backwater of a neighborhood so late at night, and all the houses were still and dark.

All except Moroni's, she noticed when she passed the edge of the duplex. One window shone with strips of warm light through some closed blinds. She chuckled. Maybe the angel Moroni was visiting Moroni.

Her blood vessels pumped with adrenalin as she ventured nude out into the street. She could feel the slightest variations in wind temperature all over her body. She remembered seeing a park half a block away. She wondered what it would feel like to swing nude. Did she dare?

On an impulse, she broke into a run. Her sandals flapped more noisily than she liked on the street, but she was already committed. It was better to keep heading for the park than turn around and go back. If someone noticed her now, she didn't want them to see her going into the duplex.

She ran into the covered picnic area and crouched behind a table. She looked around to determine if anybody had seen her. What would all these good Mormon families think if they knew she was running around naked in their neighborhood?

What would C.H. think?

She knew what he would think. But what was so wrong about this? It just felt good. She wasn't trying to flaunt herself in front of anyone. She wasn't trying to be sexual. Sensual—that's what it was. Experiencing the night with *all* her sense of touch, not just her face and arms. It was innocent, like a young child, like Adam and Eve in the garden. If C.H. didn't get it, that was his problem.

Since there was still no sign of life, she ventured out from behind the picnic table and headed for the swings. The night was a bit chilly, but her run had raised her body heat. She checked the clouds—they looked ominous and closer than before. She probably had only minutes before that damn cold front hit.

She climbed up on a swing in a standing position and pulled and tugged until she got herself swaying back and forth. The sensation was exhilarating! All the sensual feelings she was getting, the thrill of flaunting the social mores, the flow of adrenalin at taking such a risk—she'd never gotten such a buzz outside of taking drugs.

Sheila swung and swung, going higher and higher. The air blasted all over her, and she started shivering from cold. But she wasn't ready to give up her night of freedom. She slowed the swing down and leaped from it, breaking into a run as soon as she hit the ground. She ran the length of the park, right up to the curb of 300 East.

Car headlights were only half a block away and coming closer. She ducked behind the small restroom building. The car honked and its passengers hooted and waved as they hung out the windows, but they passed by. Sheila laughed.

With the car gone, she ran the length of the park again. She got plenty warm, even forming a thin layer of sweat on her skin. She sat on a swing once more but didn't swing. The wind was stronger now and chilling, especially with her perspiration. A cold drop hit her arm and then her face. She looked up and found the clouds on top of her.

Drops started hitting her all over. Time to go! She hopped off and jogged back home. Moroni's light was still on, but there was no sign of activity—there or anywhere. The rain peppered her skin with icy needles. It was uncomfortable and thrilling at the same time.

She paused at the edge of her driveway and looked around the neighborhood. There was no indication that anyone was the wiser. She was almost disappointed.

Reluctantly, she ran inside. Without the cold and rain, she might have stayed out until the first hint of dawn. It wasn't like she had to go to work in the morning or anything.

She grabbed a blanket and turned on the TV. The heater was on the cold end of its bipolar cycle, so she sat in her new chair and wrapped the blanket around herself. The TV still didn't offer many choices, but at least the stupid thing came with a remote so she could keep switching from channel to channel.

Before long, the heater blasted away and the room became too warm. She opened up the blanket and exposed her body to the air. It felt nice, and she fell asleep that way on the chair.

Chapter 11

As C.H. walked into the bookstore, Milt was on his knees near the entrance setting up a floor dump of paperback books to be displayed. C.H. had the late shift until closing, so the store had already been open several hours.

Milt looked up. "Good news!"

"What?"

"I've hired a couple of new people." He stood and gestured toward the cash registers. "That's Olive over there. She'll be the new lead cashier."

C.H. almost caught his breath at the sight of Olive. Her name was all wrong for her—she was anything but olive in color. Her hair was golden blonde, long, and pulled back in a pony tail. Her skin was so fair that it looked almost translucent. Her eyes radiated with blue irises. If C.H. hadn't known Milt better, he'd swear the man had chosen Olive for her looks alone.

She was already working solo at the register, checking out a customer. She seemed to exude the same confidence as an employee who had worked there for years.

"She's pretty bright," Milt said, and it took an instant for C.H. to realize he meant her intelligence, not her radiant appearance. "She catches on fast. And she has experience working at a bookstore in Denver."

"Who's the other new employee?" C.H. asked, forcing his eyes off Olive.

"John. I've got him in back packing up returns right now. College kid looking for part-time work." Milt adjusted the floor dump display just so. "Come on, I'll introduce you to Olive."

They stood behind the counter for a moment as Olive finished up with her customer. "Olive, this is C.H. He'll be training you in your management duties."

"You're the one who's leaving," Olive said as she extended her hand.

C.H. shook it. "Yes, end of next week."

"Maria will become assistant manager after you leave," Milt said, "and Olive will take her place as lead cashier."

"I'm looking forward to working with you, even if it's only a short time." When Olive smiled at C.H., her radiance increased even more. He stifled a regret that he was leaving.

"If you train her well for the next couple of days," Milt said, "I'll let you have Saturday off, and she can cover for you."

C.H. nodded. "Thanks. That'll be nice."

"Now come back and I'll introduce you to John."

As they walked toward the back room, he wasn't so sure it *was* nice that he would have Saturday off when Olive would be there. He couldn't believe how he felt right then. She set his heart pumping like any silly crush he'd had in high school. He was just a sucker for blondes.

Was there any possibility she could be wife number three?

Suddenly C.H. realized what he was doing. Lusting after a woman—at first glance even—and he was married! He couldn't ever remember doing that before, not since marrying Dani. He'd seen attractive women and admired them, even found himself thinking unsavory thoughts about them, which he immediately drove out of his mind. But he never dreamed of courting and marrying one, all within minutes of meeting her. He hadn't even married his first polygamous wife yet, and already he was dreaming about pursuing another. How easily his mind had adjusted to the new reality!

What really shook him was the fact that he had no idea if this was a good thing or a bad thing. A married man lusting after a woman who wasn't his wife—that was always a bad thing. It was committing adultery in his heart, and adultery was the last thing he wanted to do to Dani.

But when he was allowed, by decree of God, to marry other women, then it wasn't adultery anymore—was it? He wasn't imagining having illicit sex with her. He was dreaming of *marrying* her, and that was something entirely different, something he was allowed to do these days. Surely God wouldn't pick out every one of his polygamous wives, would he? Surely he'd be allowed to choose one or two for himself, wouldn't he?

It still felt bad. Marrying the first plural wife was hard enough on Dani—and himself. He shouldn't already be planning the next one. To start daydreaming about every attractive woman he came across—even one as striking as Olive—was no more virtuous as a polygamist husband than as a monogamist. Celestial marriage wasn't a license to bed anyone who came along. This was marriage—serious business! He should take each courtship slowly and carefully. Everyone involved would have to make tremendous adjustments.

Now he felt glad he wouldn't be here Saturday with Olive. He was relieved they'd be working together only a short time. He had enough on his hands trying to love Dani and Sheila at the same time.

A knock sounded on Sheila's door.

Who the hell could that be? It was too early for C.H. to be back from work.

She'd slept past noon in the chair and had been awake for only half an hour. She hadn't even put on a stitch of clothing yet. As she slid into a T-shirt and pair of jeans, skipping underwear in the interest of time, she wondered if it might be Dani. The two women hadn't seen each other since Sheila moved in, and she was dreading the moment when they'd meet.

She opened the door and raised her eyebrows when she saw Moroni standing there. He was a pleasant sight. His blond hair hung long but not long enough to touch his shoulders. He was tall and would have been lanky if it weren't for his toned muscles. He was dressed in faded jeans with frayed edges, a tight tank top, and some kind of running shoes. His eyes were brown and piercing—they were piercing her right now. Sheila shuddered slightly.

"How are you today?" he said, presenting a pink rose from behind his back.

She smiled with a mixture of amusement and gratification. She couldn't remember the last time a man had given her a flower, even though she figured it was a spur-of-the-moment whimsy as he passed a nearby bush. Not even C.H. had given her one yet.

"I don't think we've been formally introduced," he said. "My name is Moroni Samuelsen. I live across the street from you."

"Yes, I know." Taking the rose, she noticed a slight trembling in his hand. How cute! He was nervous. "Thank you, Moroni. My name is Sheila Matthews." She felt a touch of pity for him, having to go through life with such a silly name.

"Sheila. Nice name." He grinned warmly.

Especially compared to yours, she thought. "I guess I'd better put this in water."

There wasn't a vase to be found in her apartment, so she grabbed her tallest glass and filled it with tap water. With a steak knife she cut the stem at an angle and dropped the rose into the glass and set it on her kitchen table. "Great centerpiece for my dining room," she quipped.

Moroni had let himself in and was standing in the kitchen doorway, the frame clearing the top of his head by only inches. "Looks nice," he said.

"Do you want something to drink? I haven't got much right now, but—"

"Whatever you've got."

"I don't have anything alcoholic," she said as she opened the refrigerator. "But with a name like Moroni, I guess you're Mormon anyway."

A faint smirk crossed his face. "My parents are. My dad was stake president. But all I ever got to was deacon—I think."

Holding two cans of Dr. Pepper, Sheila peered at him. He'd become inactive at only twelve or thirteen years old. Hell, that was even younger than her. She felt a desire to hear his story.

"You don't need to dirty up any glasses for me," Moroni said when she opened the cupboard. "Out of the can is good enough."

His piercing gaze seemed to throw out a constant challenge, so she gazed back at him unflinchingly. "Should we sit in the living room?"

Her living room was furnished with a sofa and two easy chairs—cheap and tacky, but pleasant enough to sit in. He sat off-center on the sofa, an obvious body-language invitation for her to sit next to him. She sat in the nearest easy chair.

Where were you two days before C.H. showed up at my door, Moroni? I'd have been interested then.

She studied him as they both popped open their cans and took the first drink, sizzling with carbonation. Moroni was attractive, no question about that. Taller than C.H., *much* blonder, more amusement at the world in his expression. She had yet to see C.H.'s nude torso, but she suspected that Moroni beat him in that category too, with his hint of washboard abs. At least C.H. hadn't developed a stomach bulge yet.

Given an even choice, she'd have chosen Moroni.

But it wasn't an even choice. She knew C.H. She knew what kind of character he had, what kind of husband he was to his wife. About Moroni, she didn't know jack sh— uh, anything. Except that he thought of a flower when he wanted to come on to a girl.

She carefully let a silent belch escape her mouth, then said, "Why Moroni?"

"Huh?"

"Why do you go by Moroni, if you're not active in the church? Why not use your middle name?"

He laughed. "You mean Frederick?"

"Fred's not so bad. Better than Moroni."

"I don't think so."

She pulled up her leg and tucked it under herself. "Well, how about Moe, then, or Ron? Bud, Mack—anything but Moroni."

He shrugged. "It's kind of my rebellion against society. A reprobate like me named after an angel."

She grinned. He was getting more and more fascinating with every word. "So you're a reprobate?"

"My parents think so."

"So what you really mean is your name's a rebellion against your *parents*."

He smiled and nodded. "You're pretty smart. Does that sound childish, rebelling against my parents?"

"If so, then I'm just as childish."

They both took a drink of their sodas.

"How are you related to C.H.?" he said.

Good question. She wasn't sure what to say. Why hadn't they thought of a cover story for her by now? C.H. wasn't very good at this sneaking around stuff. Neither was she for that matter. She hadn't worried about covering up things in her life. She wasn't ashamed of how she lived.

"Oh, we're some kind of cousins three or four times removed—I don't know. We've never bothered figuring it out."

As she said it, she realized it wasn't a very useful cover story. Moroni wanted to hit on her—that was obvious. Somehow she needed to convey to him that she wasn't available. She needed time to think, so she stalled by asking, "What do you do with yourself, Moroni?"

"I work in an auto shop at State Street and Thirty-Ninth South."

"Car mechanic, huh?" She glanced down at his hands. Yep, there were the flecks of oil stains. "And what do you do for fun?"

"I like to ski and camp and hunt—most anything outdoors."

Damn Bambi killer! But the rest sounded good.

"And you..." A strange look entered his eyes as he gazed at her, like he was springing a trap. "You like to do things outdoors too, right?"

She wondered why he would assume that.

"Like going to the park in the middle of the night and swinging," he added.

She gasped. "You saw me?"

He smiled with his lips slightly parted and nodded.

She could feel her face burning, and it irritated her that she was blushing in front of him. So that was why he dropped by. He saw her running around naked and figured she was an easy score. Her chest roiled with anger at his presumption—but she also felt a touch of excitement that he'd seen her.

"I'm sorry," he said with a twinkle in his eye that indicated he wasn't the least bit sorry. "I embarrassed you. I didn't mean to."

She scowled. "No, it's alright. You didn't embarrass me."

"I just thought it was refreshing to see a girl who wasn't afraid to do something daring." He crossed one leg over the other. "I hope you don't think I came over here for sex or anything like that. I just wanted to get to know the girl who would do that kind of thing."

Her scowl softened. Sure, it could be a ploy to put her off guard. But it also made it harder for him to actually have sex with her, since he'd taken a stand on the subject. Either he was sincere, or he thought so highly of himself that he figured she'd end up wanting sex with him anyway.

And if C.H. hadn't been in the picture, he would have been right.

"I haven't done anything like that before," she said. "It was just a spur of the moment thing."

"To do it at all says a lot about somebody."

Something in his voice made her feel more confident that he *was* sincere, that he really had been impressed with her boldness and not just her nakedness. She wondered if there was any chance C.H. would have reacted that way.

No way. He was a good Mormon boy. A girl prancing around the neighborhood naked? Even if it was in the middle of the night and dark, someone still might see her. Someone *did* see her.

So what? What was so wrong about just being naked? It wasn't like she and Moroni were having sex because of it. It wasn't like he intended to see her or she intended to let him. It was just an accident.

True, this accident never would have happened if she hadn't done such a daring thing. But she couldn't go through life never daring anything just because something might go wrong. No one would ever do anything that way.

Moroni was staring at her. "Well, I suppose I should take off," he said. "Just wanted to come by and say hello." He stood.

She realized her face had a grim expression. She relaxed it. "I'm sorry. I was just thinking about something. I didn't look like that because of you."

He smiled wide. "No problem. It was my fault anyway, shocking you like that. I hope you're not pissed at me. I really didn't come here expecting sex just because I saw you naked last night."

She nodded. Yes, he was either sincere or *real* good.

Before she could close the door behind him, he paused and turned. "But if you do it again, I'm not saying I won't watch again." He gave another charming grin. "And I hope you do it again."

She sucked in her breath, trying to ignore the sexual tension she felt. "You'll have to watch every night because I'm not making any appointments."

"Understood." He turned and walked away.

Nice butt, she thought.

Sheila closed the door and leaned her back against it. Suddenly she felt stupid. Why did she keep doing that? She should know better than to let some guy disarm her like that with just a silly rose as a friendship offering. So what if he was cute? That was the sort of idiocy that got her into so much trouble in the past. Moroni might look hotter than C.H., but C.H. was *good*. Wasn't it about time she treated herself to a man who would be good to her, instead of the next self-absorbed hunk who came down the road?

"Moroni, go to hell!" She marched into the kitchen and dumped the rose and the water in the garbage.

That night, Sheila fought off the urge to swing naked in the park again. *Too cold now,* she told herself.

All day while C.H. was at work, Dani immersed herself in history—as much as she could with two little boys. It wasn't quite like school, but it was closer than she'd been in years. Reading history again felt good, but it would have felt even better if she didn't have such an intensely personal reason to do it.

She read about Nauvoo, Illinois, in the 1840s, about Emma Smith, wife of the Mormon prophet Joseph Smith, living a harrowing life. Rumors of something called "celestial marriage" or "spiritual wifery" buzzed throughout the city. Joseph took many wives, the rumors said, by command of God. Secretly.

It was too much for Emma to handle. She oscillated between accepting Joseph's polygamy and denying that it existed. In the end, the denial won out. The church and its polygamy followed Brigham Young out west to Salt Lake Valley. Emma chose to stay behind rather than admit that her husband had married any woman except her.

Dani wept as she read. She wept for Emma because she understood how she felt, and she wept in shame because she'd been so critical in the past of Emma's decision to leave the church.

"Emma, I love you," she whispered at one point. "I love you for what you went through so you could be an example to me." Emma's broken heart had caused her to deny the revelation that Joseph had received. It had caused Joseph to obey God in secret, and it had caused her to sever herself and her family from the restored gospel of Jesus Christ after Joseph's murder. Emma had made the wrong choices for perfectly understandable reasons, and now Dani could learn how to do it right.

For all the breaking Dani's heart was doing, she would not deny the revelation C.H. had received. She would not force him to disobey God or to obey God in secret. She would certainly not turn her back on the church over it, nor would she lead her two boys away from the gospel.

She read on into the Utah period, when polygamy was publicly announced and practiced openly. The things she read weren't much comfort. Polygamy was an arduous lifestyle, especially for the women. Many marriages didn't succeed. She wondered how happy the ones that stayed together were.

When new wives were married, the first wife was there at the ceremony. Dani shuddered at the thought. She hadn't been aware of that fact. The last thing she wanted to do was be at C.H. and Sheila's wedding. She wondered if Brigham Young would insist on it. He'd better not! It was enough of a sacrifice that she let the marriage happen.

But the worst was yet to come. She read about how young many of these polygamous wives were when they married. She realized that societal norms were different back then—in the nineteenth century, they considered a young teenaged girl to be of marriageable age. Dani had no problem with a young boy marrying such a young girl. But in the polygamous society of Utah, it also meant that older men—already married several times over—would wed girls as young as fourteen. Try as she might, Dani couldn't bring herself to accept that—not even with her historian's perspective.

Now that she thought about it, she remembered that modern polygamous splinter groups were still doing that, right now in the twenty-first century. Older men were marrying barely pubescent girls. Dani couldn't think of that practice as anything but child abuse.

Would God expect C.H. to marry such a young girl?

The moment Dani thought it, she knew somehow that he *would* require it, even though it made no sense. Just because they did it in the nineteenth century didn't mean he should have to do it in the twenty-first. Just because fundamentalist Mormons did it didn't mean he had to do it. They were apostates, but C.H. was not. Surely God wouldn't demand that of him in this day and age.

Yet somehow, a terrible dread inside told her that he would receive that very command. It made her sick.

And she knew who that young girl would be. Cyndy, the sweet fourteen-year-old who had a crush on her husband. It was too obvious not to see it.

Would Cyndy be the third or the fourth wife? The fifth, the sixth—how many wives would C.H. end up with? Until Dani started reading, she'd been imagining him switching between her and Sheila. That was a big enough challenge, but Dani thought she could handle it, someway, somehow.

But how would she deal with things when C.H. was torn between half a dozen wives? What would she do when C.H. walked up to her and said, "God just commanded me to marry cute little Cyndy, our underage babysitter." Would he wear an expression of dread to match the feeling she had in her heart? Or would he be covering up anticipation, a trembling thrill at being allowed to live some repulsive male fantasy?

Dear Father in Heaven, Dani prayed as she lay curled up with her arms wrapped around her legs. *Please don't ask him to do that. You can't possibly ask him to do that. I couldn't handle it. He'd be arrested. The church would look as bad as all the splinter groups. You couldn't possibly require this.*

She felt no comforting answer from the Spirit, only a dreadful feeling in her bosom. She became all the more convinced that God would require it. But why? This wasn't some apostate splinter group using a feeble religious excuse to sexually molest children. This was the Church of Jesus Christ of Latter-day Saints.

There was no way God could demand this of him.

"Father, please," she called out desperately, eyes shut tight. "I couldn't let him do it. If you command him to, I—I'll *have* to rebel. I'm sorry, Father, but I can't help it."

Forging temple recommends and marrying Sheila didn't seem like such terrible things after all, compared to what she feared lay ahead.

C.H. got home from work at 9:20 in the evening. He found Dani curled up asleep on the sofa. Picking up a library book from the floor, he saw that it was about polygamy in Utah.

He set the book on the coffee table, nodding his head. Of course his historian wife would read up on polygamy, finding out as much as she could about it. His heart ached for her. While he was thinking about marrying Olive, Dani had been sitting home trying to deal with the whole thing. How did God ever decide he was worthy enough for this calling?

It couldn't just be because he was descended from Brigham Young. So were twenty zillion other people in Utah. Out of all of them, why should he be singled out? What was this obsession he felt all his life about a special mission, just because he hobnobbed with an imaginary friend called Brother Brigham? The only thing that gave it any credence at all was his patriarchal blessing.

Who knew the ways of God? There must be some quality in him that God wanted for this most unusual of callings. It didn't necessarily mean that C.H. was the most righteous of all Brigham's living descendants. It just meant he possessed some unique quality that fit this particular time and place.

He went looking for his sons and found them asleep in the bedroom. One of those rare, sweet moments for Dani when they both left her alone. He was about to close the door when he saw a familiar glow forming in the middle of the room. He stepped into the room before he shut the door.

Speak quietly, Brother Brigham, he thought. *Let the boys sleep so Dani can sleep.*

"Cory Horace," Brigham said when he had materialized. "The time has come."

"Time to marry."

"Yes. You will not be working this Saturday. That will be the day you marry Sheila."

He thought of his desire to spend the day working with Olive.

"Here's how you'll accomplish the marriage between you and Sheila," Brigham continued. "You'll submit your real names for temple work as if they were your deceased ancestors. Then you'll do the ordinance work for the names you submitted. To everyone else, it will look like you're doing the work for your ancestors, but you'll actually be doing the work for yourselves. Even though the officiator will think he's sealing a dead couple together, in the sight of God he'll be marrying you."

C.H. stared at the floor, which glowed faintly with Brigham's golden light. Yes, he could see how it was going to work, even though he felt uncomfortable doing it.

"You'll fill out your recommends with fictitious names. Since your actual names will be used in the ordinances, those fictitious names will be of no consequence."

One more lie on the temple recommends, in addition to the two forged signatures. C.H. was relating well to Nephi these days, who had been obliged to kill someone to obey the command of God. Clinging to that scriptural account was the only thing that kept him from feeling terrible about what he was doing.

"So I did the right thing?" he asked, sitting on the bed. "About getting those recommend forms?"

"You did what you had to do," Brother Brigham replied. "Remember how difficult it was for Joseph Smith to institute the practice of polygamy. You should expect no less difficulty yourself. There was no other way to get a recommend for both you and Sheila."

Brother Brigham's words comforted him a little, easing some of his guilt. He also felt comforted by the subtle change in Brigham's manner over time, less a prophet speaking in the name of God, more the grandfather he was. Having issued the commandment, Brother Brigham was now guiding him through the challenging process of obeying it. C.H. wondered if Brigham would ever become so informal as to sit on the bed next to him.

"I'll do everything you instruct," C.H. said.

"I have one more instruction," Brother Brigham said with a faint scowl. "Quit talking to me so formally, *grandson*."

He let a short laugh escape his lips. "Okay, *grandfather*."

Chapter 12

The next day was another late shift for C.H. He and Dani ate breakfast together as Petey sat in his highchair, playing with his food more than eating it.
Glenn lay asleep in the crib, his belly full of milk. C.H. needed to tell his wife
about Brigham's latest news, but he took his time figuring out how to broach the
subject.

"Brother Brigham appeared to me again last night," he finally said.

Dani looked up from wiping Petey's mouth. "What did he say?"

"Sheila and I will get married Saturday."

Dani gazed off at nothing. "Two days," she murmured.

Two days before she had to share her husband, he figured she meant. "I'll
spend as much time as I can with you for the next two days."

Dani nodded absently.

Was there more on her mind than that? "What are you thinking, sweetie?"

She looked at him again. Her face was calm—no, blank. A poker face.

"Oh, just taking it all in." She suddenly came to life and scooped a forkful of
eggs. "But before you start spending all this time with me, you should probably
go over and tell Sheila the news."

"That's true." He took his last bite and kissed Dani on the cheek. "I'll come
back and be with you for a while before I go to work."

When C.H. helped Sheila move, it was the first concrete act bringing their
marriage closer to reality. Today was the second. He was on his way to tell her
their marriage plans—to set the date. Saturday—two days away! Saturday night
would be their wedding night. And Sunday he'd go back to work in the morning.
Some honeymoon. At least it would be his last Sunday working at the bookstore.

He realized he never really proposed to her—not in any romantic way.
Women liked that kind of thing. Heck, *he* liked that kind of thing. He liked being
romantic. This was a perfect time to do it.

On his way around the duplex, he passed a rosebush with only pink roses on it. He'd have preferred red, but this would have to do on short notice. He picked three of them, cursing a thorn that pricked him. Three roses for the three words, "I love you." At least that's what everyone said at BYU.

He plucked off the thorns, broke the stems to even lengths, and adjusted the roses as a bouquet in his hand. Hiding them behind his back, he knocked on Sheila's door.

When she saw him, she smiled. "Good morning, my love," she said. She had on a T-shirt and jeans but was barefoot.

"Good morning." He swung the roses around and held them in front of her. "For you."

Her forehead wrinkled as she looked at them, and her smile disappeared. "Oh, you got me flowers." She smiled again. "Well, bring them in and let's put them in some water."

He followed her into the kitchen where he noticed a small stack of used dishes. She grabbed a glass from the counter and filled it with water. "Sorry I don't have a vase," she said. "But you already knew that, didn't you?"

He was about to place the roses in the glass, but Sheila said, "Here, let me take those." Using a steak knife already lying on the counter, she cut off the ends at an angle and plunked the roses into the water.

She kissed him and then took his hand and led him into the living room where they sat on the sofa together. "Aren't you supposed to go to work today?"

"Later." Wondering how to start, he realized he had no ring for her. Geez, some romantic! Why hadn't he thought of a ring for her yet? That was the first thing he thought of when he decided to propose to Dani. Was it just all the distractions lately, all the incredible things that had been happening?

Or was it, he thought with consternation, that he never quite thought of this marriage as real?

What should he do? Confess his thoughtlessness? Or preserve her feelings and—he was honest enough to admit to himself—his face? He could pretend like he planned all along to pick out the ring with her.

No, then he'd have to take more time away from Dani.

Saturday—they could pick out a ring on Saturday before the wedding. That was it! Nice and neat.

And deceptive.

She began to caress his arm, and then she leaned her head on his shoulder. "I can't wait until we're married. Then we don't have to stop at things like this."

"Sheila," he began, and a wave of jitters swept over him. He cleared his throat. "Sheila, I wanted to do this right." He got down before her on one knee and held both her hands. "Sheila, darling, will you marry me?"

Her eyes gleamed, but she smiled her half-smile. "This is so sudden!" she quipped as she flipped her hair back with her fingers.

C.H. shook his head as he laughed. "Will you marry me—this Saturday?"

That caught her off guard. She gazed at him for a moment. "This Saturday? It's time?"

"It's time. We'll be married in the temple this Saturday and have our wedding night." He took a breath. "We can pick out a ring for you together that morning."

But the ring part barely seemed to register. "This Saturday...in the temple." She looked at him with an intense expression. "What's it like in the temple? I mean, what happens?"

"Well." He let go of her hands and sat beside her again. "You realize I can't say a lot about it, right?"

"Yes, I remember that. Sacred but not secret. Of course, it ends up meaning the same thing, since either way you don't talk about it."

He chuckled, then wondered how much he should say about the process Brigham explained to him. "God's streamlining things for us, faster than the usual church policies, so we'll be doing it a little differently."

She raised her eyebrows. "What does that mean?"

"Since I'm already married, the church wouldn't ever go along with marrying us." He gave her a serious look. "We'll be using fake names and pretending we're doing work for our dead ancestors. Except the ancestors will be us."

She laughed wickedly. "This'll be fun, duping the church."

"But it'll all be kosher in the eyes of God," he said quickly.

"I'm not complaining. It just makes it more fun acting devious. Especially when it's all sanctioned by God, so we won't go to hell."

"Then you'll love this." He took another breath. "You know the church won't let you in the temple until you live worthily for a year."

"Yes, I remember that too."

"So I...uh...borrowed some temple recommends for us to use. We'll be putting our fake names on them."

She laughed out loud. "Borrowed, huh? This is getting better all the time. What the hell—if God wants to break his own rules, that's fine with me."

She gazed at him with a grin on her face and then broke out in another laugh.

"What's so funny?"

"I'm trying to imagine you pilfering temple recommends."

You should have been there, he thought. *You'd have laughed your head off at how I panicked.*

She inhaled and let out a noisy sigh. "So, seriously, what goes on in there? A bunch of covenants, right? What covenants am I going to make?"

"Well..." He rubbed his chin and thought. "I'm not sure how much I'm allowed to tell you."

"Come on, if I'm supposed to swear to a bunch of covenants, don't you think I have a right to know what they are?"

"Yes, actually, I do. It's really nothing different than what you promise at baptism, only more detailed and...pointed."

"Give me some hints, at least."

"Well, there's the law of chastity, and—"

"That means I don't sleep around. I stay true to my husband." She squeezed his arm.

"Right. And the law of sacrifice..."

"Are we talking lambs and stuff here?" She brightened up. "Hey, maybe I can sacrifice Steven!"

He ignored her sarcasm. "You promise to be willing to sacrifice everything for the church."

"Yeah, okay, that's typical. What else?"

"You promise to consecrate everything you have to the building up of the kingdom of God."

She looked around the room. "Fine with me—they can have it all."

"You have to obey my every whim."

"Now just a—" She noticed his grin and slapped him on the shoulder. "I'll obey you if you obey me."

"Your wish is my command."

"That's better. *You* have to swear that in the temple too, right?"

He looked away from her. "I'm not saying."

"Alright, enough of this. Just tell me honest, straight out. You know me pretty good. Is there anything I have to promise that I'll object to?"

Her eyes were expectant but suspicious. Was there? He didn't think so. Nothing that wasn't more or less how Mormons defined righteous living outside the temple too. He didn't think anything would come as a great surprise—not the covenants, anyway. As for the rest—well, why shouldn't she be as amazed as everyone else on their first visit?

"I think you'll be fine," he answered.

"Alright." She wagged a finger at him. "If you're wrong, you'll pay for it on our wedding night."

He remembered their first kiss in her old apartment, all decked out for satanic rituals. She burned with passion as much as he did that night. It sounded like an empty threat to him.

"Sheila, you never answered my question."

"What question?"

He got down on one knee again.

"Oh." She looked down at her lap, chagrined. "That question." Looking up, she said, "Ask me again."

He took her hands. "Will you marry me?"

"Yes." Her eyes glistened. She fell to her knees next to him and embraced him tightly. "I love you," she whispered in his ear.

"I love you," he whispered back.

Their embrace lasted forever it seemed like. Slowly they parted.

"I need to get ready for work," he said, feeling reluctant to leave but remembering his promise to Dani.

"C.H.," she said, fingering his shirt sleeve, "what about garments?"

"Oh, yeah, you'll need those. We can get them Saturday, the same time we go shopping for a ring."

"I mean, what's the rules about wearing them?"

"Night and day, basically."

"*Night* and day?" She scowled. "That sounds like all the time."

"Well, there are exceptions." He smiled mischievously. "Like Saturday night, for example."

But apparently that wasn't what was bothering her. "*All* the time?"

"Like I said, there are exceptions. But for the most part, yes, all the time."

"Who decides what the exceptions are?"

"Well, the General Authorities mention certain times, but I suppose it's a personal decision. What you feel good about."

She nodded, thought for a moment, and then nodded again.

"You're not looking forward to wearing them, are you?" he said, feeling foolish for how long it had taken him to realize that was her concern.

"I just—I'm not used to the idea yet. But—" She kissed him on the cheek. "If it means being with you, I guess I can get used to them."

"Just like the rest of us," he said, hoping there would be something comforting in that.

"Yes, just like the rest of you."

C.H. pulled the early shift on Friday, so he headed for home at five p.m. He worked hard training Olive for the past two days. She still looked magnificent—there was no getting around that. And he liked her friendly demeanor, mixed with confidence and a little stubbornness, just enough to avoid suffering fools gladly. So far he hadn't found anything about her to dislike. But he kept his attraction to her theoretical, as he'd done with Sheila. She was another beautiful woman in the world, and that was all.

Spirits in the Young household were pleasant enough when he arrived home, but as the evening wore on, they grew somber. Today was his last day as a normal husband. Tomorrow he would take Sheila to the temple and marry her. Tomorrow night would be his wedding night with another woman.

The somber mood didn't surprise him one bit. What surprised him was how mild it was. Dani was subdued but didn't seem upset. He imagined all sorts of reactions from her as the wedding day approached: anger, weeping, hysteria, coldness. Instead, she sat next to him whenever the boys let her, clinging to his arm and caressing it as they watched TV. Of all the reactions he imagined, it never occurred to him that she might be quietly affectionate with him.

He wished she *would* react differently, with anger or weeping or hysteria. He was already feeling terribly guilty. Tomorrow she'd be alone all day with their two children as he took another woman to the temple and married her. She'd be alone with their two children all night as well as he took Sheila to the hotel room where they'd consummate their marriage.

He wanted to feel sorrow for her, wanted to feel hesitation about the role he was obliged to play, wanted to concentrate his full attention on her for their last remaining night together as traditional husband and wife. But his mind pulsed with anticipation about the things Sheila and he would do tomorrow night. Sheila's image filled his brain, her deep-set eyes, her dark-red hair, her smirking half-smile. He imagined her in that black teddy she wore during the satanic ritual, her small but well-rounded breasts barely covered by the fabric, the creases of her buttocks extending well below the lower hemline. As Dani stroked his arm, he filled with arousal as he pictured Sheila dropping the teddy, standing radiantly naked before him, rushing forward to embrace him and engulf him in deep kisses, her hands darting back and forth over his skin.

Through his sexual excitement wove a grimy vein of guilt. Why couldn't he concentrate on Dani tonight of all nights? Was he such a sexually obsessed deviant that he couldn't put off his anticipation of lovemaking with Sheila for one more night? He could have his fill of her tomorrow. Tonight he should—he *must*—concentrate on Dani.

But he couldn't. The arousal heightened his guilt, and the guilt motivated more arousal to dilute its painful grip. Conflicting emotions fed on each other, escalating as Dani quietly and with calm gentleness caressed his arm.

When the boys were both asleep in bed, she snuggled hard against him out on the couch, her caresses intensifying. She began to nibble, then to kiss his neck, his earlobes, his mouth. She swung around to sit on his lap, facing him, and kissed more passionately. He responded quickly, already well primed. Before long, they shed all their clothes and made love on the carpet. C.H. pumped all the arousal he felt for Sheila into Dani until climax released the passion.

The passion, but not the guilt. Without the arousal, the guilt hit him hard. He made love to Dani with passion that came from fantasizing about Sheila. He felt dirty down to his bones. He felt as if he cheated on both of them at once. As Dani stroked his cheek and gazed into his eyes with an expression of contentment and—he imagined—forgiveness for what he would do tomorrow, he couldn't take it anymore. The guilt welled up into a complete sense of worthlessness. Command or no command from God, he couldn't go through with this marriage tomorrow. It all felt too ugly now.

"Dani," he said softly. "I can't do it."

Her eyebrows trembled for an instant. "What do you mean?"

"I can't marry Sheila."

"It's okay," she whispered as her lips touched his cheek. "I've accepted it."

"No, it's ugly. It can't be right."

"God commanded you."

"I don't care. I can't—I won't do this to you."

She sat up and pulled on his arm to urge him into a sitting position, then she scooted toward him on the carpet until they could interlock their legs. "You have to do it. And I'm prepared for it."

He tried to protest, but she stopped him with her hand on his mouth.

"Cain, I promise, I'm ready for this. Sheila loves you, and she's counting on you to marry her."

He pulled his face away from her hand. "Dani—"

"Marrying Sheila isn't what bothers me. I've accepted that."

It took an instant, but only an instant, for him to realize what she said. He studied her face, her eyes gazing at him tensely. "What *is* bothering you?"

"Promise me..." She pressed her cheek against his and whispered into his ear. "Promise me you won't marry Cyndy."

"What?" he whispered back with a hiss.

"No matter what, promise me you won't marry Cyndy. Even if God commands it."

He pulled back to stare at her. Her eyes were moist, and her jaw and lips clenched tightly.

"Why do you think God would command me to do that?"

"Just—please, promise me. Promise you won't marry any underage girl."

Why was this bothering her? God hadn't commanded it, and C.H. couldn't imagine him commanding it. That would be too much for the church to accept. It would be too much for society to swallow—not only a fourteen-year-old wife, but a fourteen-year-old *third* wife. It would be sexual abuse of a minor. God couldn't possibly expect that of him.

"I promise, sweetie."

Dani hugged him, and he felt a warm tear drop on his bare shoulder. He was glad he could do this small thing for her, easing her irrational fear. But he couldn't blame her—at a time like this, any wife could be excused if she got a little irrational.

Keeping this promise would be the easiest thing in the world to do because God would never command him to do such an unthinkable thing.

Chapter 13

When Sheila woke up, she thought, *That's the last night I get to sleep naked.* After today, she'd be obliged to wear garments every night. She wondered what they'd feel like.

No, that wasn't quite true. She wouldn't have to wear garments tonight. It was her wedding night. Like hell she'd wear garments on her wedding night.

But that would only delay the inevitable. Tonight, tomorrow night—what was the difference? Either way, she wouldn't be sleeping nude for the rest of her life.

She dragged herself out of bed, warmed herself as she crouched nude over the heater vent, then headed for the kitchen. With the temperature in the apartment quickly growing too hot, she felt on the verge of breaking out in a sweat. When she swung open the refrigerator, the blast of cold air felt wonderful. She grabbed a two-liter jug of Diet Dr. Pepper, twisted it open with a *whoosh*, and filled the thirty-two-ounce cup she left by the sink. The crackling of the carbonation enhanced the craving she felt. She guzzled until a trickle escaped the corner of her mouth and dripped onto her bare breast, making her tremble at its cold touch.

That first gulp every morning tasted so good. Dr. Pepper was almost beginning to taste as good as coffee. And it was a damn sight easier to prepare.

She sat at the kitchen table and leisurely drained the cup. It was all the breakfast she needed each day because thirty-two ounces filled her stomach. As she belched and waited for the caffeine to trickle into her system, she wondered if anything else in her new life would be as easy to make peace with.

C.H. woke up wondering what he should do. It occurred to him that it might be nice to make love with Dani one more time while she was his only wife, especially since he did it all wrong last night. But he had no idea if she'd feel the same. It might seem to her like he was trying to get as much sex today as he could.

He leaned over in bed, careful to avoid Glenn. "I just want to be with you one more time when you and me are all there is." He whispered so softly that she didn't stir from her sleep.

Glenn decided for him. His little voice began to whine, and Dani, without even opening her eyes, turned over so she was facing the two of them, pulled out a breast through the opening in her nursing garments, and positioned Glenn. C.H. climbed out of bed, went to the bathroom, then went into the kitchen to make breakfast.

Dani heard the pans banging and knew what C.H. would do. Breakfast in bed. She liked breakfast in bed—but not today. Today it would be an act of pity, motivated by guilt. She couldn't handle that.

In fact, he'd be doing pity acts of kindness all morning. She thought she'd like to spend one more moment alone with him when he belonged only to her, maybe even enjoy one more act of love. But when she heard the banging of the pans, somehow she knew she couldn't handle it. If he would really be with her—only her, in mind as well as body—it would be different. But how could he do that?

She remembered her wedding day. She'd tried to concentrate on everything going on around her, but all she could think of was being with him that night as husband and wife. It would be their first time together with anyone—both of them. Between her love for him and her attraction to him and her intense curiosity about sex, she could think of nothing else. If it was that bad for her, how much more so must it be for a man?

She wasn't about to accept charity kindness from him while he thought of having sex with *her* all day. She struggled out of bed, trying to keep Glenn balanced with one arm, and shuffled to the kitchen door. She caught C.H. just as he was about to crack the first egg.

"Cain, wait."

He looked up and smiled. "Good morning. You don't want eggs?"

"Why don't you take Sheila out to breakfast instead?"

He immediately scowled. "I thought—"

"I know what you thought. But this is your wedding day. You should spend it with her."

He frowned at the egg in his hand. "I don't want to."

"*I* want you to." She gazed at him intensely, willing him to understand how determined she was about this.

He slowly set the egg back in the carton and shut off the stove, and then he looked at her with a cloudy face. "Are you sure?"

"I'm sure."

He nodded, returned the eggs and package of bacon to the refrigerator, and then came up to her and kissed her. "Okay."

Dani sat on the sofa and switched on the TV as C.H. got dressed and left. As she cycled over and over through worthless programming, she began to wonder what would have been so terrible about pity acts of kindness.

When the knock came at her door, Sheila's heart leaped. C.H. was there to start their wedding day together. For a moment she toyed with the idea of opening the door while still nude—wouldn't that leave an impression! But, no, she better not. It would matter very much to him that they weren't married yet, and he'd probably been fantasizing about that first moment of nudity together during their wedding night. If she did it now, she could spoil his fantasy.

It could also mean Moroni got an unexpected eyeful if she guessed wrong who was on the other side. She definitely didn't want to send *that* signal, even though the thought of opening the door nude to him was just as enticing.

She slipped on her T-shirt and jeans and opened the door. It was C.H. after all, standing there with his church clothes on a hanger. She eyed them with amusement.

"Dani told me to bring them with," he said.

She thought she knew why. Dani didn't want him coming back home to put them on. She didn't want to know when they were heading for the temple. Sheila probably would have done the same thing.

When he invited her to go to breakfast, she thought of the quart of Diet Dr. Pepper in her stomach. But she decided that, by the time she got ready and they made it to the restaurant, most of that liquid would be waiting in her bladder to exit, and she'd be able to make a reasonable dent in her food.

But she *was* elated that he decided to spend all day with her instead of being with Dani in the morning like he originally planned. Sheila understood why he wanted to do that, but damn it, this was *their* wedding day, and it was only right that *they* be together today. Sheila would be as much of a wife as Dani, and she deserved as much consideration. He hadn't spent part of his and Dani's wedding day with Sheila.

When he asked, she suggested the Belgian Waffle restaurant. She'd gone there often with Steven, but she made all her boyfriends take her there, so it wasn't just a Steven thing. It was better than Denny's or some other lame place she was afraid C.H. might think of. And it was certainly appropriate that she go there with her last boyfriend of all, the man she was about to marry.

He waited in the living room while Sheila got ready, and then they drove to the Belgian Waffle in the Corolla. While they perused the menu, she told him to order a Belgian waffle, and she'd order a mushroom, tomato, olive, and cheese omelette. Side dishes with those two orders would be ham, hash browns, a bowl of fruit, a muffin, and coffee—but they could substitute for the coffee. They could split up all that food between the two of them and have a nice big breakfast with lots of variety. He loved the idea.

Twenty minutes after the food arrived, they were both stuffed and asking for doggy bags. As they sat quietly waiting for the food to settle, he said, "What should we go shopping for first?"

"Let's see, diamond ring or ugly underwear? Tough choice."

They headed for Fashion Place Mall and looked through the jewelry shops until Sheila found the ring she loved: half a carat with a crushed-diamond halo and swirls in the gold band. Nothing too ostentatious for her delicate fingers.

Watching him shell out hundred-dollar bills was breathtaking. Tucking the little ring case into his pocket as they walked out to the car, he said, "Now we need to get you some garments."

She felt a little like she was being marched off to prison as he took her to a Distribution Center. The choices were more daunting than she expected. What fabric? What size? What style? "I haven't the slightest idea," she said.

They guessed at a size for her, and she decided mesh sounded the sexiest since it was almost sort of see-through.

Back in the car, they looked at each other. "I can't believe I just bought garments," she said. "Never in a million years."

He looked pleased. Maybe wearing garments *would* be worth it if it made him so happy. She leaned over, put her arms around him, and nibbled his ear. "Let's get married."

"Now?"

"Now!"

They originally planned to shop in the afternoon and go to the temple early in the evening so he could be with Dani all morning. Now that reason was gone, and Sheila couldn't see any other reason to wait. Starting their wedding night in the afternoon sounded great to her. Strains of the oldies song "Afternoon Delight" played in her head. Her parents used to play it a lot, since they had "afternoon delight" on their wedding day before the reception.

They drove back to her apartment so they could put the leftover food in the refrigerator and change into their Sunday clothes for the temple. Sheila scowled as she eyed the shiny new car in the driveway. Shouldn't he be taking her to their wedding in that, instead of this beat-up Toyota? But he insisted that he leave that one with Dani since she'd be alone all day and all night with two little boys. Sheila wasn't going to make an issue out of that. Dani could keep the nice car all to herself, since she was willing to share *him* with her.

They parked in the driveway around back. Inside, Sheila grabbed him and planted a huge kiss on his lips. "I can't believe we'll be married in a few hours." She started nibbling on his earlobe. "I don't know if I can wait."

"Sheila!" he growled.

She laughed. "Being the good Mormon boy right up to the last minute?"

"When the last minute is in the temple, absolutely."

She grinned mischievously and played with his top shirt button. "And what makes you think you could resist if I really tried to seduce you?"

"Please don't try," he whispered.

She laughed again and pressed her lips against his, then mumbled through her kiss, "Don't worry, I won't." She could feel his arousal pressing against her as they embraced. It was awfully tempting, but she knew he'd hate her forever. She broke the kiss and said, "Let's go!"

Sheila was born a Mormon, yet had never seen the inside of the Salt Lake temple. As they stood next to the reflecting pool and gazed up at the spires, the golden statue of Moroni, the glittering doors, and the inscription *Holiness to the Lord*, she filled with excitement. She always wanted to see the inside of this temple, find out what the temple ceremony was all about. Probably the only thing she regretted about leaving the church.

"You'll be taking on serious covenants with God." He held her hand as they gazed up. "It's better not to do it in the first place than to take them on and break them."

It would also be a deal breaker for their marriage, Sheila knew. If she wasn't willing to accept the temple covenants, she knew she couldn't marry C.H.—period. It was part of the deal. A fleeting image of Moroni—not the angel, but the neighbor across the street—crossed her mind. A consolation prize. But she quickly brushed that image aside. She knew nothing about him and wasn't about to trade C.H. for him.

"Is there a covenant to attend church regularly?"

He smiled at her. "Not specifically in the temple."

"Then I'm ready."

They started walking. "Just remember," he said, "there are people standing around everywhere in white clothes and name tags. You can always ask any of them what you're supposed to do next. You got your recommend?"

"Yes."

"And your name card?"

"Yes, Dad."

They entered just as a noisy motorcycle zoomed past on North Temple. She began to tingle all over. She was leaving the wicked world and entering the House of the Lord. At least that's what she was supposed to believe.

Did she believe it?

She was basing all her belief on a single visit from an apparition who claimed to be Brigham Young. C.H. said it *was* Brigham Young. At the time, she was willing to accept his claim because she was shocked and didn't know what else to believe. After that, her belief was supported by the benefits of having a place to live rent-free and being able to marry a man she loved, even though he was already married. Those two things were enough for her to suspend disbelief, to ignore the question—right up until she set foot in the temple.

But now, as she strolled hand-in-hand with C.H., as she presented her forged temple recommend to the person at the reception desk, as she entered the temple itself, as they stood in separate lines—male and female—to rent the clothing they would need, and as they parted ways to the dressing rooms, the question increasingly forced itself on her mind.

Whatever else you've been, girl, you've never been a hypocrite.

When she stopped believing in the Mormon religion, she stopped being a Mormon, unlike some people she knew who couldn't face up to the social stigma or who wanted to keep the business advantages of belonging to the dominant religion in the state. Many of her former acquaintances looked down on her as she began to drink, take occasional sniffs of cocaine, and sleep with men she wasn't married to. But she renounced her baptismal vows before doing all that—if not on paper, at least in her mind.

Some of the friends of those acquaintances were doing the same things as her, then prancing off to church every Sunday and renewing the very baptismal covenants they were mocking during the week. Yet her acquaintances never seemed to look down on *those* friends. Who was worse?

Am I being worse now? Am I like those friends now? Am I accepting all this because I need a place to live and want to sleep with my dream lover, even though he's married?

She knew the answer. It was the same reason she took up with Steven and other assholes. She always chose the immediate desire without counting future costs. Even turning her back on handsome Moroni wasn't a change in that pattern, like she deluded herself into believing. She wanted her convenient rent-free apartment and the considerate lover she dreamed about. Moroni was an unknown variable who was just mucking up her plans.

So did she believe all this or not? Did she believe in God, in Joseph Smith, in the visitation of Brigham Young? Or was she just a hypocrite, like some of the businessmen in Salt Lake City who played the Mormon role on Sunday and cheated their colleagues on Monday?

A short, ancient woman in a long white dress pointed a gnarled finger toward a locker in the dressing room. Sheila followed her directions mechanically, her stomach beginning to churn.

She always prided herself on not being a hypocrite. It was the thing she hated above all else about Mormons and one of the things by which she defined her self-image. *I am not a hypocrite.* But as she crept toward the locker she was assigned, she began to feel more and more certain with each step that she *was* a hypocrite, and it sickened her.

Did she really believe? She couldn't say with certainty that she did. But did she disbelieve? She searched hard into her heart for an answer to that. She hadn't actually left the church over doctrine per se. It was the hypocrisy she'd seen. *If that's what a Mormon is, I'm not a Mormon,* she distinctly remembered thinking the day she consciously severed ties.

The hypocrisy she saw, and her desire to live a lifestyle contrary to the teachings of the church—that's why she left. Not because she stopped believing the theology. On the other hand, she wasn't sure she ever truly believed it in the first place. It was just things she was taught in her youth. After leaving, she never thought much about the theology. So no, she couldn't find any definite *disbelief* of Mormon doctrines in her heart.

What she did find in her heart was the image of C.H. gazing at her with affection. She loved him, and all signs indicated he loved her. He respected her, even in the clutches of desire, not that selfish, lustful urge she'd seen in most boys since puberty. C.H. believed the whole Mormon thing—hook, line, and sinker—and she realized she couldn't bear the thought of *him* being wrong about something so important. If Sheila didn't believe in it, then she'd have to acknowledge that he was a dupe.

Was that enough for her to not be a hypocrite—to believe because he believed? She was sincere about trying to living the Mormon lifestyle—mostly. At least she'd been forthcoming with him about the parts she wasn't ready to live yet. And she *had* experienced something in Steven's apartment, something out of the ordinary. She decided she *would* believe, for now.

But was it enough?

Sheila opened the door to the dressing cubicle where her locker was. There were four lockers lined up in a row. Two were slightly open—

—with keys in the locks!

She stood dumbfounded and stared. She couldn't believe it. Locks in the Salt Lake temple, as if people worthy to enter the temple would steal things out of the lockers. She realized that some temple goers *must* steal things out of the lockers, or those locks wouldn't have been put there in the first place.

She laughed out loud, then hurriedly covered her mouth as nearby temple patrons glanced at her. Talk about hypocrisy! People told their bishop to his face that they were honest so they could go into the temple and steal things out of the lockers.

Suddenly Sheila wasn't feeling so much like a hypocrite after all. She was head-over-heels better than some Latter-day Saints.

With an exuberant heart, she changed into her white clothing and joined C.H. in the chapel, giving him a big, heartfelt hug.

The afternoon in the temple was a blur to Sheila. They baptized her in a large tub on the backs of twelve ox statues. In an area near the dressing room, they dabbed her with water and consecrated olive oil as they pronounced blessings. Moving with a white-clothed audience from room to room—the walls and ceilings of the first three were covered with beautiful murals—she watched as temple workers acted out the Adam and Eve story, with God, Jehovah, the devil, and other characters playing roles. Numerous times she stood along with everyone else to make gestures and recite lines in unison, including several covenants. Not suspecting it was her first time through, the helpful temple workers and women sitting on either side must have wondered why she seemed so clueless. Occasionally she made eye contact with C.H. over on the men's side, widening her eyes to communicate her overwhelming helplessness.

Finally it was over, and she sat in the gorgeous celestial room of the Salt Lake temple, her future husband next to her, both of them watching the chandelier glitter above. More than once, the little old ladies patrolling the room shushed everyone when conversations became too loud.

"What did you think?" C.H. asked in a whisper.

"Um, it was interesting," she said, trying to be tactful.

"Go ahead, you can say it." He grinned at her. "It was weird! I remember my first time. I was blown away."

She smiled with relief. That was one of the things about him that appealed to her—he was a paradoxical mix of uncompromising orthodoxy and pragmatic cynicism. If all Mormons were like him, she probably never would have left the church. "*Bizarre* was the word I had in mind."

But it wasn't over yet. There was one more thing to do—the one thing she had endured all the other hocus-pocus to accomplish. They still needed to be married in the sealing room.

The room was nice enough. Sheila remembered hearing about the reflecting mirrors facing each other on opposite walls, representing eternity as everyone stared at infinite copies of themselves extending back into oblivion. It did have a transcendent sort of impact on her. With some other couples watching who were there to do sealings for the dead too, the officiator instructed them to kneel at an altar facing each other, and he spoke some words that Sheila couldn't concentrate on. Even though the officiator had told her to watch him, she kept her gaze on C.H., who dutifully looked at the officiator. She couldn't believe she was finally marrying him! She felt like she was on the verge of passing out from lightheadedness.

He said yes to a question, and Sheila immediately recognized it as the Mormon temple version of "I do." A question was directed at her, something about accepting him as her husband. She responded with an enthusiastic yes, making sure not to say "I do," even though that was the answer she wanted to give.

More words that she barely heard, wild and crazy blessings from God. She stared at C.H., amused at how he looked in his relentlessly white temple garb—like an albino Scotsman more than anything. A curly lock of hair hung over his forehead from the elastic of what looked like a shower cap to her. She could hardly wait to play with that curl as they lay naked together in the hotel room. For a moment, she thought she should feel guilty for thinking something like that in the temple, but she decided she couldn't possibly be the first bride to do so. Not every woman getting married here was an innocent Molly Mormon—not with locks on the lockers.

When everyone chanted amen together, a thrill shot through her as she realized she was married. Not in the sight of the church and not in the sight of the law, but in the sight of God, according to C.H. and the Brigham ghost. If it was enough for her husband and his first wife, it was enough for her. It wasn't like she ever cared before what the church or the law said about her sexual relations. At least she had God on her side this time—that was a big improvement.

C.H. beamed as he reached to kiss her over the altar. The witnesses looked amused, but Sheila didn't care. That magical phrase that she'd heard all the time growing up—"kissing over the altar"—had finally become a reality for her, something she thought would never happen. She kissed him deeply and lavishly.

"This couple may have been dead when you came in," the officiator said, "but I'll bet that kiss resurrected them!" The others in the room laughed.

"Can we go now?" Sheila asked in a whisper. C.H. nodded.

She could hardly stand the time it took to change into her dress. And it was wasted effort because she had no plans of staying in the uncomfortable dress for long. She just hoped she could wait long enough for the hotel room door to close before she ripped it off again.

Noticing other women glaring at her, she realized she'd been humming "Afternoon Delight." Beyond caring, she hummed louder. She was married now. Let them throw her out if they wanted!

Chapter 14

Dani heard the car pull into Sheila's driveway. Against her own better judgment, she peeked through the curtains in time to see the Corolla drive off again. She caught a glimpse of C.H. and Sheila in their Sunday dress as they turned the corner and headed away.

She glanced at the clock. Barely past noon. They were going to the temple to be married now, not later that evening. Damn! Why had she sent him to be with Sheila all day?

Dani expected to feel miserable only tonight—the wedding night. But now that she knew they were getting married this afternoon, she would have to start feeling miserable sooner. When would they first make love? Would they wait until dark, like a respectable wedding night should play out? Or would they do it the minute they left the temple and walked into the hotel room?

Why hadn't she realized that if they got together earlier in the day, they could get married earlier? *She* had to make an appointment with the temple when she got married because it was a real wedding. Sheila needed no such appointment—they could just show up and do the sham work for their dead selves.

A sleeping Glenn woke with a cry from the bedroom, and soon she could hear Petey too. Dani's heart sank even deeper—two crying little boys were more than she felt like handling right then. She hurried into the bedroom and found Petey sitting up in the bed, rubbing one eye with a fist and whining. Dani bundled up Glenn, took him into the living room, sat on the sofa, and nursed him, letting Petey find his own way into the living room. He climbed up next to her, stood on the cushion, and started hanging onto her arm and whining in her ear.

No, she wasn't ready to deal with this at all. She reached for the phone—causing Glenn to lose contact with her nipple—and dialed Cyndy's number. Aiming her breast back into Glenn's mouth, she listened to ring after ring, until finally their voice mail replied.

She thought of Sister Vandermeer, but they'd been relying on her too much lately. The poor woman already had plenty to do—lots of other women in the ward probably had bigger problems than Dani.

Bigger problems? What other woman had a husband getting married to another woman in the temple at that moment? A rape or an abducted child or a murdered loved one—those would be bigger problems. But aside from those kinds of things, who had a bigger problem than Dani?

No one, that's who. She dialed the number. The phone rang multiple times, with no answer.

She slammed down the phone. Petey whined in her ear. "Shut up, Petey," she said softly but ominously.

Why was she feeling these bad feelings? She thought she'd prepared herself. She was ready to accept this thing God had commanded them to do. She felt a measure of peace last night.

Was it because she was so worried about C.H. marrying an underage girl that the idea of his marrying Sheila seemed tame in comparison? Was it because she figured she had all day to psych herself up before their first time together? She thought she wouldn't be sharing her husband with someone else until that night, but now she had maybe an hour or two—no more—before he was no longer hers alone. With that moment finally here, was she finding out that it really was more than she could handle?

Why couldn't Cyndy or Sister Vandermeer answer? She needed to be alone to think things through. Petey's whine was grating on her nerves. She'd depended on those two for babysitting for so long that she wasn't sure who else she could call right now. Even just to talk to Sister Vandermeer about it—that might be enough. But that, of course, was out of the question. No one was supposed to know about this. There was no one Dani could talk to except Sheila, and Sheila was the last person on earth she wanted to talk to, even if she *were* available.

Maybe she should have gone to the wedding, as was the first wife's right. Maybe it was better than sitting home wondering. She was surprised that Brigham Young never insisted that she be there. She would have refused, but shouldn't he have insisted in the first place?

If only she had someone to talk to.

Maybe she could look up one of the polygamist wives among the fundamentalists, just to find someone who'd understand. However, not only was that a bigger step than she was ready to take—confiding in a woman who was part of an apostate group—but she wasn't quite sure where to find one. Ever since she moved to Utah, she'd heard about fundamentalists and polygamists and the compounds they lived on. But she had no idea where any were. It wasn't like they'd be listed in the phone book.

Maybe she could talk to that one organization—what was it called? Something that started with a *T*. A group of former polygamist wives who were against polygamy. *Reformed* apostates—there was some improvement, she smirked.

But they'd be against the very arrangement that God had commanded her husband to enter into. They'd try to talk her out of it, not help her deal with it. She laughed at the irony. The apostates would be more understanding and helpful than the women who left the apostate groups. More understanding than her own Relief Society president.

And why was that? She felt a tightening in her heart—even tighter than it already was. Why would women who believed in apostate doctrines be the ones she needed to turn to for understanding and support?

C.H. had stolen some temple recommends, forged them, and was using them to take an unworthy woman to the temple to marry him, even though he already had a wife. All because an apparition who called himself Brigham Young told him to. Both she and C.H. had seen the apparition. He said he tried the handshake test on him, and Brigham passed.

But Dani hadn't. She took C.H.'s word for it. She wanted to believe him, to support him. That's what she was supposed to do. That's what she covenanted in the temple to do. And she had many reasons to believe—the visitation, the existence of the money, no command that C.H. leave the church and start a new one. Nobody showed up looking for the money, just like Brigham said.

And yet, the scriptures were full of spiritual visitations that were real but not from God. Satan visiting Moses. Satan tempting Jesus. Satan silencing Joseph Smith right before the First Vision. Satan appearing before the children of Adam, commanding them not to believe the things their father taught them. Devils appearing as angels of light and duping people into acting contrary to the teachings of the established church.

The Brigham Young apparition had appeared with a golden glow—an angel of light—commanding C.H. to do something that was strictly forbidden by the established church, something that got people excommunicated. If the bishop found out, C.H. *would* be excommunicated in a heartbeat, and probably Dani too, since she went along with it. Last night, she even encouraged him when he wavered.

Her hands shook as she held Glenn, and her tears began to flow. She felt deathly sick to her stomach. Why? Why had she done it?

The money, the visitation, the plausible way Brother Brigham had explained everything. According to LDS doctrine, it *was* possible—theoretically—for something like this to happen. Brigham Young hadn't exactly gone outside the line of authority in the church—not exactly—because he wasn't telling C.H. to defy that authority. He was telling C.H. that he'd *become* that authority through proper procedures—out of the ordinary procedures, but proper. Brigham hadn't commanded him to form his own church. He just told him to wait until the church chose him.

If it were all a satanic bluff, why would Brigham set it up the way he had? It couldn't possibly work. Eventually the plan would fall apart, glaringly, obviously. What would be the point?

Like a punch to the gut, she saw what the point would be. A decent member of the church was on his way to the temple to marry a second wife who wasn't even worthy to enter the temple and would be using a temple recommend that he'd stolen and forged. After defiling the temple, he'd then proceed to break his temple covenants and commit adultery tonight—or even this afternoon.

And if it were all a fraud, the hundred and fifty thousand dollars couldn't possibly be legitimate. They'd been spending thousands of dollars of illegal drug money all over town.

All this done to a family committed to Jesus and the church through baptism and married in the temple. How much more point did Satan need?

A line out of scripture blazed into her mind and burned with searing force: *They shall deceive the very elect.*

Dani knew it wouldn't stop there. Brigham *would* command C.H. to take another wife. His first pick was Sheila, someone already attracted to him—of course!—to help grease the wheels of this insane arrangement. Who was the next most obvious choice? Who was another convenient girl who was attracted to him and might let that attraction interfere with her good judgment?

Fourteen-year-old Cyndy. Naive, starry-eyed Cyndy. Her crush on him was written all over her face every time she looked at him. A nice, harmless, youthful crush—so Dani and C.H. had thought all this time. Harmless? Fodder for Satan to deceive a good man to commit yet another despicable sin—sexual relations with a child—all the while believing he was doing the will of God.

Quite an achievement for a few visitations as an angel of light. Yes, there was a definite point to doing all that, even if the deception wouldn't last. It was enough to get both of them excommunicated.

Oh, dear God, why did I let this happen?

Glenn cried, bringing back her attention. Petey stood next to her, gazing into her eyes with a sad look. "Mama crying?"

She'd let Glenn's head fall to her lap so he couldn't reach her nipple. Her face was wet with tears, and she dabbed at them with her free hand. "Mommy's alright, Petey." She peered into their faces, her two little boys who were supposed to grow up with a righteous, intact, celestial family because their parents had done everything right—married as virgins, married in the temple, stayed active in the church, at least as active as C.H.'s job let him be.

"What the hell have we been doing?" she moaned.

"Bad word, mommy," Petey said. "Bad word." He slapped her lightly on the mouth.

She laughed and sobbed in one burst of sound. "Yes, Petey, bad word. Mommy's sorry."

Ignoring Glenn's crying, she grabbed the phone to try Sister Vandermeer again. She had to find her husband and stop him. But no one answered the phone. She tried Cyndy again. No answer there, either.

She couldn't wait! The boys would have to come with.

Maybe that would be better anyway, she thought as she bundled them into the SUV and headed down the road. With his sons looking at him, maybe C.H. would be more inclined to come to his senses.

As she buckled the boys in, a gnawing anger built up inside her. Anger at her husband, Cain Hell Young. How marvelously appropriate that nickname was now! How could he do this to them? He was the one some devil decided was worth visiting. He was the one who accepted it and assured Dani it was true. He was the one off marrying another wife now. How wonderful for him! He would get to have sex with a girl he had the hots for since he met her. He probably hatched the whole scheme in his dirty, dark little mind all those days at the bookstore as he undressed Sheila with his eyes, lusting after her. Somehow he faked Brother Brigham's appearance just to convince Dani to go along.

Sheila wouldn't need any convincing. She was used to screwing men she wasn't supposed to. Maybe she was even in on the scheme. It was all Dani could do to keep a string of profanities from escaping her lips in front of Petey. She'd been duped by a conniving, faithless husband and the whore he wanted to sleep with. Hell, they probably had sex months ago—they just got tired of sneaking around and dreamed up this crazy scheme to get the wife to go along.

But even as she thought all that, she knew it wasn't true. In the first place, she knew him too well. In the second place, who would dream up a crazy scheme like that? Who'd believe it?

She burst out crying. *She'd* believe it. What a damned fool she was!

As she drove out of their neighborhood, she was still angry. Angry at what? She knew C.H. wouldn't dream up something like this just to have an affair. He wouldn't want the affair in the first place. She knew him too well. He had his faults, but infidelity was not one of them. So why was she still angry at him?

Because if he hadn't made it up, that meant he *had* been deceived by a devil and dragged his whole family down with him. How could he be so stupid? How could he let this happen to his family?

What was it about C.H. that made him an enticing target for some devil to think he'd be successful with such an outrageous deception?

Because C.H. expected a special mission all his life. His dad pumped that idea into his head, his patriarchal blessing promised it, and he was born into one of the most aristocratic families among Mormons. And Brigham Young had been his childhood companion. C.H. thought he deserved some kind of special treatment.

It wasn't sexual lust that brought his downfall. It was pride.

She zoomed down State Street, swooping in and out around slow vehicles, barely noticing the front of a Salt Lake City police car peeking out from behind a storefront. She slowed down just in time to avoid being clocked at twenty miles over the speed limit. Reaching Temple Square, she parked in a red zone. What did a silly parking ticket matter when her husband was about to ruin their lives?

She fought to get the boys out of their car seats, then dragged Petey by one hand and clutched Glenn desperately with one arm until she reached the reception desk inside the temple entrance. All the temple workers standing or sitting in their white clothes stared at her as she barged into the temple, dressed casually and with two little kids.

"Please," she said to the man at the desk. "My husband is in there right now. I need to get hold of him. He's—"

She couldn't believe it. She almost said he was marrying another woman.

"—it's an emergency."

"What's his name, Sister?" the man said.

"Cai— Cory Young."

"Is he in an endowment session right now?"

"I—I don't know." Dani glanced around at the gawking temple workers. A line of temple visitors was already forming behind her. She was on the verge of passing out from embarrassment. "He was going to do all the ordinances for...a family name. He could be in a session, or—" She couldn't look the man in the eye, so she lowered her gaze. "He might be doing the sealing."

"Hold on, Sister. Please wait right here." He gestured at a chair behind her. As she sat, the gawking people around her went back to their business. A second man at the desk processed visitors in line, and other workers directed them where to go. The man Dani had spoken to stepped into a room where she saw him pick up a phone.

Glenn was asleep, thank heavens. Petey sat on the floor looking around. The people who had moments ago stared at her were now tactfully ignoring her, except one petite old woman dressed all in white who kept looking her way every once in a while and smiling. A pity smile, Dani supposed.

Pity. Why hadn't Dani let C.H. stay home and do pity kindnesses for her?

The man came out of the room, and she struggled to her feet with Glenn in her arms. Petey stood and walked next to her as she met the man halfway.

"We don't have a record of a Cory Young *doing* any work here..."

She didn't understand. Hadn't they come here yet? Did she dare feel relief?

Or had they gone to the Jordan River temple for some reason? Her relief quickly turned into despair. To have to drive all the way out there!

But wait. She didn't have to drive. She could call down there and ask—

Then she realized how stupid she'd been. She could have called the Salt Lake temple instead of wasting time driving. Why hadn't she thought of that?

For some reason, she felt like she had to confront him in person because he wouldn't believe her if she didn't. But she realized she wasn't sure he would believe her even then. She'd be pulling the rug out from under his future. Instead of becoming president of the church, he'd have to go back to being an assistant manager in a bookstore. Instead of having two beautiful wives to make love to, he'd have to go back to one—the same one he'd made love to for years already, not some fresh, exciting conquest. Instead of fulfilling a special calling from God, he'd be just an average LDS member again.

"But we *do* have record of some work done *for* a Cory Young today," the man continued.

Dani's mouth dropped open, and she quickly shut it and play-acted a smile. She'd forgotten about the name switch! He was using a fake name for himself.

"Yes, that's right," she said. "Cory Young is the relative he's doing the work for. I was—I got confused there."

"I understand," the man said. "But I'm afraid he completed the work for that name about half an hour ago. Do you think he might still be here, doing work for another name?"

Despair gripped her. It was done. They had come and gotten married. But only in the eyes of Satan.

"Sister?" the man said with concern in his voice.

"No, I'm sorry. Thank you. I think I know where he'll be now."

She grabbed Petey's hand and started walking out.

"I hope everything turns out alright," the man said.

She nodded and forced a smile. "Me too."

Dani drove home, threw in a Disney tape for Petey, and dropped Glenn crying into his crib. Then she started calling hotels. She hadn't wanted to know what hotel they were staying in, but now she was regretting a whole lot of choices she'd made based on jealousy.

Would he register under his real name? Should she be asking for Mr. and Mrs. Smith?

But she found him in the Little America Hotel under C.H. Young. She was about to ask the operator to ring the room, but then she stopped. She *should* ring the room so she could stop him from making a big mistake. But the thought of interrupting them in the middle of—

She couldn't bear it.

"How long since they checked in?" she asked.

"It's been over an hour," the operator said.

Over an hour. Dani shuddered. Long enough to be well into foreplay, but there was still a chance they hadn't actually consummated the marriage yet.

She had to try, no matter how nauseated she felt right now. "Could you please ring the room for me?"

The phone started ringing. Dani wished desperately that he'd answer and dreaded that he'd answer. What would she say to him? She wanted to confront him face to face to make sure she could convince him. But there was no way she'd barge into that hotel room now. And she didn't have time anyway. She may already be too late.

Another ring.

Would he answer? She imagined them lying naked together in bed, kissing passionately. The phone rings. C.H. reaches for it. Sheila pulls back his hand and says, "No! No one's disturbing us now." His hand falls back onto Sheila's bare skin and begins caressing.

Dani shut her eyes tight and shook her head, trying to get that image out. A third ring. He wasn't going to answer it—she knew he wasn't. What if it *were* an emergency? Well, it was—but what if there were a problem with one of the boys or something? What if she were trying to get hold of him from the hospital? What if the hospital were trying to get hold of him because she was in an accident with the boys and they were all in the hospital and she was unconscious and the hospital needed his permission for life-saving surgery? And he was refusing to answer the phone so he could keep pawing that Satan-worshiper!

The fourth ring sounded. Dani slammed down the phone angrily. This was the last straw! That bitch could have him! No one, from her visiting teachers to the Relief Society president to the bishop to her own mother, could blame her for leaving him under these circumstances.

Her mother. An intense desire to see her mother, to be with her, to talk to her—to be held and comforted by her—overwhelmed Dani. She ran into the bedroom and pulled out all the suitcases they had—old, beat-up things they collected here and there over the years. She stuffed the boys' and her clothes in them, caring little for how neatly they were packed, and sat on the lids to shut them tight enough to latch. She dragged the cases out and threw them in the back of the SUV, then went back into the bedroom and dumped over the clothes basket, spilling dirty laundry onto the floor. A lot of that laundry was hers and the boys', but she didn't care. They could buy more. She grabbed the strap of the backpack, marched out, and tossed it onto the front passenger seat.

Finally she gathered up the boys—Glenn was still crying, and Petey whined to see the rest of the movie—and strapped them into their car seats. She returned to the house to shut the door and stood a moment, staring into the living room.

She lived there her whole married life with her husband and two sons. They struggled, but they were happy together. Yet now, she couldn't conjure up any of those happy memories or feelings. All she could think of was how Brother Brigham and Sheila had invaded their home and destroyed it. There was no happiness left here anymore. She would leave it to C.H. and Sheila and Cyndy and whoever else he recruited to defile their lives and the temple with, and good riddance!

Dani slammed the door without bothering to lock it, climbed into the SUV, and drove off. She kept reminding herself to watch her speed—she didn't want to deal with any cops right now. She drove north on I-15 and then west on I-80, heading for the airport. As she drove, she realized this would have been the same route C.H. took to pick up the backpack in the first place. Which mile marker did he say? Forty-something.

She toyed with the idea of driving out there and tossing the backpack out where it should have stayed in the first place. Then maybe their lives could get back to normal, back to the way things were when they were broke and happy. And she might have done it if C.H. wasn't in a hotel room right now screwing Sheila's brains out.

No, there was no going back. The damage was done.

She pulled off the exit to the Salt Lake International Airport. Ignoring the parking entrances, she stopped the van in the loading zone. She grabbed a cart, loaded the suitcases and the backpack, strapped Glenn into his stroller, and let Petey help push the cart to the ticket counter.

She bought first-class tickets to Minneapolis, Minnesota. When she pulled a wad of hundreds out of the backpack, the clerk raised one eyebrow. She checked the luggage in, but kept the backpack and a diaper bag with her. She held her breath when the backpack went through the X-ray machine, but no one said anything.

As they headed down the concourse, she started having second thoughts. What was she doing? Leaving her husband? She never dreamed such a thing would ever happen. Yes, he made some incredible blunders lately, but marriage meant dealing with the bad along with the good.

Yes, he was—she swallowed hard as she thought it—having sex with another woman right now. But he was doing it out of a misguided notion that it was the right thing to do—not because he felt like cheating on Dani. He really believed God had commanded him to do this. And Dani had gone along with it too, giving her blessing to the situation. If he'd been duped, she had too. How could she blame it all on him?

She should go back. She could still tell him what she figured out and convince him he was deceived. Once he accepted that, he'd be mortified at what he did. He'd be in anguish over how much he hurt Dani. He was a good man—she knew it—even after doing this. If there ever was a situation where adultery could be easy to forgive, this would be it.

Someone tapped her on the shoulder. "Ma'am?" said a deep voice.

She turned to find a large, frightening man in an official uniform. There was a gun holstered at his side and a badge on his chest. Immediately she felt lightheaded and couldn't focus her eyes enough to read what kind of a law enforcement officer he was.

"Ma'am, what do you have in the backpack?"

Dread filled her from head to toe. He knew damn well what was in the backpack, and that was why he asked. Her mouth and throat went dry. Her face puckered in an attempt to cry, but the tears wouldn't flow. The man stared at her mercilessly. She noticed two other men standing behind him wearing the same uniforms.

"I'm going to have to take a look inside that backpack, ma'am."

"You don't—" she started. It came out as a rasp. She cleared her throat and tried again. "You don't have the right to search me."

"Uh, yes I do, ma'am." He reached over and gently slipped the backpack from her shoulder, where it hung by one strap.

"Police, Mommy," Petey said. Dani couldn't move.

The officer opened the pack and rummaged through it. "You'll have to come with us, ma'am."

She didn't know if she could avoid fainting or throwing up and wasn't sure which would happen first. One of the other officers walked up and took the stroller from her. The other took Petey by his hand.

"No!" she cried. "Not my children."

"They'll be okay, ma'am," the officer said. "We'll take good care of them."

"Mommy?" Petey moaned, and he started to cry.

"No." But it was only a whisper now, as she watched her children disappear down the corridor with the two officers. The first officer slipped his hand around her arm and led her away. Dani couldn't see anything around her.

What an astronomical blunder she made! Running away from home. That's all it amounted to, something as simple and stupid as that. She started out trying to save her husband, then got furious with him. If she just hadn't gotten furious, none of this would have happened. If she'd only stayed home and waited it out, she could have told him after he got back. She could have forgiven him.

Instead, she got angry and ran right into an international airport with a back-pack full of hundred-dollar bills. How stupid could one person get? She knew about profiling. Now they were carting her away on suspicion of drug dealing. God was punishing her for running out on her husband right when C.H. needed her the most.

The officer brought her into a room where another officer waited. They took her purse and emptied its contents onto a table, then the diaper bag. They rummaged around in her personal effects. They had her empty her pockets. Then two female officers entered and the male officers left. One of them held a latex glove in her hand. Dread shot through Dani.

"You'll need to remove all your clothing," she said.

She couldn't believe this was happening. Slowly she unbuttoned her blouse, slid it off, slipped out of her shoes, pulled off her jeans, and burned with shame as she stood before them in her garments. What would they think of a Mormon who'd gone through the temple being detained for drug dealing?

"You'll have to remove your underwear too," the officer said. There was no sense of compassion in her voice.

Dani didn't think she could do it. She already felt violated, and their cold stares made her feel dirty. Her body started trembling violently, and she couldn't get it to stop.

"Ma'am, if you don't remove your underwear, we'll need to."

Barely able to control her shaking hand, Dani pulled off her garments and laid them carefully atop the pile of her clothes on the floor. Then she stood with one arm over her breasts and a hand covering her pubic area. She had never felt so vulnerable and ashamed in her life.

The other officer picked up the pile of clothes, laid them on a table, and started searching through them. The first officer began putting on the glove.

"You'll need to bend over," she said. "If you like, you can lean on the table."

Dani took a deep, shuddering breath, then stepped toward the table. She lurched and would have fallen if the officer hadn't caught her arm and steadied her. The officer kept her upright as she led her to the table. Dani leaned over and rested on it with her forearms, thinking about the last time she stripped for someone, the last time someone handled her naked—C.H. making love to her. She wished she could remember how that felt, but all she could feel now was the shame. She couldn't imagine feeling anything else ever again.

Dani felt a terrible pressure down below. Finally her tears burst out.

Chapter 15

"Cynthia McGarry."

Cyndy jumped as a thrill shot through her body, prickling the hair on the back of her neck. She glanced at her door. It was still closed and locked, protecting her from Ryan while she did her homework. Who was in the bedroom with her? She stared at the poster on the wall above her desk. Some kind of strange light was making it look yellowish.

"Cynthia, I am Brigham Young."

"Not funny, Ryan!" She turned to see what he'd rigged up to pipe his voice into her room, altered to sound lower.

Near her bed stood a man dressed in a robe, glowing with a yellow halo surrounding his entire body. Cyndy gasped. He *did* look like Brigham Young!

"Cynthia, do not be afraid," the man said. "I've come here to give you a message from God."

This was too much. Cyndy squinted her eyes, trying to figure out if there was some way Ryan could be doing this. Gosh, it looked so real! If this were Star Trek, she'd figure it was a holographic projection. But this wasn't Star Trek.

"You're really Brigham Young?" she said weakly.

"Yes, Cynthia."

"Why would you come to me?"

"I have a message for you from God."

If this was Ryan, he was truly dead meat this time. Although she had to admit, if it *was* Ryan, she was impressed. How was he doing it?

"What's the message?"

"You've heard of plural marriage, haven't you?" The man smiled.

This was sounding very suspicious. "You mean, like polygamy? Sure, I've heard of it."

"God is restoring plural marriage. He wants the church to practice it again. You've been chosen to be one of the first. It's a great blessing."

No, this was getting dumber and dumber. It had to be Ryan. She decided to have some fun. "You want me to marry two husbands?" she smirked.

The Brigham guy raised both his eyebrows. "That's not what I mean. You are to become a plural wife of Cory Horace Young."

"Who?"

"Brother C.H. Young."

That was the clincher! Ryan was always making fun of her about this. "Ryan!" she shouted to the walls. "I'm going to kill you!"

"Cynthia McGarry!" the Brigham guy bellowed, shocking her. "This is no joke!" The halo around him began to glow more intensely. "I am Brigham Young. I have been sent from God to command you to marry C.H. Young. Do not trifle with the things of God!"

Something was wrong. This didn't sound like Ryan at all.

"You will go to Brother Young's home right now and tell him that God sent you and commanded you to marry him. Do so at once!"

Brigham Young vanished into thin air.

Cyndy gaped at the empty space. Holy cow, was that real? Suddenly she remembered that Ryan had gone over to his friend's house after school. A shiver ran through her spine. Was that really Brigham Young?

If it was, she was supposed to march over to Brother Young and tell him— *oh, my gosh*—tell him that God said to marry her. She grabbed the back of her chair to keep from falling over with lightheadedness. God wanted her to marry Brother Young!

She'd been praying for—but no, she hadn't prayed to marry Brother Young. She'd prayed to have a husband some day *like* Brother Young.

Hadn't she?

She had to admit, every time she prayed she was thinking of Brother Young. And not just his face either. She'd been picturing having him as her husband. Maybe she *had* been praying that she could marry Brother Young without realizing it.

But God had realized it and answered her prayer. Gosh, was he bringing back polygamy just so she could marry Brother Young? That was too much to believe! He must have wanted to bring it back anyway, and Cyndy was just incredibly lucky to get in on it.

She shook her head. No, this couldn't be true. It was stupid. Somehow Ryan had snuck over with his friend and pulled this trick on her. They were probably laughing somewhere nearby right now.

There was one way to find out. She marched into the hallway, picked up the phone, and consulted the list of phone numbers her mother kept nearby. When the friend's mother answered, Cyndy said, "May I speak to Ryan?"

"Just a moment," said the mother.

Wrong answer! She was supposed to say they'd come over here.

Maybe they rigged this up earlier and were working the trick from the friend's house by remote control. It was an elaborate trick. They had to have prepared well in advance.

"Hello?" Ryan said.

"Ryan, you didn't fool me," Cyndy said with her best condescending voice. "I know it was you."

"I don't know what you're talking about, goombah."

"That Brigham Young trick. I know it was you. Give it up."

"You're a bigger idiot than I thought." *Click.*

Something was wrong. He didn't act right. Sure, he denied it—that was a given. But he should have been snickering, he and his friend in the background. He should have been playing it up good, enjoying every minute. This didn't sound like Ryan when he was playing a trick on her.

She looked up at the ceiling and cowered. If it *was* real, it wasn't Ryan and his friend who were watching her right now, laughing. It was Brigham Young and God watching, and not laughing but scowling. Brigham Young said, "Don't trifle with the things of God." Well, she'd been trifling alright.

"Sorry, God," she murmured with a cringe. But she still didn't want to risk letting Ryan have the last laugh. She wanted to flip him off all around her room, just to make sure the hidden camera caught it. But in case God was watching and not Ryan, she didn't do that.

There was only one other way to find out. Go to Brother Young's house and give him the message. It would be a ridiculous thing to say—unless God had really commanded it. Then Brother Young should know somehow. Maybe Brigham Young was appearing to him right now, telling him what was about to happen.

"I know it's you, Ryan," she called out once more just in case, then rushed out of the house. If Ryan had worked things out well enough to see her on her way to Brother Young's place, then she'd just have to live with him getting the last laugh. He'd have earned it with a fantastic trick like this. She'd just have to start planning her revenge.

C.H. was terrified. He tried to hide how he felt as he and Sheila pulled into the driveway of her apartment. But she wasn't stupid—she could probably tell.

Everything had been so wonderful. Sheila had insisted they head to the hotel room right after they left the temple. She hummed a tune on the way that seemed familiar to him, but he couldn't place it. At the Little America, they barely got the door to their room closed before Sheila smothered his face in passionate kisses.

It was over quickly, and he was drenched in sweat as he lay back on the bed, panting—and starving. They ate at the hotel restaurant, then went back up to the room and had a real wedding night. Sheila put on a stunning negligee, and they took their time, relishing every moment.

They fell asleep after the second time. In the morning, lying next to Sheila nude, he felt arousal blanket him again. He kissed and caressed her awake, and they made love once more before showering and getting ready to check out.

He would have liked to take Sheila to Hawaii for a honeymoon or something. But there hadn't been time to prepare anything, and he felt obligated to keep going to work that last week. She said she understood, although she didn't seem too happy about it. So they had room service bring up breakfast, after which they drove back to her apartment.

The bad feeling started during breakfast. Watching her as she ate, he wondered what the uneasy feeling in his gut was. She was his wife now, and they'd enjoyed a wonderful wedding night together—wedding afternoon and night and morning. He'd looked forward to it and enjoyed it while it happened. But as he stared at her face, her lovely face and eyes and hair, he had an ugly feeling that he didn't want to touch her that way again. All that desire for her had been lost.

How did this happen? He thought he loved her. He remembered his and Dani's morning after. Their night of intimacy only deepened his feelings for her.

What had gone wrong with Sheila? How was he supposed to be her husband for the rest of his life feeling that way?

It must have been some residual guilt about doing something he always thought of as wrong—having sex with a woman when he was already married to someone else. Had Joseph Smith and Brigham Young felt this way after their first polygamous intimacy? He decided he would ask Brother Brigham the next time he saw him.

He desperately hoped the feeling was temporary. It was as if he lusted after some desirable woman, then felt no respect for her after he conquered her. He knew some boys like that. But he'd never been that kind of a person, not even with milder behavior like mere kissing. He would never make out with a girl just to do it—there had to be feelings behind it. Well, except for that one girl, whose name he couldn't even remember. But the dead feeling he had afterward caused him to never make out casually again.

It was the same feeling he had for Sheila right now. He conquered her, and now he was ready to cast her aside emotionally. He hated himself for feeling that way. He never would have chosen to feel that way—never would have dreamed he *could* feel that way toward her. He thought his love had been genuine.

God, please let this be temporary, he prayed. Just some leftover emotional baggage about polygamy.

He didn't like what the feeling might be saying about his character. But more so, he didn't like how the feeling might end up hurting Sheila.

He tried to hide his feelings from her, but he knew he wasn't successful. She acted reserved during breakfast and on the drive home. She must have sensed something was wrong.

Inside her apartment, she embraced him. "C.H., I'm pretty tired. You need to go to work soon, and I'm sure Dani would like to see you before you go. Would you mind if I just went to bed right now?"

He felt a rush of relief—relief at the chance to get away from her until he could work out this feeling and relief that maybe she hadn't noticed after all. Maybe she *had* only been tired. "Sure, I understand. I'm pretty tired too."

They kissed goodbye, a warm kiss but far from the passionate ones they exchanged over the last twenty-four hours. Just tired—that had to be it.

Sheila kept her smile plastered on her face until the door shut behind C.H., then breathed out a heavy sigh of relief. Thank God he was gone! She flopped down onto her cheesy couch. She refused to cry, but she couldn't help one tear trickling down her cheek.

The heater was in the sauna stage of its cycle, so she jumped up and ripped off all her clothes—including the creepy-crawly garments—and flung herself onto her bed. It was still unmade, and the sheets against her bare skin felt great.

What a night that had been! She was looking forward to it so much. She thought she had everything worked out for her life, as long as she ignored the little aberration of being a second wife—a decent and sexy man for a husband, a place to live, more than enough money to live on. She was so eager to have sex with him that she didn't even want to wait for night. Afternoon delight.

And what did he do? Just about the most amazing premature ejaculation she'd ever experienced with a man. He barely got started before he was done, then he didn't even offer to stroke her or anything to satisfy her. He just said he was hungry and wanted to get something to eat.

Well, she could overlook that. After all, it must have been one exciting moment for a good Mormon boy to have sex with a second wife. But later that evening, when they took their time having sex, he still didn't bring her to climax. She tried to make some suggestions, but he really didn't know what he was doing. He *acted* like he knew what he was doing, plodding along like it was something Sheila was supposed to enjoy. Probably Dani liked it that way, and that's why he expected she'd like it—but Sheila had been with a number of men over the years, some pretty kinky ones, and that tame missionary-position shit C.H. was doing couldn't evoke more than a yawn from her.

Then he pawed her in the morning, waking her from a restful sleep with his slimy kisses and bumbling strokes. She endured it as best she could, then during her shower she gave herself the orgasm she'd been craving.

And fantasized about Moroni across the street while she did it.

She tried to keep up a pleasant demeanor as they ate breakfast and drove home. Was she glad they hadn't planned an elaborate honeymoon now! She just wanted to get away from him. All the excitement and anticipation she felt about spending her life with him was gone. She could hardly remember what it even felt like.

What the hell was she doing? Becoming a Mormon all over again, giving up wine and coffee and cocaine and swearing and maybe even ending up in church someday—all for *him*? What was she thinking? He was a naive, prudish twit who said he loved her but kept trying to fashion her in the image he wanted. He didn't love her for who she was, just for what he could turn her into Pygmalion-style: a straight-laced Molly Mormon. The very idea made her want to retch. She knew plenty of girls who married men with the expectation of fixing them, and she vowed never to do that to any of her men. But she never anticipated pairing up with someone who would try to fix her.

Steven's occasional punches were nothing compared to the emotional abuse C.H. would put her through.

She wished desperately she had a cut of cocaine in her grandmother's jewelry box. It might even be worth looking up Steven and crawling back to him just to get some. She wondered if Moroni was into that kind of thing. He seemed like he might be the type.

She decided she was through with this charade of a marriage. The only reason she ever bought into it in the first place was that appearance Brigham Young made in Steven's apartment. What the hell was that about anyway? Did she really believe it was Brigham Young making a visitation to *her*? It seemed so ridiculous now. More likely some netherworld demon smelling her satanic ritual and poking around to see what was going on.

Sheila, she told herself, *you're way out of your element here. Time to get back to doing what you know.*

Time to give Moroni a visit.

She wished she could trot across the street naked. That would certainly make a strong impression on him. Unfortunately it would also make a strong impression on the neighbors and on the cops they would be sure to call. She pulled on her customary clothes—a T-shirt and jeans and sandals—and stared with amusement at the garments lying in a bunched-up pile on the floor. At least she'd gotten an inside look at the temple for her trouble.

In the bright autumn sunlight, she headed for Moroni's house, hoping she wouldn't see the Youngs on the way. The Corolla was still parked in the driveway, so C.H. hadn't gone to work yet. She hoped he didn't see her heading over to Moroni's. That was a confrontation she didn't want until she had her future settled elsewhere.

The SUV was still gone though. She wondered where Dani might be. Wouldn't she be thrilled when she found out she could have him all to herself again! Until he conned some other fool woman to marry him.

She felt in a good mood as she crossed the street, in spite of the brisk cold wind on her bare arms. She hadn't realized how oppressed her new lifestyle had made her feel until she shucked it. That turkey Moroni had better be home and not ruin things. He wouldn't be in church—that was for sure.

She rang the doorbell. Only seconds passed before the door swung open and Moroni stood there shirtless. His eyes widened, then he grinned.

"Didn't expect you."

"Can I come in?"

"Certainly." He stepped aside and swung the door wide for her.

The minute she entered, she could smell it—smoldering weed. She was about to whisper thanks to God, then laughed when she recognized the irony.

"What's so funny?" he asked as he closed the door.

She turned to face him. She wanted to see his reaction. "I smell your weed."

His smile disappeared. "Is that a problem for you?"

"Yes." She tried to force her half-smile into a scowl. "I don't have any."

The smile leaped back onto his face. "That's easy to remedy."

As he disappeared through a door, she studied the room. Not exactly tidy, but not the mess she'd endured in so many other men's homes. Beyond the smell of weed, she could detect a metallic, musky undertone, a masculine smell. He had his skis laid out on the coffee table, getting them waxed up for the first good snowfall. Posters of models Sheila didn't recognize adorned the walls, some of them naked. On an end table were three issues of *Hustler* magazine.

But the most impressive part of the room was one entire wall covered with electronic toys: a huge wide-screen TV, a receiver and Blu-ray player with flashy LED displays, and surround-sound speakers large enough to crush a small child. In the corner was a gaudy electric guitar.

Sheila instantly claimed this place as her new home.

Moroni returned with a lit joint in his mouth, two more fat joints in his hand, a lighter, and his tank top slung over one shoulder. He set it all down on the end table with the *Hustler*s and started to pull the tank top over his head.

"Why are you doing that?" she asked.

"Huh?" he said through the head opening, his arms halfway through.

"Why are you putting that on?"

He popped it back off his head, his long blond hair spraying everywhere. "I figured you'd be more comfortable if I had on a shirt."

She liked his considerateness. Maybe she could have the best of both worlds with Moroni, a little of C.H. without the prudishness. "What makes me uncomfortable is wearing a shirt when you're not." She grabbed the bottom of her T-shirt, whipped it over her head, and tossed it onto a chair. "But I like this solution better."

Pretty silly logic, she knew, but he wasn't complaining. Staring at her with a wide grin and wide pupils, he threw his tank top next to her T-shirt, sat down, and stubbed out his joint. She sat on the floor next to him, and he kept glancing at her, especially her breasts, trying to be furtive and failing miserably. *Now that's how a man should act*, she thought.

"So what have you got there?" she asked, pointing at the two large joints.

"Weed from hell. Some new stuff I just got last night. A friend of mine said it's potent shit."

That shot some red flags up the flagpole for her. "I'm not smoking anything you're not."

"No problem." He placed both joints in his mouth and lit them, pulled one out and took a deep drag on the other and poked it into Sheila's mouth. "Enjoy."

"Okay, but not this one." She pulled the joint out of her mouth and switched it with the one in his. He laughed and coughed a little.

"On second thought," she said, plucking the joint out of his mouth, "you pick." She hid both joints behind her back and swapped them from hand to hand, taking care not to burn herself.

"Trusting soul, aren't you?" he said. "I can get you the regular shit if you're that worried."

"Just pick one." She brought out the joints. "A girl's got to be careful, you know."

He shrugged and grabbed the one on the left. "Not with me. I'm harmless."

They drew long drags from their joints. The tangy aroma was like an old friend come home. She wondered if Moroni could be a source of cocaine too. She held the smoke in her lungs until her body forced it out and repeated the process several times. Soon her head began to swim. This *was* strong shit!

She stared at Moroni, who was grinning at her. His hair was still in disarray, and Sheila started to giggle. He reminded her of Einstein.

"Never thought I'd see Albert Einstein shirtless," she said and fell back laughing.

Moroni looked at her askance. "Never thought I'd see *you* shirtless."

"What do you mean? You saw me completely naked."

"Not up close. Weren't you supposed to be hooked up with that C.Q. guy? Or are you still claiming to be a cousin?"

"Huh? Oh, you mean C.H." She dismissed the idea with a wave of her hand. "Naw, that's over."

"So I'm your rebound guy, is that it?"

That made her feel a little panicky. What if he threw her out? "No, no, it's not like that. I dumped *him*. I was already thinking about you before that— you're part of the reason I left him."

He seemed to like that. "Makes more sense. I don't know how he could dump a girl like you." He looked down at her breasts.

"Do you like to sleep naked?" she asked.

"Sure."

"Good."

It was time to make this personal. She stood up, but her legs wobbled, feeling like they would fall right off at the hip. She stepped carefully, and the floor seemed to give with each footstep, as if it were made of sponge. When she plopped into Moroni's lap, he leaned back in his chair to accommodate her, his eyes wide. She knew he was thinking how lucky he was right now. "Do you know I was naked right before I came here? I wished I could walk over naked without getting arrested."

"I'd like to have seen that," he said with a stream of smoke coming out of his mouth and nostrils.

She stroked his frizzy hair with one hand. "You still can." She set her smoldering joint in the ashtray, unbuttoned her jeans, and kicked them as far away as she could.

He peered at her and started to chuckle. "You're something else, babe." He leaned forward. "Of course, I meant I wish I could see you walking naked across the street."

She tingled all over, and her body felt light enough to float. His dare sounded like fun.

"This ain't no weed," she mumbled, picking up the joint and staring at it. "What'd you give me?"

"Sure it is," Moroni said.

"Weed and what else?"

"A little dust for my angel."

That made her laugh. She was Moroni's angel, the Angel Moroni, she'd seen an angel, C.H. tried to make her an angel...

"Come sit on my lap again," he said, beckoning her over.

"I thought you wanted to see me walk across the street naked."

"Sounds great."

"You'll have to join me."

"Sure, babe."

"I mean naked. You have to come outside naked with me."

He set his joint in the ashtray. "What about the neighbors?"

Sheila scowled and dropped onto his lap again. "To hell with the neighbors! What business is it of theirs anyway?" She ran her hands over his tight arms and chest and abdomen, and then she fumbled to unbutton his pants.

"It's cold out."

She kissed his cheek and nibbled on his ear. "Aren't you a big, strong, tough guy? Gonna let a little cold stop you?"

She stood up and backed toward the front door. "Come on, tough guy," she taunted, beckoning with a hand.

Moroni half-grinned, half-leered as he stared at her. He grabbed the joint and stuck it back in his mouth and sucked deeply. Then he removed his pants and his brightly colored briefs. Sheila liked what she saw—bigger than C.H.! She giggled and ran for the door, checking back to make sure he followed. He did.

The blast of cool autumn air when she flung open the door made her catch her breath, but it felt great. What a rush of sensations! A boy rode by on his bike as she stepped out, and she waved at him. Moroni came up from behind and put his arms around her, pressing them against her breasts. She shivered with excitement and with the sudden warmth of his body heat. He kissed the nape of her neck, then moved around to her ear and nibbled. She giggled and would have lost her balance if it weren't for his muscular arms.

Someone down the street shouted at them, but she didn't pay any attention.

Not quite understanding how, Sheila found herself lying on her back with the chilly grass pressing against her and Moroni on top. She swore she could feel every individual blade stroking her skin. The cold of the lawn on her back and the warmth of Moroni's weight caused her to tremble ecstatically. She was floating in space with the sun before her and the void behind, as if she were the planet Mercury, keeping one face to the sun.

There were people talking not too far off. She wished they would shut up. "Go have your own sex!" she cried at them—or did she just think it? Why didn't they just go into Moroni's house and enjoy the *Hustler* magazines instead of gaping at them? Didn't they have any sense of decorum?

Her breathing came in desperate gasps. This was better than anything C.H. had done. This was even better than with Steven! He never made her become a planet flying through space. And when the time came for her to explode, her planetary body burst into a quadrillion pieces, shooting everywhere and every-when—all of space and time couldn't contain it. Countless blinding streaks of light turned the jet blackness of the universe into noonday. Brighter than the noonday sun. She giggled. Maybe *that's* what Joseph Smith saw.

Someone ripped Moroni from her, causing her to cry out at the sudden loss of comforting warmth. Others helped her up and threw somet kind of fabric around her. "Are you alright, ma'am?" said a voice.

She began to cry. Why had they taken Moroni away from her? She wanted to remain locked together as they swam through the cosmos. She wanted to embrace him tightly as they floated down from their explosion. Who did this to her?

She tried to focus on the figure in front of her. There was dark clothing. And a shiny thing on it. A badge. The police. She gasped and tried to run, but she tripped and fell.

"Ma'am, calm down, everything's okay now," the officer said. "We've got him."

Got who? What was he talking about? Did he mean they got Moroni? Of course they did, and she wanted him back. Why did he say everything was okay, when Moroni wasn't in her arms?

Hands rested on her shoulders and guided her toward dizzily flashing lights, red and blue. "Get in here, ma'am," a woman's voice said. "We'll take you to the hospital."

The hands guided her into a car, and the door closed beside her. Sheila's surroundings began to come into focus. She heard a police dispatch radio rasping, echoing throughout the cosmos she was still swimming in—swimming alone, a million pieces of herself wandering the sky, searching for Moroni to put her back together again. Those dreadful red-and-blue lights spun everywhere.

Then she saw him. Moroni was beautiful, regal, as he strutted along. Colored shadows played over his nude body as they led him in handcuffs to another car and threw a blanket over him.

What was going on? Why was Moroni in handcuffs? Sudden panic set in. She didn't understand what was happening. "Where are they taking him?" she cried.

"It's alright, ma'am," some disembodied voice said out of the void. "He can't hurt you now."

She searched around desperately, tears streaming down her face. She was in...in a cop car! Panic overwhelmed her. There had to be some way to escape.

The door on the other side of her opened, and someone sat next to her. She couldn't control the shaking that engulfed her body.

"Oh, honey, please calm down," said a woman's voice. "They've got the man in custody. You're safe now."

No, she wasn't safe at all. She needed to get away.

"We'll take you to the hospital. They'll check you out and make sure everything's alright. Then you'll get some counseling to help you deal with this."

"Counseling?" she uttered weakly.

"Yes, for the rape."

Rape? The voice thought she'd been raped? Fear shuddered through her. She didn't remember being raped. She only remembered floating through space and exploding into a million pieces.

"In a way, you're lucky," the voice went on. "Although it sounds ridiculous to say that under the circumstances. But you probably won't even have to testify, since there were so many witnesses."

She tried to shake the clouds of confusion from her mind. She hadn't been raped. She *wanted* Moroni to take her.

Hadn't she?

She was sure of it.

Wasn't she?

"Rape," Sheila echoed, trying out the word.

She saw a face full of pathos before her. It brought Sheila to tears, although she didn't understand why. What was making that face so sad?

"A boy in the neighborhood saw you trying to escape out of the house," the face said. "He saw how your attacker ran after you and grabbed you, then forced you to the ground and raped you. An adult two houses down confirmed it." The face leaned closer, and Sheila felt a hand rest on her shoulder. "Did he tear your clothes off in the house?"

Sheila tried to think. She wasn't sure. Someone must have taken off her clothes. Before she flew into space.

"She's really out of it," said the voice, more distantly. "He must have slipped her something."

"Rape," Sheila murmured. "Somebody raped me." She meant to ask it as a question, but she wasn't sure it came out that way.

Just when Special Agent Robinson was most enjoying his late Sunday-morning sleep, his phone rang. He reached over and fumbled for it with his eyes half-shut. His wife rolled onto her side, facing away from him. "Yeah," he croaked, "what is it?"

"We've got word about an incident next to the Youngs' home," the agent on the phone said.

"An incident?" Robinson let his head plop back onto his pillow. "What kind of an incident?"

"The Matthews girl living behind them went across the street..." The agent paused, and Robinson could hear paper rustling. "...to visit Moroni Samuelsen.

Later she was seen running from the house nude and chased by Samuelsen, who was also nude. They ended up having sex on the lawn. They were high on something. Apparently it's being considered a rape."

That opened his eyes. "Thanks," Robinson said. "I'll get on it."

He disconnected. This was too much. After everything else going on there, a rape right out on the lawn involving drugs? It was time for Special Agent Robinson to head out there personally and investigate. He climbed out of bed, causing a moan to escape his wife's lips, and hurriedly dressed.

Chapter 16

C.H. breathed a sigh of relief as he left Sheila's apartment. He needed to spend some time sorting through his feelings about her.

How soon he could do that, he wasn't sure. He had to face Dani next—for the first time since making love to Sheila. That would be an ordeal in and of itself. He had no idea how it would go.

Should he tell her how he felt about Sheila now? Would that make her happy? Or would she be angry that, after going through all this—including having sex with Sheila—he might back out of the whole thing?

He didn't know if he had the strength to deal with that right now. As he started up the car, he flirted with the idea of driving off somewhere on his own so he could think. He backed into the street and put the car into drive, but then he stopped. No, he couldn't be that cowardly with Dani. She was the one suffering the most through all this. The least he could do was be a man and face her.

More than that, he was tired of hiding things, especially from his wife. He would just go in there, and whatever happened happened. He'd let her know exactly how he felt. It wasn't like she'd leave him—not Dani. Not if she hadn't already left him through all this.

He drove around to their driveway and found the SUV missing. Dani wasn't even home. Where would she go on a Sunday morning? There was still an hour or so before church.

He'd have felt happy to have the house all to himself if it wasn't so strange that she was gone right now. He couldn't think of anywhere she be likely to go.

Inside the house, he found the TV and VCR on. Snow flickered noisily on the screen. She must have left a tape running and forgotten to shut everything off, as if she left in a hurry. Had there been an emergency?

There was no note anywhere. He wondered if he should start calling hospitals, but he felt foolish doing that with so little information. Maybe she just got bored and went for a drive. If there really was an emergency, she'd call soon.

What he needed right then more than anything was sleep. He still had a few hours before he was due at work. He kicked off his shoes and headed for the bedroom. When he heard the doorbell ring, he didn't know if he'd slept for minutes or hours. He certainly didn't feel rested.

He hadn't locked the door, so it wouldn't be Dani. Sheila, perhaps? No, she wouldn't come by right after their wedding night and risk meeting Dani.

Unless something serious was up. Like she wanted to call the whole thing off because she sensed how he felt. That would be a relief, but what would God think about it? Well, if Sheila wanted to back out, there was nothing he could do. No point trying to hide his mixed emotions from God, who already knew about them of course.

The doorbell rang again, and he hurried out and opened the door. To his surprise, there stood Cyndy.

"H-hello, Brother Young," she said. She looked nervous.

"Hi, Cyndy. What can I do for you?"

She looked around the neighborhood like she was trying to hide something. "I have something important to tell you."

"Okay."

"Do you know what it's about?" she asked, sounding hopeful.

"Not a clue."

Her face wrinkled with disappointment. "Can I come in and talk?"

He needed to get ready for work, and for an instant he wondered if it was wise to be alone in the house with a fourteen-year-old girl who had a crush on him. After all, he was slated to be the next president of the church. Rumors could start flying fast and grow all out of proportion.

On the other hand, with the way he felt about Sheila now, maybe he wouldn't end up as president anyway. Maybe that calling would be given to another— someone who would follow God's commandments more enthusiastically. He felt sorry for the poor soul who might replace him.

But this was Cyndy, a friend of the family. He'd been alone with her a number of times before with Dani's knowledge, and nothing had ever come of it. "Sure, Cyndy," he said. "Come on in."

He led her into the living room, motioned for her to sit on the sofa, then sat in the chair. She fidgeted as she gazed at the floor. "I don't know where to start."

Man, was she nervous! He wondered what she had to say. Had she done something wrong and didn't know who else to talk to? "It's alright, Cyndy. You can tell me anything. I'll understand."

She peered at him, as if deciding whether she could believe that. Then she looked down again. "I saw Brigham Young."

"*Wha-at?*" He slowly stood up.

Tears formed in her eyes. "I knew it. I'm going to kill Ryan!"

"Wait a minute. You really saw Brigham Young?"

"I...saw something. It looked like him. I think my brother played a trick on me." She dabbed at her eyes.

Sitting back down, he said, "Did he say anything to you?"

"Brigham Young?"

"Yes."

She got even more nervous, if that were possible. "You're not going to believe this, but...well, he said we should get married." Then she spat out fast, "But I think it was just Ryan."

He barely heard the last part. Brigham Young had told Cyndy to marry him. It was Dani's greatest fear, and he was certain it would never happen.

Yet it made sense, in a roundabout sort of way. He knew there'd be more wives to come, and Brother Brigham had emphasized the urgency of time. That another wife would have been selected by now was not strange—some of the old-time polygamists had married several wives at once. And the timing was perfect. Just as C.H. was considering abandoning the whole thing, God placed a clear-cut choice in front of him: Will you obey me or not? Will you marry the next woman I command you to take as a wife?

Woman? She was a girl, barely past puberty.

But what about his promise to Dani? She asked that he not marry any underage girl, *specifically* Cyndy. So, of course, the next wife God wanted him to marry was Cyndy. It was the test of Abraham all over again, a choice between God and the person C.H. loved most. It was Joseph Smith's dilemma all over again, obey God or obey his wife.

Yes, it made perfect sense. He was being tested to the hilt before the mantle of the prophet was bestowed upon him.

"I believe you," he told Cyndy. "I've seen Brigham Young myself. He didn't tell me about *you*, but he told me I'd be practicing polygamy and marrying more wives."

Her eyes popped wide open, and relief seemed to sweep across her face. "Like that lady who moved in behind you?" she asked timidly.

"Yes, I just married Sheila. She's my second wife."

"And I'd be your third?"

He nodded. He would have thought a command like this would freak someone like Cyndy out. But then again, she did have a crush on him. Maybe this was a dream come true for her.

"So how do you feel about all this?" he said.

Her lower lip began to tremble. "I..." Her tears started again. "I..." She shook her head. "I feel too embarrassed to say."

"It's okay, Cyndy. You can tell me anything. Anything at all. You don't need to be embarrassed with me."

She peered at him through swimming eyes, her lip still trembling. "I love you, Brother Young."

He sighed. Any other time he'd have felt obligated to let her down slowly. But this time, apparently, the crush was the very thing needed to help along the commandment of God. Troubling as it felt, he knew he should encourage it. "I see. I wish I could say I love you, but I don't know you that well yet." Noting the sudden look of alarm on her face, he added quickly, "I'm sure I could grow to love you. You're a very pretty girl, and a nice one. You've been very good with our boys. I guess if God really does want us to get married, I would like that very much."

He felt like a child molester grooming his next victim, but his words pleased her. She nearly smiled, and her face beamed through her flagging tears.

"I'll have to get my own confirmation from God, though," he added. "I can't take another wife unless I get a direct commandment."

She nodded, then startled as a patch of glowing light formed in the air between them. Brother Brigham materialized, facing C.H.

"Cynthia is correct, Cory Horace," he said. "She is to be your next wife. You are to marry her immediately."

He froze in place. This was happening too fast! He wasn't even sure he wanted to stay with his second wife, and here he was expected to take a third wife—an underage wife. The world would consider him a sexual predator.

But first he needed to deal with the biggest reservation of all.

"I promised Dani I wouldn't marry someone who's under age."

"I know," Brother Brigham said. "Nonetheless, it is the command of God. Will you obey God or your wife?"

It was if Brigham had been listening in on his thoughts—for all he knew, Brigham *had* somehow listened in. Anything was possible with God. Including, apparently, being commanded to marry a fourteen-year-old child.

There was no point in mentioning the other reservations. If the biggest one hadn't made Brigham flinch, the rest certainly wouldn't. All he could do now was make his choice: obey God or his wife.

He wanted to see how Cyndy was taking this, but Brigham stood between them. C.H. rose and walked over to her. She was staring at Brother Brigham with her mouth open. Apparently, the first time she saw him, she didn't take it seriously—not entirely. She thought her brother was playing a trick on her. But she took it seriously enough to come over and make sure.

Now it must be sinking in that she *had* seen Brigham Young and that he *had* commanded her to marry the man she loved, even though he was already married. Would she be happy or terrified as the reality hit her?

He sat next to her. In her face he saw awe, a little confusion perhaps, and possibly some anticipation. But there wasn't a hint of fear. Cyndy wanted to marry him.

Should he marry her?

Should he choose God or Dani?

Would Dani understand? Or would she leave him?

Knowing Dani, she would be furious if he broke his promise to her. But in the end, she would understand. He had to obey God. There was nothing else he could do. He shouldn't have made that promise in the first place. And, to be honest, she shouldn't have demanded it of him. The only way he would marry an underage girl was if God commanded it.

But nothing said he had to have sex with her, not until she was of age. That should help Dani feel better and appease anyone accusing him of being a predator. He wondered if Cyndy would even want sex anyway. A fourteen-year-old girl probably didn't think of marriage in those terms, just in terms of how romantic it would be. The prospect of having sex with him might actually frighten her.

He knelt down on one knee and took her hand. "Cyndy, will you marry me?"

Her tears burst out, and she threw her arms around him. "Yes," she whispered in his ear.

He stood and lifted her to a standing position. "Okay, Brother Brigham, we'll obey God. When should we get married, and how? She's too young to go to the temple."

"You will be married now," Brigham said sternly. "You will *not* be going to the temple this time, not at first. I will marry you right here."

Cyndy's hand was shaking. C.H. felt a little trembling in his own body. This was certainly going fast! Was he really ready to do this?

Yes, as long as he didn't have to have sex with her until she was eighteen.

Brother Brigham launched into a series of words that sounded fleetingly like the sealing ceremony in the temple. C.H. supposed the words were different because they were not being married in the temple and Cyndy was a minor. Brigham spoke more of a promise for an eternal union rather than a declaration of one.

"You may kiss now as husband and wife," he finally said.

Cyndy blushed beet-red. C.H. turned to her and, stooping down, kissed her on the cheek.

"That was a pretty chaste kiss," Brigham said with a smirk. "You're married now."

The smirk made him feel uneasy. Brother Brigham hadn't done anything like that before. It made him seem like an intruder on this private moment. Maybe he didn't fully understand how strange it felt in this day and age to marry such a young girl.

"We'll kiss more passionately when you're not around," he said, trying to suppress an angry tone.

"You should leave on your wedding night now," Brother Brigham said. "I will explain to Danielle and Sheila what's happened."

That didn't sound like a very good idea. He wanted to be the one to tell Dani. To do otherwise would look cowardly.

"Cyndy," C.H. said, "do you want to go to a hotel room with me?"

She studied the floor, red-faced as ever. "Um..."

"I don't think she's quite ready, Brigham. I think we'll put off the wedding night for now."

Brigham scowled. "I'm sorry, Cory, but you are obliged to consummate the marriage now. To do otherwise makes a mockery of God's command."

"She's not ready." C.H. felt somewhat amazed that he was talking back to an angel of God. His decision not to have sex had been the only thing that brought him to obey the commandment in the first place. Besides, Cyndy wasn't ready. As her husband, he was obligated to protect her sensibilities. "This is a private matter between husband and wife. Not even an angel should interfere with this."

The glow around Brigham intensified into a dark yellow-orange radiance. "It is not I who commands you, but God!" he said ominously. "Are you saying God does not have the right to interfere in this?"

Brigham's eyes glared with a ferocity that frightened him. Cyndy pulled back and cowered behind him, keeping her hand in his. Something felt very wrong.

"Where's Dani?"

"Danielle is fine," Brother Brigham said. "You'll be hearing about—from her fairly soon.

Very, very wrong. "What's going on here, Brother Brigham?"

"You have just been married to your third wife, and you must now consummate the marriage. The need is urgent to restore celestial marriage."

"It's already been restored," C.H. said with some belligerence. "I just restored it last night."

"You will consummate the marriage now!"

"No, Brother Brigham," C.H. said, trembling. "Cyndy is not ready, and I won't traumatize her by forcing her."

Brother Brigham's expression became ugly. The phone suddenly rang, causing both C.H. and Cyndy to jump.

"Do not answer that!" Brigham bellowed. "You must consummate the marriage *now*. It is the will of God."

He didn't know what to do, except stall for time. "Then let us be alone in the bedroom."

"No!" Brigham roared. "You have demonstrated your faithlessness. You must act here in this room—at once!"

Cyndy began to whimper, burying her face in C.H.'s side. He put his arm around her and squeezed. "It's okay, Cyndy. We won't do anything you don't want to do."

"Will you defy the command of God?" Brigham shouted. His face twisted with wrath, and the glow around him boiled, deepening to a crimson red. The daylight shining through the window darkened considerably. The phone continued to ring.

Something shimmered behind Brother Brigham in the darkness. C.H. thought he saw a face, then another—ethereal things floating in the shimmering. The faces looked dark and terrible. Some glowered, some smirked, and some leered. C.H. held Cyndy's head against his side so she wouldn't look up.

"Will you obey the command of God?" Brigham bellowed.

Dread filled him as he realized this apparition could not be Brigham Young. What a fool he'd been, believing it!

Brother Brigham gestured toward the specters behind him. "Will you fight the hosts of heaven?"

"You are not the hosts of heaven," he whispered, his body tingling with fear. He felt Cyndy press her face harder against him.

Brother Brigham laughed.

But how could this not be Brigham Young? "You refused to shake hands with me," C.H. said.

"Refused?" Brigham said. "I don't recall *refusing* to shake hands with you."

"But—you did—"

"I said I'd rather not." He shrugged one shoulder. "But if you had insisted, well—" He laughed an appalling laugh. "I guess you really wanted to believe."

"This can't be..." He felt on the verge of fainting. How had he been so easily duped?

Brother Brigham snickered. "You think we don't know what the Doctrine and Covenants says? Of course we'll try to avoid shaking hands, if you let us. All you had to do was insist. You've got the priesthood. How could we resist your command?"

C.H.'s head swam so he could hardly stand. "But—what about the interview with the bishop? The basketball—the injury. You couldn't have known that would happen if..."

Brother Brigham chuckled with satisfaction. "A risk, I admit. But a little whispering at the opportune moment into the ear of a frustrated boy—it's amazing how easy it is to get boys to do things while playing sports that they normally wouldn't do, like trip another boy into the wall."

He'd really been deceived! It was more than he could endure.

"You think we don't know you?" Brother Brigham said, glaring. The hosts behind him laughed and snarled and growled. "We know you better than you know yourself. We're *assigned* to look after you." He grinned smugly. "We come to know our charges very well—their deepest, darkest secrets, their most intimate desires, their most vulnerable weaknesses. We know who will be susceptible to what temptations, to what deceptions." He laughed boisterously. "By the great Lucifer himself, were you susceptible!"

The room seemed to spin, and C.H.'s vision telescoped until all he could see was the frightening visage of Brother Brigham. The apparition took one step closer.

"By the way, I told Cain about your little joke with his name. He was very amused. He can't wait to meet you."

"I—" He fought to get out the words. "I'm no son of perdition."

"No, I suppose not," Brother Brigham said with a hint of disappointment, taking another step toward C.H. "But you *will* be in the neighborhood for a while. Say, oh, about a thousand years, enjoying the buffetings of Satan. Don't you think?"

"Get away from me, Satan," C.H. rasped.

"Well, *my* name isn't Satan, but I get your point." He grinned a ghastly grin. "And how do you expect to enforce this?"

"I—command you," he gasped out, "by the power of the priesthood—"

"What priesthood?" Brother Brigham said. He lifted a mocking finger. "Ah, perhaps you mean that priesthood that comes from Father. But don't you think Father said amen to your priesthood long ago? You just married a second wife in the temple—and she wasn't the least bit worthy to enter. You defiled the temple, and then you had sex with her. You committed adultery. You accepted apostate teachings."

"I—uh—" C.H. couldn't speak. Cyndy had slid to the floor and was hugging his legs so tightly that he almost fell over. She was gazing up at Brother Brigham, her face contorted with fear.

Brother Brigham took another step toward him, and the hosts followed behind. "I want to thank you for a good time. I haven't had this much fun since I appeared to Korihor as an angel of light. I'm sure you read all about that in the Book of Mormon."

C.H. shook his head. He couldn't believe what was happening. Tears welled up in his eyes. Utter blackness seemed to permeate the room. Had the sun gone out? Had the black glory of Outer Darkness filled the room?

"Of course, I was hoping to take this a little further." Brigham stepped still closer. "I was hoping to add sex with a young girl to your list of accomplishments. Still, it was a fulfilling experience."

C.H. had to do something. "By—by the—power—" He tried to force out the words between gasps. "In the—name—of—"

"Don't bother," Brother Brigham said, taking another step. "It won't work. You're an apostate."

"I'm not," C.H. rasped. "You deceived me."

Brother Brigham grinned as he leaned forward and came within inches of C.H.'s nose. "Whatever."

He pounced, and C.H. screamed.

Chapter 17

Cyndy felt like the darkness would engulf her. She'd never felt so horrible in her life. Suddenly Brother Young screamed, then Brigham Young and all the creepy faces behind him whooshed into his body. There must have been dozens of them, many even hundreds, and suddenly they were gone. The darkness seemed to wash out of the room instantly. Sunlight shone through the window again.

Brother Young jerked violently and thrust himself back, hitting his shoulder on the arm of the sofa and then rolling to the floor. Cyndy's embrace around his legs broke, and she caught her fall with her hands. Sprawled out awkwardly, she gaped at Brother Young.

He shook all over. His eyes stared off at nothing, wide and wild. Strange sounds came from his mouth, like he needed to throw up and was trying to hold it back. Suddenly a deep growl started low and quiet in his throat, building up louder and louder, more ferocious. He raised himself on his arms, his face contorted like the tragedy mask in theater. The growl grew into a roar, louder and more gruesome than the lion Cyndy once heard at Hogle Zoo. He rolled over and thrashed, banging his thigh against the coffee table, and then he rolled again, pushing aside the table. His arms and legs flailed everywhere, his body jerking like the dead frog in biology class when she shot electricity through it.

Cyndy clamped her hands over her ears as the roar echoed through the room. Brother Young rolled several times toward the TV set, then rolled back toward her. She scampered onto the sofa as he twisted sideways and rose to a sitting position. He howled once more, and Cyndy covered her ears again.

His fierce eyes fixed on her. He growled at her like a villain in a silly horror movie, but it wasn't silly now. Cyndy had never seen a human being look so ugly. His eyes were dark and glaring, his face contorted in a grimace of anger and hate, and his body trembled like he was shivering in a freezer.

The ugly face leered at her. "Come here, little girl," he said in a rasp that was

Brother Young's voice, but harsh and vicious. "Come and play with me."

Cyndy was too frightened to move. She didn't know where to go. Brother Young sat between her and the door. His eyes looked horrible, as if a crazy person stared out from behind them. She had never been so terrified in her life—and of the man she loved!

"Come and play, Cyndy," Brother Young snarled. Then he tried to grin. "We're married. Let's play house!"

She felt like his gaze could rip the clothes from her—in fact, she felt naked already. Reflexively she curled up with her arms and legs in front of her. She had to keep blinking to clear her eyes—she wanted to burst into tears but didn't dare take her focus away from him.

All those horrible faces—she knew they were inside him. They had all gone inside Brother Young. He was possessed by hundreds of devils!

What should she do? She had to tell somebody. She had to get some help.

Brother Young's body convulsed again, almost dancing in place on the rug. His continuous growl pulsated with each bounce, like an engine trying to start.

This might be her chance.

She bolted for the door. Brother Young reached out. His hand clawed at her, but he missed, only scraping his fingernails on her jeans. He bellowed worse than any werewolf in any movie she'd ever seen. To her relief, the slamming of the door cut the noise short.

She saw several cop cars across the street, lights flashing. Were they here for Brother Young already? No, that was crazy. They couldn't know what happened. But why were they there?

Whatever—she had to get help. She started for them but then stopped. What could cops do about someone possessed with a bunch of devils? What would they care about that? Why would they even believe her? No, she needed someone else, someone who'd believe her and could do something about devils.

She needed Bishop Schmidt.

She raced for his house a couple doors passed her own. What if he wasn't home? What if he was at church?

"Please, Heavenly Father," she panted out loud as she ran. "Let me find him home."

She turned the corner. There was no car in the bishop's driveway, but it could be in the garage. She leaped up the three steps and almost slammed into the door, banging it with her hands and forearms. Then she punched the doorbell with her finger several times.

The door opened, and his wife stood there. "Cyndy," she said. "What's wrong?"

"Is Bishop Schmidt home?" she gasped desperately between breaths. "I need the bishop."

"He's just about to leave for church. But he's running late—"

Cyndy pushed past her and ran in. "Bishop! Bishop! Help!"

The bishop appeared from a hallway, dressed in suit pants and a white shirt with no tie yet, carrying his shoes in one hand. He looked at her with alarm. "Cyndy, what's the matter?"

"Bishop, you gotta help me!" She leaned over to catch her breath and keep her head from getting too dizzy. "It's—it's Brother Young. He needs your help— *now!*"

He trotted into the living room, sat down on a chair, and lifted a leg to put on a shoe. "Where is he? What's wrong?"

"No!" Cyndy cried, grabbing the shoe out of his hand and tossing it against the wall. 'You gotta come *now!*" She pulled on his arm until he stood.

"For heaven's sake, Cyndy, what's wrong?"

"He's possessed. Devils got him. A hundred devils."

"What?" The bishop gave her a skeptical look.

"*I'm not kidding!*" She pulled him to the door.

"Cyndy, where is he?" the bishop's wife asked.

"Home. He's rolling all over the floor and shaking."

The bishop cocked his head. She must have said something that caught his attention. "Alright, Cyndy," he said, fishing some keys out of his pocket. "Let's go."

He started pulling her, leading her through a door into the garage. "Get in," he said, pointing at the nearest of two cars. She climbed into the passenger seat as he got in, started the car with one hand, and pushed the button of the garage-door opener with the other. The door wasn't quite up as he started backing out, and the antenna bent forward and then wobbled as they pulled into the street. The bishop jerked the car into drive and squealed the tires.

Checking both ways for cars, he ran the stop sign at the end of the street. He zoomed ahead but hit the brakes as soon as he saw the cop cars. With his expression looking even more puzzled and concerned, he parked one house down from Brother Young's.

"Come on," he said, throwing the car into park and shutting off the engine. He jumped out and Cyndy followed, watching his shoeless feet run along the sidewalk. The soles of his black socks became gray with dust.

"What are the police here for?" he asked her.

"I don't know."

They jogged up the driveway. Cyndy could have sworn she heard the bishop mutter a quiet "Damn!" as he stepped on a bit of gravel. When they heard a crashing sound come from the house, he paused, and Cyndy stopped beside him.

There was another crash and then another, and suddenly something flew through the window, smashing the glass.

"Holy—" the bishop said. A book lay in front of them, *Orson Scott Card* written across its face in large letters.

"Stay out here." He ran to the front door and headed inside.

No way, thought Cyndy. She was still frightened, but not nearly so much now that the bishop was here. She darted through the door and stopped short next to the bishop, letting out a gasp.

Brother Young stood in the middle of the room, glaring at the bishop. He was completely naked, and his clothes were strewn about the floor in shreds. His whole body was covered with scratches and scrapes. Blood oozed from an ugly gash on his upper cheek.

As all three of them stood frozen, Cyndy noticed more things. The screen of the TV was smashed in. The chair was toppled onto its side. The Blu-ray player was in shambles on the kitchen floor. The fingers of Brother Young's left hand hung limp and crooked, and there was a fist-sized hole in the wall behind him.

"What do you want?" Brother Young said in that same dreadful voice.

"Who are you?" the bishop asked, eyes wide.

Brother Young grinned. It looked like a grimace of pain more than amusement. "I'm Brigham Young."

The bishop slowly shook his head. "No, you're not."

Howling, Brother Young picked up the coffee table and heaved it at the bishop. Cyndy couldn't believe how strong he seemed. Trying to duck, the bishop deflected the table with his arm. He cried out in pain and rubbed his elbow.

"I am Brigham Young!" Brother Young raged.

"I command you in the name of Jesus Christ to tell me who you are," the bishop said in a firm voice.

Brother Young cried out with a gurgling sound. Then he inhaled deeply and fixed his gaze on the bishop. "I am Legion," he hissed, his eyes glowing with arrogance.

"Legion," the bishop whispered as his face went white.

Cyndy remembered that name from a story in Sunday School. Jesus asked a possessed man what his name was. "Legion," the man said, "because there's a bunch of us"—or something like that. Jesus cast out the devils and they jumped into some pigs, who ran over a cliff and died. Could these be the same devils?

She remembered what Brigham Young said to Brother Young. Pointing at Brother Young, she said, "The main one's the same devil who appeared to, uh, Cori—in the Book of Mormon, Cori—Coriantumr, I think."

"Korihor?" said the Bishop.

"Yeah, that's him!"

The bishop peered at Brother Young, and Cyndy thought she saw him trembling. "I command you—"

"*No!*" Brother Young shrieked.

"—in the name of Jesus Christ—"

With both hands extended, Brother Young charged the bishop, and Cyndy screamed.

"—and by the power of the Melchizedek Priesthood—"

Brother Young wrapped his good hand around the bishop's throat and squeezed. Grabbing the wrist with both hands, the bishop managed to pull off the hand.

"—I command you to depart—"

The heel of the broken hand pressed against the bishop's throat, cutting off his voice. Cyndy jumped forward and stomped Brother Young's foot as hard as she could, but he didn't flinch. As soon as the bishop pushed away the hurt hand, the good hand grabbed his throat again.

Cyndy stomped on the other foot and then kicked Brother Young's shins. He hissed at her but didn't back off.

Enough of this! She bashed her knee as deep as she could into Brother Young's groin. He lurched back with a powerful gasp, his eyes bulging.

"I command you, Legion, to depart from this man at once!" the bishop rasped as fast as he could. Holding his throat, he coughed heavily.

The howl that came from Brother Young's mouth reverberated through the room, hurting Cyndy's ears. Brother Young convulsed, toppled, and bashed his head on the side of the TV stand. The room darkened as multiple howls rang out, then suddenly a creepy silence fell upon everything and the sunlight returned.

Leaning against the wall, the bishop panted and held his throat. Brother Young lay still on the carpet, blood seeping from his new wound. Cyndy began to cry. Maybe he was dead! She went over to him and knelt down.

"Cyndy," the bishop said, his voice still hoarse. "What happened here?"

A blast of static caused Cyndy to look up. Someone appeared in the open doorway. It was one of the cops from across the street. Peering around the room, he looked at the bishop, Cyndy, then Brother Young on the floor. He lifted a radio to his mouth and said, "We need an ambulance. Fourth East just south of I-80." Still talking, he stepped out to report the exact house number.

Cyndy felt Brother Young's chest. His heart was still beating, and his lungs were breathing.

"What's going on here?" The cop came back inside. "What happened to this man? Why is he naked?"

Cyndy looked at the bishop. He gazed at her for an instant and then looked at the cop. "I'm not sure." He took a step toward her.

"Please stay where you are," the cop said. "Young lady, please move away from the body."

"He's alive," she growled as she stood and joined the bishop.

Another cop showed up, and the first one moved to Brother Young and stooped down. He felt his neck, opened an eyelid, and examined the gashes on his head. "How is he?" the other cop asked.

"Well, he's alive."

"I told you," Cyndy said, scowling.

Another person appeared in the doorway, a man dressed in a suit. The second officer moved further into the room to let him in. The man studied the room, then walked over to the bishop and Cyndy, flipped open a wallet, and showed a badge.

"I'm Special Agent Robinson from the Federal Bureau of Investigations. Are you Cory Young?"

"No, I'm his bishop." The bishop pointed at Brother Young. "That's C.H. Young there."

"And this girl?"

"I'm Cyndy McGarry," she said quickly, not wanting the bishop to answer for her.

More police started showing up, and the FBI agent said, "Will you two please come outside?"

They followed him out. Poking his shoe tip at broken glass and peering at the book lying on the lawn, the agent asked, "What happened here?"

It was the third time that question had been asked, and Cyndy was still at a loss how to answer. How could she tell the police and an FBI agent that a devil had appeared to her, called himself Brigham Young, married her to a grown man, and then possessed that man? They'd take her to the loony bin.

A devil? But if Brigham Young was really a devil...

She didn't want to think the next thought. *I'm his wife!* she cried in her head.

"I'm not sure," the bishop repeated.

The FBI agent looked at Cyndy. "Can you tell me what happened?"

Cyndy looked back and forth between the two men, having no idea where to even start.

The bishop cleared his throat. "Cyndy here came rushing over to my house and told me that C.H. was in trouble. She asked me to come over and help. When I got here, he was carrying on like—like he was having a nervous breakdown or something. I—"

"No!" Cyndy cried. The thought of the cops and the FBI thinking Brother Young was crazy was too much for her. "It wasn't a nervous breakdown."

"Cyndy—" the bishop began.

"He's a good man, and he's not crazy."

"What is your relationship with him, Cyndy?" the FBI agent asked.

She took a deep breath and glanced at the bishop. His expression seemed to tell her to shut up. But she was tired of being treated like a child, tired of hiding all these feelings she had. It was time she declared herself so they could start treating her like the mature woman she was. "I'm his wife," she said proudly.

The bishop's jaw dropped. The FBI agent's face jerked toward the bishop. "Is this true, sir?"

"I don't know what she's talking about," the bishop said. "His wife is Danielle, and she's much older than Cyndy."

"Danielle is his first wife," she said.

The agent's eyebrows went up. The bishop gaped at her.

"So you're the second wife?" the FBI agent asked.

She shook her head. "The lady in back is his second wife."

The agent pulled a notebook from his jacket and thumbed through it. "That would be...Sheila Matthews?"

"I don't know her name," Cyndy said.

The agent looked at the bishop. "I have no idea who Sheila Matthews is," the bishop said.

"You're his third wife?" the FBI agent asked Cyndy.

"Yes, his third wife."

"And you're his bishop?"

Bishop Schmidt scowled at Cyndy, and she lowered her eyes. "Yes, I'm his bishop."

"Cyndy's too?"

"Yes."

The agent studied them both. "How did C.H. get so banged up?"

The bishop opened his mouth, but she didn't want him talking about any nervous breakdown again. Why shouldn't they just tell the truth? So what if the cops didn't believe it? The truth was the truth. Like they said in all her church classes, be honest, tell the truth, and everything will work out.

"Some devils possessed him," she said, refusing to look at Bishop Schmidt.

"Devils, you say?" the agent said.

"Lots of them." She gestured with one hand. "Like in the Bible. Legion."

"And that's what banged him up?"

"The devils possessed him, and he went crazy. I mean, they went crazy inside him, but now they're gone."

The agent turned to the bishop. "What do you say happened?"

Bishop Schmidt nodded his head with a sigh as he gazed at Cyndy. "It's like she said. She came over and got me to help. I found him acting violently, and...

and I cast out the spirits. He fell and hit his head on the TV stand. It knocked him out."

The FBI agent tapped his notebook. "I'm going to have to ask the two of you to come with me for further questioning. Cyndy, we'll need to have your mother or father there with you."

Cyndy began to tremble. She was going to be questioned by the FBI, like a desperate criminal? Her eyes welled, but she fought to hold back her tears—they'd just think she was a child. In the distance she could hear the siren of an approaching ambulance.

"Is this necessary?" the bishop asked. "We've told you pretty much what we know. You can ask us right here, and we can fill in any details."

"Details about polygamous wives and being possessed by devils and performing exorcisms?" the agent said. "Do you want to know what I think happened here?"

The bishop remained silent. Cyndy wanted to know—but she also didn't.

"I think we've got one of these Mormon polygamy rings going. This C.H. Young has married three wives, including this minor girl. You claim to be his bishop. I think there's been some kind of feud going on between cults, and you've beaten this man, perhaps in an attempt to kill him. Through Sheila Matthews we have a possible connection with drugs as well. No, sir, I don't think we can take care of this with a few questions while we stand here. Now, if you two will please get in that car." He gestured across the street at an unmarked car.

"Let's go, Cyndy," Bishop Schmidt said with a grim look on his face. He took her hand, and they started to walk, the FBI agent following right behind.

Cyndy knew she was in trouble. How had this happened? She only told the truth. Would the bishop yell at her the first chance he got? She thought of his wife, waiting at home for him to return so they could go to church, where the whole ward expected him to be.

She kept trying to hold back her tears. The agent said they'd have to get her mother. What would she think? Her daughter married a married man and got arrested by the FBI. Not even the regular police—it had to be the *FBI*.

The agent opened the back door and let them climb in, then he closed it behind them. He stood beside the car for a while, talking to some cops.

"Cyndy, what in the world's going on here?" Bishop Schmidt asked as soon as they were alone.

"It's like I said." She knew the yelling was about to begin.

"You married Brother Young?"

"Well..." She shrugged her shoulders. "Brigham Young married us. I mean—he called himself Brigham Young." She felt a wave of despair. The thought she didn't want to think was pressing in on her.

The bishop looked at her with intense eyes. "You mean to tell me an evil spirit appeared to Brother Young and said he was Brigham Young?"

"I guess so."

"How do you know?"

"Well, the spirit appeared to me too."

"It appeared to *you*?"

Cyndy nodded, chagrined. Did that mean she was evil?

"What's this about being married?"

"The spirit said we were supposed to get married. He said polygamy was being restored and Brother Young had already married another wife. I thought it was Ryan playing a trick on me and—"

Try as she might, she couldn't hold back the tears any longer. She felt so stupid. An evil spirit had come into her bedroom, and she thought it was a trick her brother was playing on her. Then she believed the evil spirit and went over to marry Brother Young, as if God would really command her to do that.

"How many wives does Brother Young have?"

"Just three, I'm pretty sure. That's what the spirit said." *Just* three wives? Boy, did *that* sound stupid!

"Oh dear. Oh my gosh." She could tell he was holding back stronger language.

Quietly she said, "We were married by—by that—" She looked at him as the tears flowed freely. "We're not really married, are we?"

"No, Cyndy, you're not," the bishop said sorrowfully. "Did you two, uh, do ...anything?"

"No. The spirit tried to get us to, but I was afraid, and Brother Young said he wouldn't do it because I wasn't ready."

"How did all this happen?" He had a faraway look, so she didn't think he was asking her. "How did it get so out of hand? Why didn't I know something was wrong? Where were his home teachers? I don't even know who his home teachers are. I'll bet they haven't been visiting him."

"Bishop, I don't want anything to happen to Brother Young. I love him."

"Oh, dear child. Oh, what a mess!" He put his arm around her and squeezed. "I don't want anything to happen to him either. But I don't know what's going to happen. This is all such a mess."

"It's all my fault, Bishop! I wanted to be his wife. I didn't realize it, but I wanted it so bad! I wished for it every night—I even prayed for it. It's all my fault."

"No, no, dear Cyndy. It's not your fault at all. Don't you worry—nothing will happen to you. We'll sort through this mess together and figure out what happened. Then we'll figure out how to make it right again. I promise you, we'll make it all right again...someday."

The FBI agent got into the car. "Alright, Cyndy, where do you live?"

She told him, and he started the car and pulled into the street.

"But it might not be easy, sorting all this out," the bishop said, a little quieter now that the agent was in the car. "It might be very hard."

"Bishop, are we evil—me and Brother Young?"

The bishop's eyes were moist when he looked at her. It made Cyndy feel better to know that an adult could feel like crying too.

"No, dear girl, you're not evil."

"But an evil spirit came to me."

"He was trying to deceive you."

"What about Brother Young? Is he evil?"

"No. He just lost his way somewhere along the line."

"I do love him, Bishop. I know we're not married, and I know we can't be because he's already married. But I still love him. I want him to be okay."

The bishop smiled at her, a doleful smile. "We'll make everything okay again, I promise. Can you be strong with me, and brave?"

Cyndy nodded. "To help Brother Young, I will."

They pulled into the driveway of Cyndy's home. She trembled uncontrollably, and the bishop put his arm around her. She felt so ashamed that she was trembling.

"Don't be afraid," he said. "Just tell the truth about what happened. We'll start sorting this out. With God's help, we'll make everything all right one day. I promise."

The FBI agent watched in the rearview mirror, but remained silent.

"Now go and get your mother," Bishop Schmidt said. "Everything will be okay."

Cyndy nodded and stepped out of the car.

Chapter 18

C.H. squirmed in his chair and glanced at the clock on the wall. It was only four minutes since their appointment was supposed to have started, but to him it felt like hours. His hand, still in the cast, was throbbing. He pulled out his bottle of prescription painkiller, removed a pill, and walked to the drinking fountain to swallow it.

Never in his life did he imagine he'd be sitting in an LDS Family Services office waiting for marriage counseling.

He returned to his seat. Across from him Dani sat. This was the first time they'd been in the same place since she returned home and asked him to leave. During the past two months, he appeared in court about the money he'd found and spent without reporting it and received a fine and six months of probation. He attended a disciplinary council. The three men of the bishopric deliberated for some time before calling him back into the bishop's office. One counselor held out for sending him to the stake for excommunication, but in the end they agreed on disfellowshipment because C.H. had believed he was doing the right thing and had not intended to sin, no matter how foolish his belief had been.

A grim woman sat off to the side in the waiting area. She had two young boys with her, and they were playing with toys on the floor. They were calm now, but earlier they had broken into a fight, and the woman had ignored them.

Dani kept staring at the two boys. She hadn't spoken a word since she arrived, and she would not look at him. Taking that as a cue, he didn't say anything. He couldn't deny that they were in serious need of counseling.

All because of him and his astounding stupidity.

How did he ever get suckered into believing it was true? Had he really wanted it to be true that much? He wouldn't have thought so.

The counselor finally appeared from the hallway. He had thinning gray hair and an old-fashioned salt-and-pepper moustache that made him look like a Jules Verne character. The man smiled and said, "Are you the Youngs?"

C.H. nodded and stood. Dani stood, glanced at the counselor, and then looked down at the floor as she walked.

The counselor extended his hand. "I'm Brother Ingols."

"Cory Young. And this is Dani."

She nodded but didn't extend her hand.

As Brother Ingols led them back to an office, C.H. saw Dani steal one last glance back at the two boys. The counselor sat in a plush leather chair behind a desk and motioned to several other chairs around the room, which all looked comfortable. "Take your pick."

Dani sat down. C.H. figured that where they sat in relation to each other would mean something to Brother Ingols, so he took the chair right next to her. The room filled with a cologne smell that must have emanated from the counselor.

Brother Ingols donned some narrow reading glasses and picked up a clipboard. "Okay, how were we paying for these sessions? Do you have insurance?"

C.H. sighed. "No. I'm just working part time right now."

"Was the ward going to pay for it?"

"Yes," C.H. said. "Out of fast-offering funds."

Brother Ingols scribbled something and handed the clipboard to him with the pen. "Sign at the bottom, please."

He signed and handed it back. The counselor opened a folder on his desk. He picked up one sheet of paper from a small stack of them inside and scanned it. "Most of the time when a bishop refers a couple for counseling, he'll fill us in on a few details." His eyebrows rose. "But in your case, there were more than a few."

"So you know all about it?" C.H. asked. Dani studied the floor intently.

Brother Ingols looked over his glasses. "I know what your bishop knows. I'd like to hear what you have to say about it."

He already resolved not to beat around the bush and make the counselor dig for embarrassing information. "I was deceived by an evil spirit—that's the gist of it. He appeared to me and convinced me...well, that he was Brigham Young. He commanded me to do some things that were pretty bad."

"Yes, that's all in my notes." The counselor glanced down at the paper. "How do you feel about everything?"

"I feel like a complete moron, that's how." C.H. pursed his lips and looked down, feeling shame. "There must have been something really wrong with me, to be fooled so easily." He glanced at Dani out of the corner of his eye. "Everything's my fault—I know it."

"We're not here to lay blame." Brother Ingols shifted in his chair. "That's already been taken care of by your bishop and the judicial system, right?" He took off his glasses and slipped one earpiece into his mouth. "Our purpose here is to save your marriage."

C.H. thought he saw a tear trickle from Dani's eye, but he avoided looking at her. He already knew he'd hurt her badly. "What do we do?"

"Let's hear what Dani has to say." He locked at her expectantly. C.H. wanted to look at her too, but he didn't think that would help her talk, so he stared at his hands in his lap.

A painful silence followed. Unable to hold off any longer, he looked at her. Her lower lip trembled as her mouth curved down severely. Tears glistened fiercely in her eyes.

For two months C.H. felt like he was going to hell. Now he felt like he was already there.

A tear finally slid onto her cheek, and Dani rubbed at it. She shook her head and blinked. More tears fell out. Brother Ingols stood and handed her a tissue from a box on his desk. She took it and wiped her face.

"How do you feel about your husband?" he asked, sitting back down.

The sobs broke out as she shook her head. She pressed the tissue to her nose. In a whisper she said, "I—"

Brother Ingols cocked his head to hear.

"I hate him."

A shock passed through C.H., and he felt his own tears forming. Many emotions churned simultaneously—despair at what she said, grim satisfaction that he was getting what he deserved, fear of what his life would be like from now on. And sickening nausea.

Brother Ingols stood again and handed her the whole box this time. "Well, you've been through an awful lot. That's certainly understandable."

"A lot?" she squeaked out. It would have sounded funny at any other time. "Do you know what they did to me?"

"They detained you at the airport and searched you. But they released you without pressing any charges. Of course, they kept all the money."

"I don't give a *damn* about the money!" she spat, shooting a vicious look at C.H. "The money's where this all started. They took my children away."

"But they gave them back when they released you," Brother Ingols said calmly.

"The next *day*. Do you have any idea where they kept my little boys all night?"

The counselor sat quietly. C.H. wanted to throw up.

"And they made me take my clothes off."

C.H. couldn't look at her anymore. He closed his eyes, feeling tears squeeze out between the lids.

"Yes, I know," said Brother Ingols.

"And they...they stuck their...they jabbed—"

"I know," said Brother Ingols. "I saw the police report."

C.H. heard Dani's breathing grow short and heavy. "I feel like I was raped," she whispered.

After some silence passed, C.H. opened his eyes. Dani's tears had stopped, leaving her face streaked. She glared off into space. It was unbearable to see her hurting like this. But he had to bear it because he did it to her.

This must be what hell is like. A wrenching torment that would never dull, would never end, would eat him alive forever. It was even worse than when those hideous beings stole his body because it would never end. He almost felt sorry for Brother Brigham, now that he had a taste of what that creature would go through for eternity. But that demon didn't deserve any compassion, just like C.H. didn't deserve any.

"Dani," Brother Ingols said gently. He waited. "Dani?"

She broke her stare and looked at him.

"Do you love Cory?"

The look in her eyes was dull and lifeless. "I hate him."

"Yes, but do you *love* him?"

The contorted face returned—puckered chin, down-turned mouth, trembling facial muscles. She said nothing.

"You're here, aren't you? Trying to save the marriage?"

"For my two boys," she said sharply. "I don't want to take their father away from them."

Brother Ingols took a deep breath and sighed. "*Did* you love your husband at one time?"

"Yes!" she said with vehemence.

"But not anymore."

Tears fell again. "I can't feel it through the hate." She pulled a tissue out of the box and dabbed at her eyes. "He had sex with another woman. He invited that monster into our lives. He was supposed to protect us and be the righteous priesthood holder in our family, and he destroyed us!"

"And you went right along with it, didn't you?"

Dani's face jerked toward Brother Ingols. "That's not fair. I *trusted* him. I *supported* him."

"Like a good wife should."

The statement hung in the air. C.H. felt his gut churning. Was the counselor accusing Dani of complicity after saying there would be no blaming here?

"As I understand it," the counselor said, "the wife is as responsible as the husband for the spiritual environment in the home."

C.H. wasn't going to let him get away with it. "It's all my fault. She's right. She was just believing in me."

Brother Ingols pierced him with a steady gaze. "And you were just believing in what you thought was right."

Anger began to surge in him. "I was deceived by a devil! Why would the devil even try if there wasn't something wrong with me?"

"The point is that you were both deceived. You both need to take the blame."

"*No!*" C.H. cried as he jumped up. "Don't you dare talk about her like that. It was all my fault." He dropped to his knees before Dani and took her hands, knocking the box of tissues to the floor. "Dani, I'm sorry. I can't believe I did all this to you. I'm so sorry."

She stared at him in shock. He buried his face in her hands. "I can't beg your forgiveness. It's too much to ask. But I'm so, so sorry." His cheeks felt the dampness of his own tears on her hands. "I love you so much. I'm so, so sorry."

His grief engulfed him and silenced him as he broke out in muted sobs that shook his whole body.

Brother Ingols' voice broke in. "You've never asked for her forgiveness, have you?"

C.H. shook his head without lifting his face from her hands.

"You've never told her you're sorry."

"How could I? What I did was so, so terrible. Saying I'm sorry seems like such a feeble thing—"

"It's not," said Brother Ingols.

Slowly C.H. lifted his head until he could look into Dani's eyes. Her face was wet and her expression deeply somber. But her eyes looked at him with something new. The dullness was gone.

"Have a seat, Cory, and let's talk some more," Brother Ingols said. "But don't let go of that hand."

C.H. obeyed. Dani peered down at their intertwined fingers.

"Dani," Brother Ingols said. She turned her face toward him. "Do you love your husband?"

She looked at C.H. He peered deep into her eyes. He couldn't find forgiveness there. He didn't think he could see any love. But what he saw was...

Reconsideration?

Peering back at him without flinching, she sighed. "I don't know. Maybe."

It was more hope than he deserved, more than his wretched guilt could deal with. But his heart jumped a beat anyway.

"But I still hate him too."

"That's okay," said Brother Ingols.

"And I'm still only doing this because of my sons."

"That's enough for now."

"And..." She gazed back at C.H. "I don't know if I can forgive him."

Brother Ingols waited a beat. "Do you believe it's all his fault?"

Tears formed in her eyes again. How many tears would it take to wash all this away?

Almost inaudibly she whispered, "No."

"Then he may need to forgive you too."

C.H. spoke out nobly, "I already for—"

Brother Ingols raised his hand. "No, don't say it out of guilt now. Say it when you really mean it."

What was he talking about? He did mean it. There was nothing to forgive, so of course he could forgive her...

Or was that the point? Maybe there *was* something to forgive?

Her hand felt soft and delicious in his. He realized he hadn't touched her like that since his unholy marriage to Sheila. What he wouldn't give to make all that time between then and now go away.

Brother Ingols reached for the folder and his glasses. He read a bit and then spoke conversationally, as if nothing had happened. "You're working part time, now, Cory? At the same bookstore?"

"Yes. They'll make me full time as soon as they have an opening."

"But you won't be an assistant manager."

"Not until an opening comes up."

"In the meantime, the ward's helping you with fast offerings."

"Yes."

He looked up. "Now, don't go feeling guilty about that. That's what it's there for. You're feeling enough guilt as it is, and you've got your whole life to be generous with fast offerings when you get back on your feet."

He felt some relief, which surprised him. He'd been so busy feeling bad about his sins against Dani that he hadn't noticed any guilt over church assistance—yet.

"What about this Sheila Matthews?"

C.H. and Dani looked at each other. "We don't know," Dani said. "We haven't heard anything from her."

"You don't know where she is or what happened to her?"

"No," said C.H.

"Good! Keep it that way. I'm not saying she's any kind of villain in this, but it wouldn't be a very good influence right now if she were back in your lives."

"Fine with me," Dani said.

"Cory," Brother Ingols said, looking at his notes. "You're living in a room in the basement of Bishop Schmidt's home, right?"

"Yes."

"And Dani, you're still at home with the boys."

She nodded.

He dropped the paper and peered at them. "How long are you going to put up with that arrangement?"

C.H. shrugged. He hadn't thought about it. Dani wanted him out, so he went. "I guess when Dani says I can come back."

Brother Ingols looked at her. "Planning on saving this marriage by remote control, are we?"

Dani scowled back at him.

"I wish—" C.H. took a breath. "I wish you wouldn't be so hard on her."

Brother Ingols switched his piercing gaze to him. "I'm concerned that all the blame's being dumped on you, Cory. How do you expect to have a decent marriage if you slink around like the black sheep of the family for the rest of your life?"

"I cheated on my wife," C.H. growled, feeling the anger rise up again.

"Did you?"

He hated how the counselor's eyes pierced. They reminded him of that portrait of Brigham Young all those years ago hanging in his family's home, the things his father said standing before it that planted the seed in his boyish mind that caused him to be such an easy target for a devil.

"Did you sneak around behind her back? Go to sleazy motels? Lie to her about working late?"

C.H. glared, but the anger inside was softening.

"Did she give you permission to sleep with this woman?"

"Yes," said Dani suddenly. "I did."

C.H. looked at her with surprise. She had a totally new expression on her face. He couldn't read it, but it wasn't anger, sorrow, or hate.

Brother Ingols nodded. "So how can it be cheating? Unintentional adultery, maybe, but not cheating."

"Unintentional adultery," C.H. smirked. "What in the world is that?"

Brother Ingols smiled and set down the paper and his glasses. "Well, we've got a lot of work ahead, no doubt about that. Are you willing to give this a shot, Dani? For the boys, I mean."

She nodded. "Yes. For the boys." C.H. thought he saw a faint smile play at the corners of her mouth.

"And you, Cory?"

"Call him C.H.," Dani said.

"No!" C.H. said. "I'm not using that name anymore. It reminds me of—" He looked at the counselor, feeling self-conscious. "Cain Hell."

Brother Ingols looked at him with a bemused expression.

"But I hate the name Cory," Dani said, looking at C.H. "Even more than I hate you."

"Are you willing to give this a shot, *C.H.?*" Brother Ingols said.

"Yes." It was the easiest answer he'd ever given in his life.

Brother Ingols nodded with satisfaction, then swiveled around his chair and looked out the window. The sunlight played across his face like artistic movie lighting. C.H. wondered why the man didn't just wear a tweed suit and vest to go with the rest of his look.

"You know what I'd like to see right now?" said Brother Ingols.

"What?" C.H. said.

"I'd like to see you two kiss."

C.H. felt his face go red, but it wasn't embarrassment. He was afraid Dani would refuse. He didn't know what to do, force the issue or let her make the first move.

And nothing happened.

Without moving his gaze from the window, Brother Ingols said, "In this room, I always get what I want."

Abruptly Dani grabbed C.H.'s chin and pulled his face toward her. She stared at him with hard eyes for a long time. Then her eyes softened, and she touched the scar on the side of his head where the TV stand had gashed him.

"It's going to kill you to kiss him?" Brother Ingols said.

She leaned forward and pressed her lips to his, gently.

It electrified C.H., like their very first kiss.

D. Michael Martindale is a storyteller. It doesn't matter which medium the story is told in—whether it be film or television or books or music—what's important is telling stories that people enjoy.

He was born in Minnesota and has been telling stories since before he could write. He started out by drawing comic strips and having his mother fill in the dialog balloons for him. He developed a taste for science fiction and fantasy, and although he's written screenplays in all sorts of genres, he continues to gravitate back to speculative fiction.

Martindale earned an Associate Degree in Film Production at Salt Lake Community College and a Bachelor Degree in Screenwriting and Cinematography at Utah Valley University.

For a period of time, he focused on telling stories about his religious community, Mormons. He considered the quality of Mormon literature subpar and preachy and wanted to tell stories about his people that he'd want to read, quality stories that were honest and edgy and not the least bit preachy. He's glad to see that the quality of Mormon art has been improving over the years.

He served three years on the board of the Association for Mormon Letters, a nonprofit organization that promotes Mormon literature and other arts, and acted as their Writers Conference chairperson for four years. He wrote a number of articles and book and film reviews for their literary journal *Irreantum.*

He worked for a time as a staff writer for *The Sugar Beet*, an Internet publication of Mormon satire patterned after the infamous website *The Onion.* Many of these online articles of alleged Mormon "news" were eventually collected into the popular book *The Mormon Tabernacle Enquirer.*

The editor of *The Mormon Tabernacle Enquirer* decided to start his own publishing company, Zarahemla Books, and chose as its flagship publication Martindale's second novel *Brother Brigham*, which he categorizes as "Mormon speculative fiction." *Brother Brigham* went on to receive substantial critical acclaim and was even used as reading material in a college comparative religion class one semester. He also had a science fiction short story "Bokev Momen" published in the anthology *Monsters and Mormons*, which is included in his collection of short stories *Twisted Mind.*

Inspired by *Jesus Christ Superstar*, he composed the musical *General Prophet Joseph Smith*, based on the events leading up to the assassination of the Mormon prophet Joseph Smith. He produced a concept album recording of it on CDs, and is currently developing a film adaptation of it. He calls it "Les Mis for Mormons."

Martindale has written two other novels. His first, *The Power of the Seeker*, is the beginning installment of a science fiction series called *The Reincarnate.* It remains unpublished, and he describes it as "crap." He may rewrite it someday. His third novel is a fantasy called *Celeste & the White Dragon* which he's in the process of bringing to publication. It's the first volume in a series, as of yet untitled.

He's already writing the first draft of his fourth novel, the prequel to *Celeste & the White Dragon*, which currently has the title *Seven Sisters*, but he makes no guarantee that title will remain the same. He envisions more volumes to the series and wonders if he'll live long enough to produce them all.

For nine years Martindale has focused on screenwriting and film making as a director and editor. Film is his favorite medium in which to tell stories. He wrote, produced, directed, and edited eight short films and a feature-length fantasy film called *Geeks and Goblins, Elves and Elliot.* He has multiple other screenplays ready to be developed into feature-length films, including an adaptation of his short story "Solar Butterfly" that also appears in *Twisted Mind.* Additionally, he's been on the development team for three television/web series.

He resides in Salt Lake City, Utah, and is the father of three grown children and the grandfather of the best granddaughter in the world. Do not debate him on this.

Twisted Mind:
6 Science Fiction Stories
by D. Michael Martindale

From the twisted mind of D. Michael comes six science fiction stories that disrupt the status quo of our world in the spirit of The Twilight Zone and Black Mirror. Whether the new world that arises is better or worse is a question each individual will have to decide for themselves.

A Growth in the Backyard
Eternal Rectangle
Solar Butterfly
Bokev Momen
Mary Mother of Nanites
Eyes of the Beholder
Bonus story: **Time Forks**

twistedstories.worldsmithstories.com

Twisted Soul
4 Slipstream Novellas
by D. Michael Martindale

From the twisted soul of D. Michael come four slipstream novellas that explore the twists and turns of human spirituality and psychic powers. The hidden worlds they reveal may inspire or disturb, but the souls that experience them will never be the same again.

Alexandra
A Face in the Window
First Mormons in the Moon
Godblind
Bonus novelette: **The Dreamcatcher**

twisted.worldsmithstories.com

Celeste & the White Dragon
by D. Michael Martindale

Queen Tamara, thrown into a dungeon by the rogue sorceress Gwendolyn, is about to give birth. There's something about her baby that makes Gwendolyn want to possess it, and when Tamara delivers, Gwendolyn will kill her and take the baby.

But Tamara's chambermaid Zenia will not let that happen. At great risk to her life, she rescues Tamara and helps her flee out of the kingdom of Gallea. But in the midst of Fenweald Forest, Tamara dies while giving birth to the baby, and Zenia discovers the terrible secret that makes Gwendolyn want to possess it. She puts her life in peril seeking a way to hide the infant.

A great search for the child begins, with kings and sorceresses and wizards and accursed monsters and village witches all struggling to find and possess the young princess, whom Zenia names Celeste. The fate of three continents depends on who succeeds.

celeste.worldsmithstories.com

www.ingramcontent.com/pod-product-compliance
Lightning Source LLC
Chambersburg PA
CBHW070447260626
47161CB00004B/1228